Praise for
Josephine Cox

'This is vintage Cox. Passionate and touching, an irre-sistible read. It's a perfect book to while away an after-noon. Just make sure you hide *Born Bad* away from your mum and grandmother because they'll love it too.'

—*News of the World* (UK)

'The latest emotionally charged story from the mega-selling author won't disappoint her army of fans.'

—*Bella* (UK)

'Cox's talent as a storyteller never lets you escape the spell.'

—*Daily Mail* (UK)

'Another masterpiece.'

—*Best* (UK)

'A born storyteller.'

—*Befordshire Times & Citizen* (UK)

'Any regular readers of Josephine Cox will tell you that the second you start to read one of her books you are actually living the scenario along with the characters.'

—Sue Brunton

Also by Josephine Cox

Queenie's Story
HER FATHER'S SINS • LET LOOSE THE TIGERS

The Emma Grady Trilogy
OUTCAST • ALLEY URCHIN • VAGABONDS

ANGELS CRY SOMETIMES
TAKE THIS WOMAN
WHISTLEDOWN WOMAN
DON'T CRY ALONE
JESSICA'S GIRL
NOBODY'S DARLING
BORN TO SERVE
MORE THAN RICHES
A LITTLE BADNESS
LIVING A LIE
THE DEVIL YOU KNOW
A TIME FOR US
CRADLE OF THORNS
MISS YOU FOREVER
LOVE ME OR LEAVE ME
TOMORROW THE WORLD
THE GILDED CAGE
SOMEWHERE, SOMEDAY
RAINBOW DAYS
LOOKING BACK
LET IT SHINE

THE WOMAN WHO LEFT
JINNIE

BAD BOY JACK
THE BEACHCOMBER
LOVERS AND LIARS
THE JOURNEY
JOURNEY'S END
THE LONER
SONGBIRD

Born Bad

~

JOSEPHINE COX

AVON

An Imprint of HarperCollins*Publishers*

An edition of this book was first published in the United Kingdom in 2009 by HarperCollins Publishers.

First U.S. edition

ISBN 978-0-06-171897-7

10 11 12 13 14   OV/RRD   10 9 8 7 6 5 4 3 2 1

This book is for my Ken, as always

To all the caring people in my life;
family, friends and business colleagues,
I give my wholehearted thanks and huge love

~

For my lovely sister Win who has shown
determination and courage in a difficult situation.
Love you loads, sweetheart, take care, Josie x

CONTENTS

PART ONE

~

Weymouth, July 1956

Love Hurts

CHAPTER ONE

Harry Blake felt as though he was the last man on earth. It was a lonely, disturbing feeling.

In this rare moment of quiet, the long-ago memories were like moving pictures in his tortured mind; vivid, aching memories of love and loss, of pain and joy and the people and places that had shaped his life so far.

Even now, in this moment of solitude, with the soothing throb of the ocean in his ears and the bright sunshine bouncing off the water, he could not rest easy.

Today was one of those perfect July days when the heart soars and dreams are allowed.

But not for Harry. Not today. Maybe never again.

All about him, ordinary people were enjoying their ordinary lives. Above him, the seagulls mewed and swooped, and sounds of laughter echoed across the sands. Harry was oblivious to all of that.

This was a day for families, a day for fun and being together. But not for him, *and not for her.* No amount of laughter or sunshine could change what was happening in his life.

He had no say in the events unfolding. Events which, in a few short months, had changed his world – and that of his loved ones. Only once before had he felt so lost and alone, and that was many years ago when he was a fresh-faced lad of eighteen.

Back then, he had made a decision which had haunted

him ever since; a hard decision, forced on him by youth and circumstance. Because of his decision, lives had been fractured – including his own – and for that he would always blame himself.

Today though, he was caught up in a completely different nightmare. This time, he had played no part in its creation, because unlike before, he had no way of influencing the outcome. This time, it was all too final. Too cruel.

Deep in thought, his gaze absentmindedly followed the sailing-boats. Wending their way through Weymouth Harbour, their tall white sails billowing as they thrust along on the crest of a gentle breeze, they were a magnificent sight.

Vaguely aware of the playful children building castles in the sand, a kind of rage cut like a blade through his heart. She should be here, he thought. Sharing it all with us.

He could see her now, the chocolate-brown hair and the pretty dark eyes that crinkled in the corners when she laughed, her long slender legs swinging as she perched on their garden wall, and her smiling eyes uplifted to the sunshine.

Sara was a good woman, a woman of kindness and humour, and now, for reasons he would never understand, something had happened. It was happening right now, at this very moment. Relentless and unforgiving, it would go on until the end.

Nothing he could do would halt the inevitable.

'Daddy!' The little boy's voice cut across his dark thoughts. 'Please may I have an ice cream?'

Composing himself, Harry turned and nodded.

Excited, the boy jumped up and down. 'And can I have strawberry sauce?'

'Go on then.' Harry wondered at the way life could still go on, when inside, his world was falling apart. 'Here's a shilling. Try not to get it all over your shirt.'

Pushing the chocolate-flake into the ice cream, the big man serving behind the beachfront café counter passed the cornet to the boy, joking, 'Your daddy doesn't want an ice cream, then?'

Holding the cornet carefully with both hands, Tom curled his tongue along the ice cream. 'He can share mine if he likes!'

''Spect he's got his mind on other things, eh?' Leaning down to hand the nipper his threepenny bit change, the man glanced across at Harry, thinking how sad the young fella looked. He could only have been in his thirties, yet he was bent and haggard like an old man. Curious, the older man observed Harry a moment longer, before turning away to serve his other customers.

A few moments later, still heavy of heart yet openly smiling and chatting for his son's sake, Harry led Tom along the Esplanade and on towards where the car was parked near the statue of George III. 'Are we going to see Mammy now?' the boy asked eagerly.

Harry took a moment to answer, his gaze sweeping the child's appearance. His thick mop of dark hair stood up as though in fright, and the pink strawberry sauce was plastered around his mouth. Oh, how he loved this child, and Sara . . . *his* Sara . . . *his precious, wonderful Sara*!

Swamped with emotion, he took the boy by the hand and ran him across the road.

'Just look at the state of you!' he said huskily. 'We'd best clean you up, before your mammy sees you.'

Slurping on his ice cream, the boy ran and skipped, laughing heartily while his father pretended to chase him.

The boy did not fully realize the situation, but things had begun to change some time ago, when he had sensed a sadness in his parents. When he was near they smiled and pretended that everything was all right. But when they thought he was not looking, they would hold each other for a long time and never let go. Then his mammy went off to hospital, and the house felt so lonely without her.

When, just now, the sadness touched him, he thought of Jack.

Jack was a frog he had caught from the brook in his long-handled net.

He loved that frog; he fed it and cared for it, and even made a little pool for it to swim in, with plants to hide under, and when he called its name it would come hopping out to see him. One day, Jack went away and he never saw him again.

Tom was upset for a time. Then his daddy got him another frog who looked exactly like Jack, and that was fine. He remembered it clearly. When he was sad about Jack, his daddy had put it right, so now whenever he was sad, he believed his daddy would put that right too.

There was nothing to fear, no one to hurt him, because his daddy was here. In Tom's little world everything was warm and wonderful, and that was how it should be.

As they walked on, Harry chatted to his son, and for a while his heart was quieter. His world had crumbled about him, but so far, the child had been protected.

'Daddy, look!' The boy brought Harry's attention to the flower barrow. 'Yellow roses.'

Remembering, Harry smiled. 'Mammy's favourites,' he mused aloud. If she could have red, pink or yellow roses, she would always choose the yellow ones.

'Can we take her some?'

Leading the boy to the stall, Harry fished a handful of coins from his trouser-pocket. 'Why don't we get her a dozen, eh?'

A short time later, the two of them were nearly back at the car, Harry deep in thought, and the boy alongside, clutching the bunch of roses in one hand and his melting ice cream in the other.

With his sticky fingers, the boy threw the remains of the cornet to the seagulls. When they quickly swooped down and carried it away in their sharp beaks, the child was fearful. 'You won't let them hurt me, will you?'

Harry reassured him. 'I would never let *anyone* hurt you.' Lifting the boy into his arms, he inwardly cringed at the knowledge that soon, the boy would hurt like never before.

As he was bundled into the Hillman Minx, Tom asked, 'Are we really taking Mammy home today?'

'Yes, son.' Starting the ignition, Harry fought back his tears. 'Your mammy's waiting for us right now, so we'd best get a move on.' He cleared his throat.

'Daddy?'

'Yes, son?'

'Why did Mammy send us away today?'

As he moved off from the kerb and into the traffic, Harry recalled how Sara had been adamant that she needed a little time, that she wasn't ready and they must come back later. 'I think she wanted to make herself look pretty for us,' he said eventually, and smiled to himself.

His darling wife could be a bossy tramp when needed!

'When we get Mammy, can we go to the park?'

'That would be nice, but I don't think so – not today, son.'

'Why not?'

'Because . . .' Harry swallowed hard before going on. 'Maybe we'd best leave it for another day.'

'Look, Daddy! New baby ducks.'

'I know, and I'm sure Mammy would love to do that, but . . . like I said, another day, eh?'

'She *will* like her roses though, won't she?'

Harry nodded.

'Can we go to the park for my *birthday* next week then?'

'Mmm.' Harry's thoughts were elsewhere.

The boy took his dad's mumble as a yes. 'Mammy said she's got five candles for my cake. I'm a big boy now.'

Harry smiled wistfully. 'You certainly are.'

'I'm starting school next week.'

'Not next week,' Harry gently reminded him. 'It's next term – in September.'

'Oh.' The boy was downhearted.

'Hey, Tom, don't be like that.' Harry glanced at the boy in his mirror. 'It's only a few weeks away. It'll be here before you know it.'

The boy grinned. 'I've got my red cap – and my black blazer,' he said proudly.

Harry played along. 'Soon you'll be all grown up.' He recalled the day when Sara went shopping with Tom for his uniform, and how excited their son had been. Dear God! That was such a short time ago. So much had happened in between, it seemed like a lifetime.

His thoughts retreated into the past. They say your bad deeds come home to haunt you. Was it true? he thought. When he had caused all that pain eighteen years ago, was the payback always lurking in the shadows?

Deep down, he had always known his past would return with a vengeance. After all, it was what he deserved.

But Sara did not deserve it.

And neither did their son.

For one sorry, fleeting moment, someone else crossed his mind – a girl named Judy.

Flooded with guilt, he thrust her from his mind. That was a lifetime ago.

And this was now.

~

The nurse was a happy young thing, with dark expressive eyes and a broad Scottish accent.

'Just look at yourself,' she said, holding the mirror up to Sara's face. 'See how bonny you are.'

While Sara checked herself in the mirror, the nurse went on, 'Nurse Bridget has done a fantastic job with you. She knows more about make-up and fashion than I could learn in a lifetime.'

'And I'm very grateful.' Sara could not believe the difference in her appearance.

Nurse McDonald chatted on. 'You do know she's off to a fancy job as a make-up artist in one o' them posh London salons? Apparently, when she was a bairn, she always wanted to be either a nurse or a beauty consultant. It was her dad who persuaded her to go in for the nursing. "Nurses are always in demand," he told her, "so you'll never be out of a job".'

She groaned. 'Have ye ever known a man not to interfere?' She didn't wait for an answer. Instead she chatted on, 'Bridget reckons her dad's a born interferer, like all men, always thinking they know best.'

Sara was sympathetic. 'Dads are like that. I suppose he was only thinking of Bridget though. It sounds like he really wanted her to have a solid future.'

'Aye . . . could be. Anyway, she's leaving on Friday, and she's happy as Larry. Don't get me wrong, I'm glad for her, but at the same time I can't help but envy her. There she'll be, dabbling in cosmetics and meeting rich, famous people. And there'll be me – stuck here changing beds and emptying bedpans.'

Sara smiled at that. 'Ah, come on, Aileen. You would never want to be anything but a nurse, would you?'

During her long and gruelling stay in hospital, Sara had come to know this kindly girl, and like all the other patients she had great respect for the staff who cared for them; each and every one a true professional. But Aileen McDonald was special; a dedicated nurse, born to care for others.

Sara reminded her now. 'You may not realise it, but you have a real gift . . . a magical way that puts us all at ease.' She glanced about the ward. 'There isn't one single patient here who doesn't love you.'

The other young woman glowed with pride. 'Do you really think so?'

Sara nodded. 'Ask anyone here, and they'll tell you.'

'So, I'm good at being a nurse but I'm a real dunce at make-up, is that what you're trying to say?'

Sara chuckled. 'We're all gifted in different ways. Nurse Bridget has the talent to brighten a patient's face, while you have the God-given talent to brighten a patient's spirits.'

Embarrassed and humbled by Sara's remark, Nurse Aileen gave her a peck on the cheek, 'Alright,' she conceded, 'I'll admit, I'm no genius when it comes to make-up . . . in fact, sometimes when I'm in a rush, I can't even put my lipstick on straight, and once when I was in an almighty rush, I got on the bus with one eyebrow plucked and the other looking like a shaggy dog. When I got out my mirror and tweezers to finish the job, I got some very peculiar looks I can tell you!'

Laughing at that, Sara then reached forward from her wheel-chair and picked up the hand mirror from the bedcover where she had lain it. Taking a second glance at herself, she said, 'I still can't believe that's me!'

The discreet sweep of mascara and eyebrow pencil made her brown eyes appear bright and sparkling, whereas before they had been dull and lifeless. Also, the delicate mask of cream foundation skilfully hid the dark hollows beneath her eyes, making her look even younger than her thirty-two years. Amazingly, with careful use of tinted face powder, Nurse Bridget had somehow managed to flush Sara's pale skin into a soft pink glow.

Ravaged by a debilitating illness and the harsh, invasive treatment over the past months, Sara's long flowing locks were gone, and in their place was a cap of fine, closely cropped hair.

This morning, Nurse Bridget had done her best to breathe life into it, and now, after much tweaking and brushing, she had created the illusion of a natural shine. Moreover, when the wispy ends were trimmed away, the hair appeared thick and healthy.

Admiring her transformation, Sara patted the beautiful

burgundy-coloured dress she was wearing. 'I do love this dress,' she murmured. 'Don't you think my Harry has good taste?'

Nurse Aileen nodded approvingly at the dress with its boatneckline and pretty buttons, and the clever blouson design that hid the pathetically thin shape beneath. 'I think you look wonderful,' she said, 'and yes, your Harry does have good taste.'

Nurse Aileen recalled how thrilled and excited both Harry and his son had been, earlier that morning. 'We can't wait to take you home, sweetheart,' Harry told Sara.

'We've got cake and everything!' the boy informed her. 'Daddy's made a surprise for you. He's built a special place in the garden where you can sit.'

'Tom!' Harry had groaned. 'You weren't supposed to tell. It's not a surprise any more now, is it?'

When Tom looked downcast, Harry had hugged him hard. 'It's all right, son. All that matters is that Mammy likes it.'

Tom jumped up and down. 'You will, won't you, Mammy?' Sara promised that she would love it.

Harry and Sara had laughed at his innocent antics, while the nurse had looked on, her heart sore. She had seen the pain in Harry's eyes, and sensed his anguish, which he somehow managed to hide whenever Sara was watching.

'He's handsome too, don't you think?' Sara's quiet voice interrupted her thoughts.

'He certainly is,' the nurse agreed.

Sara's mood grew serious. 'Life is so unfair, isn't it?' she asked softly. Then, even before Nurse Aileen could answer, she swiftly changed the subject. 'So?' Her smile was quick and bright, though her voice was quivering. 'You really like the dress he chose?'

Nurse Aileen played along. 'Aha, I really do,' she answered truthfully. 'That burgundy colour is so right for you, and the belt is perfect.' Wide and hugging, the shiny black belt gave Sara the illusion of shape.

Close to tears, Sara thanked her. 'I feel like a *real* woman.'

'That's because you *are* a real woman,' Aileen told her. 'Don't you ever forget that.'

Sara gave her a peck on the cheek. 'You're such a good friend. I don't know how I can ever thank you.' She had not forgotten the endless hours this dear, devoted girl had spent talking with her, exchanging secrets and making her laugh through the pain.

'Sara?' the nurse's gentle voice interrupted her thoughts.

'Yes?'

'Why did you make me send them away earlier – Harry and Tom?'

Sara gave a long drawn-out sigh. 'Just for once, I didn't want them to see me looking pale and ill.' She paused, her dark eyes swimming with tears. 'I know it can't last, but thanks to you and Nurse Bridget, just for a while I can pretend there is still something of the woman I once was.'

Her voice broke as she remembered how it had been. 'I so much want Harry to look at me and see the girl he married . . . even if it's only for a few fleeting moments.'

Nurse McDonald had noticed how Sara was fidgeting. 'You don't need to be in pain,' she reminded her again. 'I can give you something to make you more comfortable.'

Sara shook her head. 'Not today.' Her quick little smile was incredibly beautiful. 'Today, I mean to be fully conscious and strong. I need my family to see past the illness, and imagine me as I used to be.'

Bowing her head she spoke in a whisper, as though to herself: 'If they can do that, this effort will all have been worthwhile.'

The nurse quietly persisted. 'All the same, Harry would not want you to punish yourself.'

Sara reached out and took hold of her hand. 'Won't you just be happy for me? I'm going home! After all these weeks, I can't believe I'm really going home.'

She took a moment to let herself believe it. 'Time with my family will be so precious . . . to listen and talk, and *laugh* with them.' When a rogue tear escaped down her cheek, she quickly brushed it aside. 'You do know what I mean, don't you?'

Filled with admiration, Nurse Aileen McDonald assured her that she understood. And she did.

During her time on this ward, she had witnessed much suffering, but this time, because of Sara's relative youth and selfless determination, she felt a deep anger at life's cruelty.

Seeing how the little nurse had fallen into a sombre mood, Sara quickly rebuked her. 'You mustn't be sad,' she chided. 'Think how lucky I've been in my life. How many women have had the good fortune to know the love and devotion of a fine man? I've been blessed with a wonderful son and, until only recently, I have never known real pain; but even that is a small price to pay. So, please, Nurse Aileen, no being sad, and no crying – not for me!'

'Has anybody ever told you how bossy you are?' Aileen quipped.

Sara laughed aloud. 'Harry tells me that all the time,' she admitted happily. 'He calls me a bossy tramp, but what do I care? Look at me . . . I'm being cosseted, and I feel beautiful! Most of all, I'm able to refuse the treatment, so I can enjoy the company of the two people I love most in all the world for one whole day at home.' Aware of the other woman's concern, she looked up apologetically. 'I'm right, aren't I?'

The nurse shrugged. 'If that's what you want, who am I to argue? But I need a promise from you.'

'What kind of promise?'

'Let me come home with you. I've talked with Matron and your doctor, and they have given their permission.'

'No!' Sara was adamant. 'We've already been through this, and the answer is still no.'

'Very well, but,' Nurse McDonald held up the paper bag in her hand, 'you must keep these close to you at all times. If the pain gets too bad, they'll help you cope, until you get back here.'

13

Sara's gaze was drawn to the big blue cross on the side of the bag. She knew what it contained, and she hoped the powerful medication would not be needed until she got back here at six o'clock, as agreed. 'Hmh! I can see I'm not the only bossy tramp round here.'

'Exactly right!' The nurse wagged a finger. 'You would do well to remember that.' Taking control of the wheelchair, she thrust it forward. 'Until six o'clock tonight, then, and not a minute later, mind. I'll be right here, waiting for you to come back through that door.'

Sara laughed. 'I don't doubt that for one minute,' she joked.

As the two of them wended their way along the ward, the other patients waved, and wished her well. 'You behave yourself now,' they merrily instructed. 'No gallivanting, and no giving that handsome husband of yours a hard time!'

'Have a lovely day, m'dear.' Miss Bateman was formidable and difficult, and normally she kept herself to herself. On this occasion though, she felt the need to be gracious.

'See you later, pet.' That was Alice Arnold, a kindly soul, recovering from pneumonia. 'Give that little lad of yours a big hug from me!'

The well-meaning advice continued, lighting her way, until the ward doors closed behind her.

When they reached the reception area, Sara carefully scribbled her signature onto the prepared documents.

'Are you really sure you want to do this, Sara?' The young doctor understood her reason for wanting to spend a normal day with her family, and he was reluctant to spoil it. But he was not happy with the situation.

'It *is* what I want to do,' she smiled up at him, 'more than anything else in the world.'

He nodded his acknowledgement, because if he spoke he might show his emotion, and that would not be professional.

'Sara has her medication.' Nurse McDonald pre-empted his next question.

'Do you have the direct ward number,' he looked down at Sara, 'in case your husband needs to contact us?'

She patted the pretty blue handbag that Harry had delivered only that morning. 'It's all in here,' she assured him. 'But I'll be fine, you'll see.'

'Very well. Have a lovely day, and we'll see you back here this evening.' Deeply humbled, the young man strode away. There was little else he could do.

~

Having arrived at the hospital, Harry swung the car into the one remaining parking place. 'Come on, little fella.' He lifted Tom out of the car. 'Your mammy's waiting for you.'

When Tom caught sight of Sara, waiting in her wheelchair at the entrance, there was no holding him. 'Mammy! Mammy!' Arms open, he ran to her, brimming with tales and needing a hug.

Harry could not take his eyes off Sara. 'You look so beautiful!'

For the first time in an age, he could see the girl he had married; that glowing girl with the wide, wonderful smile, and those quiet brown eyes. 'You look . . . stunning!' Try as he might, Harry could not find the right words.

Sara felt a rush of pride. 'I'm glad you approve,' she retorted cheekily. 'I hope you realise it took a wagonload of make-up and an army of people to produce this new me.'

Much to everyone's concern, she then helped her son clamber onto her lap, while he chatted excitedly of seagulls and ice cream.

Safe and content in her embrace, Tom wrapped his small arms round her neck and kissed her full on the mouth.

Fearing that Tom's enthusiasm was bound to take its toll, Harry gently removed the boy from her lap. 'I tell you what.' He handed the flowers to Tom. 'You give these to Mammy, then you can help me to push the wheelchair to the car. What do you say?'

The child glanced up, looking for his mammy's approval. When she nodded, he ran to the rear of the wheelchair, feeling tall and proud next to Nurse McDonald. 'Do you think you're big enough?' she asked with a mischievous glint in her eye.

Tom stretched to his full height. 'I'm bigger than Johnny Mason.'

'Oh, and are you strong enough, my little man?'

The boy flexed his muscles. ''Course I am!'

Nurse Aileen kept him chatting while Harry enjoyed a quiet moment with his wife.

'Are you sure you feel able to come home with us?' he asked her, his heart full.

Sara pressed her finger to Harry's lips. 'I've been looking forward to it all morning,' she whispered, and he knew not to argue with her. Besides, though it was a bittersweet thing, after endless weeks of seeing her in a hospital bed, it was so wonderful to be taking her home.

A few minutes later, after thanking Nurse Aileen, the little group left the hospital.

Having got Sara to the car without any difficulty, Harry opened the rear door for Tom, then pushed the front seat back as far as it would go. Gently lifting Sara out of the wheelchair and into the car, he was devastated to realise how thin and weightless his wife had become.

He sensed her looking up at him. Her eyes held his gaze, and though not a word was spoken, the bond between them was a powerful thing; so much so, that he believed he would suffocate. 'I love you so much,' he whispered in her ear.

'Show me how much.' The pretty brown eyes twinkled mischievously.

Deeply moved, he gazed on her a moment longer, then he leaned forward and, steadying himself with one hand, he placed the other to the side of her face, and then he kissed her – a long, wonderful kiss that told her everything she needed to know.

'We need to go to the park!' Full of childish anticipation, Tom was clapping his hands. 'I want Mammy to see the ducks!'

Sara laughed. 'You two have already been gadding about the beach and now you want to go to the park?' Sara was glad that Harry had not yet told their son the truth, but there would be time enough, she thought. It was only right that her darling boy should enjoy the magic in his carefree world, for just a while longer.

She worried about them both; especially Harry. He would have no one to console him, while Tom would always have his daddy. She thought of Irish Kathleen, and not for the first time she prayed with all her heart that Harry would keep his promise and return to Fisher's Hill, the place where he was born. He still had friends there; people who had cared for him as a boy, and whom he had badly missed over the years.

Sara knew that for Harry, going back to face his demons would not be easy. But it would be a fresh start for both him and young Tom.

She truly believed it was the right thing for her husband and son, and it was what she herself wanted. Harry always kept his promises, and she knew he would keep this one; albeit reluctantly.

'Mammy! You *have* to come and see!' Tom was insistent. 'You *have* to come and help us feed the ducks!'

'That's enough, Tom.' Harry could see how tired his wife was. 'I told you we might have to leave it for another day. Your mammy needs to rest. We must take her home.' Harry was desperate to get her settled and comfortable. 'We'll maybe go later – see if your mammy feels up to it then. All right, son?'

On the verge of tears, Tom nodded. 'All right.'

As he drove away, all manner of things were running through Harry's mind. Should he tell the boy today . . . tell him right now, or later when they were all together at home? No! The doctor said not to tell him until it was absolutely necessary. 'No need upsetting him a minute before you have to,' that was what he had advised. Yet Harry felt the weight of it like a mountain on his shoulders.

He thought it was wrong not to warn the boy, yet like the doctor, he was coming round to the idea that it might be best if he left it for a while – not too long though. Maybe it could wait until tomorrow, after Sara was back in the hospital.

Yes, that was it, he decided. He would tell young Tom tomorrow.

Giving Sara a reassuring squeeze of the hand, he headed out of the hospital grounds, towards home.

As they travelled along, Sara kept glancing in the rearview mirror; she could see the disappointment in her son's eyes. Harry was right, she *was* tired, and she could hardly wait to see her home after all these weeks. But, it was so hard, seeing Tom's forlorn little face.

Her mind was made up. 'Head for the park, Harry,' she said. 'I really would like to go and see the ducks with you and Tom.'

Tom gave a whoop of joy. 'I told you! I *knew* Mammy wanted to see the ducks. Please, Daddy. Please!'

'Stop it, Tom.' Harry couldn't think straight. 'Be quiet for a minute.' Turning briefly to Sara, he asked, 'Are you sure you're up to it?'

Sara took a moment, before giving her answer. 'You said this would be *my* day,' she reminded him gently. 'You said I could do whatever I wanted.'

'I know, but I meant—'

'I know what you meant. "Within the boundaries" is what you meant. But what's the sense in having boundaries?' She gave him a long, quiet look that spoke volumes. 'If I don't go right now, I may never get another chance.'

Harry knew she was right, but he could not bring himself to speak of it. Besides, there was nothing he could say that she didn't already know; that they didn't *both* already know.

Behind them, Tom was yelling with excitement.

'I should have known the two of you would gang up on me,' Harry groaned. 'I never could get the better of you pair.'

~

The park was fairly busy, with young mums pushing their big coach-built prams along and occasionally stopping to point out the ducks and swans to the babies inside. People went strolling by and older men sat on the benches, enjoying their pipes and newspapers; and right there, leaning over the rails, a young woman was feeding her half-eaten sandwich to the clamouring ducks.

Having parked up, Harry switched off the engine and lifted the wheelchair out of the boot. 'Stay where you are, Tom,' he told the boy. 'I'll get Mammy out first, then we'll go for a walk round the lake.'

'I want to come out now!' Tom was far too excited to remain in the car. 'I want to show Mammy the duck with the hurt wing.'

'Just hang on a minute, eh?' Harry wagged a finger at him. 'I can't keep my eye on you and get your mammy out all at the same time.'

Shifting forward in his seat, Tom wound his arms round his mother's neck. 'Are you happy, Mammy? Are you glad we brought you to see the ducks?'

Sara took hold of his hands. 'This is the happiest day of my life,' she said, and kissed the small warm fingers.

When Harry lifted her into the wheelchair, she held onto him. *You won't forget your promise, will you?* Weak as she was, her hold on him was vice-like, and the steely look of determination in her eyes took him aback.

'What do you mean?' he said. He knew well enough what she meant; but he could not bear to think about it.

Sensing his dilemma, Sara's heart was sore. The suffering had been long and hard, but right now in the depths of her soul, she was content – all but for one thing. 'I need to know that you and Tom have a place to go, when . . .' She paused, before going on more brightly. 'If your friend Kathleen is half as wonderful as you described, I can rest easy, knowing that you and Tom will have someone who cares.'

Deliberately averting his gaze, Harry looked out across the lake. He didn't want to talk about it, but it would not go away. *It would never go away!* A dark anger flooded his soul.

'Harry?' Her voice drifted into his thoughts. '*I need to know,*' she repeated.

Still, Harry did not look at her. Instead he closed his eyes, taking a moment to recover, before placing his two hands on the arms of the wheelchair. He met her gaze with the deepest concern. 'You mustn't fret. I made you that promise,' he spoke with quiet sincerity, 'and I'm telling you now, hand on heart, you can be sure I mean to keep it.' There! It was said, and the saying made it all the more real, and now the tears swam across his eyes so he could hardly see.

'Thank you.' With her slim, delicate fingers she wiped away his tears with a gossamer touch. Her smile was infectious. 'Now then, my lovely, handsome man, before our son jumps right through the floorboards, can we *please* go and find these blessed ducks?'

Beside himself with excitement, Tom was leaping up and down in the back of the car.

A few moments later, Sara was settled in the wheelchair. Despite the warm July day, she was swathed in a rug with her feet tucked up nice and cosy; she remarked on the fresh sweet smell of the land and the water. Then she sat back, taking in the magnificent scenery, while Harry pushed her along the walkway and Tom skipped on ahead, shouting and laughing, and frightening every creature for miles around.

Sara's pain was constant, but not yet unbearable, and for that she was thankful; though at the same time she was mindful of the medicine bag in the pouch behind her seat. Oh, but it was such a treat to be in the fresh air, where she could breathe easier, and the skies seemed never-ending. And what a joy, to see the wide meandering lake, and the mixed, colourful shrubbery beyond. 'It's so special here,' she told Harry excitedly. 'I don't know if I ever told you, but this park has always been a favourite of mine.'

'Mine, too.' Tom fell over but soon jumped up again.

With Tom giving a running commentary, Harry pushed the wheelchair all the way round the lake, his attention evenly divided between his wife and his son. But all the time he was acutely aware of Sara's medication, secreted away yet readily accessible.

Every now and then they stopped while Tom coaxed the ducks onto the grass with pieces of bread. When they waddled towards him at full speed, quacking and screeching, Tom would run away screaming like a banshee, making his mother laugh out loud.

When Harry got Sara close enough to stroke her fingers down the long slim neck of a graceful and unusually tame swan, she was beside herself. 'Oh, Harry, he's so soft . . . the feathers are so beautiful, just like silk!'

They had been there for no more than half an hour, when Harry caught Sara shivering. 'Are you in pain?' he asked immediately. As ever, he was right there for her.

'No,' she quickly assured him. 'I felt a bit of a chill, that's all.'

'Right, come on, Tom. That's enough for now,' Harry announced. 'It's time to go home.'

Sara agreed. 'It's been wonderful, though,' she told them both happily. 'I would not have missed it for the world.'

On the way back to the car, Tom was thrilled to see a family of swans gliding over the lake. 'Daddy! Mammy! Look!' Before they could stop him, he ran across the grass to sit on a nearby bench, from where he had a good view of the birds. His voice sailed through the air. 'COME AND SEE THE SWANS!'

Angry that he should have run off like that, Tom ordered him back. 'We need to leave! Tom, get back here *now*!'

Surprising him, he felt Sara's hand in his. 'Leave him be, my love,' she murmured. 'He's just excited.'

'I'm concerned about you catching a chill.'

A couple of times on the way round the lake, Harry had seen her wincing with pain. When he reminded her that the medication was in the pouch, along with a flask of water, she told him she was fine, and that he worried too much.

'Wheel me to the bench, Harry.' Seeing how he was about to protest, she grabbed his hand. 'Just for a minute . . . please?'

With Tom still yelling, and Sara so insistent, Harry reluctantly gave in. 'A couple of minutes, that's all,' he conceded. 'Then you're both going back into the car and no arguments.' Slipping off his jacket, he fastened it securely about Sara's shoulders and neck.

'Honestly, Harry! You've got me trussed up like a turkey,' she grumbled, while in truth, she had never been happier.

For a few precious moments, the three of them took delight in watching the swans fly past until they were just tiny specks on the horizon.

Tom was still leaping up and down, doing acrobatics on the bench, while Sara laughed at his antics. 'Look at him, Harry.' The child was a sheer delight to her. 'It does my heart good, to see him so happy.' She ached for her son, knowing that soon, he would be faced with a terrible truth.

She looked up at her husband, her adoring gaze drawing his image into her soul. 'Harry?'

He stooped to her. 'Yes, sweetheart?'

'Thank you for today,' she told him. 'You've given me the best day of my life.'

Deeply moved, Harry held her close. 'Oh Sara, I miss you so much,' he confessed brokenly. 'I miss holding you when we go to bed, and waking up next to you in the morning. I miss watching you when you potter about in the garden . . . and hearing your awful singing when you're doing the dishes.' They both smiled at that. 'All those familiar things that we took for granted, I miss them *desperately*. But most of all, I miss our life together.'

Choking on his words, he gulped back the emotion. 'Sorry, sweetheart. I try to be strong, but now and then it swamps me. I feel ashamed, because it's *you* I should be concerned about. Not myself.'

'Don't be too hard on yourself, Harry. It's out of our hands now, and however much we want to, we can't change that.'

As Sara ran the palm of her hand over Harry's bowed shoulders, not for the first time she realised that, in a different way, Harry's pain was every bit as crippling as her own.

'All those things you said – I miss them too,' she confided lovingly. 'But you and me, Harry, we should be counting our blessings. We've been given so much – a happy life together, a darling boy, and now just look at us: here we are, sitting in the sunshine, holding each other, when there are so many people in this world who will never know how wonderful that feels. When you think about it, Harry, we haven't done so bad, have we, eh?'

Harry shook his head in admiration. 'You never cease to amaze me. You've always been able to see the best in a bad situation,' he said. 'And that's another thing I love about you.'

Just then, Tom jumped off the bench and began running down the steep bank, towards the lake. 'No, Tom! Get back here!' Harry shouted. But the boy kept running, veering this way then that, and thinking it was all a game.

'Go on, Harry.' Sara had every faith in him. 'Go get him!' And when Harry took off at the run, she yelled encouragement. 'Come on, you can do it! You've got long legs and he's only little!' Harry had to laugh at that, and when Tom shot off towards the shrubbery, he paused for breath, before setting off again. '*All right Tom, that's enough! Game over, come on now!*'

Breathless now, it crossed his mind that he wasn't as fit as he should be. '*Tom! Your mammy's waiting to go home!*'

It wasn't long before he had the runaway in his arms. 'You and your mammy are two of a kind,' Harry panted then threw him over his shoulder, until Tom squealed with laughter. Then when Harry tickled his ribs, the boy was almost hysterical.

They went along the path and up the bank, towards the spot where Sara was waiting, 'This boy takes after you,' Harry called ahead. 'Disobedient and wilful, that's what he is.'

As they drew closer, Harry continued to lightheartedly tease and grumble. 'Oh yes, he's definitely taken after his mother. It's no good, Sara, you're gonna have to get him under control, because he doesn't listen to a word I say . . .' He stopped in his tracks. *Something was wrong! He could sense it.*

Swinging Tom from his shoulders, he ran forward. 'Sara! . . . Oh dear God . . . my SARA!' But Sara was gone from this world, and when he took her in his arms, he knew her pain was over.

Passionately, he folded her to his heart, remembering the words she had said only minutes ago. 'This is the best day of my life.' But it was small consolation. Sara had left them behind, and he was devastated.

Instinctively, Harry caught his son to him, and together they held her – until a passing couple came to their aid.

When he thought about it later, Harry could never remember covering those last few paces to Sara. He recalled the very moment when he realised something was wrong. He felt the weight of his son on his shoulders, and he remembered swinging Tom to the ground.

But that was all; until he had Sara in his arms.

Too young, too vibrant, she had lost her fight to live.

She was at peace now; and in that agonising time when he held her, Harry thought she was more beautiful than he could ever remember.

The following week in the pretty church overlooking the shoreline, there were many tears at Sara's untimely departure and great joy at having known her as Harry and little Tom, proud and broken, led the congregation outside, to the well-tended, colourful garden. There on the bank on a glorious August day, they laid her to rest, facing the view she had always loved.

There followed a well-set-out tea in Sara's cosy home, where the neighbours had pulled together and taken charge.

Afterwards, when everyone was gone, Harry spoke with his son. 'Your mammy is safe now,' he promised him gently. 'Someone very special is looking after her now.'

Tom flung his arms round his daddy and sobbed until it seemed he would never stop. After a time, he fell asleep in Harry's arms, whereupon with great tenderness, his father carried him to the couch and covered him over.

With those tiny arms around his neck, Harry had felt the unforgiving burden of grief like never before.

Looking down now on that small, innocent face so much like his mammy's, Harry's heart turned over. 'Look out for us, my darling,' he wept, and glanced towards the window as though talking to some unseen person. 'Help me to make the right decisions.'

~

On the last day of August, Harry and his son stood at the door of their home and watched their furniture being loaded up. 'Have you kept back everything you need, son?' Harry wanted the boy to be sure.

Tom held up the raggedy lop-eared dog. 'I've got Loppy,' he said, and gave the shadow of a smile.

'Are you sure he's all you want to take with you?'

The boy confirmed this with a nod.

'It's your last chance, Tom. If there's anything else you need, you have to say so now, before the wagon leaves.'

'I only need Loppy.'

'Okay, if you're sure.'

Striding down the drive, Harry spoke with the burly driver.

'You can take it away now,' he instructed. 'Oh, and you won't forget, will you,' he pointed to a large tea-chest marked Personal, 'that that one does *not* go in the sale. It goes into storage.'

The driver perused his clipboard. 'I've got it all written down, sir. Don't worry, everything will be taken care of.'

'And you've got the forwarding address for the documents and such?'

The driver tapped his clipboard. 'Like I say, it's all written down here.'

'Good.' Taking his wallet from his back pocket, Harry slipped the driver two pound notes. 'Thanks. You and your mate have done a good job.'

The driver stuffed the notes in his pocket. 'Much appreciated, sir.'

'You will be careful with it all, won't you? I mean, try not to damage anything?' Buried under cardboard boxes, he could see the well-worn armchair that both he and Sara had sat on many times; in particular he recalled the evening when she had perched on his knee in that very chair and told him she was expecting their first – and now only – child.

'We'll treat your belongings with respect, sir.' At the onset of this job, the driver had been acquainted with Harry's circumstances, causing him to be grateful for his own happy marriage and five healthy children.

Harry thanked him before, with heavy heart, he turned away.

~

Having gone from room to room, satisfying himself that everything was locked and secure, Harry got Tom and the suitcases into the car and drove straight to the churchyard.

The gardener, Roland Sparrow, was waiting in the porch; pencil-thin and whisky-faced, he gave a nervous cough as Harry approached. 'I've not been waiting too long, Mr Blake,' he preempted Harry's question. 'Five minutes at most.'

Taking off his flat cap, he then addressed him with a mood of respect. 'Might I say before we start, the boss informed me of your loss, and if you don't mind, I would very much like to offer my condolences.'

Harry acknowledged his concern. 'Thank you, Mr Sparrow, that's very kind.' Quickly changing the subject, he asked, 'Did you bring the copy of instructions I left at your office?'

'I have them here,' came the answer. 'Very thorough they are too. Most folks either don't know how, or don't bother, to take the time and trouble drawing plans and naming flowers, but you've done it all, and it makes my job that much easier, if I may say so.'

'And are you comfortable with everything?' Harry had taken a long time, thinking about what Sara would have wanted.

'I have, and what's more I think it'll turn out to be the prettiest little garden in the churchyard. Keeping the place beautiful, it's what I do.'

Looking down his glasses, which were precariously perched at the end of his narrow nose, he read from Harry's list. 'Let's see now . . . the planting of different coloured heathers for autumn and winter; daffodil and tulip bulbs all around the border for spring, and a girdle of low-growing pink and blue perennials for the summertime.

'By! It'll be well pretty! Oh, and just think of the perfumes in the summertime!' His voice adopted a reverent tone again. 'I understand you've chosen a black marble cross, with two inbuilt flower vases?'

Harry confirmed it with a nod.

'Well, I can tell you now, the vases will be filled every two weeks with seasonal flowers, and they'll be regularly topped up with water 'cause that's what I do.'

'So, I can count on you, then?' Harry needed reassuring.

Mr Sparrow beamed with pride. 'I shall tend your lady's garden with great care, you can depend on it.'

Harry concluded the discussion. 'You'll find all the names

and telephone numbers you need on your list, and I will be in touch with your office with regards to everything. Also, I'll be back as often as I can, so as to keep an eye on things.'

'That's absolutely understood, Mr Blake. And I'm sure you'll find everything to your satisfaction.' Sparrow glanced about the well-tended churchyard. 'I've been doing this work for nigh on twenty years. It's what I do, and though I say so meself . . . nobody does it better.'

'I'm sure.' With that, they parted company.

Harry watched the older man amble away. He did not particularly enjoy the idea of someone else tending Sara's grave plot, but for now it had to be that way, if he was to keep his promise to her.

'Is the man getting yellow roses for Mammy?' Cradling his precious raggedy dog, Tom had stood silent throughout the conversation. Now though, as he looked up at Harry, the tears were not far away.

Harry swung the boy into his arms. 'That's right, and because we'll be nearly two hundred miles away, Daddy's paying him to take care of your mammy's garden when we can't be here.' It hurt him to see how the boy was so hopelessly out of his depth. 'Is that all right with you, young man?'

'Will he put the yellow roses where Mammy can see them?'

'I'm sure he will, yes. Mr Sparrow is a good, kind man. He would want Mammy to see her favourite flowers.'

He and Tom then went to stand before Sara's grave for what seemed an age. They talked of the past and spoke of the future, and they gave their heartfelt promise to come back whenever they could.

After a time, they made their way out of the churchyard in silence, lost in thoughts of that wonderful woman who had briefly touched their lives, and made them all the stronger for it.

Leaning back on his rickety wooden bench, the gardener saw them leave; he saw how the little boy clung to his father, and he saw the grief in the latter's face, and he shook his greying head.

'Time will help,' he muttered. 'Wait and see if I'm not right.' His own young wife had died of blood poisoning twenty years or more since, and at the time, he had thought he would never get over it. But he'd now been married to the excellent second Mrs Sparrow for over fifteen years, and couldn't be happier.

He then slid the whisky flask out of his back pocket and took a healthy swig. 'Phew! Puts hairs on a man's chest that does, and no mistake!' he said to the gravestones.

Returning the flask to his back pocket, he began merrily whistling as he went about his work.

Roland Sparrow was used to seeing folks come and go. He tended their graves and he drank to their health.

After all . . . *it was what he did.*

At the gate, Harry glanced back. In his mind's eye he could see Sara as plain as day; laughing in that carefree way he loved, her long hair blown by the breeze while she chased Tom across the park. She was always so brimful of life and energy.

He smiled at her memory now, and through the rest of his life, that was the way he would always remember her.

~

The final stop was the estate agent.

'So the house is empty now, is it, sir?' The agent was a fresh-faced young fellow with a blue and white spotted tie and a smile as wide as the Mersey Tunnel.

Harry handed over the keys.

'We'll be in touch.' The young man's smile was comforting. 'Matter of fact, the gentleman who viewed your property a week ago has sold his own place and now he's arranged to view your house again.'

'Sounds hopeful.' Harry had agonised about selling their home, but it was all part of the promise he had made to Sara.

'It's best if you do it straight away.' She had been insistent. 'Before Tom starts school.'

'I'll let you know how it goes.' The young man's voice penetrated Harry's thoughts. 'Is that all right with you?'

Harry apologised. 'Sorry . . . er, yes. Yes, that's absolutely fine. I'll wait to hear from you.'

A few moments later, taking hold of Tom's hand, Harry then embarked on the journey he never dreamed he would make. He would not be making it now, if Sara had not made him promise.

The memories of his youth had never really gone away; Sara knew that. When he first met her, he told her everything, and she was a tower of strength to him.

The memories were suffocating, of the way it had been. Wonderful memories. Crippling memories.

After he lost his parents in a fire, there was the lovely Irish Kathleen, always there, wise and caring. She had been like a mother to him.

Sometimes tragedy frightens people away, like the mates he used to hang about with – Bob, Alan, and the unpredictable Phil Saunders, who had always been his rival. Where were they now? What had become of them? Had they done well, or fallen by the wayside?

He smiled, despite his sombre mood. Wasn't it strange how life swept you along, whether you wanted it or not. Like the ebb and flow of the tide, it was meant to be.

Without him even realising it, the girl grew strong in his mind.

'Judy.' After all this time, her name came softly to his lips. Back then when they were young, she had meant the world to him. When it all went wrong, he had moved away – to the mayhem of war and manhood. And then some turbulent years later he had met his darling Sara and moved to Weymouth to build a life with her. Warm and forgiving, she had been his saviour, giving him stability and a son.

Why though, had Sara desperately wanted him to go back?

Back to that place where he had grown up and found his first love? What woman would want that? But then, Sara was special.

In that moment, he wondered about his first love, and a great sadness filled his heart. Had Judy found happiness? Was she safe? Had she forgiven him? Or did she want to punish him for what had happened all those years ago?

Time would tell, he thought.

Truth was, the prospect of seeing her again was deeply unsettling.

CHAPTER TWO

With only a short distance to go up the A418 from Aylesbury before they reached Leighton Buzzard, Harry found himself snarled up in traffic. 'I think we'll take a short break,' he said. A quick glance at the boy and he decided it would do them both good to take another breather. It was a very long journey from Weymouth to Bedfordshire and they had been driving for hours. Besides, the nearer he got to Fisher's Hill, the more his nerves were getting the better of him.

Twenty minutes later, as Harry negotiated his way through the lanes and backways, Tom spotted a food van in a lay-by. 'I'm hungry, Daddy,' he said.

'Okay,' Harry conceded. 'It's been a while since we ate.' Drawing into a little gravelled area, he got Tom out of the Hillman. 'Come on, then. Let's see what they've got.' To tell the truth, he welcomed the stop. His back was aching, and he had a real thirst on him.

At the van Harry lifted Tom into his arms. 'Right, big man. What d'you fancy?' He pointed to the items arranged on glass shelves behind the counter. 'And don't get anything too messy,' he cautioned. 'I don't want it all over you . . . or the car!'

Tom chose a ham roll. Harry chose ham and tomato; and each had a bag of potato crisps, a Wagon Wheel chocolate biscuit, and a bottle of orange juice. On the way back to the car, they chatted about this and that, the main topic being the little man who could hardly see over the counter to serve them.

With only a short distance to Fisher's Hill, Harry was still questioning the situation. Was Kathleen only acting out of loyalty by writing back in response to his letter, and saying they could stop with her? And would Judy's life be turned upside down again, because of him?

He could not go home, and he had no other family, so if he didn't go to Kathleen, where would he go? All the same, wouldn't it be better if he let sleeping dogs lie? He could take them to a hotel; maybe arrange to rent a house until he found something more permanent.

'I think we'll pull off the road for a while, Tom,' he told the boy. 'After all, we're in no hurry.' He felt the need to slow everything down.

Taking a left turn, he found himself in what looked like a lane to nowhere. 'I remember this place.' He and Judy had been here many times on their bikes. 'I used to go fishing in the stream at the bottom,' he said. 'Me and . . . my friends.' The pictures were so alive in his mind – of him and his mates – climbing trees, chasing rabbits, and doing all the usual stuff that growing boys do.

And then, later on, there were the quieter, more memorable times, when he and Judy came walking hand-in-hand down this very lane, wide-eyed and starstruck; hopelessly in love.

Now, when the guilt poured in, he deliberately pushed the memories to the back of his mind.

Parking the car, he collected Tom and the food, and the two of them meandered down the bank, to follow the splashing sound of water.

Overhung with ancient willows, the stream was magical. The frothy white water tumbled over the boulders and wound its way down to the valley, and all around the birds could be heard singing.

Mesmerised, the two of them stood for a moment, just watching, and listening. The graceful willows swayed ever so gently in the teasing breeze, and the sound of water against stone was uniquely soothing.

Harry allowed the memories to flood back. 'Shall I tell you something?' he murmured to Tom.

Intent on the little bird hopping from boulder to boulder, the boy nodded. 'Mmm.'

'When we were your age, me and my friends used to leap across this stream.'

Wide-eyed and open-mouthed, Tom gave his father his full attention. 'Did you?'

'We did.'

'And did you get a smack for being naughty?'

Harry laughed out loud. 'We did, yes! Every time we fell in and got wet, our mams got cross and our dads gave us a clip round the ear.'

Deep in thought, he grew quiet for a while. 'We still came down here though.' He pointed to an old oak tree on the other side. 'We even made a den in the branches of that tree.'

Stretching his neck, Tom strained to look into the tree branches. 'I can't see it.'

'Well, you wouldn't, would you?' Harry felt a pang of sadness. 'It was a long time ago. It's probably rotted away by now.'

'Can we see?' Having caught the excitement in his father's voice, Tom was curious.

Harry considered Tom's request, and he too began to wonder. 'Yes, why not? Let's go take a look.'

'How can we get across?'

'We'll paddle – would you like that?'

Tom threw his two arms up in the air. 'Yes, I would!'

So they kicked off their shoes, rolled up their trousers, and dipped their bare feet in the stream, with Tom screeching at the shockingly cold water which lapped over his ankles.

For the first time in an age, Harry laughed out loud. 'Wow! That's a good feeling, don't you think so, Tom?'

'It's freezing, Daddy!'

'Do you want me to carry you?'

'No! I want to paddle!'

So with Harry holding tight to Tom's hand, the two of them paddled across the stream and clambered out on the other side, all wet and refreshed, and much lighter of heart. 'D'you know what, Tom?' Harry took a deep invigorating breath. 'I'd forgotten what that felt like.' It had taken him right back to another time, one without responsibility or worries.

'We might do that again some day?' he suggested, and Tom was all for it.

After rummaging about in that big old tree, they found remnants of Harry's childhood. Amazingly, the main plank which had forged the base of their den was still virtually intact. 'Lift me up, Daddy!' Tom was beside himself with excitement.

Warning him to stay very still, because of the rotting wood, Harry lifted him up to stand on the plank, and when the boy looked down on what had been Harry's kingdom, Harry felt deeply nostalgic. He could see himself up there, not much older than Tom was now, being master of all he surveyed.

The most surprising find of all, was when Harry lifted his boy down. He was not consciously thinking of it, so it must have been a deeper instinct that brought his gaze to the widest girth of the trunk.

'Good Lord!' His heart soared in his chest when he saw the outline of two entwined shapes deeply engraved in the timber.

'What is it, Daddy?' Tom wanted to know.

Seeming not to have heard, Harry went forward, with Tom right behind, and there, crudely carved within the two entwined hearts, so faint he could hardly read it, were the names of *Harry* and *Judy*.

An unexpected storm of emotion flooded Harry's being; for a moment he had to turn away, so Tom would not see.

'Daddy, show me! Show me, Daddy!'

Taking a deep breath to compose himself, Harry snatched

the boy into his arms and strode away. 'It's nothing . . . just some old carvings, that's all.' But it wasn't all. It was wonderful, and shocking, and the strongest reminder yet, of how it had been between him and Judy.

He remembered it now, as if it was yesterday.

It was the summer after Judy's family had moved into the street, when they were just childhood friends, riding their old bikes around the countryside, coming here and making their mark on the world.

As they hurried away from that place, Harry could hear his son chatting about the tree and the stream, telling his dad how he wanted to come back again. Harry had nothing to say. He was being drawn back into another world, one from which he had flown long ago.

Having paddled back to the other side, Harry tried desperately to shut the images out of his mind. 'Hungry now, are you?' he asked Tom.

'Starving!'

'Right.' They dried their feet on their socks, then put their shoes back on, and Harry unwrapped the food.

'There you go, son. Time to tuck in.' He handed the boy his bread roll, relieved that Tom had got back his appetite. 'Good, is it?' These past few weeks, neither of them had felt much like eating.

With his mouth full, Tom nodded.

'I didn't realise how hungry I was,' Harry commented, tearing off another chunk of his bread roll. 'When we've finished, we'll get back on the road.' He swallowed the last bite. 'There's a box of tissues in the back of the car. We can finish drying our feet on them.'

The boy looked up. 'Daddy?' he asked.

Harry didn't hear. He was thinking of that carving, and Judy. Then he was thinking how much Sara would have loved this beautiful place.

'Daddy!' Tom repeated, more loudly this time.

Startled, Harry turned, his glance softening as he gazed down on that small, innocent face, 'Sorry, son. I was miles away.'

'What town is that?' The lad pointed across the bank, towards the swathe of houses.

'It isn't a town, son. It's a village – name of Heath and Reach.' This whole area had been his stamping ground. 'The nearest town is Leighton Buzzard,' he pointed towards the curve of the canal, 'about four miles in that direction.'

'Leighton Buzzard? That's a funny name. So, is that where we're going?'

'Nope.' Harry shook his head.

'Where are we going then?'

Again, Harry turned away, his mind filled with things belonging to the past. Things that had never really left him.

The boy tugged on Harry's sleeve. 'I'm tired.'

Smiling patiently, Harry slid an arm round his narrow shoulders. 'I know,' he conceded. 'It's been a long journey, but we're not far off now.'

'Where are we going?'

'Oh, Tom, I already told you three times on the way here. We're going to a place called Fisher's Hill. The place where I grew up.'

'Oh yes.' The boy dropped his quiet gaze to the water's edge. He didn't want to go somewhere strange. He wanted to go back to his own house. He wanted his mammy, and the garden where he played at soldiers behind the trees.

But it was gone now. All gone, and the child's heart was heavy.

'Will I like it in our new place, Daddy?' he asked tearfully.

'I hope so, son.' Harry was anxious, for both of them. 'Yes, I believe you will like it. I *know* you'll like Kathleen. She's a lovely person. When I was growing up and something really bad happened, Kathleen was very good to me.'

'Was that when your mammy and daddy got burned?'

Shocked, Harry swung round. 'Tom! Who told you that?'

'I heard you talking with Mammy,' Tom answered candidly.

'Oh, I see.' In an odd way, Harry was strangely relieved, though he wondered how a small boy could have remembered something like that.

'Mammy asked you to promise you would go back, and you said you didn't want to, because you had those bad memories.'

'That's right, son. I did say that.' He was sorry that Tom had been living with those thoughts, and then felt the need to clarify something. 'Can you remember anything else – apart from the bit about the bad memories?' he asked.

Tom shrugged his shoulders, but gave no answer.

'Well, when I told Mammy that I didn't want to go back to where I grew up, she reminded me that I shouldn't just remember the *bad* memories, because there were good memories as well. Memories of love, and friendship, and of that kind lady called Kathleen, who took me in after I lost my parents. That's really why Mammy wanted us to go back.'

'Because she was going away, wasn't she?'

'Yes, son,' Harry said in a choked voice, 'because she was going away, and she did not want us to be without friends.'

Tom considered that, before, with the innocence of a child, he asked, 'Will Kathleen really like me?'

Harry smiled at that. 'Of course she'll like you. She won't be able to help herself.'

There followed a brief span of silence while each of them took stock of the situation, 'Daddy?'

'Yes, son?'

'Kathleen won't pretend to be my real mammy, will she?'

'No. She would never do that.'

'I wish Mammy could be with us.'

'I know, son.' Harry's voice fell to a whisper. 'But she can't. I'm sorry, Tom, but we have to get used to that.'

'I miss her.' The tears threatened.

'I know you do, and so do I.' He drew the boy close. 'If there was any other way, you know I would make it right. But I can't, so from now on, it's just the two of us.'

'Will Mammy be all right without us?'

'Don't worry. She'll be fine.'

'Is she with the angels?'

'I imagine so. Yes, that's where she is . . . with the angels.'

The boy's next question shook Harry to the roots, for it echoed his own deepest fears. 'We'll never see her again, will we? Not ever.'

For the moment, Harry could not bring himself to answer. The truth was, he still had not come to terms with her loss.

He looked down on that small, bewildered face, and he felt helpless. 'We have no way of knowing if we'll ever see her again, Tom,' he answered quietly. 'But even if we can't see her, I bet she can see us. Wherever we go, she'll be keeping an eye on us; wanting us to be strong, wanting us to look after each other.'

Tom was amazed. 'Does she know I got my feet wet in the stream?'

Harry smiled. 'Maybe she does, yes.'

'When we go back to the car, will she come with us?'

'I don't know, son.'

Tears were inevitable as they tumbled down the boy's face. 'I want my Mammy . . . I want her *now*!'

Grabbing the boy into his arms, Harry pacified him. 'Hush now. I want her too, but we can't have her back, except in our hearts and minds. That's something, isn't it, Tom? That really is . . . something.'

Sensing his father's desolation, the boy wrapped his arms round his neck. 'I'm sorry, Daddy.'

'I'm sorry too, son.' Brushing back the boy's brown hair, he put his hand under his chin and lifted Tom's face to him. 'I love you, Tom. I'll take good care of you, just like Mammy wanted.'

After a while he led the boy by the hand and together they walked back across the field and over the bridge. 'We'd best make tracks.' He didn't want it to be dark when they got there. 'Kathleen will be wondering where we are.' It was so long since he'd seen that kindly soul, he had almost forgotten what she looked like.

'What if she doesn't like me?' Tom began to fret again.

Harry gave the boy a loving glance, observing the eager eyes and the endless mop of brown hair, and the little face that could never be described as handsome, but was honest and giving. In that moment, he saw the mother in the child, and the pride was like a flame burning his chest.

'Will you stop worrying!' he said fondly. 'She'll love you to bits!'

'She's not my mammy though.' A familiar little frown crumpled the boy's forehead. 'You have to tell her.'

'I will, of course I will, but she already knows that. Look, son, trust me. Kathleen would never try to take your mammy's place. But she is a kind and wonderful person who is sure to want your happiness, every bit as much as I do.'

'Is she young and pretty, like Mammy?'

Harry shook his head. 'No, she's not young. But as I recall, she did have a pretty face . . . kind of warm and smiley.'

'Is she very old?'

He laughed. 'Old enough, I suppose.'

'Grandad was old, wasn't he?'

'I don't know that he would have agreed, but yes, I dare say he was.'

'Are *you* old, Daddy?'

Harry thought on that for a moment. 'Well, thirty-six isn't really meant to be old,' he had been shaken by the realisation of how short life could be, 'but yes, today, I *do* feel old.'

'Am I old?'

Harry laughed at his innocence. 'God, yes! You're as old as Methuselah.'

'Who's Musoothella?'

Chuckling, Harry settled the boy into the back of the car. 'He was a very wise person.'

'Am *I* a wise person?'

His father gazed on him tenderly for a moment. 'You know what?'

'What?'

Harry gave a wistful smile. 'I think you're probably the wisest person in the whole wide world.'

'Wise as Kathleen?'

'Well, nobody's as wise as Kathleen, but near enough, I reckon.'

Harry gave an involuntary shiver. Today had been a typical late-summer day, with long spells of bright sunshine and a warm, gentle breeze. Now though, with the onset of evening, the clouds hung menacingly low, and there was a sudden nip in the air. 'We might just get there before dark,' he muttered, covering Tom with the tartan travelling rug and pressing Loppy into his arms.

He then gazed back a moment to where they had been. Only the fleetest of moments, but he held it safe in his mind for all time.

Quickly now, he climbed into the driving seat and glanced in the mirror, to see the boy's head lolling to one side. 'That's right, son,' he murmured. 'You get some sleep.'

Before starting the engine he glanced at the sleepy boy, 'Aw, child! You give me so much joy . . . and I have nothing to give you in return.'

Driving away, he wondered what lay in store for them both. In the wake of recent events, he had made a hasty decision. Now with every mile that took them closer, the doubts grew stronger.

He had been a youth of eighteen when he left Fisher's Hill. He didn't altogether leave because he wanted to; war was in the air, and joining up seemed like the right thing at the time. He had left his home under a cloud, trailing with him a deal of heartache and regrets, with the intention of never returning.

In the eighteen years between, he had never forgotten the place that he loved so much. He moved away, travelling far and wide, and eventually settled after the war in Weymouth, with his new sweetheart, Sara, but Fisher's Hill and Judy remained a part of him, with the bad memories always overshadowing the good.

Even now, it was hard to believe that he was just a heartbeat away from Fisher's Hill.

When he had first contacted Kathleen after Sara's funeral, he was amazed and reassured to find that she was still alive, still the same lovely, homely person, and that she would welcome him and young Tom with open arms.

In his grief, he had needed something familiar and comforting, and it did his heart good just to see her familiar handwriting.

How many of his old mates might still be living there? He was thinking especially of Phil Saunders. Had he stayed? Had *any* of them gone back after the war – if they got through intact – and if they had, would they welcome him with open arms, or would they reject him, as he had rejected them all those years ago . . .

And what of his old sweetheart, Judy? Was she still there? Had she met someone – and if so, were they happy, or like himself, had she been badly scarred by what happened back then? He hoped not. Oh, he truly hoped not.

Aching with regrets, he slowed the car into the side of the road, where he remained for what seemed an age; thinking, remembering. Hurting all over again.

'What's wrong, Daddy?' Opening his eyes, Tom peered at him through the mirror.

'Nothing's wrong, son.'

'Why aren't we moving?'

'I just need a minute,' he replied. 'A minute, that's all . . . to get my thoughts together.'

Collecting a comic book from the passenger seat, he handed it back to Tom, watching in the mirror as the child began to quietly look at it and read a few words to himself.

'Judy might not be there,' Harry muttered under his breath. 'I didn't want to ask about her, and Kathleen never volunteered any information.' He hoped that was a good sign. 'I expect she's moved on . . . made a new life for herself.'

The man that Sara had moulded ached for his wife.

The boy inside the man longed for the one called Judy.

After all these years Harry could still see how heartless he had been. In spite of what had happened, he had truly loved her, back then, when he was just a youth.

Now though, he was a man with a man's responsibilities. He had lost the woman he loved and married, and he had a child to care for. He had no right to fret about the past because right now, at this moment in time, he was only concerned with building a new life for himself and Tom. That was his priority. He had to keep reminding himself of that!

At the junction he saw the sign, and his heart lurched:

Fisher's Hill – 2 Miles

He wondered if it would be wise to ring Kathleen and say he had changed his mind, that he was not coming back after all, but that he would keep in touch.

Then he was ashamed to himself. What's the matter with you? he thought. So you want to turn tail and run, is that it? It wouldn't be the first time, he admitted to himself, shamefacedly.

No! The choice was made. He had to go on. Kathleen was waiting, looking forward to seeing him and Tom. She was the only one who had stood by him, the only one who believed in him.

Thankful that Tom had drifted back to sleep, he realised how fortunate he was to have a friend like Kathleen.

Kathleen would give Tom a woman's love and comfort, he knew. He believed that beyond a shadow of doubt, because hadn't she done that for him? She had always been there for him. It was Kathleen who had seen him through that dreadful time with Judy, and she had never once judged him.

When his father took off with another woman and his mother turned to drink, he had felt so alone, but as always, Kathleen gave him comfort.

Some months later, drunk and violent, his father came back, pleading that he was ready to try again. That night, while Harry was out with his mates, his parents got into a fight and somehow a fire started – 'from a lit cigarette on the bedclothes' the investigators said.

Witnesses claimed that the fire exploded into a raging inferno. The emergency services arrived within minutes, but it was too late. 'A tragic accident' was the verdict.

That same night, Kathleen took him in and brought him through the nightmare of losing both his parents.

Through each and every crisis in his colourful, rebellious youth, Kathleen had been his only salvation; a tower of strength.

During the war, and his proud time of serving with the Bedfordshire and Hertfordshire Regiment, she was like a mother to him, keeping him safe, he felt, with her parcels and prayers. More than one thousand men were killed from the regiment, but Corporal, then Sergeant Harry Blake was not one of them. And now, when he had turned to her yet again, after years of deserting her and all that reminded him of his time at Fisher's Hill, she had welcomed him with open arms.

Stronger of heart, he drove on. Tom half-opened his eyes. 'Are we there yet, Daddy?'

'Not yet, Tom, no. Go back to sleep if you're tired.' He saw how the boy was still drowsy. Since Sara was taken, neither he nor Tom had slept through the night.

Minutes later, he pulled off the main road and drove very slowly up the lane leading to Fisher's Hill.

He had come this far and now, whatever the outcome, there was no way back.

Returning here, to the place of his youth, to his family roots, his first sweetheart and the tragedy of losing his parents, was the worst feeling. Yet coming back had always seemed inevitable, somehow. It was something he had needed to do, unfinished business, and when Sara was lost to him, turning to Kathleen seemed the most natural thing in the world.

As he drew closer, his heart was clenched like a fist, his throat so dry he could hardly swallow. He felt much like a man might feel on his way to the gallows. It was right that he should suffer, he thought cynically. *A kind of penance for his sins.*

One glance at the sleeping child in the back made him ashamed. It was Tom who mattered; not him.

Determined to concentrate on what lay ahead, he inched the car forward, his anxious gaze drawn towards the houses. As far as he could see, nothing had changed; every little detail was exactly as he remembered it. The brown-bricked houses were still there, strong and sturdy snuggled up side by side, with their little front walls and concrete paths, tidy well-kept gardens and net curtains at the windows; many of them twitching as folks peered through to take a look at the Hillman Minx moving at a snail's pace up the hill.

His troubled gaze went to the house on the corner. Number 12 – there it was on the door in large brass numbers just as he remembered.

He wondered if he was being watched. Was Judy there, still living at home? Was she hiding behind the curtains, her sorry eyes trained on him in that very moment? Or had she really gone for ever, from the house, this street, and his life?

He had no way of knowing, because in the many recent telephone conversations between them, Kathleen had never once mentioned Judy, and neither had he. It was for the best, he thought.

In spite of himself, and even when he had met and married

his lovely Sara, Judy had lingered, in the boy, and in the man; and the questions never went away. After he was gone, did she realise how he had had no choice but to do what he had done . . . for *both* their sakes? Or had she despised him to this day, and found contentment with someone more deserving?

'Let it go, Harry,' he told himself firmly. 'It was a lifetime ago.'

But he couldn't let it go. Against his better instincts, his quiet gaze lingered on the house. In his mind's eye he could see himself and Judy, laughing at silly, childish things; dancing to music on the wireless or just curled up on the sofa. He pictured them both running down the path, hand-in-hand, incredibly young and blissfully happy. Then he remembered the bomb-shell that ruined it all. If only he'd known! But he had never even suspected. So why then, should he feel so guilty?

He closed his eyes, the memories too painful. 'I did love you, Judy,' he told that young girl. 'Don't ever doubt that.'

Braking, and putting the car into neutral, he turned to look at the sleeping child. 'Your mammy knew what I had done,' he whispered. 'I told her everything, yet she took me into her life without question, accepting me as I was. She gave me a new start . . . taught me how to love again.'

The tears burned his eyes. 'I'm sorry you lost her, Tom,' he murmured. 'So sorry.' Leaning over, he stroked the child's soft hair. 'Your darling mammy was a wonderful woman and I loved her with every fibre of my being. You'll always miss her, and so will I, but I promise you . . . whatever life throws at us, we'll face it full on. You need have no worries, because I'll always be here for you.'

He raised his eyes to the shifting skies. 'Oh, Sara! I know you believed I should come back here, but now that I'm only a short distance away from where it all happened, I can't help but wonder if I'm doing the right thing. Did you think that I might find the forgiveness I crave? Or was your intention that I should settle the past once and for all, whatever the conse-quences?'

He closed his eyes, but the chaos in his mind was rampant, until he turned yet again to gaze on his son. Sara had entrusted him to take care of the boy and, for now, that was all that mattered.

For a moment he dwelled on all that was good in his life, and he felt at peace. 'I'll take good care of him, Sara, my love,' he vowed. 'With all that's in me, I give you my word.'

Composing himself, he put the car into gear and drove on up towards Kathleen's house. As he drew closer, the street enveloped him. It was as if he had never been away.

~

Kathleen O'Leary had been keeping vigil at the window. When she saw the car approach, she pressed close to the pane, her anxious gaze searching for the young man she had known all those years ago. When she recognised him, her heart leaped.

Flinging open her front door, she ran down the path to greet him; a small round woman with a mop of wild auburn hair and a crinkly, homely face that made you smile. 'Harry, me darlin'! I've been watching out for youse both . . .' Her Irish lilt was music to his ears. 'Sure I was worried you might change your mind, but now look, here you are at long last!' He had not changed, she thought. He was taller, wider of shoulder, and life had etched itself in his face, but it was him – Harry Boy – the lad she had cared for all those years ago. Her surrogate son.

She grabbed Harry as he got out of the car, and for a long time, they clung to each other. He had not realised just how desperately he needed to see that familiar, welcoming face and to feel those chubby comforting arms about him. The bright eyes were the same, and the wide, ready smile, filled with such kindliness.

'Aw, Harry Boy . . . will ye look at yourself? Isn't it the strong fine man you are!' She held him at arm's length, her quick brown eyes travelling the length and breadth of Harry's physique. 'Ah sure, you've not changed a bit. You're the same handsome, capable fella with the same dark eyes and wild mop of chestnut-coloured hair.' A tear brightened her eyes. 'You've a sadness about ye though,' she murmured. 'I can see I'll have to bring back that winning smile, so I will.'

'Oh, Kathleen.' Harry was deeply touched by her concern. 'You can't know how wonderful it is to see you again.' Moved by a well of emotion, he clutched hold of her shoulders. 'We'll never be able to thank you enough.'

'Give over with you! Sure, I'm only glad you've arrived safely, so I am.' She covered him in a beaming smile. 'And I am so longing to see the darlin' child.'

Peering into the back of the car, she gleefully clapped her hands together. 'Oh now, will ye look at the little fella. Sure, it doesn't seem a minute since yerself was just a lad.' She rolled her eyes. 'I'm sure I don't know where the years have gone . . . and now here ye are with a wee bairn of yer own.'

Gently waking Tom, and helping him out of the car, Harry watched as Kathleen took him into those fat little arms, her face wet with tears. 'Oh, but I'm glad you're back, Harry,' she told him fondly. 'An' now you've brought a little angel with you . . . Tom, a grand name, and a grand little face.' She kissed the sleepy upturned face, and thought how lost the little boy must be without his beloved mammy.

Thinking of Harry's young wife, taken all too soon, she caught his quiet gaze. 'I'm sorry, me darlin', about what happened. It's been hard going for you and the wee bairn, I know that.'

Harry nodded, tears in his own eyes. 'I feel lost, Kathleen,' he admitted brokenly. 'Me and the boy both.'

Smiling through the emotional moment, she grabbed them both into her embrace. 'Ah sure, ye have *me*, so y'do,' she said warmly. 'I'll look after youse, don't you worry about that.'

'You're a woman in a million,' Harry told her. 'I don't know what Tom and I would have done without you. And all those years back, whenever my life took a bad turn, you were always there, ready to put me back together again.'

He had been away for so long, and yet he remembered it all, as if it was only yesterday.

Since the day he left Fisher's Hill, he had regretted the hurt he caused; though given the same circumstances, he believed he would have to do the very same again.

Standing here outside Kathleen's house and looking down that familiar street, he felt oddly out of place. It was as though he was looking through a darkened window into the past. It was the strangest feeling, with his emotions torn in every direction.

Sensing his turmoil, Kathleen assured him, 'I kept my word, Harry. I never told anyone that you were on your way back.'

Harry nodded. 'And Judy? How did she get through it? What happened to her, Kathleen? I need to know.'

The small woman slowly shook her head. 'Judy is long gone from the street.' Glancing at the child, she suggested quietly, 'Best if we talk about it later, eh?'

He understood. 'You're right,' he answered. 'This isn't the time.' He had not expected to be disappointed at the news of Judy's leaving, but he was.

Kathleen saw his reaction. 'You've had a bad time of it, you and the bairn,' she murmured. 'I know how hard it must have been for you to come back here.' Her quick, warm smile was like a ray of sunshine. 'But if it's peace of mind ye're after, sure you've come to the right place.'

Harry nodded in agreement. It had taken all his willpower to come home, but he was here now, and more importantly, it was what his darling Sara had wanted.

Not for the first time, he counted his blessings. He had rekindled his friendship with dear Kathleen, he had his precious son, and the unforgettable memories of Sara, and he was immensely grateful. Yet, even with all of that, he still felt incredibly alone.

Both his parents were long gone; there were no brothers or sisters or any other relatives that he knew of, and his happy-go-lucky schoolmates, with their passion for girls and motorbikes, by now had probably moved away and had wives and families.

Here in this ordinary place, he had lived with the consequences of drunken, violent parents. He had experienced terror of a kind that no child should ever encounter. But he had forged deep friendships, and found his first real love in a girl called Judy. It had been an overwhelmingly beautiful experience, and to his dying day he would never forget how it was. But it was never meant to last, and for that he would be forever sorry.

Then, when he was at his lowest ebb, he had found another love – oh, not like before, because a man's first love is too deep and fulfilling to ever forget – but little Tom's mother, Sara, was a wise and beautiful creature with a generous heart. He came to love her deeply, but it could never be the same, all-consuming love he had felt for Judy, the young, sweet girl who had wakened his manhood and opened his heart like summer after winter.

Sara though, had been his salvation. She was forgiving and thoughtful, and he regarded himself as a very fortunate man to have had such joy and beauty in his life.

Over and over, he recalled the night when he had confided in Sara, revealing how it had been between himself and Judy, and of the awful manner in which their relationship had ended.

Sara did not blame or scold, nor did she judge. Instead, she listened to him, but it was never forgotten; not by him, and he knew not by her. Yet she stood by him, like the gentle person she was.

But it was never enough! He needed to confront the demons. He needed forgiveness from the very person he had hurt. But that was not to be, and so he had learned to live with the guilt.

'Come on now, Harry Boy,' Kathleen said cheerfully, as she waddled back up to the house. 'Let's get your man inside.'

Hoisting his yawning son into his arms, Harry took a moment

to follow, his attention still trained on number twelve. So, Judy had gone, and now he might never be able to make amends.

He let the past take him for a while.

Then he turned and hurried after Kathleen.

CHAPTER THREE

THE MINUTE HE walked into Kathleen's cosy little parlour, Harry felt at home. He stood, the child once more deeply asleep in his father's arms, and took a long look about him.

On the whole, it had not changed from the place he had fondly remembered all those years. The wood-panelled door was still the same, with its brass knocker and big iron handle, and the prettiest stained-glass window right at the top.

Once inside the tiny parlour his senses warmed to the familiar scent of snuff. He recalled how Kathleen had a weakness for it. When she thought no one was looking, she would take the smallest pinch of brown powder from the little silver box, pop it on the back of her hand, then she'd sniff it up her nose until her eyes watered and the ensuing sneeze took her breath away. Harry had always thought it comical, how after a pinch or two, the snuff formed an odd kind of moustache round her top lip.

It was oddly comforting to think she still enjoyed that secret 'little pinch o' snuff'.

The old leather chair that used to sit beside the fireplace was gone, and in its place was a smart brown chair with wide arms and long wooden legs. The old chair had been special to Kathleen's husband, Michael.

Harry had not forgotten the news which Kathleen imparted when they first spoke on the phone. 'I'm sorry about Michael,' he said awkwardly now.

Her smile momentarily disappeared. 'Me too,' she murmured. Then, in her usual robust manner, she deliberately changed the subject, took a deep breath and brought Harry's attention to the new décor. 'As you can see, I've changed a thing or two these past years.'

Looking about, Harry noticed the new lemon-coloured curtains, where before there had been pretty floral curtains of pink and green. The rug before the fireplace had been a crescent-shaped one, a rag rug that Kathleen had made herself. Now though, there was a smart, oval red rug with a border of cream-coloured roses; and the old brown horsehair sofa had been replaced with a dark blue cloth-covered one, with big round wooden feet and wooden arms where you might easily rest your cup of tea.

Kathleen's idea of comfort was as old-fashioned as the darling woman herself. Her home was a welcoming place where folks could put up their feet and rest awhile, or stay a week, whichever suited.

'We've got gas fires now,' Kathleen proudly informed him. 'Oh, and we've got rid of the old bed,' she revealed. 'Lord knows, I've been cracking me head on them iron knobs for long enough. Sure, it's a wonder me old brains aren't scrambled.'

She went on with a grin. 'As you well know, my Michael loved that bed, creaks and all. For years I fought him tooth and nail for a new one, but the stubborn old eejit was having none of it.'

Recalling the fierce but friendly arguments concerning the bed, Harry was curious. 'So how did you manage to persuade him?'

Kathleen gave out a raucous laugh, then quickly shushed herself. 'Michael had a night out with his mates down the pub, dominoes and drinking till the early hours, the buggers! The ting is, he staggered home totally blathered, setting off the dogs and waking up the street, he was! Then he was singing and now he was threatening at the top of his voice: "Me name is Michael O'Leary, an' I'll knock out the lights of any man who gets in me way!"'

Harry had to laugh. 'So, *did* anyone challenge him?' Going to the sofa, he gently laid the child down.

'No, thank the Lord. Sure, they'd have more sense than to tackle the likes of him! Well, anyway, I heard him arriving – in fact, I wouldn't be at all surprised if the whole world didn't hear him! He fell in the door, crawled up the stairs and crumpled into bed. Five minutes later he was away with the fairies.'

Harry had always thought Michael to be a lovable old rogue. 'But if he was asleep, he couldn't cause you any trouble, could he?'

'Aye, well, you'd think so, wouldn't you, eh?' she sighed. 'Had a nightmare, he did, thrashing about in a fight with some fella down the pub. The old bed was a-shaking and a-heaving, and suddenly it collapsed. The bedhead fell over and trapped Mikey by the neck. He was yelling and bawling, and saying how he could "feel the vengeance of the Lord".'

With a hearty chuckle she finished the tale. 'I told him to shut up his yelling, or he would feel the vengeance o' me yard-broom across his backside!'

Harry was laughing as he had not laughed for weeks, until he thought of poor Michael. 'He wasn't hurt bad, was he?'

'Aw, bless ye, Harry Boy . . . sure he wasn't hurt at all; or if he was, he didn't admit it.'

Taking a breath, she went on, 'The very next morning he was off for a game o' pool with his mates, but before he left, he called Patrick Mason. He asked would he call round and see if he could mend the bed. A while later, Patrick came and took a look. "I'll have it good as new in no time at all!" he said.'

There was a definite twinkle in her eye. 'I asked him how much would it cost to have it mended, and he said four pounds, so I gave him six and told him to say it was beyond repair. So there it is! Everyone was happy. Michael had the satisfaction of knowing that he was a better man than the bed, Patrick found a few quid in his pocket, and I got the new bed I'd been after for years. So there youse have it!'

She laughed out loud. 'Sure I couldn't have planned the whole thing better if I'd tried.' Making the sign of the cross on herself, she muttered humbly, 'Poor Mikey . . . may the Lord rest his soul.'

'And may the good Lord forgive *you*, Kathleen O'Leary.' Harry mimicked her Irish accent well. 'You're a wicked woman, so ye are.'

Her burst of laughter was so infectious that Tom stirred in his sleep. 'Away with ye, Harry Boy!' she cried. 'A woman has to beat the men at their own game, so she does.'

Her Irish eyes dimmed over. 'All the same, it's a pity he never lived long enough to enjoy the new bed,' she sighed. 'If he hadn't gone into that beer-drinking contest, he might still be here to this very day.' Then she gave a cheeky grin. 'Mind you, I reckon he had a fine old life, and if you ask me, he's up there with his mates – the lot of 'em drinking and carrying on like they ever did . . . bless their merry hearts!'

It was a tonic for Harry to hear her stories and her laughter, for it took him away from the grief and the loneliness of these past weeks. 'You'll never change, will you?' he said affection-ately. 'Honestly, Kathleen, you can't know how good it is to be here with you.'

Smiling bashfully, she brushed away his compliments. 'I dare say the pair of youse are starving hungry, so while I go and get us a bite to eat, you'd best wake the bairn up, or he won't sleep tonight.'

With that she left him to it, and hurried off to the kitchen.

Soon the little house was filled with the smells of wholesome good cooking. 'Come on, you two.' Harry was out in the back garden with Tom when she called them in. 'The table's all set and the food is ready, so it's just the two of youse I'm waiting for.' She ceremoniously ushered them inside, then told them to tuck in. 'You've got fat pork sausages new from the butcher this very morning, with vegetables so fresh they stand up on the plate, and potatoes mashed from my very own kitchen garden.' She gave Tom a wink. 'I've got a juicy apple pie for afters,' she whispered, 'all smothered in thick creamy custard. What d'you think to that, eh?'

Tom whispered back, 'Can I have a big piece with crust?'

Kathleen laughed aloud. 'As big as ye like,' she answered with a wink, and though he tried really hard, Tom could not manage a wink back, so he gave her a big gappy smile instead – which then opened the conversation as to how he lost his front tooth.

Tom explained that the fairies had taken the tooth and left him a whole shilling under his pillow, along with 'a note, saying they were building me a new tooth straight away!'

'Ah, well now, isn't that grand?' Kathleen gave a knowing wink at Harry, who was watching the two of them with a quieter heart than of late. 'I've lost four back teeth meself, so I have,' she said. 'How much d'you think they'll charge me to get new ones?'

Tom was amazed. 'I don't know.' He frowned. 'You've got big, grown-up teeth, and the fairies are only little.' He looked at his father, then he looked at Kathleen, and in a sombre voice informed her, 'Maybe you'd better go to the blacksmith.'

Trying not to laugh, Kathleen asked innocently, 'The blacksmith, eh? And what does he do?'

'He makes big shoes for big horses – I read it in the book Mammy got me for Christmas.'

For a second or two, the silence spoke volumes. 'Oh, I see,' said Kathleen, lightening the mood. 'So you think I'm big as a horse, do you?'

'Oh, no.' Tom shook his head vehemently. 'But he's got bigger tools than the fairies, and he could make your big new teeth on his fire.'

'Right.' Kathleen plopped another sausage onto his empty

plate. 'So that's what I'll do then,' she promised. 'I'll get my new teeth from the blacksmith. Shake on it?' She held out her hand.

'Shake on it!' Tom's happy grin said it all.

When conversation was done, and everyone was full to contentment, Kathleen left Tom and Harry chatting while she went upstairs. A few minutes later she returned with a flowery pinnie wrapped round her ample middle. 'I've run a bath for the child,' she told Harry, 'so now you take it easy, while I get Tom ready for his bed.'

Dismissing Harry's protests, she took the boy by the hand and chatted with him all the way up the stairs. 'So now ye can tell me all about these fairies who had the cheek to take your lovely tooth and make you wait for a new one. If you ask me, they want a good telling off!'

Harry smiled at her antics. 'She's not changed,' he chuckled to himself. 'She's still the same Kathleen as ever was.'

While Kathleen and Tom were getting to know each other, Harry set about clearing away the dishes and wiping down the table. He put the kettle on to boil water for the washing-up.

Kathleen was none too pleased when she bustled in. 'Hey, you're not here to do my job,' she chided. 'You leave that to me, and get yourself up them stairs. There's a wee bairn in his bed, waiting to say goodnight to his daddy.'

Tom thanked her. 'I'm surprised he let you wash him,' he said. 'It's usually a big struggle at bathtime.'

'Ah well now, the trick is to keep the water out of his eyes and keep him busy, with stories of hobgoblins and things of a child's imagination.' Regret coloured her voice. 'I never had childer of my own, but I've looked after a few in my time, I can tell ye.'

'Including me,' he reminded her.

'Oh, my!' She had that mischievous look again. 'So I did,' she tutted. 'Isn't that dreadful? I'd completely forgotten about you.'

Smiling to himself, he crossed the room. 'You'll find him in the box room,' she called out. 'He'll be watching for you, I'm sure.'

It was a while before Harry came down, and as he walked towards her, Kathleen thought he seemed more at ease. 'Is the bairn sleeping?' she asked.

'Like he hasn't slept since—' He pulled himself up short. 'Yes, he's sleeping soundly, thanks to you and your magic stories.'

'It's always wise to have a few magic stories up your sleeve; you never know when you might need them,' Kathleen said.

Harry glanced at the pile of dishes to be put away. 'D'you need a hand?'

'No, thank you. What I need is for you to sit down and put your feet up. Sure I'll have these dishes sorted in no time, then, if you're up to it, you and me will have a heart-to-heart. Would you like that? Or are you feeling a bit weary, what with the long drive an' all?'

Harry was not ready for sleep. In fact, he desperately needed a catch-up with Kathleen. He had so many questions, and so much to tell. 'Yes, I'd like that – if you're sure?'

'I said so, didn't I?' She shook her dishcloth at him. 'Go on then. Take yourself away to the sitting room and I'll be with you in no time at all.'

Harry gratefully took his leave. He went into the front room and sat awhile, thinking how welcoming Kathleen's little house was. He thought about the past and the present and the future, and he grew increasingly restless. It was only a matter of minutes before he got out of the chair and, passing the kitchen, strolled out of the back door and into the garden where the evening shadows had begun to move in.

For what seemed an age he stood by the door, his gaze sweeping that pretty, tiny garden he had known so well as a boy.

Few things had changed. The apple tree was still there, its

far-reaching branches touching the bedroom windows as always. The wooden gate that led onto the back lane was still wonky, and the bolt that secured it was still hanging by a thread.

The garden path was new though; where before it had been hardcore and broken concrete, it was now paved with pretty square blocks. The vegetable patch was obviously still in use, because the fork was standing up in the soil. And the patch of grass under the window was forever worn where Kathleen walked when cleaning the windows.

Walking to the far end of the garden on this, the last day of summer, he sat on the same iron bench that he had sat on as a teenager; though it was succumbing to rust in places. As he looked about at all the familiar things, he felt a great sense of homecoming.

He closed his eyes and he could see Judy, the girl who had awakened him to beauty and love, and whose image he had never really lost.

In that split second, steeped in memories, he could not see his beloved Sara. That was when the tears broke loose and he could not stop them. Instead he leaned forward, head in hands, and sobbed at the cruelty of it all. 'Sara.' He said her name over and over. He had never wanted anything more in his life than to see her right there, where he could stretch out his arms and hold her so tight she would never leave him again.

From the kitchen window Kathleen saw, and her heart ached for him. 'Oh, dear boy,' she murmured. 'Stay strong. The pain will surely ease, but maybe not the loneliness . . . ever.' She knew all about that, since the loss of her own dear Michael.

Not wanting to intrude on Harry's private grief, she waited a while. She had the pot of tea all ready on the tray, and a plate of biscuits for dunking. Now though, she poured the tea down the sink and slipped the biscuits back into the box.

Going to the sitting room she took out a bottle of the finest brandy from the bottom cupboard, collected two glasses from her best cabinet and, armed with her cure for all ills, she made her way to the kitchen window. Harry, she could see, had come through a very bad time, and was only now appearing to be more in control of his emotions.

'Ah! There y'are, Harry Boy,' she slowed her step, wisely allowing him time to recover. 'When I couldn't find you in the house, I thought you might be in the garden.'

'Sorry, Kathleen, I should have told you where I'd be.' Thankful for her timely intervention, he suspected she had seen him, and was grateful that she made no mention of it.

Falling heavily onto the bench, she gave out a cry. 'Jaysus, Mary and Joseph! It strikes cold to the nether regions, an' no mistake!'

Harry grinned. 'Here – swap places. I've warmed my seat up.' He spied the bottle of brandy and the glasses. 'So, what's all this then?'

'A party in a bottle,' she laughed. 'It's September tomorrow, me laddie. The night air is a bit thin an' we don't want to end up with raging pneumonia, now do we, eh?' She brandished the bottle. 'This little beauty will chase away the cold, while we sit and talk.'

Placing both glasses in his fist, she told him, 'Hold the little divils still while I open this 'ere bottle.'

She twisted with all her might until suddenly the top was out and the brandy breathing. 'Nothing better than a drop o' the good stuff to warm the cockles,' she promised, pouring out two good measures.

That done, she replaced the top and stood the bottle on the ground beside her. 'Bottoms up, Harry me boy!' Raising her glass, she toasted, 'Here's to you and that darlin' boy of yours – and brighter days ahead for us all.'

Harry drank to that. 'To all of us! And you're right,' he recalled her earlier remark, 'we *do* need to talk . . . if you're not too tired, that is?'

'I don't mind if we sit out here all night,' she replied. 'It may be a bit nippy, but the moon is lovely and we've got our friend the brandy.' She settled back in her seat. 'You and me need to clear the air . . . especially you, Harry Boy. A trouble shared is a trouble halved. Isn't that what they say?'

For a time they sat together, two old friends, thrown closer together by life's cruelties. They had always been easy in each other's company, and though the two of them had long been separated by time and distance, right now, seated together on that familiar iron bench in that little garden, it was as though they had never been apart.

'I missed you, Harry Boy.' Kathleen did not look up. Instead she took a sip of her brandy. 'For a long time I waited for you to get in touch, after the war ended, or maybe turn up at the door, but you never did. When the years passed and there was no word, I didn't know what to think. I had no idea where you were, or what you were doing after you were demobbed.'

Harry explained, 'I just kept going. I didn't know or care where I would end up.' When Sara came on the scene, he was little more than a tramp. 'You can't imagine how often I wanted to get in touch, but I was too ashamed.'

'Don't fret about it,' she chided. 'You're home now, you and little Tom.' She glanced up at him, her voice charged with emotion. 'Judy waited for you, every day she was at the window, hoping you'd come striding down the street.'

There was a moment of quiet, before Harry answered in a choked voice, 'I never meant to hurt her. You know that, don't you, Kathleen?'

'I do, yes.'

'I did love her . . . so very much.'

'I know that too.'

'Do you think I was wrong in leaving like that?'

After carefully considering his question, Kathleen answered in her usual forthright manner. 'Yes, if truth be told, I *do* think you were wrong. But who could blame you? There you were, just a lad, when all's said and done, and it must have seemed like you'd got the world on your shoulders. You weren't ready or equipped to deal with what Judy told you.'

Harry admitted it. 'I was knocked for six. I had no idea how to deal with it.'

'I'm not surprised. What Judy did was silly, plain wrong – and you were right to feel afraid and deceived. But she did it out of love for you, Harry Boy. Oh, don't get me wrong! I'm not denying that she created a frightening situation, and that the two of youse desperately needed someone to turn to. Thankfully, I was here for Judy, but you made it impossible for me to be there for you, and to tell you the truth, it took me a long time to forgive you for running off to enlist like that.'

When he made no comment, she went on, 'You ought never to have gone away like that, in the depth of night, without telling a soul where you were going.'

She cast her mind back, to the way he and Judy had gone into the garden to discuss their future, and how he came back into the house, pale as a sheet and without a word to say. She heard him pacing his room half the night. In the morning when she called to him, he was already gone.

'Kathleen?'

'Yes?'

'Do you honestly think it might have been better if I'd stayed?'

The little woman shook her head. 'No, I don't think that,' she told him. 'In fact, to tell you the truth, taking everything into consideration, I don't believe you had much of a choice. I dare say you did the only thing you could . . . in the circumstances.'

Harry recalled the moment that Judy had delivered her shocking revelation. 'Judy lied to me. Time and again, she deliberately deceived me. If she truly loved me, how could she do that?'

Even now, he could not believe that it had gone so far. 'Fourteen,' he groaned. '*She was only fourteen!* Why did she let me go on believing she was sixteen! Didn't she realise I could have been sent to prison?'

That night, when Judy had confided in her, the very same thought had entered Kathleen's mind. 'I can't condone what Judy did,' she conceded, 'but she loved you, Harry. She was obviously carried away by her feelings for you, and then it was too late to tell you she wasn't old enough for a full relationship.'

'If only she'd told me earlier, we could have put it all on a different footing. I loved her enough to wait until she was older. But she led me to believe that everything was all right and I, like a damned fool, swallowed every word she said.' He shook his head. 'It wasn't just that she lied about her age,' he confided. 'That was bad enough, but the *other* thing . . .' His guilt was tenfold. 'I just couldn't cope.'

Kathleen could see how deep it had gone with Harry, but from the anger and the hurt he was showing now, she was left in no doubt but that he still had feelings for Judy, every bit as much as he did back then.

'She told me she had never loved anyone else, not in the way she loved you.' Kathleen paused, before going on in a softer voice, 'Deep down you already know that, don't you, Harry?'

Harry had told himself the very same over the years. 'What really matters is that I should have stayed and faced it like a man. The truth is, I didn't know what to do. Like a coward, I panicked and ran.' Agitated, he got up to pace back and forth like a trapped animal. 'You think that too, don't you, Kathleen – that I did a cowardly thing?'

Kathleen shook her head. 'You're wrong,' she assured him. 'You were a fine boy then, and you're a fine man now. You were never a coward; you never could be, because it's simply not in your make-up.'

'So if it wasn't cowardice, what was it that made me run? Why couldn't I face it head on?'

'Because the enormity of the situation was beyond you, that's why.'

'Did she tell you everything?'

Kathleen confirmed it. 'The following day, when Judy realised you were gone, she told me everything. I'll admit, I was just as shocked as you – on both counts! Like you, I assumed that she was at least sixteen or seventeen. She certainly looked it. None of us had any reason to doubt her word.' She recalled the moment when Judy admitted to having lied about her age.

Then came the *second* bombshell, which rocked Kathleen to her roots, and there was something else too. All the while Judy was telling her, about the fact that she was only fourteen, and that Harry had made her with child, there was something about Judy's story that made Kathleen feel uneasy.

To this day, she suspected that Judy had deliberately hidden the real truth from her, and from Harry.

Like Harry, Kathleen had always loved and trusted Judy, but on that occasion she was made to ask herself: what did they really know about Judy? After all, the Roberts family had not been in the street long enough for folks to really get to know them.

Nevertheless, her affection for the girl had not wavered.

Remembering now, she smiled. 'From the very first I thought Judy was special. She was such a pretty, shy young thing who hardly had two words to say for herself. Of course, it was rumoured that her mother ruled the family with a rod of iron.'

Harry had heard that too. 'Judy talked about her father a lot, but she hardly ever mentioned her mother. In fact, she hardly ever talked about her past, or where they'd come from. I got the impression that her mother kept her on a short string, that she didn't care for her to meet other people.'

'She always found a way to be with you though,' Kathleen reminded him. She made a wide gesture with her hands. 'Oh, and didn't she love this little garden! The very first time you brought her home, you spent the whole evening, talking and laughing and making plans, here on this very bench.'

Harry recalled every magical minute of it. 'Like you say, Kathleen, she really was very special.' His manner darkened. 'And when she needed me most, I let her down.'

'Maybe you did, but if Judy had not lied to you about her age, the whole sorry matter would never have happened.' She called him to sit down beside her again, then announced: 'I'm the one who should be sorry.'

'What do you mean?'

'Because neither of you found it in your heart to trust me. If you'd come to me, I might have been able to find a solution.'

'What solution, Kathleen?' Harry was on his feet again. 'I loved Judy more than I can say. I thought she loved me too, but how could she, if she was prepared to let me go on believing she was old enough to have a full relationship? She knew I could have been taken away by the authorities, and still she went on lying to me.'

He sat beside her. 'She was fourteen,' he groaned again. 'Can you imagine how I felt when she told me that, and then, as if that wasn't enough to contend with, she told me she was pregnant with my child!'

Even after all this time, he could still feel the horror of that night. 'She said if her mother found out, she would kill us both! I know I should have reacted differently, but all I could think of was to get away. Oh, it wasn't all about her parents, or the police. It was about Judy being so young, and the child.'

'She told me that you gave her the money to pay for an illegal abortion.'

Harry was deeply ashamed. 'I didn't know what else to do, and she insisted it was for the best. But she was wrong. We both were.'

He walked to the window where he stood silent for a while. 'Believe me, Kathleen.' He turned to address her. 'I swear I would give anything to turn the clock back.'

'Sure, don't I know that already?' She had seen the regret in his face and in his voice whenever he mentioned Judy's name. 'It's all in the past now. What's done is done and can't be undone. You went on to make a new life and so did Judy. Don't punish yourself, Harry Boy. You need to remember, you were not alone in making the situation. So, please, listen to me.'

She tugged at his sleeve. 'If you don't let the bad memories go, son, they could well destroy you.'

He gave a harsh laugh. 'You could be right.'

'Don't forget, you have the boy to think of. Moreover, from what I've learned of Sara, she would not want you to torment yourself this way, would she, eh?'

'No.' Harry was brought up sharp by Kathleen's wise words. 'Sara would not want that.'

'It seems you found a good woman in her. Tell me, Harry. What was she really like?'

The memory of Sara was bittersweet for Harry. 'She was wonderful. Understanding . . . forgiving. If you'd known her, you would have loved her.'

Until now, Harry had not realised how much he needed to talk about Sara. 'When I saw the relationship was getting serious, I told her all about Judy. I was afraid of losing her, but knew I had to take that chance.'

'So – did you tell her everything – about the bairn, and how Judy lied about her age?'

'I did, yes. After what happened with Judy, I was determined from the start that there would be no secrets between me and Sara.'

'Sure, that's as good a way as any to start a relationship.' Kathleen fully approved.

'I told her how Judy's family was new into the street and that no one knew much about them. I described how we were drawn to each other from the first moment we met, the day she dropped all her shopping right in front of me. I explained how we naturally drifted into a serious relationship, and that it never occurred to me to ask about Judy's age, especially when she had the look and manner of a much older girl.'

He could picture Judy in his mind so clearly. 'I told her how sincere and lovely Judy was, and how for some reason known only to herself, she let me believe she was older than her years.'

'You did right to tell Sara.' Kathleen had no doubts on that score. 'As for Judy, we were all fooled with regards to her age. I mean, she never went to school, at least not as far as we knew. So, it was natural to assume that she had left all that behind her. Anyway, lots of people left school at fourteen.'

'But I should have known,' Harry groaned. 'Somehow, I should have known.' He recalled one particular thing that had bothered him at the time, but Judy had explained it away, and he had had no reason to doubt her explanation.

Now though, having recalled the incident, he began to wonder.

He chose not to disclose this to Kathleen because it was a delicate, womanly thing, and he would find it embarrassing to talk about.

The truth was, that first and only time he and Judy made love, she was unusually nervous; almost as though she didn't want to. In fact, he was so concerned he backed off, but Judy was adamant. 'It's what I want,' she insisted.

Afterwards though, he felt as if he had betrayed her.

As it turned out, in the end, it was Judy who betrayed him.

Kathleen asked now, 'How did Sara react to what you told her?'

'Much like you . . . with compassion. She took it in her stride and urged me to track Judy down. "Put it to rest, once and for all," is what she said, but at the time, I thought it might be best to leave it behind us.'

'So, what made you come back now, after all this time?'

'It was Sara. When we were told she was not long for this world, she made me promise that I would contact you, and ask if Tom and I could come home.'

'She was very wise, your Sara.'

Harry chuckled. 'Sometimes, when I thought I was on my own, she would be watching, almost as though she knew what I was thinking. She felt my guilt. She knew I wanted to make amends with Judy, but didn't know how.' He was convinced of it. 'Otherwise, why would she be so insistent that Tom and I should come back here?'

Practical as ever, Kathleen went on to dash his hopes. 'Maybe it was all for nothing,' she suggested thoughtfully. 'Especially with Judy long gone from the street.'

Harry could not hide his disappointment. 'Where did she go?'

'I don't know. All I know is after you'd gone away, she came to see me – in a frantic state she was. She told me everything. She admitted that she was only fourteen, and that she was with child. She said you had given her money and she'd already arranged to visit some old woman who, she claimed, had a repu- tation of dealing with unwanted babies. I tried my best to stop her. I even threatened to go and see her parents, but she warned me not to, because if her mother found out, she would skin her alive. So, I offered to find her a private clinic, if she really thought that was the right thing to do.'

'So, what did she do?' Harry's guilt was tenfold.

'I truly believed she was listening to what I had to say. I got her to promise not to do anything until she'd thought it through. I asked her to come back as soon as she felt able, and between us, we would find a way to deal with it.'

Saddened, she shrugged her shoulders. 'When I didn't see her for a while, I assumed she was still giving it some serious thought. Then a short time later, she told me she had already been to this woman, and that everything was all right now.'

Harry blamed himself. 'If I hadn't given her the money, she would never have done it.' Now he wanted to know, 'Where can I find this woman who gets rid of unwanted babies?'

Kathleen bristled. 'If I knew that, Harry Boy, I would be speaking to the authorities.'

'And are you really sure that Judy was all right afterwards?'

Kathleen nodded. 'Like she said, everything was dealt with.'

'Do you have any idea where she is now?'

''Fraid not. All I know is, soon after Judy came to see me, she and her family moved away. I don't know why they left the street, or where they went. If I did I would tell you, so I would.'

Harry believed she was telling the truth.

'How can I find her?' he asked now. 'Where should I look?'

'Do you really want my opinion?'

'Of course.'

'Leave it be. Let her go, Harry Boy. Sometimes, raking over old coals can get you badly burned. They may look dead, but somewhere underneath, the flame often burns on.'

'Kathleen!' Harry felt that she was hiding something. '*Do* you know where Judy is?'

The little woman shook her head. 'Wherever she is now, she's obviously managed to put it all behind her. Happen you must do the same. Years have passed and things have changed. It's time to look forward now. You need to build a future, for you and your son.'

The two of them talked well into the night, moving back indoors when it grew too chilly outside.

Harry wondered if there was work to be found locally, and Kathleen gave him a few pointers. 'Well, there's the Plysu factory in Woburn Sands,' she said. 'They've extended the business and need more people. Oh, and I heard that Jacobs' Store in Bedford needs a new tallyman. Old Ernie Wright's done the job for over twenty years, but he's retired now.'

She was convinced. 'That one should suit you down to the ground. You'll get a good wage and you'll be out and about, meeting all kinds of folks. What's more, you'll be able to work out your own route and timetable.'

She laughed out loud. 'Old Ernie met a lot of naughty women on his rounds, including his second wife. He used to stop at every house and have a cuppa . . . though he never accepted a

69

slice o' cake until he got here.' She gave another cheery, infectious giggle. 'That's because he knew the best cake lived at *my* house!'

Harry was highly amused, and for a time they got sidetracked; but then he needed to bring the conversation back to work. 'So, what *is* a tallyman?' he asked. If it was anything to do with figures he'd be fine, as he had often worked as a bookkeeper after leaving the Army.

'If you call at the store, sure they'll tell you all about it. And you know what? I reckon you're just the fella they're looking for.'

'Oh, you do, do you?' He was certainly interested. 'In that case, I might just go and have a word with them.'

Later that night, when Harry and Tom were fast asleep, Kathleen sat at the kitchen table supping her bedtime drink.

In her mind she went over the conversation with Harry. 'It's a curious thing,' she muttered, clearing away her cup, 'how the love and devotion of two young people can create such a lifetime of heartache.'

Turning out the lights, she shuffled her way up the stairs and into her room, where she softly closed the door.

A moment later, with her arms raised to close the curtains, she took a few seconds to marvel at the night skies. She had always thought the heavens were uniquely magnificent. With a myriad of twinkling diamonds against a forever carpet of midnight blue, there could be no other creation like it in the whole world.

She stayed awhile, letting the beauty sink into her senses, then she quietly addressed the heavens. 'Well, Judy, here we are,' she whispered. 'Your boy is home again. Sure, he's a tortured man, and he's looking to find his first love. So, what are we going to do, Judy m'darlin'? How will it all end, I wonder. And where are you now? What have you done with your life? More than that, did ye find happiness . . . or are ye haunted, just like yer man?'

She sat on the edge of the bed for a long time, thinking and wondering; recalling the very last conversation she had had with Judy.

After a time, she undressed and slid between the sheets, but she was deeply troubled, and not only because of the things she and Harry had openly discussed.

More importantly, it was the very things she had deliberately kept from Harry, that wounded her most and which made her deeply ashamed for the first time in her life. Bad things touching on abortion, family and wickedness. And especially the fact that Judy had come to see her another time; with news that had lifted her old heart in forgiveness.

She had toyed with the idea of telling Harry, then thought it kinder, and wiser, to let him believe what she had just now told him. It wasn't her secret to reveal. Moreover, her suspicions were now substantiated. Yet doubts still tormented her.

She still didn't have the whole story. At one point she had almost got the truth out of Judy; until the poor girl grew afraid and ran away.

'Harry has a right to know my thoughts,' she whispered to the darkness, 'but oh, dear Lord, how can I ever be sure?'

She knew one thing though. Harry had already been the victim of deception. If the truth was even more disturbing, and Judy had not entrusted him with it, she would not be surprised if he turned his back on her and Judy for all time.

Turning over, she closed her eyes, but sleep eluded her. There were things on her mind that should be spoken out loud.

After a time, she climbed out of bed and went softly on tippytoes down the stairs. She entered the kitchen, closed the door behind her and made herself another cup of cocoa. Then she sat at the table, rolling the cup about in her hands and thinking what to do.

'Not telling him of my suspicions is tantamount to betraying him yet again!' she chided herself. 'That's exactly what Judy did, and that's what drove him away for all these years. He deserves to know!' The truth played heavy on her mind.

She was all for telling him, and then she was not, and now she was desperately trying to justify keeping him in the dark. 'If I tell him now, it will cause more heartache, so it will.'

Pushing her cocoa aside, she left it untouched and crept back to her bed. Rightly or wrongly, her decision was made. She intended to keep her own counsel, for the alternative would be too cruel for everyone concerned.

'He'll find her, or he won't!' she muttered as she clambered back under the bedclothes. 'Either way, I can't be the one to stir up trouble. He's had enough upset in his life, without me adding to his burden now.'

Before drifting into a restless sleep, she turned her sad gaze to the window.

'Forgive me,' she begged some unseen entity. 'I can't voice my thoughts just now, but for Harry's sake, I only hope and pray I'm doing the right thing by remaining silent.'

CHAPTER FOUR

THE FOLLOWING MORNING, Harry was ready to go looking for work. 'Are you sure you don't mind keeping an eye on Tom?' he asked Kathleen. Though reluctant to leave his boy behind, he had been pleased to see how the pair of them were getting on like a house on fire.

'Do I *mind*?' Kathleen was wounded. 'Aw, sure, looking after the little fella will be a joy, so it will.'

'I'll be quick as I can,' he promised Tom.

'I don't mind, Daddy.' Tucking into one of the apple tarts Kathleen had baked that very morning, Tom proudly informed him, 'Kathleen's taking me on the bus to Bedford. We're looking for new shoes for when I go to school.'

Harry was puzzled. 'What about the shoes your mammy bought for you?'

Tom frowned. 'My feet won't stop growing, and now the shoes are squeezing all my toes up. Kathleen says when I grow up like you, I'll probably have feet the size of meat plates.'

'Is that right?' Fishing in his wallet, Harry declared, 'We can't have my son walking about with his toes sticking out the end of his shoes!' He gave Kathleen enough money for shoes and socks, and a bit extra for a meal and bus fare.

'So, am I not allowed to buy the boy a new pair of shoes?' Kathleen feigned an air of indignation. 'Kathleen O'Leary's money is not good enough, is that what you're saying?'

Harry played her little game. 'Well, I'm sure I didn't mean to offend you.' He held out his hand. 'Give it back?'

'What! You really want me to give it back? Shame on ye, Harry Boy! You're a heartless divil, so ye are.' She winked at Tom, who was beginning to realise it was just a game. 'Tom, what d'ye think?' she asked. 'Should we keep your daddy's money or not?'

'Keep it! Yes!' Laughing and screeching, Tom jumped up and down.

'Behave yourselves, you two.' Harry swung Tom up into his arms. 'I can see I'll have to keep an eye on the pair of you,' he said, wagging a finger. 'If I'm not careful, you'll be running rings round me.'

A thought occurred to him. 'Look, Kathleen, if you're taking Tom into town, you might as well jump in the car with me,' he suggested. 'I can drop you off at the end of the market, if you like.'

Kathleen graciously declined. 'I promised Tom we would go on the bus and he's looking forward to it.'

'Yes!' Tom was like a cat on hot bricks. 'I want to go on the bus with Kathleen, please, Daddy?'

A short time later, Harry was out of the door, into the car, and away down the street, waving all the way. 'Keep your fingers crossed for me!' he called out.

'We will,' the pair replied in unison.

Kathleen's directions were easy to follow, and within the hour, Harry had gone through Bedford Town and out towards the prison, where he took a sharp left. The store was directly in front of him, exactly where Kathleen had predicted.

Straddling the entire corner and snaking down a consider-able length of the back street, the building made an immediate impression. With its great arched entrance, fancy tiles under-foot and sturdy windows, it was an obvious relic from Victorian times; and there on a massive sign, written in large black letters on a deep mustard background, was the proud announcement:

JACOBS' EMPORIUM

ESTABLISHED 1945

EVERYTHING YOU NEED FOR HOME AND GARDEN

Drawing the Hillman Minx into the kerb, Harry switched off the engine and got out of the car. After locking the car, he stooped to regard himself in the wing mirror.

Satisfied, he straightened his tie, polished the uppers of his shoes against the back of his trousers and, taking a deep breath, he strode to the door and rang the bell at the side. There was still half an hour to go until opening time.

The painted dolly-girl had seen him coming and was eager to tend to him. 'Good morning, sir. Are you looking for anything in particular?' Judging from her enthusiasm, she would have liked it to be *her* that Harry was 'looking for'.

'I'm here to see Mr Jacobs.' Now that he was only minutes away from the interview, Harry's nerves were beginning to get the better of him.

'Ah.' The girl looked him up and down. 'You must be Mr Blake, applying for Mr Wright's old job.'

'Yes,' Harry answered.

'You're younger than him.'

Harry was taken aback. 'Is that a problem?'

'Oh no, quite the opposite as far as I'm concerned.' Allowing him a coy little smile, she explained, 'It's just that, well, we've had all kinds wanting the job, but they were all in their late fifties, and scruffy into the bargain.' She leaned forward to impart quietly, 'If you ask me, they were all layabouts – probably been given the sack for not working as hard as they should. I expect they thought being a tallyman would be an easy option.'

'And is it?'

'Hmh!' She gave Harry a critical look. 'Don't you believe it,' she told him sternly. 'It's damned hard work. That's why poor Ernie retired early . . . because he was worn out.'

'How so?' Harry had never been afraid of hard work.

'Well, it's just *people*, innit?'

'In what way?'

'Well, there's those who can get really stroppy and threaten you, and those who always find some excuse not to pay. Then there's the "other" kind.' She gave him a knowing wink. 'If you know what I mean.'

'Well, no, not exactly.' From the look in her eye, Harry guessed it was something cheeky.

'They're the ones who prefer to pay for goods in other ways than money,' she giggled. 'I reckon if we took you on, you'd soon find out about the other kind.'

'Chatting again, Amy? Get back to your work at once!' The voice of authority echoed across the floor.

The girl was startled. 'Yes, Mr Jacobs. Sorry, this is Mr Blake. I was about to bring him up to you.'

Bernie Jacobs was a sizeable man with a squashy face, which was mostly covered by his huge, black-rimmed spectacles. A fair-minded man, he had hands the size of shovels, and a beer belly that would go twice round the gasworks.

'I've warned you about wasting valuable time!' he reprimanded the girl. 'I distinctly asked that you bring Mr Blake up the minute he arrived. Instead I find you gossiping with him!'

'I really am sorry, Mr Jacobs.' She secretly rolled her eyes at Harry. 'It won't happen again.'

'It had better not!'

Addressing Harry, the boss welcomed him to the store. 'So you're here for the position of tallyman, is that right?'

Harry confirmed that.

'Good!' He looked Harry up and down, mentally applauding the way he was turned out. More importantly, he thought Harry's manner was exactly right for the part – nice and easy, but with a layer of authority. Bernie was not one to go on first impressions, and today was no exception, though so far he liked what he saw.

As he continued to appraise Harry's demeanour, his whole face began to shift; first the mouth went loose, then the plump cheekbones lifted the glasses up to the forehead, and now the podgy little eyes, all crinkled and beady, started blinking; all features on the move like some slow, giant sloth.

If it wasn't so mesmerising, Harry mused, it would have been frightful. 'Like something out of a horror movie,' Amy commented to him later.

Suddenly, the face relaxed, and everything fell back into place. 'Well, Mr Blake, I must say you look more capable than some I've had to contend with.' He turned on his heel, calling for Harry to, 'Follow me, young man!'

As they filed past the girl, she discreetly caught Harry's attention, gestured to Mr Jacobs and made a face that would frighten the dead.

It took all of Harry's self-control to keep from laughing out loud.

'Be seated.' Mr Jacobs gestured for Harry to park himself in the upright chair at the near end of the huge desk. When Harry was comfortable, the older man ceremoniously settled his mounds of fat in the wide, executive leather chair. 'Hmm!' He looked at Harry, then he glanced down, then he looked again, then he began cracking his knuckles, making a sound that put Harry's teeth on edge. 'Hmm!' Then again: 'Hmm!'

Harry felt the urge to speak. 'Excuse my ignorance, Mr Jacobs, sir, but I'm not quite sure what a tallyman does.'

'Really?' The face crumpled like a sagging balloon.

He then proceeded to address Harry in that authoritative, nasal voice which was beginning to grate on his nerves. 'A tallyman is the very backbone of this business,' he announced proudly. 'It has been that way since I opened just before Christmas in 1945.'

Harry duly waited, while the older man lost himself in a sea of memories and pride.

All of a sudden, appearing self-conscious, he noisily cleared his throat. 'As I was saying, the tallyman has been the link between Jacobs' Emporium and the public at large, for as far back as the store itself has existed. He, or she as the case may be, is representative of our quality of service, and professional standing in the community.'

Harry urged him on. 'Yes, I understand all that. But what exactly does the tallyman *do*?'

The face blushed pink. 'Oh, dearie me! I've been wandering again. So sorry! It's a bad habit of mine. Anyway, what were we saying . . . ? Oh yes.'

He went on hurriedly, 'We currently employ seven sales-people, three of whom are permanently based in the store. The remaining four salesmen are what I call "mobile", in that they also carry out the responsibilities of the tallyman.'

Taking a deep invigorating breath, he elaborated, 'A customer will come into the store and browse though our range of furniture and fittings, wherepon one of our salesmen, be it a dedicated floor person, or a tallyman, will then approach and assist, and when the customer makes a purchase, the paperwork is carried out in the usual way. From there, it depends on whether the client pays in full, or whether they prefer to pay in instalments, and we have numerous customers who do exactly that.'

Harry waited patiently while Bernie Jacobs paused for breath.

'On payment by instalment, the salesman will enter it all into his ledger, and the customer is issued with a little blue book, together with the number and amount of weekly payments required.' Leaning back in his chair he folded his arms. 'Every week thereafter, the tallyman will call at the customer's house, to collect payments, and issue a receipt.'

Harry needed to clarify. 'So even though the tallyman would be partly based in the store, he will still be required to collect from his regular customers?'

'Exactly right. Most tallymen prefer to be out on the road at the latter end of the week, say Friday. There will, of course, be a company car and necessary expenses. You must remember, the tallyman is an important ambassador for Jacobs' Emporium, and as such I expect, and indeed insist, on the highest of moral and professional standards.'

He gave a nervous little cough. 'I'm afraid there have been one or two indiscretions recently. The salesman responsible was very quickly given his cards and shown the door. D'you understand what I'm saying, Mr Blake?' His words were an obvious warning.

Harry nodded. 'I believe I do, yes.' He recalled the young woman's words: 'Then there's the "other" kind if you know what I mean?'

Mr Jacobs was now asking Harry about his past work and present ambitions. Harry outlined how, after the war, he had worked on building sites for a firm of builders for a while, then graduated to the offices, 'where I dealt with all manner of things; like stock control, wages and accounts, liaising with the customers . . .'

'Yes, I'm aware of that. After you telephoned Amy, she made a note of what you said. I have it here.' Collecting the page from the desk, Mr Jacobs remarked, 'I'm impressed with your many achievements, but,' he referred to the point in question, 'it says here that you returned to working on the building sites for personal reasons.'

'That's right, yes.'

'May I ask why you would do that – go from office work back to labouring? Of course, you do understand that before I can make a decision, I will need to contact your former employers?'

Harry explained, 'I went back to the building sites because it made fewer demands on my time. Although I enjoyed my work at the office, it meant I was there for long hours . . . sometimes at weekends too, when I badly needed to be at home. Whereas on the sites I could work the hours I chose. There were no telephones or accountants to deal with, and I could arrange my working day to suit the situation.'

'What situation would that be then?'

Bracing himself, Harry revealed the reason. 'My wife was diagnosed with a terminal illness; we both knew it was only a matter of time. I had to earn a living, yes, but she came first. I needed to be with her, you understand. Not only to console and support and to make the most of every minute available to us; there were practical things, like long stays in hospital, and our son to take care of.'

Pausing, he swallowed hard before going on to explain how, when she lost her fight against the illness, he had come back to the place where he had grown up. 'That's the long and short of it,' he concluded. 'A very dear friend has taken me and my son in, until we find a place of our own. And now I need a new job.'

'Hmm.' The older man had listened intently to what Harry had to say, and now he had to make up his mind. 'Wait outside,' he instructed. 'Amy will get you a cup of tea. Have a walk about. Talk to people. See what you think. I'll call you in presently.'

With that he ushered him out.

'It looks good to me!' Amy was delighted to have the company of this fine, good-looking fellow. 'He kept you in there longer than the others,' she announced cheekily. 'I reckon he likes you.'

Harry made small talk for a time, then he wandered away and talked with the salesmen. 'As bosses go, he's not all that bad,' John told him. 'A bit pompous at times, but fair and straight when needed.'

The same sentiments were echoed by everyone Harry chatted with, although: 'He's a hard taskmaster.' That was Louise, the only woman in sales.

Harry went upstairs to the bed department, and was amazed at the sheer scale and diversity of items on offer. He went across to the soft furnishings area with its wonderful displays of curtains and bedlinen, and the best selection of cushions he had ever seen, and now he was back downstairs amongst the displays of furniture, all set out as different rooms in the house. There were kitchens and living-rooms – here a piano and there a wall of pictures and paintings.

'It's like Aladdin's Cave!' He was surprised when Amy crept up on him. 'I swear, I've never seen anything like it.'

She laughed. 'You haven't seen outside yet then. There's lawn mowers and ladders, and everything else you might want in your backyard or garden.' Tapping him on the arm she informed him. 'You haven't got time to look now though, because His Majesty has summoned you.' Making Harry smile, she gave a little curtsy. 'Follow me, my good man.' Not relishing the idea of another reprimand, she then set off at a brisk pace.

After showing him into the office, she returned to her desk, delighted to offer Harry congratulations half an hour later. 'So, you got the job?'

'How did you know that?'

'From your beaming face when you came out.'

It was still beaming as he walked onto the street. 'I've got work, Sara my darling,' he murmured.

Three months' trial, a generous travelling allowance, and he was virtually his own boss.

It was an excellent start.

~

Kathleen and Tom were also pleased with their day.

'You've worn me out, so ye have,' Kathleen groaned as they headed for the café on the High Steet. 'I can't believe a little fella like you could take longer than a cartload o' women to choose a pair of shoes: Jaysus, Mary and Joseph! Sure, ye could make a living at it.'

'*I'm* not tired,' Tom announced proudly.

'Oh, are ye not?' Kathleen quipped. 'Well, aren't you the lucky one, 'cos I'm dropping on me feet, so I am.'

'I've got money.'

'Sure, I know that already,' she answered. 'Didn't I see yer father give it to ye?'

'I can buy *you* some new shoes, if you want,' he offered grandly.

Kathleen laughed out loud at that. 'Aw, ye little darlin'.' She gently ruffled his hair. 'Shall I tell ye something?'

'What?'

'Right now, I don't think I'd even get a pair of shoes on me feet.'

'Why not?'

''Cos me poor oul' feet feel like two fresh-baked loaves.'

'D'you want to sit down?'

'Ah, sure I wouldn't mind that at all.'

'I need an ice cream.'

'Ah! So what you're really saying is we should find a café, where I can sit down and you can have an ice cream, and we'll both be happy, is that it?'

'I don't know.' The little boy was confused.

'Ah, but ye're a joy to behold, so you are! Look, there's a café right there, and a little table for you and me, right by the window. What d'you say then?'

'Yes, yes!' Tom did his usual leaping up and down.

Kathleen chuckled. 'Y'know what, m'darlin'?'

'What?'

'Ye're a fella after me own heart, so ye are.' She tightened her hold on him, and as fast as her sore old feet would take her, she rushed him across the road. 'Will ye look at that!' she cried merrily. 'Sure, me feet are getting that excited, they're almost running!'

Unbeknownst to them, a small skirmish was unfolding some way down the street. 'Get away from me, you dirty beggar!' Shoving the woman aside, the man hurried on. 'People scrounging in the street. Whatever next!'

'I wasn't scrounging!' The woman was close to tears. 'I was just asking the time, you miserable old devil.'

Clad in a plain dark dress fastened at the waist with a broad belt, she looked nothing like a beggar; yet she appeared waiflike, and there was an air of desolation about her that could be mistaken for hunger of a kind.

In her early thirties, she was painfully thin, with long, fair hair and small, distinctly pretty features. Her soft grey eyes told a story; of great sadness, and fear.

As she darted her anxious gaze up and down the street, the fear was like a living entity in those sorry grey eyes.

When the hand fell on her shoulder, she gave a small, frightened cry. 'It's all right!' The man was a friend. Grey-haired and weathered, he was old enough to be her father.

These past years, because of her situation, he and his wife, Pauline, had taken it on themselves to watch out for her. 'I saw you just now,' he said as he led her away. 'That bloody stupid man! He mistook you for some kind of beggar, didn't he?'

She wasn't listening, because now her attention was drawn across the street to the café, where Kathleen and Tom were settling themselves at the table. Kathleen was standing, talking to the little boy, and when suddenly she looked up, the young woman was shocked to her roots. 'Oh, my God! It really *is* her! IT'S KATHLEEN!'

The man followed her nervous gaze. 'Who's Kathleen?' he asked. 'Is she a friend?'

Now she was talking to herself. 'She's got a child with her. Whose child is that?' Seeming confused, she turned to the man. 'She's got a child! *Kathleen's got a child.* Who does it belong to?'

As though a light had flicked on in her mind, she gave a soft, uneasy laugh. 'Is it . . . is it?' Giving a wry little smile, she shook her head. 'No! It can't be, can it?'

The man gave her a gentle shake. 'Stop it now. You're doing yourself no good being out here like this.' He felt her hand. 'You're freezing cold, lovey. We'd best get you inside.'

She gave him the sweetest smile. 'Did you see though? Irish

Kathleen's got a child with her.' She had no way of knowing what it meant, but it gave her a warm feeling inside.

'Would you like to go over and see her, this Kathleen? You could ask her whose child it is. That would put your mind at rest.'

'No!' Shrinking from him, her eyes swam with tears. 'I was wrong about the child. I know that now. Besides, Kathleen would not want to see me.' Just then in that raw moment, she remembered it all. 'She was my friend once, but I lied to her.'

'I see.' Although he didn't see at all. Nor did he understand her reluctance to say hello to someone who had once befriended her. 'All right then. You don't have to see her if you don't want to.'

'I want to go now, please.'

He had seen her like this before and it was a sad thing. It was even sadder to see her so obsessed with the child. It concerned him greatly.

'We'd best go. I'll make you one of my special cups of hot chocolate – do you a power of good it will.'

She nodded. 'In a minute.' Alan was landlord of the Bedford Arms, the pub on the corner. She trusted him and his dear wife Pauline above all others, but she would not be drawn on Kathleen.

'Did you have a falling-out with that lady?' he persisted.

'I did not fall out with her! I already told you, she was my friend.'

'Then you really should talk to her. After all, you need all the friends you can get.'

'I've got you, haven't I?' She gave him a hug. 'And Pauline?'

'Yes, of course you've got me, and you've got Pauline, but you can never have enough friends, and this Kathleen does look a kindly old thing. You ought to get in touch with her . . . make amends for whatever it was that made her send you away.'

'She didn't send me away. I left. We *all* left.' Unwilling to get into any further conversation, she threaded her arm through his and set him walking. 'Hot chocolate sounds nice.' She licked her lips at the thought of it.

He chuckled. 'You're a stubborn little devil when you choose,' he muttered. 'But I suppose you know best, after all.'

Back at the Bedford Arms, she made her way to the Ladies toilets, where she washed her face and combed her hair and peeked at herself in the mirror. The image that came back was pitiful. The long fair hair was dull and lank, the skin blotchy with tears, and the grey cloudy eyes had lost their sparkle.

'Who are you?' she asked of the image.

'Judy Saunders,' came the reply.

'No! Not Judy Saunders.' She shook her head slowly from side to side. 'Who are you . . . *really*?'

She gave a harsh little laugh. 'You're a bad woman, that's who you are. You lie and you cheat, and you've done terrible things. It's good that you're married to a man you don't love. It's good that you're paying the price.'

Bunching her fist, she thumped it into her chest. 'You should be dead!' When the tears began again, she couldn't stop them, and then she was laughing, soft, wild laughter like someone insane.

Running the cold water tap, she cupped her hands and splashed the water over her face for a second time. For what seemed an age, she stared at herself again in the mirror; what she saw was a shadow, without substance, without life.

'Judy Saunders.' She gave a snort of disgust. 'Look at yourself! You *look* dead, you *feel* dead, so why are you able to walk about, taking up valuable space; bothering ordinary good folks in the street? You are nothing! NO ONE! You're not loved and you're not wanted, so why don't you just end it? Go on, Judy. Do it properly, here and now.'

'Judy!' The woman's voice startled her. 'Alan's made you a hot drink. What are you up to? Come on.' The woman's voice became anxious. 'JUDY. Come out of there!'

The young woman quickly composed herself. 'It's all right, Pauline. I'll be out in a minute.'

She looked at the scars on her arms, her empty gaze following the long meandering red lines where the knife had split open the flesh. She was shocked. Whenever she caught sight of the scars, she was *always* shocked.

It was hard to realise how low she had sunk.

Taking a moment to loosely flick her hair, she then lightly stroked her lips, pinched her face to give it a glow, and finally she unrolled her sleeves to cover the scars.

One last look in the mirror to make sure she looked something approaching normal, then she painted on a smile, and was ready to face the world for another day.

Lately though, the days seemed to get longer and heavier. And the burden of living was almost too much to bear.

CHAPTER FIVE

P HIL SAUNDERS WAS looking for trouble, but that was nothing new. 'Who's for a pint down the pub?' Stripping off his overalls he scanned the room, his hard stare alighting on his work-mates who had yet to respond. 'What? None of you fancies a pint? I don't believe it!'

'Looks like you're on your own, matey.' That was Jimmy Clayton, a stick-thin man in his late forties, with a straight-forward, no-nonsense manner.

'Oh, really?' Incensed, Phil Saunders squared his broad shoulders. 'And what's *that* supposed to mean?'

'It means what it says.' The other man made a wide gesture with outstretched arms. 'Look around. Do you see anybody rushing to join you?'

'Oh, so now you speak for everybody else, do you? Anyway, what makes you think I give a sod whether any of you come or not? Matter o' fact, it's just as well, 'cos I'm a bit particular about my drinking partners.'

'There you go then.'

Clayton's attitude was riling Saunders, who took a step closer. 'Seems to me like you're itching for trouble, mate.'

'You're wrong. I don't want trouble. The thing is, I've had to work alongside you all week. I've put up with your foul temper and constant complaining, because I've got no choice. But the last thing I need is to go drinking like we're "mates", because we're *not* mates and we never will be.'

Saunders continued to goad him. 'The truth is, you wouldn't dare come down the pub in case you might have to dip into your wages; the little wife wouldn't like that, would she, eh?' He gave a sneering laugh. 'I bet she waits at the door every Friday with her greedy little mitts held out, waiting for the wages *you've* sweated for.' He sniggered. 'I bet she even gives you pocket money.'

For what seemed an age the smaller man looked Saunders in the eye, his jaw working up and down and his fists clenched together.

'Want to punch me, do you?' Saunders stuck his face out. 'Go on then, matey, you try it. We all know who would come off worse, don't we, eh?'

'Leave it, Phil.' That was Arnie Reynolds, a big bumbling lump of a man. 'There's no need to rile him. If Jimmy doesn't want to come for a drink, that's his choice, and whatever his reason, it's not for you or any of us to question.'

Taking a deep noisy breath through his nose, Saunders let it out through his mouth, together with a torrent of words. 'You're all the bloody same. Can't stand on your own two feet. Lily-livered, the lot of you.'

'Hey! That's enough o' that.' Stuart McArthy was a Scot with an attitude, though unlike Saunders he was not a bully. 'I for one happen to have a real thirst on me, so why don't we stop the gabbing an' make our way to the pub.'

He had a word of advice for Jimmy. 'He's right though, Jimmy lad. A man needs to show the little woman who's boss. Otherwise she'll run rings round you.'

Saunders laughed out loud. 'That might be good advice for a real man, but y'see, our Jimmy wouldn't know how to be a real man. He's a coward through and through – ain't that right, Jimmy Boy?' A man in his prime, Phil Saunders considered himself to be a cut above the rest. 'You won't catch *me* pandering to no bloody female! Never in a million years. Anyway, what's so different about *your* woman that you treat her so special, eh?'

'She's my wife . . . the mother of my children, and if that isn't enough, I happen to love and respect her.' Like every man jack there, Jimmy was well aware of the way Saunders treated his wife, Judy. 'You might want to think about that,' he added.

'I think you'd best explain yourself!' Saunders said dangerously.

'I don't have to explain anything. You asked me why I treat my wife so special and I'm telling you.' Leaning forward, Jimmy lowered his voice. 'I don't treat my wife like a piece of rubbish. Nor do I take my temper out on her.'

With an animal-like growl, Saunders got him by the throat. 'You bastard! What the hell are you insinuating, eh?' He locked his fingers tighter, until Jimmy's face felt like it was boiling. 'Are you saying I don't love my Judy . . . or that I don't respect her? Is that what you're saying?' He squeezed his hands tighter. 'I've a good mind to finish you here and now!'

Jimmy truly thought he would never see another day. He couldn't breathe. His eyeballs felt as though they would pop right out of his head, and his tongue was clamped so hard between his teeth, he could feel the pain right through to his chest.

When in that moment, the other two men leaped forward and tore Saunders away, Jimmy fell to the ground, coughing and spluttering; thankful that he might live to tell the tale.

'I thought you said you were off to the pub,' intent on cooling the situation, McArthy asked of Saunders. 'So, are you coming, or do I go without you?'

'I said so, didn't I?' Glancing at Jimmy who was now up on his feet and smoothing down his hair, Saunders' smile was pure evil. 'It's good to see there's at least one man in the place besides me who knows how to spend his own hard-earned money.'

Jimmy did not rise to the bait a second time, although he

managed to croak, 'You're a lucky man, Saunders, if you can afford to chuck your money about. As for me, I've got better things to do with mine. I've a family waiting for me, with a clutch of kids that need my every penny.' He addressed the other two men. 'See you.'

Saunders' goading voice followed him. 'Get going then, you pansy – unless you want me to help you through the door!'

'See you tomorrow.' The others had no axe to grind with Jimmy. If they had to choose out of him and Saunders, Jimmy was the better man.

'What about you then, Bill?' Saunders addressed the man next to him. Tall and willowy, Anderson was a reliable work-mate who grafted tirelessly, though he kept his distance and never got caught up in heated arguments. 'Gonna join us for a drink, are you?'

'Nope.' A man of few words, his conversations were short and to the point.

'Why's that?' Saunders was still heated from his set-to with Jimmy.

'Got my own reasons, and before you ask, I don't discuss my business with anybody.'

Saunders gave a cynical laugh. 'You're a miserable bugger!' But he said no more. He suspected Bill Anderson of having hidden depths; and that if he and the other man ever did have an affray, it might not be Anderson who came off worse. So, with that in mind, Saunders stayed true to form, by picking only on those weaker than himself.

Aware that Bill was growing impatient with Saunders, Arnie Reynolds moved towards the door. 'Cheerio then, Bill, see you tomorrow.' Turning to the others he called out, 'Stuart! Phil! Are you two coming or what?'

With the three men gone, Bill Anderson walked over to the far end of the warehouse, where he found the worried foreman taking stock.

With a good three years to retirement, Joe Peters did not

carry his age well. Having now shrivelled in size, he was permanently bent over. His spectacles were too large for his tiny face, and where he constantly screwed up his nose to keep them in place, the deep troughs of wrinkles had etched a pattern alongside his sunken cheekbones.

'You're like Will-o'-the-Wisp,' Bill said, relieved to have found him. 'One minute you're there, the next you're nowhere to be seen.' Bill had always liked and respected Joe Peters, thinking him a fair-minded and honest sort.

'I needed to check these rolls of canvas.' Joe made a quick entry into his ledger. 'We're two rolls short. Whoever checked the delivery obviously didn't do his job properly.'

'Well, it weren't me,' Bill informed him abruptly.

'Have the men gone?'

'Yes . . . just now.'

'Right, well, I'll have to deal with it in the morning.'

'Maybe the lorry driver had the two rolls away, thinking no one would notice,' Bill suggested light-heartedly.

'Maybe he did, and who could blame him, when the load isn't properly checked as it comes off? This isn't the first time, and if it's not put a stop to, it won't be the last, then we'll *all* lose our jobs!'

Bill suddenly realised the implications. 'What? Are you saying it's one of us?'

'I'm not sure, but you can rest easy, because you and Arnie are two men I would trust implicitly.'

'So, you're saying it's either McArthy or Saunders who's the thief?'

'No! I am not saying that.'

Bill was persistent. 'There is no way one man on his own could shift even one roll of that canvas.'

Looking thoughtful, the little man nodded. 'I already thought of that. It would certainly be a difficult thing to do without anyone knowing or seeing.' He fell into deep thought. 'But if there was an arrangement of sorts . . .'

'What kind of arrangement?'

The little man shook his head. 'Like you said, it might be the lorry driver's fault, after all. Or it could be that there was a mistake at the other end, and the rolls were never put on the lorry in the first place. The trouble is, there have been these other things of late . . .' He lapsed into silence.

'What things?' Bill was curious.

'Never you mind.' Briskly now, the little man bade him good night.

Before he left, Bill asked the foreman, 'Did you hear that skirmish between Phil and Jimmy?'

The little man grunted. 'Saunders is a troublemaker. If he wasn't a good worker, he'd be out that door so fast you wouldn't see his heels for dust.' He wagged a bony finger. 'I'll tell you this. He's sailing very close to the wind. One more set-to like that and it'll be his last under this roof.'

Bill nodded knowingly. He had no doubt but that the foreman was keeping a wary eye on Phil Saunders, and with every right.

'Do you need any help finishing off here?' Bill enquired.

'What? You think I'm too old and frail to do my job, is that it?' The fear of losing his work was a constant nightmare for old Joe.

'Good God, man! I was only offering a helping hand so's you could finish up and get away home.' Bill was taken aback by Joe's sharp response. 'I'd do the same for any one of us.'

'I know, and I didn't mean to snap at you like that,' Joe apologised. 'It's just that, well, three weeks ago I had to inform the manager about those boxes of spare machine parts that went missing, so he's already on the alert. I did manage to sort that one out; it was a mix-up in the ordering – but he won't be too pleased if I report that there are two rolls of top quality, heavy-gauge canvas missing, which will make us short for that big order on tents.'

'So, d'you reckon you can get to the bottom of it, without

him ever knowing?' Bill was worried. Like Joe said, this was not the first instance of its kind, though it was the most serious.

'I hope so. I intend following every avenue, until I do.'

After they parted and Bill was going through the door, Joe called after him. 'BILL!' He came scurrying towards him. 'Don't say a word to anyone about what you've been told here.' He tapped his nose meaningfully. 'Least said soonest mended, eh?'

'I won't say a word,' Bill assured him, 'and don't you worry – I expect you'll find that the driver overlooked the rolls when he loaded up at the other end.'

But as Bill walked to his car, the full impact of the incident suddenly hit him hard. Even if the driver had accidentally miscounted his load, whoever checked the rolls into the warehouse should have noticed.

It was a puzzle, and a worrying one at that. Big heavy rolls of canvas didn't just disappear. Besides, you needed more than one man to move them. He recalled something Joe had said about an arrangement.

My God! Bill thought. Was there really a thief among them? Somebody who was willing to put all their livelihoods at risk? And if so, which one was the culprit?

Naw! he decided. I can't believe that. I won't! Besides, if we had a thief among us, I'm sure we'd know.

It'll be a simple mistake, that's what it'll be.

But like Joe, he could not be certain.

It was a bad thing, and if it had to be dealt with by management, they'd all be under suspicion; each and every man jack of them.

After a process of elimination, his thoughts came to Phil Saunders. 'I'd bet my life that Stuart and Arnie are as straight as the day's long,' he muttered. 'But if I'm honest, I can't be that sure of Saunders.'

He had not known Phil as long as he'd known the others, but even in their relatively short acquaintance, over two years, he had come to realise that Saunders had depths of wickedness in him.

'Wickedness, bordering on evil!' When he said it out loud like that, it seemed rather inconceivable but where Saunders was concerned, he should know by now, anything was possible.

He thought of Judy Saunders, the man's wife. 'He's a damned bully,' he muttered. 'We all know that from Pauline at the Bedford Arms. There's talk that he once beat Judy so badly, she was put in hospital for a week.' His expression darkened. 'Bastard! He should be hung, drawn and quartered!'

Ashamed, he glanced at himself in the rear-view mirror. That was just gossip though. Pauline herself had denied any knowledge of it, but who was to say what the truth was? As the old saying had it: there was no smoke without fire.

~

The pub had closed half an hour since, but two customers lingered.

'Alan! Get him out of here!' hissed Pauline, who had no time for Phil Saunders, and even less for the woman with him. 'I've a damned good mind to turn the hosepipe on the pair of 'em!'

Pauline's contempt was heightened by their lewd laughter and sniggering, and how the girl was whispering in Phil's ear while he had his hand up her skirt. Phil Saunders was a married man with a spiteful side to him, while the girl was one of a shameless pack, got for two-a-penny in Bedford Town.

The one person Pauline cared about was Judy, who had to put up with this bastard.

'Alan!' She called her husband again. 'Just look at them! Turn my stomach, they do. And there's Judy waiting at home, wondering where the hell he is.'

'Yes, all right, I can see for myself what they're up to.' Alan stopped wiping a table and emptied an ashtray into the bucket on the floor. Like Pauline, he was sickened to see what was going on. 'You get off to bed, love. I'll deal with this.'

'I want him out NOW!' Hands on hips, she was determined to make sure he put them both out on the pavement, with the door securely bolted behind them.

'Listen to me, love, I'd rather you got out of the way. I'm not risking you getting involved in a skirmish. You know well enough what Phil can be like when he's had a few. Now, go on, Pauline. Do as I ask.' He gave her a gentle push. 'Away upstairs with you. I'll not be far behind.'

Bristling with anger, Pauline made her way across the room, passing Phil Saunders and the girl on the way. 'You no-good rubbish!' She glared down at him. 'You should be ashamed. You don't deserve a wife like Judy.'

'Who the devil d'you think you're talking to?' Phil struggled to his feet, then fell back in the seat and was laughing out loud, one arm round the floozy and the other steadying himself on the chair. 'Me and my friend here, we pay good money for our booze, and we don't bother nobody. The thing is,' he burped noisily, 'we don't want to be disturbed.' He gave a lazy wink. 'You know what I'm saying, don't you, eh?' He scowled. 'So go on, bugger off and leave us to it, why don't you?'

Before Pauline could reply, Alan was there to intervene. 'You'd best go,' he told Saunders. 'And take your "friend" with you.'

'Oh, dearie me!' Hanging onto the woman, Saunders managed to stand up straight. 'Want us out, do you?'

'That's the idea, yes.'

'What if I said we're not moving from here . . .' he turned to grin at the girl '. . . not for a while anyway?'

'I would not advise it.'

'Well, we're not going, so what d'you intend doing about that, eh?'

Alan's answer was to take hold of the woman's arm and lead her to the door, with Saunders tugging at her, cursing and swearing, and threatening all manner of punishment. 'You'll not get away with it!' he warned the older man. 'You know what I'm capable of when I set my mind to it.'

'Oh yes – I know what you're capable of all right, especially when it comes to beating up women. But you don't know what *I'm* capable of. Up to now, I've been polite, but you wouldn't want to push me too far!'

Handling the woman carefully, Alan prepared to usher her through the door. 'You'd best make your way home,' he instructed. 'The pub's shut and I'm about to lock up.'

'She's not going anywhere, and neither am I.' Coming up behind him, Phil bumped Alan aside, grabbed the girl and yanked her backwards. The two of them lost their balance and began rolling about the floor laughing hysterically. 'Shut up, woman!' Saunders gave her a playful slap. 'Come on, get me up.'

Grabbing the pair of them by the scruff of the neck, Alan pushed them out on the pavement. 'I should shift a bit smartish if I were you,' he advised them, 'before the police happen along and lock you in the cells for a night.'

Addressing the girl, he gave her a piece of well-meant advice. 'If you've got an ounce of common sense, you'll stay well away from this fella. When he's sober he's nasty, and when he's drunk, he's even nastier than that.'

His meaning was clear. 'It might be best if you didn't hang around to find out.'

Some part of his message must have got through her drink-sozzled brain, because she fought Saunders off and began to walk unsteadily down the street on her own.

When she was far enough away, Alan hoisted Phil Saunders by the collar and slammed him against the wall. 'You've got a lovely young wife at home,' he reminded Saunders. 'She's worth ten of that little tart. I don't know how you got your claws into Judy, but if I was her, I wouldn't even let you through the door!'

Humiliated and angry, Saunders began blustering. 'It's none

of your damned business. Judy is *my* woman and I'll do as I please – have you got that?'

He then fell in a heap on the ground and lay there, burping and giggling, until suddenly his mood darkened. 'That damned Judy! I know what she's up to all right, and I'm telling you now – if she ever crosses me, I'll snap her neck like a dry twig!' He struggled to his feet, breathing heavily.

Alan snatched him by the shoulders and ground out: 'You listen to me, sunshine.' Shoving his face to within an inch of Saunders's, he promised, 'If I ever find out you've laid a finger on that girl, I swear to God, I'll swing for you.' When there came no response, he tightened his hold. 'Did you hear what I said? Has it got through that thick mist of booze and arrogance – has it? ANSWER ME, YOU HEAP O' RUBBISH!'

'All right! All right! I won't hurt her,' came the sulky answer. Then he turned maudlin. 'I love her, don't you know that?'

'You don't love her,' Alan said scornfully. He was aware of Judy's story; not all of it, but enough to realise that she was as lonely and frightened as any young woman could be. 'You wouldn't know *how* to love anybody. You *control* her, that's what you do. You use and defile her, then you demand her love and loyalty in return. You don't even *know* her. You'll only ever be satisfied if you bring her down to your own level, but you'll never be able to do that, because for all her suffering and loneliness, she's a cut above you, and always will be.'

Astonished to see tears in the other man's eyes, he lowered his voice. 'Let her go, Saunders!' he urged. 'You're no good to her. Acting like this, you're no good to her. The way you are now, you're no good to anybody!' Then, hardening his heart again, he thrust him aside. 'Now get out of my sight. But remember what I said – Judy is a good friend to me and mine, and we'll be watching. So you just think on that.'

'Get off me!' When the older man released him, Phil remained where he was, propped unsteadily against the wall, shoulders sagged and a look of defeat on his sorry face.

In his fogged mind, he did love Judy, but not with tender-ness or joy. It was a spiteful love – of dictatorship, and unfounded suspicions. Deep down, he knew his wife had no feelings for him, and it drove him crazy.

Truth was, Phil Saunders had never known Judy's love; not the kind that spoke from the heart or shone in a woman's eyes when she looked at you. So he went on punishing her, because she could never give him what he craved – that elusive 'forever love' that comes only once in a lifetime.

Deep down, he knew it wasn't her fault, because how could she give him that kind of love, when she had already given it to someone else; a boy of eighteen. A boy she had deceived when she was only a kid herself.

In all these years, she had never forgiven herself for what she had done; and Phil had never forgiven her for choosing another over him.

When he too was on the brink of manhood, Saunders had witnessed at first-hand the magic that was Judy and Harry. The memories were deeply ingrained, he could see them in his mind's eye even now, the way they laughed together and looked at each other, the way they held hands as though they could never let go.

It was because of these memories that he knew in his heart, that however much he wanted it, Judy could never be his.

Yet he continued to chase the dream, until very slowly, the love he felt for her was turning into a frenzy of resentment darkening into hatred.

~

At number 16 Jackson Street in the backwaters of Bedford town, Judy lay in bed, her eyes closed – but she was not asleep, never asleep; especially not on a Friday when Phil was late home from work.

Every sound outside the house made her nervous, so nervous

that she had to get out of her bed and go downstairs. When the wall clock in the hallway rang out the first hour of a new day, she almost leaped out of her skin.

Shivering, she grabbed a jacket from the coat stand and, throwing it about her shoulders, she crossed into the tiny kitchen. 'One o'clock in the morning, and he's still out there, drinking and carrying on,' she said out loud, 'working himself up to fever pitch for when he gets home.'

It wasn't the cold that made her shiver. *It was fear.*

Unable to settle and reluctant to go back to bed, Judy prepared herself a cup of cocoa. She carried it to the table and there she sat, her eyes darting to the door at every sound. 'I should leave him,' she muttered. 'I should go away and never come back.' But where would she go, and how would she manage?

Maybe she could find work, but what kind of work? And if her last attempt was anything to go by, how long would she be able to hold it down before they sacked her for being useless? Her nerves were shattered. She couldn't focus on anything for more than a few minutes at a time, and she was incredibly uncomfortable around people.

She was constantly afraid. Afraid of being in a crowd, afraid when people approached her, and panic-stricken when she felt cornered.

So what chance did she have in the big wide world? She had no money except what he gave her, and that was pitifully little. 'I'll ask Pauline to help me,' she told herself. 'She'll get me my confidence back again. I'll talk to her – yes, that's it. She'll help me, I know she will. When I took that factory work last time, I wasn't ready. I wasn't strong enough, but I'm stronger now. I can do it, I'm sure I can.'

Her sense of excitement wavered when she remembered. 'Phil would never let me do it.' She recalled the rows and upsets she had endured each time she mentioned going out to work. 'It was because of him that I lost my job in the laundry that time,' she recalled.

She had been so happy in that little job with the other girls, but then he had humiliated her. 'He wouldn't stay away, wouldn't let me be. So they had to sack me. It wasn't their fault.'

Time and again she had tried to break free, and each time he had ruined it for her. It was like a game to him – a nasty, spiteful cat and mouse game. At first, she had tried to fight him. In the end though, he always won.

'I don't love him. I never have, never will,' she whispered. 'So why do I stay with him?' Once upon a time she had been strong. But he had drained all her strength away, until she just didn't care any more.

Halfway down the street, Saunders was embroiled in a row with the taxi driver, who was glad to be rid of this particular fare. 'Pay me what you owe me,' he warned Saunders, 'or I'll go to the police!'

The man had never encountered a more miserable passenger. 'I should charge you a damned sight more,' he complained, 'for all the earache and aggravation I've had to put up with, let alone having to stop twice and let you out to be sick.'

Sorting out the money, Saunders threw it at him. 'It's me who should be calling the police!' he grumbled. 'The fare you charge is out-and-out robbery!'

But before he could start another argument, the taxi driver swung his cab round in the street and raced off. Winding down his window, he yelled down the street, 'Bloody drunks! Lunatic! Next time I see you looking for a cab, I'll be off in the other direction.'

'Good!' Saunders waved his fist as the taxi sped away. 'You robbing swine! If I never see you again, it'll be too soon!'

One minute he was cursing and threatening, and the next he was roaring with laughter; loud, raucous laughter that actually unbalanced him and sent him careering against the front door. 'Where's that damned key?' he slurred.

He fumbled about until he found it, but then he was having difficulty fitting it into the lock. His voice echoed down the street. 'JUDY! LET ME IN, YOU DOZY BUGGER! JUDY! GET OUT HERE, WILL YOU, WOMAN!'

Judy made no move. Instead she remained seated at the table, cowering, her stomach churning as she waited for the inevitable.

It wasn't long before the door was flung open and he was inside. The sound of his voice sent cold shivers down her spine. 'Judy, where are you?' He began laughing, a soft, evil sound that she knew so well. Sometimes she really thought he was out of his mind. 'Come here, my pretty.' He chuckled. 'Your husband has need of you.'

As he stumbled down the passageway, Judy felt herself shrinking into the chair, and when he burst through the door, she wished she could be anywhere but there.

'Oh, look! There's my dear little mouse.' Putting his fingers across his face he made the image of a mouse twitching its whiskers. 'Little mouse,' he sniggered. 'Frightened, pretty little mouse.'

Judy looked away. 'I'm not playing your games,' she told him, pretending to drink her cocoa.

'Ooo, so little mouse is not playing, eh?' giggling childishly he swaggered towards her. 'You'd best be nice to me.' Drawing out a chair, he sat so close to her, she could hardly bear it.

'So tell me, little mouse, what are you doing down here? Why aren't you in bed?'

'I couldn't sleep.'

'Oh, and why was that?'

She shrugged her shoulders. 'I don't know, but I'm feeling sleepy now, so I'll get back up—'

'We'll go when *I'm* ready!' As she stood to leave, he gripped her arm so tightly he made her cry out. *'I said . . . sit!'* Putting force on her arm, he made her sit down. 'Now then, I want to know what you've been up to.'

Assuming he'd found out about the man who thought she was a beggar, Judy was frantic. Taking a deep breath, she tried to explain. 'The man made a mistake, that's all. He thought I was begging, but I was only asking the time.'

'What!' He spun her round to face him. '*Who* thought you were begging? What the hell are you talking about?'

'Nothing.' Realising he didn't know, Judy tried desperately to cover it up. 'It was nothing – a mistake, that's all. I was just there and he made a mistake.'

'Who?' Taking hold of her by the shoulders he shook her hard, until she cried out for him to stop. Then, throwing her aside as if she was nothing, he sneered, 'That says it all, doesn't it, eh? Phil Saunders' wife . . . *begging in the street!*'

The laughter stopped. 'Who else saw you, eh? Who else saw you asking for money in the streets? Damn you! I make sure you want for nothing, and that's how you repay me. Bitch!'

Bringing his fist up, he caught her hard across the face and sent her reeling backwards. 'I ASKED YOU A QUESTION!' The trickle of blood from her temple seemed to enrage him. 'ANSWER ME! WHO ELSE SAW YOU BEGGING?'

'I was *not* begging.' Dazed by the blow, she wiped away the blood with the back of her hand. 'I was asking the time, and the man just thought I was begging.'

'It doesn't make sense. Why would he think you were begging?'

'I don't know. Ask Alan,' she sobbed. 'He was there. He took me back to Pauline. I would never beg, and why would I need to?' She had to humour him, or pay the price. 'Since I lost my job at the factory, you've always provided for me.'

Clinging to him, she appealed, 'Listen to me, Phil. I was not begging. You ask Alan. He'll tell you.'

He stared at her hard and long, before stretching out his arms and crushing her to him. 'You're right.' He stroked her long fair hair. 'You'll never need to beg, while you've got me. Nor will you need to work in a place where men gawp at you all the time, itching to get their hands on you. I won't have it, d'you hear?'

He had the look of madness. 'I'll take care of you. *Me* – Phil Saunders. I took care of you when nobody else would,' his manner softened, 'because I love you. I've always loved you.'

Holding her away from him, he said, 'I'll give you a few more pounds, then you can buy yourself some nice new clothes. The old ones are getting a bit tatty and folks might blame me. I can't have that now, can I?'

He thrust his hands into his trouser-pocket. 'Here.' Shoving a fistful of money into her hand, he ordered, 'Take it – it's yours. Tomorrow morning, I want you to go out and get some decent-looking clothes, so nobody can ever say that Phil Saunders' wife is a beggar!'

She looked at the wad of notes, realising they were the best part of his wages. 'I can't take this.' She stuffed it back into his pocket. 'We need it for more important things.'

He made no move to return the money to her. Instead, he continued to stare down on her, his eyes narrowed and his face set hard.

'Honest, Phil, I'll be fine.' She saw the signs and began to panic. 'All right then, I'll just have a few pounds,' she gabbled. 'I've seen some really nice things in town. There's a little skirt and top, and a really pretty jacket . . . blue with black trim. I could buy all of those things for just a few pounds. We don't need to use all your hard-earned wages.'

For a long moment, it seemed as though he wasn't even listening, but then he gave a begrudging half-smile. 'Whatever my Judy wants is fine by me.' When he raised his hand, she instinctively flinched. 'Aw, poor little mouse, look what you made me do.' With the cuff of his sleeve he dabbed at the line of blood trailing from her temple. 'I didn't mean to hurt you, but you just get me all riled up.'

Loudly tutting, he uprighted the cocoa cup which had been spilled over. Then, taking her by the hand, he switched out the light, and pushed her up the stairs.

Judy knew full well what was coming, but she said not a word.

Instead she allowed herself to be led to the bedroom, where he roughly stripped off her nightgown and threw her bodily onto the bed.

'Who do you belong to?' It was a question he often asked of her.

'You.'

'Say it properly!'

'I belong to you.'

'That's right. You need to remember that. They *all* need to remember that.'

Tearing off his clothes, he straddled her, his hands all over her, touching her face, fondling her small, pert breasts, and now he was running his hands over her smooth, bare thighs. 'You're very special to me,' he murmured hoarsely. 'There are men out there who would give their right arm to have you.'

He sniggered. 'They can't have you though, can they? Not when you belong to *me!*'

Judy thought it was a strange kind of love that wanted to hurt and dominate. There was a dark hatred in him that filled her with terror. But still, she said nothing, for if she dared to disagree, she would be made to pay the price. Sometimes, he was incredibly gentle. Sometimes, like now, he was the unforgiving enemy.

Cruel or gentle, he raised no feelings in her, other than fear and repugnance, and a deep-seated urge to tell him the truth: of how she cringed under his touch; of how her dearest wish was to find the courage to put a million miles between them.

At times like this though, when he was in this mood, Judy knew to keep her silence.

'You're the loveliest thing I've ever seen.' He traced his finger over the hollow of her neck. 'My dear, sweet little mouse.' His passion so obviously aroused, he whispered harshly, 'If any man ever tried to take you from me, I would have to hurt him. *Really* hurt him! You do understand that, don't you?'

When again she gave no answer, he grabbed her by the mouth. 'What was that? I didn't hear what you said.'

When he gave her room to breathe, she whispered the answer he wanted. 'Yes, Phil. I do see that, yes.'

Smiling, he bent to kiss her. 'Good girl. Now then, you haven't forgotten how to please your man, have you, because that would really upset me.'

She shook her head. 'I haven't forgotten.'

'Good!'

His taking of her was self-gratifying and incredibly cruel, and when she cried out with pain, it only spurred him on.

Trapped beneath his considerable weight, Judy could almost taste the booze on his breath, and something else, heavy on his skin – a woman's perfume. She felt defiled. She should confront him, she thought angrily, walk out on him, and not worry over what he might do to her.

Like a predator, he had swooped on her when she was at her lowest; over the years he had moulded her to his will, skilfully quashing all her resistance.

After Harry was gone, the family rejected her, and the nightmare worsened. For a while, she was totally lost, until Phil Saunders took her under his wing.

At first he was kind, sometimes funny and wonderful, always there, waiting, watching, ready to take care of her; a much-needed shoulder to cry on. But then slowly, subtly, almost without her realising it, he became her jailer.

He knew exactly how to torment her mind – about Harry having deserted her, and the callous way in which her family had kicked her onto the streets. He goaded her about the other, faceless men who had used and left her, and other bad things that still haunted her, so much so that she had no self-respect, no sense of identity.

Phil Saunders had drained her of ambition and purpose. He knew her past. He knew her fears, and for his own gratuitous ends, he had played on those fears until now, she truly believed that no one else would want her – that she was less than worthless.

Like a young fool she had gone to him – willingly, blindly. More and more she grew to depend on him.

He had succeeded in that, if nothing else.

There was a time, long ago, when she lived in hope that something, or somebody, would rescue her. But they never did.

And why would they?

PART TWO

Bedfordshire, Autumn 1956

Man and Boy

CHAPTER SIX

D ON ROBERTS SAT at the kitchen table, his troubled mind going back over the years. Not so long ago he had been a strong, proud man. He had a wife and family, he held down a good job and he had a future. Now, all that was behind him.

At the age of sixty-eight, he was a stocky man with a cropped grey chin beard and round blue eyes. He still had the strength of a man not yet past his prime, and when there was no work to do around the house, he would make himself busy outside, or stride across the fields from Heath and Reach, through the woods and beyond.

Now though, seated at his daughter's kitchen table, his mind fled back over the years. He remembered the day as if it was only yesterday; that fateful day when Judy told them she was carrying Harry Blake's child.

So much water had gone under the bridge since then. His wife Norma had passed on. Shortly afterwards, he had sold his home and moved in with his eldest daughter Nancy and her family. It wasn't so bad while he was still out at work all day, but now that he was retired, he realised that it had been a big mistake.

So many regrets; so much heartache. Yet out of all the aching memories, the one that pained him the most was that shocking incident over seventeen years ago, just before the war.

To this day, he bitterly regretted how he and his wife had

turned their daughter Judy out, at a time in her young life when she needed them most.

'Sammie!' Nancy's voice shattered his thoughts.

'What?' Sammie was impatient. This was the third time her mother had called up the stairs to her.

'Have you packed your suitcase yet?'

'Not yet, no. I'm reading!'

'Oh, for heaven's sake! Why will that girl never do what she's asked to do?' Swinging round, Nancy addressed Don. 'Honestly, Dad, what's the matter with the child?'

Don smiled knowingly. 'She's young, that's all. She's got a million more important things on her mind than packing a case.' Grandfather to Nancy's two children, Don understood them far better than she ever could. 'Leave her be, and she'll do it all the quicker,' he promised. 'That's how kids are.'

'Well, she'd best get a move on. Her father's only at the garage, filling up the car with petrol. Woe betide her if she still hasn't done it by the time he gets back.'

Tall and slender, with auburn hair and an air of authority, Nancy Wells bore no resemblance whatsoever to her younger sister, Judy, long ago labelled the black sheep of the family.

'Sammie! You've got half an hour at most, before your father gets back!' she shouted up to her daughter for the fourth time. 'Oh, and you need to find David. He seems to have gone missing.'

'For crying out loud, will you stop panicking, Nancy. You've plenty of time yet,' Don said.

Nancy threw herself onto a chair, her arms spread out across the kitchen table. 'They wear me out at times,' she moaned. 'I haven't even had a cuppa this morning, let alone any breakfast.' She gestured to the sink. 'Put the kettle on, Dad,' she told him. 'You make a pot of tea, while I go and sort those two out.' Before he could answer, she was up and away, marching with a purpose towards the stairs.

Don gave a heartfelt sigh. 'Here we go again.' He got up to

do as he was instructed. 'That's a frightening sight and no mistake, our Nancy on the warpath. She never learns, does she, eh?' Lately, he had got into the habit of talking to himself.

After his wife passed on some years ago, Nancy had persuaded him to sell up and move in with her and her family. At first he had resisted, but since he was lonely at the time, it had not taken long for him to change his mind.

Since then, he had often regretted his decision. Nancy was such a particular person, pernickety and fussy about almost everything.

While filling the kettle with water, he summed up Nancy's character to a tee. '"Do this, do that . . . Don't forget to make your bed. Take the dog for a walk and make sure she has her biscuits. Oh, and put the kettle on, Dad!"'

He gave a little groan. 'I never knew how much like your mother you were.' Not that he hadn't loved Norma because, like any other married couple, they had grown together over the years.

He shook his head, grinning. 'Hmh! Like daughter like mother. *She* had a way of making me think I was still in the Army an' all!'

Through the window he could see his grandson David; a fine young fellow of twenty, with dark good looks that attracted the girls from every corner. He had a friendly, natural way with people. His dad Brian would say, 'If there was no one else around, he would strike up a conversation with a lamppost!'

Just a wink away from his twenty-first birthday, David was a responsible, contented young man with a quirky sense of humour. He had a number of ambitions which were frowned on by his parents, one being to give up his job at the garage and head off round the world with a couple of mates. Although he was sensible, there were times when he craved something more exciting than being a mechanic, and just occasionally, he showed signs of his sister Sammie's rebellious nature.

Unlike Sammie though, he had never been tempted to go

off the rails. Sammie was fiery, where he was a listener. She was boisterous where he was easy-going, and when it came to tempers, Sammie could frighten the devil himself, whereas David preferred to reason his way out of a situation.

Though she was the kindest, most caring creature he knew, there was no denying that Sammie bordered on the rebellious.

A stunning-looking girl, Sammie was fine-boned and pretty, with warm auburn hair like her mother, but where Nancy's hair was straight and smooth, Sammie's fiery locks were wild and burnished like sunshine on moorland. Her wide, honest eyes were softest brown with flecks of twinkly blue, while her mother's eyes were deep-coloured.

When she wasn't in one of her dark moods, she was a warm-natured, fun-loving girl, possessed of an infectious laugh that drew you to her and with a passion for life that left him breathless.

Nancy had been upstairs for just a few minutes, when the argument started.

Down in the kitchen, Don heard the rumpus and he despaired. 'I don't know who's worse,' he muttered into his tea-cup. 'The mother or the child.'

'I MEAN IT, MUMMY. I DON'T WANT TO GO.'

'WELL, HARD LUCK! BECAUSE I AM NOT LEAVING YOU BEHIND, AND THAT'S THAT.'

'WHY NOT? I CAN LOOK AFTER MYSELF. I'VE LEFT SCHOOL, FOR HEAVEN'S SAKE!'

'I SAID NO!'

'THEN LET GRANDAD LOOK AFTER ME.'

'ENOUGH, MY GIRL!' Nancy's voice shook with anger. 'YOU'RE COMING WITH US AND THAT'S THAT!'

Don rolled his eyes to the ceiling. 'For God's sake, Nancy, leave her alone!' he despaired. 'If you could just cut the girl some slack, you might find she'd come round to your way of thinking.'

He heard the slam of a door, then the thump of footsteps

as Nancy came thundering down the stairs, and now she was rushing into the kitchen.

'I've had just about enough of that girl,' she fumed. 'She seems to have got it into her head that it's all right for her to stay behind, while the rest of the family are off for a week in Lytham St Anne's. Well, if she thinks that, she's got another thought coming.' Hurrying across to the sink, she poured out the tea he had just brewed. 'D'you want one?'

'Got one. Thanks all the same.'

'What am I going to do with her, Dad? She's out of control. She should be grateful. Her Uncle Mac is very kind to let us use his lovely house while he and Rita are away on business.'

'Come on, sit yourself down, Nancy.' Don could see she was working herself into a state. 'I'll do that.'

Agitated, she didn't argue. Instead she slumped into the chair, listening to what he had to say.

'For a start, Uncle Mac is not just being kind, as you put it.' Don had always been proud of his younger brother, though he was under no illusions as to where Mac's loyalties lay. 'My brother has always been able to grasp an opportunity. He wants someone to look after his grand property while he and Rita are away. You and the family need a place to stay at the seaside, so it's a good deal either way. It suits you to stay in Mac's house, and it suits Mac to have you taking care of his precious assets.'

Nancy could see the logic in that. 'I thought you always admired Uncle Mac's business sense?'

'Oh, don't get me wrong. I do!' Don explained. 'Only I wouldn't want you to mistake convenience for "kindness". That's all I'm saying.'

'Well, whatever his reasoning, I for one am very grateful that we don't have to spend a small fortune to stay in some cheap hotel, when we can have a luxury house right on the coast.' Nancy gave a wistful sigh. 'I like Uncle Mac. He's funny and mischievous, and over the years he's been a great uncle to the kids.'

Don chuckled. 'That's because he's still a kid himself. Fifty-eight going on six years old, that's my brother,' he concluded. 'Truth is, I've always wished I was more like him. He's always been a genius where making money's concerned.'

Don cast his mind back to when they were boys. 'Even as a kid Mac was always ducking and diving . . . wheeling and dealing. He found an old pram on the scrapheap once. It had a wheel missing and part of the panel at the side was torn off. It took him every night for a week to repair it . . . mind you, it still looked a bit of an eyesore, but he got it back in working order. Every Friday after school, he'd wheel the old pram round the neighbourhood, knocking on doors, asking for old newspapers and magazines. Then he'd sell them to the paper factory at the bottom of Hazel Street.'

'Amazing!' Nancy said. 'It's a pity you didn't take a leaf or two out of his book,' she remarked thoughtlessly. 'You and Mum might have had a better quality of life.'

Shocked rigid, Don rounded on her. 'Your mother and I might not have had a big house and a flash car, but we came through the war in one piece, we rubbed along together well, and had a regular wage coming in. Money and chancing does not make for contentment and happiness, Nancy, my girl. You should remember that.'

Agitated, she glared at him. 'Don't be so prickly. I didn't mean it like that.'

'Then you should think before you speak.' He was really upset.

Nancy closed the subject. 'I'm more concerned about Sammie. Why does she never listen to me?'

'Because *you* never listen to *her*.' For once, Don did not mince his words. 'She talks, and you talk over the top. She's quiet and you rant and rave at her. Be very careful, Nancy, or you might just turn her against you.'

'I could never do that!'

'Then don't suffocate her. That's exactly what your mother did with Judy, and look what happened there.'

'Oh! So now you're saying that Judy going with some bloke and getting pregnant was all Mother's fault, is that it?'

'No, I am not saying that. What I'm saying is, your mother was overanxious about Judy, her being the youngest an' all. She insisted on knowing where she was going, and who with, and what time she would be back. Judy was at that difficult stage between childhood and womanhood and as far as I'm concerned, your mother should have cut her some slack. Just like you should cut Sammie some slack now. She needs space to grow. D'you understand what I'm saying?'

For a moment, Nancy appeared to be considering his remark. Lapsing into deep thought, she stared at the tablecloth and rolled the cup in the palms of her hands. Presently she looked up, surprising him with her admission of emotion. 'I do love her, Dad – more than she could ever know.'

'Have you told her that?'

She shook her head. 'Not lately.'

'Well, you should tell her. This is a time when she craves reassurance and guidance. She needs to know that you do love her . . . that you enjoy her company, and that you would really *like* her to come to Lytham.'

'It wouldn't make any difference,' Nancy answered tiredly. 'We'll still end up arguing.'

'Yes, you probably will.'

'See? Even you know we can never have a proper conversation, without ending up in a quarrel.'

'That's because you set yourself.'

'What d'you mean?'

Don felt uncomfortable, being put on the spot like that. 'Mmm . . . sometimes you have a way about you that makes you seem – well – *hard.*' He felt a bit like he was digging his own grave.

His daughter gave him a stony stare. 'Is that the best you can do to reassure me?' she snapped. 'Telling me I'm *hard*?'

Wisely ignoring the reprimand, he went on, 'You're too much

alike, you and Sammie, that's the trouble. And if you don't mind me saying, you should try *not* to argue with her, because it gives her the opportunity to argue right back.'

'What? So you're an expert on teenagers now, are you? Hmh!'

He fell silent for a moment, remembering, filled with regrets. Then he slowly shook his head. 'Oh, I know! Don't you worry about that, Nancy. I know all right. I've made some terrible mistakes, or has your sister slipped your memory after all these years?'

She gave a gasp of astonishment. 'No, of course not, Dad! Believe it or not, I do think about her, from time to time.'

Don merely nodded. 'Truth is, I never stop thinking of her.' The tears filled his eyes. 'My head is bursting with questions. Where is she? What is she doing? Is she well . . . has she gone abroad? We don't even know if she's alive or dead!' His voice broke. 'My own child! Not yet fifteen years old, and I turned her onto the streets.' He had been so angry with Judy and the things she had done. But two wrongs never made a right, he knew that now.

'Firstly, Dad, it wasn't you who actually turned her out,' Nancy reminded him. 'It was Mother.'

'Maybe. But I could have put my foot down. Instead I was too busy wallowing in self-pity, asking myself how I could have brought you up right, yet made such a hash of it with your sister. I take the blame. I should have been a better father.'

Aware that Sammie might be listening, Nancy lowered her voice. 'No, Dad! Judy should have been a better daughter. Remember how she was?' she urged him. 'All right, Judy wasn't fifteen yet, but she was older than that . . . in herself, in her ways. Face it, Dad. *She was born bad!*'

Don sat bolt upright. 'No! I can't accept that. No one is born bad, especially a child of mine.'

'If she wasn't born bad, how did she get like she did? You raised us both the same. We were always treated in the same way. And yet she went and got herself pregnant. As if that wasn't enough, she arranged an abortion . . . *she didn't even care about killing her own child!*'

Don laid a hand over hers. 'Please, Nancy, don't say that.'

'Sorry, Dad, but it has to be said. I won't have you making yourself ill over her. She was a selfish little bitch with absolutely no self-respect. Even after she was shown the door, did she try and make amends? No! Did she ever apologise to you and Mother? No! Did she change her ways and try to improve her life? No, she did not. Instead, she flaunted herself to every Tom, Dick and Harry; shaming herself, shaming the family.'

Reluctantly, Don had to concede that. 'But what I'm saying is, did *we* make her like that, by turning her out? If I'd had a more sympathetic ear and heard her side of the story, we might still have her with us.' He shook his head sadly. 'I should have gone after her and brought her back. I should have been more forceful about it.'

'But you *did* go after her,' Nancy reminded him patiently. 'And when you found her and asked her to come home, what did she do, eh?'

When he gave no answer, she shoved her face close to his. 'She told you to bugger off and leave her alone,' she hissed. 'Said that she wanted nothing more to do with any of us. *Judy disowned us!* She cut us out of her life for ever. Think, Dad! Think about all the nasty things she said to you.'

She sat back in the chair. 'Or maybe you've forgotten, is that it?'

'No, I haven't forgotten. How could I? Thinking about it later, I got the feeling that she was just lashing out; that she was hurt and angry, and if she had "disowned" us like she said, we must have deserved it.'

The pain was etched in his face. 'Trouble was, if I had brought her back, your mother would never have let her in. At least not without a fight, and what good would that have done?'

'Mother was right not to want her back,' Nancy replied vehemently. 'Judy was no good then and she's no good now. I bet you wherever she is right this minute, she'll be happily married to some idle, no-good bloke, and she'll have a dozen kids baying at her heels.' She gave a kind of growl. 'If you ask me, it's only what she deserves.'

'That's a cruel thing to say.'

'Yes, but I'm right, and you know it.'

'Ah, but what if you're *wrong*, Nancy?' It was his enduring fear. 'What if right now, Judy – my daughter, your sister – is in dire need of us?'

'Trust me, she isn't.' Nancy thought she knew her sister better than anyone. 'Judy doesn't need anybody! Not you, not me . . . not anybody! She's a survivor. She'll do what it takes to make sure she's all right. For heaven's sake, have you forgotten how she went away with your wallet and all the money in it?'

Don rebuked her sharply. 'I like to think she would never have done that if she wasn't desperate.'

'Oh, Dad! Will you listen to yourself? The truth is, she was the bad apple in the barrel. We all knew that. She let us all down, and as far as I'm concerned, she will never be a part of this family again.'

She lowered her voice again. 'You and Mother made a hard decision, but it was the only one left to you. Judy gave you no choice. And now, you have really got to stop feeling guilty.'

He nodded, but remained silent.

Nancy saw how it was with him, and the old jealousy rose in her. 'Why is it you feel so mortified about Judy? But then, she was always your favourite, wasn't she?' Even now after all these years, she could not control her feelings. 'If anyone's to blame for what she did, it's you and Mother, for spoiling her rotten and always giving in to her.'

Don was amazed. Only now did he realise how envious Nancy had been of her sister. 'That's not true, and you know it,' he snapped. 'We always treated both you girls the same.'

Realising she had said more than she meant to, Nancy soft-ened her voice. 'I'm sorry, Dad, but Judy's gone her own way now. Mother's gone too, but we're still here, and we have to make the best of it, you and me, and this family.'

'You're very unforgiving, Nancy.'

'Maybe it's just that my memory is more vivid than yours.' She wanted him to know how bitter she was. 'I wouldn't be at all surprised if it wasn't Judy who triggered Mother's illness.'

Her remark stunned him. 'Don't talk nonsense!'

'Oh, really?'

Pushing back the chair, she looked at him for a moment, despising him for his weakness. When he averted his gaze, she gave an impatient snort and stood up. 'I'd best go and see what Sammie is up to.'

After she had stormed up the stairs for the umpteenth time, his words of advice clearly forgotten, Don remained in the chair, head in hands as he leaned over the table. 'I don't care what you say, Nancy,' he murmured. 'We let your sister down, badly.'

Nothing and no one would ever convince him that he had done the right thing. What father would throw his daughter onto the street when, for the first time in her young life, she had turned to him for help?

For a long time now, especially since losing his wife, Don had relived that shocking moment when he watched Judy run away down the street, sobbing uncontrollably. Even when his wife slammed the door on her, he had stood there for what seemed an age.

At the time, he had been deadened by the news that Judy was with child. It was a terrible shock. Even so, devastating as it had been, there could be no excuse for what they did to her.

If Judy had done wrong, then so had they.

'Go on then! Run to the filth who put you with child! Let him take care of you!' That's what his wife shouted after Judy as she ran away from them.

Because of pride, and shame, and the knowledge that his 'innocent' baby daughter was now expecting an illegitimate baby, Donald Roberts had lost all reason. He should have been strong for her, but instead, he had turned away, leaving her to flounder.

May God forgive him.

~

Outside in the garden, Sammie and her brother were gently swinging on the old wooden bench. Attached to a mighty branch of an elm tree by a measure of strong chain, it had long been a source of enjoyment. Even now, when they were almost grown up, it was still a favourite spot.

'They've been arguing again,' Sammie confided in her older brother, as she threw an old tennis ball for Lottie, the white bull terrier, to catch.

'I know,' he replied casually. 'I heard them though I couldn't quite hear what it was all about – something that happened a long time ago, I reckon.' He turned his curious gaze on her. 'Did *you* hear?'

Sammie shook her head. 'Not really. When I came out to the garden they were whispering, or at least Mother was.' She gave it a moment's thought. 'Although I did hear a name. It sounded like Julie.'

David repeated the name thoughtfully. 'Julie, eh? And what else?'

'Well, nothing really. The door was closed so it was just muffled, kinda private. Mother was angry though. When she raised her voice, Grandad had to calm her down.'

'Hmh! So, what's new?' Their mother's mood-swings were something they had lived with as far back as they could remember. 'She's always angry about something or another.'

Sammie grinned suddenly. 'I did hear Mother ranting on about me not having packed my case, and Grandad told her off good and proper.'

'Good old Grandad!'

'I think I heard her say how he wasn't to blame himself . . . or something like that.'

'When it comes right down to it, you really didn't hear much of any use, did you?' Her brother laughed. 'You'd never make a spy, that's for sure.'

'Neither would you!'

'You're a Cloth Ears.'

'Cheek!' She gave him a push, then leaped off the swing and ran, dodging through the bushes with David in pursuit, their laughter echoing up to the house and the dog barking frantically with joy at all the excitement.

'Bless their hearts.' Don smiled as he watched them through the window. 'What I wouldn't give to be young like that again.'

His heart sank as he heard Nancy's voice cut across the garden. 'David . . . Sammie!' She spied them from a distance. 'Oh, there you are. Your father should be on his way back by now. I hope you two are all packed and ready to leave?'

'I don't want to go,' Sammie confided to David.

'Oh Sam, please!' David implored. 'If *you* don't come, then I won't go either. I can't stand Uncle Mac. It'll be awful on my own.'

'Then neither of us should go. Why don't we stand up to them and say we're not kids any more. We're past making castles in the sand and all that stuff. You tell them, David.' She smiled mischievously. 'I'll back you up.'

'Monster!'

'Coward!'

David chased her to the house where, in spite of their pleading, Nancy sent them upstairs to collect their bags. By the time they came down, grudgingly dragging their cases, their father was home and ready to leave.

'All set are you, kids?' Big-built and homely with a mop of light-brown hair, Brian was calm in both manner and appearance.

'It's all right for you and David,' Sammie told him. 'You both enjoy the boats and the amusement arcade, and sitting outside the pub of a night. Mother goes walking for hours, and takes a nap while you and David go off exploring, but what is there for *me* to do?'

Before he could speak, she answered her own question. 'Nothing, that's what. Except to wander up and down like a lost soul.'

'You can always come walking with me,' her mother butted in.

'I don't like walking.'

'So, do some shopping then. Buy shoes or new make-up. You've got your spending money, and savings from your paper-round. Or you could just sit on the beach and relax. That's the idea of this holiday, so we can all do whatever we like.'

'Well, if we can do whatever we like, why can't I stay here?' When she glanced at Don across the table, he slowly shook his head, as if advising her not to argue.

While Sammie took a minute to consider, Nancy launched into full sail. 'For heaven's sake, girl, don't be so difficult! There's a lot to do at the seaside, if only you would give it a chance. Besides, this is the only time we can all get away together. Don't spoil it by being selfish.'

Anticipating a full-blown row, Brian took Sammie aside. 'Look, sweetheart, I *really* want you to come with us.' He lowered his voice, 'What with being out on the road at all hours, I see little enough of you as it is.'

He saw the disappointment in her face, and sighed. 'If you really are dead set against coming with us, I'm sure Grandad would look after you.' When she opened her mouth to speak, he put a gentle finger on her lips. 'Before you decide though, you really need to give a thought to Grandad. He moved in with us not long after he lost your grandma, and since then there's been hardly a minute when he gets any time to himself. When you think about it, he doesn't get much peace, does he? Oh, I know he never complains, but how many times have you seen him set out on a long walk in all weathers, for hours on end?'

Sammie nodded. 'I know, Dad. I've watched him.'

'Well, it occurred to me that he might just need that kind of solitude, to think of your grandma, and to remember how it was. Sometimes we all need that little space to call our own, to clear our heads of the hustle and bustle around us; even you, when you sit out there on that swing, enjoying the peace away from everyone.' He smoothed her wild auburn curls. 'Do you see what I mean, pet?'

Sammie knew exactly what he meant, because there were times when she would go upstairs to her room and lock the door, just to think, and be alone; especially when her mother was in one of her foul moods.

She thought of what her father had said just now, and the way David had pleaded with her to go with them, and she realised how selfish she was being. Quietly collecting her case from the foot of the stairs, she asked, 'Can you please take this to the car, Daddy? I need to talk with Grandad.'

Relieved, he gave a ceremonious bow. 'Whatever m'lady wishes,' he answered stoutly, tipping his forehead in a mock-servile manner.

Taking Nancy's case, Brian asked David to 'Fetch whatever needs bringing, will you, son? Then we'd best be off. We need to miss the worst of the traffic on the A5.' Addressing Don, he told him, 'I'll be back in a minute.'

'Oh, wait!' Delighted that once again she had won the day, Nancy fled after her husband. 'I forgot to clean out the boot of the car.'

A few minutes later they were ready for off. Nancy and Brian asked Don if he was sure he'd be all right on his own. 'I'll be absolutely fine,' he assured them. 'You get off and enjoy your-selves.'

David gave his grandad a hug. 'Don't go throwing wild parties while we're away,' he joked. 'Loose women and booze will get you a bad name.'

Don gave a hearty chuckle. 'Chance would be a fine thing,' he said, then he shoved him out the door.

While the other three climbed into the car, Sammie threw her arms round Don's neck. 'Will you *really* be all right?' she asked, tearfully clinging to him.

'Of course I will,' Don said. 'I'll get some peace, without you lot running about, arguing and moaning, and your mother going off at a tangent at every little thing.'

'You're not just saying that, are you?'

'Absolutely not!' He gave her an affectionate smile.

Unwrapping him, she looked him in the eye. For a time the two of them were quiet, until Sammie told him, 'I love you, Grandad. I don't want anything to happen to you . . . *ever*!'

Deeply emotional, Don took a deep breath. 'Ever is a long time,' he answered, 'but nothing's going to happen to me while you're away, I promise. Satisfied now?'

Wiping away her tears, she gave a half-smile. 'Yes, Grandad.'

He took her by the hand and walked with her to the car. 'Have a lovely time, all of you.'

Helping Sammie into the car he waved them goodbye, but as Brian drove off, with four arms sticking out of the window waving back, Don felt suddenly alone in the world. He loved his family with a passion, but he loved Sammie most of all. She was a very special person; with a beautiful and loving heart.

He had only ever loved one other person in the same way he loved his granddaughter. She too, had been another bright and lovely creature: Judy, the daughter now estranged from him. The daughter he and the family had so deeply wronged.

He remembered Nancy's cruel words – 'She'll be all cosied up to some no-good bloke.' In his deepest heart, and even after all she had done, he could not believe that Judy would have sunk so low.

Collecting his cap and jacket from the hall stand, he looked at himself in the mirror there, his eyes stern with determination.

'Come on, Lottie!' Clipping the lead through the dog's collar, he led her outside. 'Once we're clear of the lanes and that mad postman in his delivery van, I'll let you loose,' he promised.

With the family away for a time, there was only one thought blazing in his mind.

He had to find Judy.

He needed to know whether his younger daughter had made good her life, and whether she had forgiven them all for their cruel treatment of her.

CHAPTER SEVEN

H ARRY WAS MORE nervous than he had been in a long time. Having suffered a sleepless night, he felt both weary and anxious, and now as he came into Kathleen's kitchen, he wasn't at all sure that he had made the right decision in accepting the job at Jacobs' Emporium.

What if it all went wrong? What if he hated the work? What if he made a complete hash of it and nobody else would ever give him a job? What if . . . what if?

Kathleen looked up as he entered. 'Jaysus, Mary and Joseph! Sure, anyone would think you were on your way to the hangman, so they would.'

She noted the slouch of his shoulders and the way he fidgeted nervously with his tie, and her heart went out to him. 'Will ye just look at the state of yourself !'

Laying down the knife, she crossed the room to him. 'Sure, I've never seen a man yet who can fix his tie.' Reaching up, she flicked the tie here, then crossed it over there, and now she patted it down. Standing back to admire her handiwork, she gave him a little push. 'Sit yourself down,' she told him. 'Young Tom is already up and dressed, and ready for breakfast, bless his little manly heart.'

When Harry began fiddling with his tie again, she slapped the back of his hand. 'Will ye leave that alone, or do I have to clip your ear an' all?'

'Sorry, Kathleen,' Harry said. 'I don't know what's wrong with me. All I'm doing today is accompanying one of the salesmen on his rounds, and I feel like a little boy on my first day at a new school.'

Kathleen laughed out loud. 'Do ye not know what us women have always known?' she asked.

'No, but I'm sure you'll tell me.' He relaxed with a smile. 'So what is it that you women have always known?'

Kathleen chuckled. 'Only that a man needs a wise woman to tell him what to do.' She patted her ample chest. 'And they don't come any wiser than Kathleen O'Leary!'

'Well, thank you for that, Kathleen O'Leary,' Harry grinned, tongue in cheek. 'I feel ten times better now, for knowing that.'

'Sausage or black pudding?' she wanted to know. 'You can't have both, because there are only two sausages and somebody's got to go without.'

Harry loved her jolly banter. It lifted his spirits. 'I'm happy either way,' he told her.

'But what would you prefer?'

'The sausage, if it's going begging.'

'Right then! You can have the last sausage. Tom's already opted for the other one.'

'No, I'm all right, Kathleen, honestly. If Tom's already claimed one sausage, you'd best have the other. I'll be absolutely fine with the black pudding.' He glanced about. 'Where is Tom, by the way?'

'Outside, chasing the cat.'

Harry went to the back door and called him in. 'Hurry up, son. I'll be away to work in a few minutes.'

When Tom came running in through the back door, Harry scooped him into his arms. 'I hear you've been chasing the cat?'

Tom shook his head. 'No, Daddy. I was just running, and the cat ran after me.'

'Oh, I see. The cat was chasing *you*.' Harry set him down. 'Well, now it's time for breakfast. After that, I'm away to my new job, and you've got the lovely Kathleen to take care of you.' He lowered his voice to a more intimate level. 'So are you happy with that, son?'

Tom's face lit up. 'Me and Kathleen are going on the train to Bedford, and we might go down to the river and feed the ducks, that's what Kathleen said.'

'All the way to Bedford? Wow! And feeding the ducks, lucky you!' Harry feigned disappointment. 'And there's poor me, having to go to work. It's just not fair.'

'I'm sorry, Daddy, but you have to go to work,' the small boy declared. 'Kathleen said you have to "shake a leg" and get out to work. Right? I'm not to worry, 'cos you need to earn us a living, don't you?' His little head was nodding fifteen to the dozen, as though encouraging Harry to agree.

Harry had to smile. 'You're right,' he answered stoutly. 'Some of us can play, and some of us have to work. Is that what you mean?'

Tom nodded. 'Yes, Daddy. That's what Kathleen said.'

Harry turned away with a grin on his face. This past year had been a nightmare. Only now, with Kathleen back in his life and little Tom taking so well to his new environment, did Harry's heart feel easier. He realised how his darling wife had known what she was doing, when she made him promise to go back to the place of his childhood. She had been so right. And he was so immensely grateful for her wisdom.

For a moment he held her memory close, and he was sad.

Then Kathleen's cheery voice came sailing across the kitchen, and all the pain of the past was pushed into that special, private corner of his heart.

With her usual hustle and bustle, Kathleen served the breakfast, and what a breakfast it was: sausage, black pudding, bacon and eggs, with a pile of newly baked, fresh-cut crusty bread, and a pint of tea on the side.

'Crikey, Kathleen!' Harry was amazed. 'It's Monday morning and I'm away to a new job. With this lot inside me, I'll be lucky to get to the first call.'

'Away with ye!' Dipping her crust into the plump egg yolk, she wagged a finger at him. 'A man needs a good start to the day.'

Harry tucked in. 'Whatever you say.' He looked over at Tom who was munching on a piece of crispy bacon. 'All right, son?'

Tom gave a little nod. He was far too busy to talk.

'Hang on, what's this sausage doing on my plate?' Harry complained. 'I thought I said I'd be happy to settle for the black pudding?'

'Ah, well now.' Kathleen looked positively guilty. 'The thing is, I'm very partial to black pudding, only I didn't like to say, and so I took yours and gave you the sausage instead. And it's no good you asking for it back, because this is the last piece!' With the cheekiest grin, she popped the chunk of black pudding into her mouth.

'Naughty Kathleen!' Tom was earwigging.

'Sure, when ye get to my age, being naughty is the only real thing you have to look forward to,' she told him.

Tom was intrigued. 'When will I get to your age?'

'Let me see . . .' Kathleen pretended to ponder. 'Well now, I reckon you could get there tomorrow. But if truth be told, ye have to work up to it, and do things, and learn things, and then you get bigger and wiser; and then you might be ready to be as old as your Auntie Kathleen. So, has that answered your question now?'

Tom gave a deep, grown-up sigh, popped the tail end of his own sausage into his mouth and nodded. Then he shook his head, and nodded again. 'Mmm!'

Sausage gone. Subject closed.

~

Having arrived in Bedford town, Harry parked the Hillman at the back of Jacobs' Emporium and made his way inside the staff entrance.

'Morning, Harry!' That was the effervescent Amy, chirpy as ever. 'Fighting fit, are you?'

Looking more like sixteen than twenty-four, with her mousey-coloured hair in a pigtail down her back and a white shirt that gave her the demeanour of a schoolgirl, she merrily informed him, 'Mr Jacobs isn't about and Len is up in the office working out his round. I'm just making a brew, so d'you want a cuppa while you wait?' She had taken to Harry the first time he walked into the shop. He was good-looking and easy-natured, though there was something about him that made her want to cuddle him and tell him not to worry, that everything would be all right.

Harry shook his head. 'I've had enough tea this morning to float a battleship,' he laughed. Still full from breakfast, he wanted to be able to tackle the streets of Bedford without puffing and panting at the slightest little hill he might come across.

He did have a question though. 'This tallyman job – what's it really like?' he asked. He'd chatted to her about it last time, before his interview, but his nerves had got in the way and he still didn't really know what he was letting himself in for.

'It's okay, I guess.' Leaning forward across her desk, she crossed her arms, and gazed up at him, as though waiting for his next question.

'What's "okay" supposed to mean exactly?' Harry was amazed that from the very first, he had fallen so naturally into conversation with this bright, curious little creature.

Amy briefly pondered, then she sat up straight and explained, 'Well, it means that some days you can go from house to house with never a problem. The sun is shining. You knock on the door, they open it, hand you the money with a smile; you sign their little tally-book, and away you go, job done – unless, of course, you're offered a piece of cake that you can't refuse.'

Harry got all that. 'Right, so that's some days. What about the others?'

Twisting her mouth into a wide wavy shape, she pondered again. 'Well, on other days, it might be chucking it down with rain and you're soaked to the skin. Then you knock on the door, and get no answer. You knock again; still no answer, but you know the customer is in, because she's done it before. So you peer through the window, and you can see her legs sticking out from behind the sofa, and you know she's hiding from you.'

Harry got the picture. 'So then what?'

'Then you call through the letterbox and you say that you'll be sending somebody round to collect the furniture if she doesn't come to the door right this very minute.'

'And will she come to the door?'

'You never know your luck. It all depends on how much in arrears she might be.'

'So if I've persuaded her to come to the door, what do I do then?'

'Well, you ask her for payment. Usually, she'll plead that she's a bit short on her housekeeping this week, and that you'll have to wait. Besides, her little Joey needs a new pair of shoes, but don't worry because she'll be sure to catch up with you next week.'

'I see. And if she's got no money, I just write it down in my tally-ledger, and that's a black mark against her, is that it?'

'Something like that, yes.'

'And if she *won't* come to the door, I just go away and she still gets a black mark, yes?'

Amy nodded. 'That's about the size of it.'

'So, if she doesn't catch up with the arrears next week, what happens then?'

'Then you report it to Mr Jacobs and he deals with it, in his own way.'

'I see!'

When he frowned, she quickly put his mind at rest. 'Jakey won't send round a gang of thugs to sort her out, if that's what worries you,' she told him with a grin. 'He's a good man and does his best to help the customers out. But at the end of the day, he's also a businessman. This store provides us *all* with a living, including himself.'

'I understand that.'

'Okay. So you will also understand that he needs a regular supply of money to buy the stock, or he might as well shut up shop. So, if he gets a bad payer, he'll make arrangements for her to pay a smaller amount until the debt is cleared. Meantime, she won't be allowed in the shop. Once the debt is paid, she can buy whatever she likes from the store, cash in hand, but she won't be allowed to buy anything else on tick.'

'And that happens often, does it?'

'Thankfully, not too often.' She took a sip of her lukewarm tea. 'Are you sure you don't want a cup?'

Harry was about to reply, when Len emerged from sorting out his round; a larger-than-life character, with bags of charm and a high opinion of himself, he was all smiles and teeth and loud with it. But there was something about him which Harry could not put his finger on, but which put him instantly on his guard.

'Well, Harry, my lad!' The other man addressed Harry with a wide, flamboyant grin. 'Good to see you.' Grabbing his hand, he shook it vigorously. 'So! You're ready to face the big wide world, are you?'

Harry had taken an instant dislike to him, but he knew better than to show his feelings, especially as he was to work with this man until he knew the ropes well enough to go out on his own. 'Ready when you are.' Harry looked him squarely in the eye. 'In fact, I'm looking forward to it.'

Len took stock of Harry; the broad shoulders and confident stance, and those deep, dark eyes which seemed to see right through him. Somewhere in the back of his mind he knew he would have to be on his guard with this one. 'Right!' He made a sweeping gesture towards the doors. 'Let's be off then, shall we?'

'Have fun,' Amy's voice called after them. 'Don't do anything I wouldn't do.'

'Hah!' Len waved a hand to her. 'The world's our oyster then, is it?'

'Bloomin' cheek!' And as Amy saw the car drive away, she murmured, 'you'll need to watch that one, Harry my love. People are not always what you might think.'

Going about her work, she began singing, softly at first, then with gusto, until a customer complained that he couldn't hear himself think. Jacob, called down to her, 'AMY! Will you stop that damned caterwauling! I can't hear myself think!'

Muttering under her breath she grumbled, 'Miserable devil. It won't be long before I get discovered and then you'll see! People will pay to hear me sing.'

Not too far away, two men were loading a sofa onto the van. 'Thank God she's stopped that bloody racket!' one said to the other. 'It does my 'ead in.'

~

'So, Harry, meladdo, d'you think you're suited to it, or have you had enough already?' Planning to baptise Harry into the roughest areas first, Len had cunningly switched the order of route. 'It's not easy, is it?' he said slyly. 'Trying to get money out of these people is like pulling teeth without anaesthetic.'

'They're probably good people, just fallen on hard times.' Harry had seen enough to know that Len had no respect for the customers. The poorer they were, the more contemptuous he was; though if the woman of the house was pretty or friendly, he turned on the charm like he'd been born to it.

'Huh! You're too easily fooled,' Len retorted curtly. 'It's one

133

thing when they come into the shop, and it's an altogether different story when you visit their homes. Many of these people are liars and thieves, straight out o' jail, some of 'em. Man, woman or child, they'll take what they want and lie through their teeth to get it.'

Harry found that hard to believe. 'They can't all be that bad, surely?'

'Well, all right, maybe I am exaggerating just a little. I just don't want you lulled into a false sense of security with their canny lies and false smiles. Be on your guard, that's all I'm saying.'

'If they're bad payers, why were they allowed to get into debt?' In the short time he had known him, Harry's instinct told him not to pay too much heed to what Len had to say. 'Surely it would have been better all round if Mr Jacobs had refused to let them have credit in the first place?'

'Hmh! Listen to you. Been at it five minutes and already you're dishing out the advice.'

Harry mentally kicked himself. 'Sorry. I didn't mean it to sound that way.' The last thing he needed was to get off on the wrong foot with the man chosen to teach him the job.

Taking a cigarette from his jacket pocket, the other man lit it and took a long, slow drag. 'In case you hadn't realised, Jacobs is one hell of a smart businessman.' Watching Harry with his beady eyes, he blew the smoke out in a perfect ring. 'He knows that if he doesn't give them credit, someone else will. Besides, if they don't pay back what they owe, it's only a matter of time before he has them in the petty courts.'

He gave a dissatisfied grunt. 'It's all decided by the local magistrate. He listens to their sorry tale, then lets them pay off the debt at a few measly quid a month. I tell you what though – if I were in Jacobs' shoes, I'd forget the courts.'

'And do what?' Harry anticipated his answer.

'I'd send the heavies round, that's what I'd do. Teach the buggers a lesson they won't forget in a hurry. Either that, or seize their belongings. I wouldn't wait months till the debt's paid up, that's for sure. Hit 'em where it hurts, that's what I say.'

Harry bristled. 'It's just as well Mr Jacobs is in charge then, and not you, eh?'

Flinging his cigarette on the ground, the other man screwed it flat with the heel of his shoe. 'Are you having a go at me, or what?' He gave a half-smile, but his pale eyes glittered with anger.

Harry shrugged. 'What makes you think that?'

'I didn't much care for that remark.'

'Just an observation, that's all.' Harry played it cool. He needed to keep this job. Also, he believed he could make a few changes if he went about it the right way. Antagonising Len was not a clever move just now.

'So you're not having a go then?'

'Is there any reason why I should?' Harry answered cagily.

It seemed an age before the other man replied.

He gave a sly sideways glance at Harry, then he licked his dry lips and burst out laughing. 'You're a card an' no mistake!' he chortled. 'D'you know what? You and me are out of the same mould. Something tells me we're going to get on like a house on fire.'

Harry gave no response but the other man's sickening observation only hardened his resolve. He promised himself that once he knew the ropes, he would never work with this man again.

In fact, he had not altogether dismissed the idea of speaking with Mr Jacobs about Len's attitude to the customers.

~

The day went by much quicker than Harry expected.

By lunchtime, they had covered all the streets west of the river. They had a light lunch in the bar of the Swan Hotel, where Len eyed up every waitress, guest and even the shy young woman who came in trying to sell bed linen to the manageress. 'I wouldn't mind trying out a bed or two with her!' he said lasciviously.

Len ogled her from the minute she set foot in the foyer, to when she followed the manageress to her office and then went and sat at the bar to partake of a glass of orange juice to drown her disappointment at not making a sale. And now, as she carried her wares towards the main doors, he said to Harry, 'You just watch me in action! I'll have her eating out of my hand in no time.'

Glancing back to wink at Harry, he stalked the young woman to the door. 'You can sell me anything you like, my little beauty,' he teased. 'Any time, any place. I'm not a hard man to please.'

The young woman looked him up and down, noting the beer belly and the drooping jowls, and she gave a kind of snort. 'Clear off, you creep!' she snarled. 'If you think I'd even give you a second glance, you're way out of your tree.' She'd had a bad day and he was making it worse.

'Hey!' Rattled by her remarks, Len took a step towards her. 'Seems to me like you need a lesson in manners, you little tart.'

When at that moment the young woman's burly boss arrived on the scene, Len swiftly made himself scarce. 'Ready, are you, Harry?' he asked. Rushing out of the back door, he left Harry to follow behind. 'You got your comeuppance there, all right,' Harry chuckled to himself.

But he had not forgotten how Len was shamefully abusing his trusted position of authority.

The next stop was Moff Avenue – a long meandering street of sturdy Victorian houses. 'We've got some good customers down here,' Len told him. 'Most of 'em pay on the dot, though occasionally, some do try it on.'

Pausing at number 3, he rat-tatted on the door. 'You'll need to watch out for the skivers,' he advised with a sideways nod of the head. 'They'll give you any excuse that comes to mind. You have to ignore all that. They're trying it on, that's all. Just trying it on.' A fleeting surge of anger blushed across his face.

'Go away, mister!' A little girl's face peered down from the bedroom window. 'Me mam's not 'ome yet. You'll have to come back next week.'

Len called back, 'You tell your mam to get down here,' he instructed. 'I want a word with her . . . *now*, if you please.'

'She can't come down. She's in bed poorly.'

Impatient, Len snapped, 'You tell her that I'm staying right here until she comes down.'

A moment later the front door was inched open. 'What the devil's going on? What's all the yelling about?' Dressed in a cream-coloured dressing gown and wearing yesterday's make-up, the woman looked to be in her thirties. She was tall and shapely with tousled hair and long painted fingernails. 'Oh, it's you!' She shook her head. 'I might have known.' She glanced at Harry. 'Who's your good-looking friend?'

Len frowned. 'Never mind about that, Maureen. It's *me* you should be worried about.'

Clutching her dressing gown together, she held it tightly closed. 'It's no good you asking for money because there isn't any. My Jim was out on the booze again last night.' She gave him an appealing look. 'You know what it's like, Len. He gets his wages of a Friday and come Saturday night, there's nothing left. I've begged and pleaded with him, but he never changes; he never will.'

Len stood his ground. 'Your domestic troubles are not my problem.'

'I know that. But I can't give you what I ain't got. You'll just have to come back next week. I'll see what I can do for you then.'

When she prepared to close the door, Len wedged it open with his foot. 'Not so fast, my beauty.'

The woman took a step backwards. 'Don't start on me,' she retaliated. 'I've got my girl off school. She's not been well.'

Len apologised. 'Oh, I'm sorry about that, Maureen. I didn't realise. But if I'm to sort out your arrears, I'll need to come in for a few minutes. Is that all right? I promise, it won't take long.'

'I'm not sure about that . . .' She hesitated, then sensing his eyes on her, she drew the gown tighter about her. 'Give me a minute then.' With that she disappeared inside, leaving the door open for him.

Addressing Harry, Len explained, 'She's one of our worst customers. This is the third time in a month that she's missed a payment. If I don't sort it this week, Jacobs will go through the roof.'

Harry had seen the look of apprehension on the woman's face. 'How will you sort it?' he asked. 'You can't get blood out of a stone.'

'Trust me, I'm sure we'll thrash out an arrangement that will suit all round. Just take the ledger, Harry. Look – there's a sweet old lady lives across the street – number 14, name of Ada Benson. She's a regular payer, you'll get no trouble from her.'

He handed Harry the ledger. 'Go and introduce yourself – oh, and don't forget to sign her tally-book. She's very fussy about that.'

Somewhat bemused, Harry took the ledger and made his way across the street, discreetly glancing back as he knocked on Ada Benson's door. He saw Len go inside number 3, and he watched the door close behind him. He had a bad feeling about it, though he didn't really know why.

'Hello, young man!' The cheery voice interrupted his thoughts, 'Have you come to see me?' Old and shrivelled, Ada Benson was still a pretty woman, with her soft curly grey hair, fine features and large green eyes.

'Yes, Mrs Benson, I'm Harry. I'm new.' Harry held out his hand in greeting. 'I'm here with Len.'

The little woman's face crumpled into a smile, 'Oh, I see.' She grabbed his outstretched hand. 'You're from Jacobs' Emporium, aren't you?'

'That's right.' Harry liked her straight off. 'I'm learning the rounds.'

Stepping back, she invited him to 'Come in, come in. I've baked a cake . . . I always bake a cake for when Len comes to call. Oh, and I've got my book ready and everything.'

Tugging at him, she drew Harry inside. 'Oh, now I've forgotten your name.' She screwed up her face in concentration. 'Oh yes, it's Harry, isn't it, yes. Come in, Harry. Please come in!'

When Harry glanced back, she asked quietly, 'Is Len over there . . . in Maureen's house?'

Harry nodded. 'Yes.'

She rolled her eyes knowingly. 'Ah well, I shouldn't worry. He'll be a while yet.'

Taking Harry along the narrow passageway to the kitchen, the little woman chuckled, 'Naughty boy Len!' She clapped her hands as though smacking a child. 'I'll have you know, there was a time when I was so pretty the men could never resist *me* either.'

As they entered the kitchen, the wonderful aroma of fresh-baked bread filled Harry's nostrils. It put him in mind of Irish Kathleen.

When he was a youngster in Fisher's Hill he spent many a happy time in Kathleen's delightful house. The smell of fresh bread never failed to entice him in. Those precious memories were as warm and welcome as the hug she gave him, and the chunky slice of brown bread smothered in melting butter and thick home-made strawberry jam.

He was so grateful that she had taken him and young Tom into that same delightful house, and showed them the same, warm welcome.

For the next half-hour, Harry was fed with cherry cake and cups of piping hot tea, and in between he was entertained by stories of Ada's colourful youth, and the young men she had met and lost along the way.

'There was never really anyone serious until I met my Cyril,' she confided. 'He and I were married for forty-two years and I talk to him every single day.'

Her large eyes swam with tears. 'When you're young, you think you're invincible. You never think you might grow old . . . oh no! That's for your grandma and grandad, but you'll never be old, or wrinkly, or ache when you walk. No, you're young, you'll always be young. You'll run and dance and never have to worry about bending down and hurting your back. Because you'll be forever you – young and beautiful.'

She tapped her bony little chest. 'In here, we stay young and beautiful for ever and ever.' She gave a little chuckle. 'Oh dear. We were so foolish, to think the years could never change us.'

One solitary teardrop trickled from her eye. 'My Cyril said that whenever he looked at me, he could only ever see a pretty young girl.' A mystical smile uplifted her face. 'I love him so very much, Harry. Oh, and I do miss him so.'

That glimpse of Ada's sadness heightened Harry's own crippling loss, and for one fleeting moment, the two of them sat quietly, Ada looking lost in the big old armchair and Harry on the tiny sofa; their thoughts drifting back over the years.

A short time later, Harry was being led back down the passageway. 'Right, well, thank you so much, Ada.' Harry was tempted to plant a little kiss on that sweet face, but a sense of protocol stopped him from doing so. 'I've really enjoyed our first meeting,' he told her warmly. 'I've signed your tally-book, I've eaten your amazing cherry cake, and I've drunk your tea. And now I'd best get on with the rounds.'

'You're a lovely young man,' Ada told him at the door. 'My Cyril would have liked you.'

When her tears threatened, Harry thought, To hell with protocoal, and he bent down to kiss her tenderly on the cheek. 'And I'm sure I would have liked him too,' he assured her.

Taken aback when she wrapped her tiny hands about his face, he looked into those bright old eyes and like her husband

Cyril, he could see the beauty and grace of a young girl. 'Shall I tell you something, Ada?' he asked softly.

She nodded. 'Please do, yes.'

'I know exactly what your Cyril meant, when he said he looked at you and could see only the young girl you once were.'

Her face lit up. 'Oh! Do you really?'

'I do, yes – and I know something else too.'

Her smile was like a bright summer's day. 'What do you know?'

'I know you will never be old . . . *never*!'

'Oh!' Like a child she clapped her hands together and he laughed out loud, and soon the two of them were chuckling together like old friends. 'Tell Len I'm glad it was you who came to see me,' she said, and Harry promised he would do just that.

When Ada closed the door, Harry began to walk back across the street. As he did so, he saw Len come sidling out of Maureen Rook's house, red in the face and discreetly straightening his jacket.

It was blatantly obvious to Harry that he had not gone into the house to help Maureen 'sort out her debts' as he had claimed. Instead, he believed the chirpy little Amy to be right; that Len had collected payment of another kind.

'Ah!' Len greeted Harry in his usual bombastic manner. 'Seen Ada, have you?' There was no mention of Maureen. 'I bet she gave you a chunk of cake and plied you with tea, until you felt it coming out your ears?' He patted Harry on the back.

Harry gave no answer, and Len didn't even notice. He was too busy preening himself.

As they resumed their rounds, Harry glanced back at Maureen's house, and there in the window was the little girl who had first called down to them. With her small hands flattened against the pane she watched them go down the street. Harry smiled at her, but she did not smile back. Instead, she kept watching them. Watching Len particularly.

Harry gave a little wave, but the girl turned away.

As he went with Len to Jackson Street, Harry thought of the child, and the way she had turned away, as though in distress.

Concerned, he promised himself that from now on, he would watch Len's every move. But he must be careful not to jump to conclusions. With something as delicate as this, he would need to get his facts right.

If, as he suspected, Len really was taking sex in payment for a signature on the tally-book, then he would first raise the matter with Len himself. If that didn't put a stop to it, he would have to speak with Mr Jacobs. If not to salve his own conscience, he would do it for those women who were genuinely unable to pay; and desperate enough to buckle under Len's powers of persuasion.

One thing was certain. Even without the hard evidence that Len was behaving shamefully, Harry's initial respect for the man who had taken him under his wing, had all too quickly evaporated.

Jackson Street was the last call on their round. 'We've only got three families along here,' Len explained. 'Most of the people who live in this street are in business themselves.'

'Nice area though.' Harry was impressed by the large Victorian houses, though one or two of them appeared to be in need of repair. 'Pity some of these fine houses have been allowed to fall into ruin though.'

Len agreed. 'I'm surprised the other residents aren't up in arms about it.' He tutted. 'Unless, of course, they're the culprits who snapped them up in the first place. Landlords get their rent money come what may, so why spend money when you don't have to, eh?'

'What can be done then?' Harry asked. 'Surely somebody has to be held accountable, if they fall into rack and ruin?'

'Not really.' Len then gave a glimpse into his own environment. 'It's a bit like where I live on the other side of the river. There was a time when my address was one of the best in the area, then the investors moved in. They bought every house that came up for sale. They extended, made one house into four flats, then they rented them out and sat back to watch their money grow. Over time, the places got run down but the council turned a blind eye, and why not, eh? As long as they keep getting their rates and they're not asked to foot the bill for repairs, why should they give a monkey's?'

Harry was deep in conversation with a Mrs Taylor, who was paying ten shillings a week off a new chest of drawers when an almighty row broke out from a house nearby.

The man's voice was raised to screaming pitch. 'IF I EVER FIND OUT YOU'VE CHEATED ON ME, I SWEAR TO GOD I'LL DO FOR YOU!'

A woman could be heard pleading with him not to be silly, saying that she didn't want to fall out with him. But still he ranted on, spitting rage and out of control.

'That'll be the couple at number 16,' Mrs Taylor remarked with a groan. 'Honestly! It's a wonder them two haven't killed each other before now. He's mad as a hatter, completely possessive, and when he gets drunk – which is often – he lays into her real bad.'

'So why doesn't somebody do something about it?' Harry was angry.

'Don't think we haven't tried. One or two people in the street have taken him to task. But when it comes right down to it, there isn't a lot you can do, is there? You should never interfere in domestic rows – well, at least, that's what the police say – and they've been out here often enough, I can tell you.'

Harry couldn't help but wonder. 'So, if he's as bad as that, why doesn't she just up and leave him?'

The woman shrugged her shoulders. 'Who knows? Bad as he is, maybe she really loves him. Or maybe she wants to leave and she hasn't anywhere to go. Or she hasn't got any friends or family, because he's chased them all away?'

'Well, it sounds like a bad situation and no mistake.' From

a discreet distance, Len had been listening to the conversation. As for the spiralling argument, he didn't care one way or the other. 'Maybe they deserve each other, eh?'

'Maybe.' Mrs Taylor glanced towards the house where the row was still raging. 'Truth is, it's gone on for so long now, she's got almost as bad as him, with the yelling and the drink and everything. Oh, it's such a shame. When they first moved into the street, she was such a sweet, quiet little thing; so pretty. These days the sadness in her face is pitiful to see. I do feel sorry for her though. I mean, day or night she can't even walk down the street without him chasing after her, bullying and yelling at her. Sometimes he gets her by the scruff of the neck and marches her back to the house.' She sighed. 'If you ask me, that young woman's life, well . . . it's like a kind of torture.'

Harry thought about the time in his life when he had done things he could never have envisaged; terrible things – working in hell-holes, fighting anyone who was up for it, and drinking himself into oblivion. After he'd come out of the Army, he'd become a drifter for a time; gone into a dark place. He had cared for nothing and no one, especially himself. That was the awful truth.

And so he knew all about pain, and that crippling sense of despair that could pull you down to the gutter.

He looked up at the woman. 'It sounds to me as if she's got an uphill climb, if she's to get away from a situation like that.'

'You're absolutely right. Trouble is, it might already be too late.' Shaking her head, she collected her tally-book from Harry. 'One of these days it'll go too far and then there'll be murder, you'll see.' With that she thanked them and closed the door.

As the two men walked down the street and on towards the car park, they could still hear the full-blown row escalating behind them. 'Gawd above! What a barney, eh?' Len laughed. 'That'll please the nobs round here, I'll be bound.' He slowed his step, so as to hear the row all the better.

The man's voice was wild with rage. 'Don't lie to me, you little slut! If you weren't giving him the come-on, why would he make a bee-line for you like that?'

'I never encouraged him!' the woman sobbed. 'I've told you, I was just there, and he came over to me. I didn't know who he was. I told him to go away and leave me alone. YOU HEARD ME TELL HIM THAT!'

'YOU'RE A DAMNED LIAR! You encouraged him. I've told you before, I'll lay you out, rather than let any man take you from me.'

There was a sharp sound, like the crack of flesh on flesh, then the woman was sobbing loudly, pleading with him. 'I wouldn't cheat on you. I've NEVER cheated on you. No! Get away from me!'

Some kind of struggle followed. 'NO! Leave me alone! You're crazy with drink . . . you're frightening me! You never believe what I say! WHY WILL YOU NEVER BELIEVE WHAT I SAY?'

There was a span of silence, which alarmed Harry.

'I think we should check it out,' he told Len. 'He sounds like an out-and-out bully! What if he's hurt her?' It was the silence that worried him the most. 'Oh, look, to hell with it, I'm going up there.'

Len was still trying to hold him back when the man started grovelling. 'I'm sorry, sweetheart. I do believe you, really I do.'

'You *should* believe me.' The woman was calm enough now. 'You know I would never cheat on you.' She laughed, a painful, hollow sound. 'I wouldn't *dare*!'

He laughed with her. 'You rascal! Come here to me.' There was another short span of silence and then, 'Get your glad rags on, pet. I'm taking you out on the town.'

There followed a short burst of teasing and laughter, before the window was slammed shut.

'See? I told you.' Len wagged a finger at Harry. 'Never be too quick to interfere in somebody else's argument, unless you want to end up being the villain between 'em.'

Harry nodded. 'You're right. That's one useful lesson I've learned today,' he said light-heartedly.

In fact, it was the second. The first had to do with Len, and unlike the row in the flat above, that particular issue was not yet resolved.

As the two men walked back to the car, the couple emerged from the building.

'D'you forgive me, sweetie?' Phil Saunders had lost his temper, and now he was worried that yet again, he had gone too far. 'I'm sorry I hurt you,' he whined. 'Do you forgive me?'

Judy had heard it all before. 'I forgive you.'

She had not forgiven him though. She never would. But what did it matter? For a long time now, her life had been empty. There was no purpose, nothing to strive for. She was with a man she could never love. Phil Saunders craved her heart and soul, but they were already given to another, long ago, in a different life.

She never doubted Phil's love for her, but his love was a selfish, grasping thing that left no room for tenderness. Possessive and controlling, he had used her shame and loneliness to his own ends. When he was sober they got along, and when he had been drinking they argued about the minutest of things.

Often the rows erupted into blows, and when they weren't arguing, he was watching, checking on her, quizzing her about the time she spent away from him. He wore her out, until now, there was no real fight left in her.

Her life was over; finished. She would not care if he ended it here and now.

She had already lost everything precious. Harry was long gone, and so too, was her beautiful baby.

Nothing mattered to her anymore.

CHAPTER EIGHT

'TWO WHOLE DAYS!' Stretched out by the pool with the hot September sun blazing down on her, Nancy still had cause to grumble. 'I never thought we'd have to share the house with *them* for two whole days.'

'Ssh!' Afraid that Mac and Rita might hear her, Brian urged, 'Try and keep your voice down.' This was the first time he'd had a chance to sit and relax with the racing page, and besides, he only had an hour to get down to the bookies. There was a horse running today which he was certain would win him a small fortune.

Nancy was still grumbling. 'They can easily have afforded to go on another flight, so why didn't they?'

'Mac already told you – the flight at Manchester Airport was cancelled because of technical problems, and there were no seats available on any other flights. Just be grateful they decided not to take the refund offered, or we'd have had to share our entire holiday with them – not that I mind one jot.'

'Well, I do,' Nancy hissed. 'Trouble with you is that you're too easy-going. You don't think about me and the children. You don't seem to realise how much we've been looking forward to this holiday.'

Brian raised an eyebrow. 'And you think I wasn't?'

'Oh stop it, you know what I'm saying. I always look forward to coming here, because it's so far removed from what I'm used to, and besides, the children would have been really disappointed if it had all fallen through.'

'What! I seem to recall Sammie not wanting to come along in the first place, and even David threatened to stay behind with her.'

'Yes, well, but then they *were* looking forward to it, and now it's ruined.'

Brian shook his head and tutted. 'For goodness sake, Nancy, don't be so melodramatic. Mac and Rita are repacking as we speak. Any minute now they'll be out the door and we'll have the place to ourselves. So, there's no real harm done.'

'That's a matter of opinion.' Lowering her voice to a harsh whisper, she confided, 'I don't care much for that wife of Mac's.'

'Why? What's she ever done to you, except lend you her house and home?'

Shrugging her shoulders, his wife gave him a haughty look. 'I just don't like her, that's all.'

'Right then, you two.' Mac surprised them when suddenly he appeared next to the pool. Short and stocky with piercing blue eyes and dark greying hair, he was nothing like his older brother Don. 'We're off . . . at long last.'

Nancy greeted him with a warm smile. 'I'm sorry you've lost two days of your trip.' While she had no liking for his wife, she had a huge fondness for her Uncle Mac.

'No matter.' Coming over to her, Mac gave Nancy a hug. 'I won't be the loser,' he informed her with confidence. 'The two lost days have been tacked onto the end of our trip, without any expense to me.' He gave a cheeky wink. 'Moreover, I intend going for compensation as well, for the inconvenience and all that.'

Nancy was impressed. 'Knowing you, I'm sure you'll get it without any trouble.'

'Good man.' Laying down his newspaper, Brian shook Mac by the hand. 'Have a good trip, and thanks again for letting us stay.'

'You're welcome, Brian, any time.' Glancing about, Mac asked, 'Where are the kids?'

'David went off on your bicycle – that's all right isn't it?' Nancy explained worriedly. 'You did say he could use it, didn't you?'

'Oh, absolutely! In fact, he's doing me a favour. I haven't ridden the thing for so long, it's beginning to rust.'

'I'll tell him to give it a good clean when he brings it back,' Nancy promised.

'And where's the lovely Sammie?' He looked towards the pool. 'I thought I saw her swimming just now.'

'Oh, she's probably changing.' Pointing across the garden to the changing-house, Nancy told him, 'You'd best say cheerio, or she'll be disappointed.'

'Right. Well, we can't have that, can we, eh?' Making his way to the changing block, he called out her name: 'Sammie! We're away now, sunshine.'

He was delighted when the girl came out; barefoot, dressed in white shorts and a pink strappy top, she looked fresh and pretty. 'Oh, Uncle Mac!' She came towards him. 'Mum said you'd be leaving soon.'

Sliding an arm about her shoulders, he walked back with her. 'My case is standing in the hallway as we speak. I'm just waiting for Rita to make herself beautiful, then we'll leave you all to it.'

In fact, it was twenty minutes later when Rita emerged. As always she was immaculate; painted nails, painted face, and dressed in the most exquisite cream-coloured tailored costume that money could buy. 'I've told her,' Mac addressed himself to Brian, 'a car journey to Manchester and then two and some hours in a plane and the suit will be crumpled to buggery. But will she listen? No, she will not!' He rolled his eyes. 'But then I'm only a man. What do I know?'

Rita ignored him as always. 'Enjoy yourselves,' she told the family as she went from one to the other, depositing fleeting pecks on the cheek. 'As for you, Sammie, if you can keep it all tidy and not make a mess on my new carpet, you're welcome to help yourself to my make-up box.'

Sammie thanked her, though she had no intention of delving about in Rita's personal belongings. Besides, she had her own modest little make-up bag, and a pretty floral comb she had bought from Bedford Market.

The family waved them off. 'Have a lovely time!' Nancy called, and Rita waved a hand out of the car window in acknowledgement. 'Stupid woman!' Nancy grumbled as they walked back to the house. 'All frills and fancies and nothing between her ears.'

Brian was not shocked at her outburst. He was well aware of Nancy's dislike for her aunt. 'That's not a very nice thing to say,' he chuckled. 'Especially after she's offered Sammie the use of her make-up box.'

'Huh!' Nancy did not take kindly to being laughed at. 'You can talk. You've never had a good word to say about Uncle Mac, and yet you're quite happy to live in his house.'

'Of course, and why not? Besides, after he's been so kind as to offer, it would be churlish of me not to accept.'

'You don't like him though, do you?'

'I never said that.'

'You don't need to.'

Brian thought about Mac. 'I admire his business skills,' he admitted, 'and I'm always grateful when he offers us the use of his lovely house . . .'

'But?'

'Truth is, of the two brothers, I have to admit I much prefer your dad.'

'But Dad's never made a fortune, and he doesn't have a cruiser. In fact, as far as I know, he's never done anything exciting or adventurous in his entire life.'

When she now stretched herself out on the lounger, Brian took note of her proud, hard-set face and the way she continued to rant and rave, even when she was supposed to be relaxing. There were times when he wondered what he had ever seen in her; and yet when she was younger she had been outgoing and exciting, and knew exactly what she wanted.

He loved her then, and he loved her still, but now it was different; his feelings for Nancy were more comfortable than exciting.

From his chair, he continued to look at her. 'Nancy?'

'What now?' Sitting up, she handed him the tub of cream. 'Put some on my back, will you?'

'I wish you wouldn't do that.' Smothering her back in the cream, he then rubbed it in.

'What d'you mean? Do what?'

'Measure everyone by their material achievements.'

'Oh, you mean Uncle Mac? Well, it's true. You can't deny, he's a genius at making money.'

'Yes, I know that, and I admire him for it. But you need to remember that being able to make pots of money is not necessarily the measure of a man.'

'Don't talk in riddles.'

'I'm just saying . . . about the way you compared your uncle to your father. Don is a good man. He's worked hard all his life and he's always been there for you. Just because he hasn't made a fortune, doesn't mean to say he's any less of a man because of it.'

Sitting bolt upright, Nancy stared at her husband in surprise. 'Oh dear. Have I touched a raw nerve?'

'What makes you say that?'

'I mean, you're not just talking about Dad, are you? You're thinking of yourself as well – how you've worked hard and never made a fortune. You're jealous of Uncle Mac, that's it, isn't it? Go on, admit it, why don't you?' Though she was teasing, he detected the note of spite in her voice.

'Me? Jealous of Mac?' Embarrassed, he looked away. 'You're talking rubbish, Nancy.'

151

When he pretended to look at the racing page again, she fell silent for a moment, then took away his paper and held it from him. 'It doesn't matter if you haven't made a fortune,' she assured him. 'You're my husband and the father of our children, and you've always provided for us, so now will you please stop sulking. We're here to enjoy ourselves. So let that be enough, Brian. Don't spoil it all by being silly.'

Brian was used to her high-handed manner and today was no exception. 'Sorry.' He got out of his chair. 'You're right. I'm just feeling inadequate, that's all. Anyway, I'm bored with just sitting around. I'll go and see what the others are up to, eh?'

'Good idea.'

As he walked away, she turned to watch him. 'You're a good man, Brian,' she muttered, 'but you and my father are two of a kind. You're both too easily pleased, too afraid to take a chance. Uncle Mac is another breed of man altogether. He's a go-getter; a man with a vision.'

She replaced his crumpled paper on the table. 'If you'd been half the man I wanted you to be, we'd have had some excitement in our dull lives.' There was more than a hint of bitterness in her voice.

Brian found David and Sammie down by the lake next to the property. 'Hey!' Waving to them, he set off at a run. 'What are you kids up to?'

Running to meet him, Sammie was excited. 'Look, Dad, we've found this little boat. We were thinking we might use it to go across the lake.' She pointed to a small rise of earth in the centre of the lake. 'There are all kinds of birds over there,' she told her dad. 'I want to see.'

Brian was concerned. 'I don't think you should.'

'Why not?'

'Because, first of all, the boat might not be altogether safe, and secondly, you could frighten the birds away and they might never come back. What's more, we don't know who the boat belongs to. We shouldn't really touch it.'

Sammie hung onto his arm. 'Oh, go on, Dad. We'll be careful. You can come too, if you like.'

He thought of Nancy's scathing words and suddenly his mind was made up. 'Right! You're on.'

Having checked the little boat from bow to stern, Brian set about starting the engine; it leaped into life and soon they were whizzing across the water. 'It might look like it's had its day,' Brian observed, 'but it seems all right enough to me.'

David was thrilled. 'Can I have a go at driving it, Dad?'

Though he was really enjoying the experience, Brian showed David the ropes. 'Slow down as you come close to the island,' he warned. 'We don't know how deep the water is out here.'

'Can I take her in, please, Dad?' Sammie didn't want to be left out.

'No, sweetheart, leave it to David. You can bring it back, how about that?'

'Okay.' Sammie was happy enough with that.

When they climbed out of the boat and onto the shore, it was immediately evident that the little island was swarming with birds; the presence of deep droppings underfoot and the noise all around them soon convinced them that they had stumbled on a little bird-Paradise. 'Go easy, you two,' Brian warned the children. 'Some of these birds might be resentful of intruders.'

It was a wonderful experience though.

They came across birds of every kind and colour, and as they tiptoed right around the little island Sammie was filled with wonder. 'Look at the flowers and shrubs. Aren't they amazing!'

Brian thought the island was like a piece of world that had escaped the hustle and bustle of time, where the birds and habitat had been allowed to grow and flourish at will. 'I wonder if this belongs to Mac and Rita?' he asked. 'Is it part of their estate, d'you think?'

David thought it was, but Sammie thought no one should own such a special place.

When they got back and tried to describe it all to Nancy,

she commented: 'It doesn't belong to your Uncle Mac. I recall him telling your grandad how he tried to buy it from some old man in the village, but he was having none of it. No matter how much money Uncle Mac offered, he could not get the old man to part with it.'

Brian was secretly glad. 'His first failure, eh?' he thought gleefully. 'Still, I expect he'll get his hands on it one day. When Mac wants something, he'll find a way to get it. He always does.'

As the evening wore on, the children swam and Brian chatted with Nancy, and after dinner, they lazed out on the verandah until Brian fell asleep and Nancy called the children in for bed. 'Your father's conked out,' she teased. 'Poor old thing. That boat ride across the lake was all too much for him.'

When he opened one eye and gave her a wicked look, she poked him in the chest. 'Not so young as you once were, are you, eh pet?'

'Neither are you,' he mumbled. He was still smarting from her comparison of Mac with himself and Don.

Business genius or not, Brian believed there was something shifty about Nancy's uncle. He was nothing like Don, who was wholesome and straight as the day was long.

Uncle Mac, on the other hand, always got it right, never took no for an answer and, according to Nancy, was a man to look up to.

Well, there was no way that Brian would ever look up to *him*.

In spite of Nancy's admiration of her dear Uncle Mac, Brian was not impressed with the man, not in any way, shape or form.

Or then again, like Nancy said, he might be just old-fashioned jealous.

~

Left alone in the house, Don got to thinking more and more about his younger daughter, Judy.

He thought about her before he went to sleep at night, and she was still on his mind when he woke in the morning.

This morning was no different. The autumn sunshine blazing in through the open window woke him early. He got out of bed, washed, dressed and cooked an egg and bacon breakfast, which he merely toyed with before throwing in the bin.

Afterwards he took his mug of tea outside, where he sat at the table, thoughtfully watching the birds feeding from the cornball.

His mind was filled with memories of Judy – of her as a baby, then as a toddler, and now she was a child going to school, and then she was . . . he could hardly say it, even in the quiet of his mind.

She was just fourteen when they discovered she had been seeing someone, having an intense relationship behind their backs.

The day she told them still seemed like only yesterday. Norma had caught her crying in her room, and suddenly the truth exploded into their ordinary little lives; that their sweet innocent child was actually carrying a child of her own!

The revelation had rocked his world and shattered his total belief in the daughter he adored. A darling girl, full of laughter and joy in everything she saw, Judy was special from the first moment she was born, when she looked into his eyes and held him there.

After the shock came the anger, like a tide of energy sweeping all commonsense and compassion away. He could not think straight. All he could see was the awful truth. When he demanded to know the name of the man who had made her pregnant, Judy adamantly refused to give his name.

To this day, Don remembered every little detail.

Out here in the warm sunshine, quietly drinking his tea and thinking of the daughter he had loved and then lost, eighteen long summers ago, Don still needed answers, but first he longed to see her; to make sure she was all right.

Even now, after all this time, that was the one question that burned in his mind; the one question that had never been answered: *who* had put her in the family way? And like the worst kind of coward, never come forward to take responsibility.

Now though, Don was ready to make his peace with Judy. 'I need you back in my life, Judy,' he murmured. 'Your mother is long gone. I'm older now, and much wiser. Who knows how long I have to put things right between us?' While he was able, he would do all in his power to make amends.

With Lottie lying heavily at his feet, he sat for a time, thinking and planning, not sure how he might go about locating her. Where would he look? Who could he ask? Of one thing he was sure. If ever he was to bring her back into the family fold, now was the time.

He thought of Nancy and of what she might say when she knew he'd been in search of Judy. 'I'm sorry, Nancy,' he murmured angrily, 'but whether you like it or not, I can't rest until I find your sister!'

A short time later he put on his boots, whistled to Lottie, locked up the house and set off down the lane. 'Let's go do some serious thinking, eh, girl?' he chatted to the dog as he went. 'First of all, I can never imagine Judy straying too far from her roots, because she was that kind of homely soul.'

He churned over every possibility in his mind, then passed it all by the dog, who too often was far ahead chasing rabbits or splashing in the water.

'Hey! Come here!' Seeing Lottie peering through the hen-coop to where the chickens were frantically cackling, he called her back. 'You'll frighten 'em off their egg-laying, staring at 'em like that with your beady red eyes!'

So the dog trotted alongside, content to go with Don, over the heathland and down to the canal, where Don sat for a time, skimming stones into the water and formulating a plan in his mind. 'I'm sure Judy will have stayed round these parts,' he told his trusty companion. 'She'll be somewhere between Fisher's Hill and Bedford town, I just know it.'

He thought it through. 'She loved the Old Bedford River, I do know that much, and she was always a curious, busy little thing, so she'll have got work, and a place to live . . . maybe somewhere in the vicinity of the river.'

He felt confident, that he would find her. 'Make no mistake, I *will* find her!' he told Lottie, who panted in reply.

Then he had another thought – and it was not a pleasant one. God forbid she'd tied herself to the devil who put her in the family way!

Whenever he thought of the man responsible, he wanted to strangle him with his bare hands. Then there was the child, who by now would be what . . . seventeen?

So many years, he thought sadly. And then: what if the father had turned his back on his baby, as Don had turned his back on Judy? A cold fear engulfed him. Had she been left to bring the child into the world, all on her own?

When he thought of the worry and heartache his adored daughter might have endured, his guilt was tenfold.

'Morning, Don.' The bargee's voice sailed across to him. 'Forgot yer fishing rod, 'ave yer?' The man was huge, with a round belly and round face, and a quiff of grey hair standing up on the top of his otherwise bald head.

'Morning, Ed.' Don returned the greeting. 'I'm not fishing this morning,' he explained. 'Got Lottie with me, see, and she's a devil with the barking. I might come back later on, and leave her at home.'

'Ah! So I might see you on me way back then?'

'You might. You might not.'

'Well, if you're still here, you can come aboard and share a drop of ale with me.'

'Sounds good. Thanks, Ed.'

'See you then.'

'Yeah, see you, Ed.'

Don waved as the other man went out of sight. 'He's one of the old sort,' he told the dog. 'Sound as a pound!'

Chatting with Ed had lifted his spirits, and oddly enough, had made him all the more determined to find Judy.

'Come on, old girl!' Bringing the bitch to heel, Don turned to retrace his steps. 'We've got things to do.'

The phone was ringing as he came into the house. Don had never got used to the blessed thing. 'Hello?' he answered warily.

It was Nancy. 'Hello, Dad, it's only me. Just to let you know that Uncle Mac and Rita have gone now, and we've got the house to ourselves.'

'That's nice.'

'Oh, and I'm sorry if I upset you . . . about Judy.'

'Mmm.' He was still riled by her harsh words. 'So you take back what you said then, do you?'

'No! I can *never* take it back. I still believe she's living in sin with that man in some filthy dump, content with her lot, and not caring a hoot about the rest of us. I'm just sorry that you and I had a falling-out about it. I could see you were upset.'

Don did not want this discussion. 'Best forget about it, eh?' he said gruffly.

There was a span of silence before Nancy asked, 'Are you all right?'

'I'm fine. Why shouldn't I be?'

'So, have you really forgiven me?'

'Nothing *to* forgive,' he assured her. 'Water under the bridge and all that.'

'All the same, it's infuriating how she can still get you and me upset, after all this time.'

Swiftly ending the conversation, Don told her, 'Got to go now. Me and Lottie have been for a walk. She got in the canal and now she needs cleaning up.'

Nancy laughed. 'Little devil! All right, we'll talk some time in the week. Okay?'

'Yes, okay, Nancy. Say hello to Brian, and give my love to the children. Bye then.' He quickly dropped the receiver into its cradle.

Now that his mind was made up, he didn't want to waste a single minute. Bringing the dog inside, he locked the outer door, then went upstairs to his room, with the dog following hard on his heels. 'No, girl!' He gestured to the bottom of the stairs. 'You go down and guard the front door and leave me to my business.'

While the dog reluctantly trundled downstairs, Don made for the wardrobe, from where he collected his suitcase.

In the zip part at the back, he found half his life tucked safely away; fond letters from his wife; a smaller version of their wedding photograph; cards he'd taken to her while she was in hospital and four cherished trinkets of her jewellery: wedding, engagement and eternity rings and a pretty blue necklace he'd bought for their twenty-fifth anniversary.

As he touched each and every one of Norma's possessions, the memories came alive, and he was momentarily saddened. But then he found the other batch of photographs and he became excited. Taking them out, he looked at each one individually; there was himself and his wife at the seaside soon after they were married; then the one with their first child, Nancy.

'Somewhere in here there should be . . .' He drew out an envelope. *Eureka!* This was what he'd been searching for: a fat brown envelope, positively bulging with mementoes.

He rummaged through the collection, until he found what he was looking for – photos of Judy as a baby, then as a toddler, and now she was dressed in her very first school uniform. The one he had in mind was a later one, taken in the garden of this very house during a visit to see Nancy, just a month before Judy gave them her devastating news.

'It's got to be in here somewhere,' he mused. 'Thank goodness I didn't listen to Nancy and throw the lot out.' His elder daughter could be cold of heart when she set her mind to it, he thought.

Ah! Here it was! Jubilant, he drew the single photo from the batch. The last one he ever took of her, it was a lovely, natural photograph of Judy, looking impossibly young and naïve. She was wearing a lemon, daisy-patterned dress. Her long fair hair was down to her waist and she was laughing. How could she be laughing? Against his instincts, Don felt a surge of disgust. Looking as though she had not a care in the world, when she must have known she was about to shatter all their lives!

In the photograph, the sun was shining much like today. Don had acquired a new camera that very morning, together with a yearning to capture photos of his family together, at a time when everything was so precarious as the clouds of war gathered.

For an age he stared at Judy's image, the tears filling his eyes and the pain of her departure draining his heart. 'You were such a pretty little thing,' he whispered, the tips of his fingers tracing her face, as he fondly recalled that day. He wondered, with a stab of agony, what his younger daughter looked like now, eighteen long years later.

A lifetime.

When suddenly Lottie began whining to be let out, Don slid the photograph into his pocket, replaced the suitcase and hurried downstairs. 'What's wrong, you bad girl? Can't you wait a few minutes while I sort myself out?' Tutting, he unlocked the door and threw it open. 'Go on then! And don't go running off, mind. I need you to guard this house while I'm gone.'

He watched the dog disappear behind the shrubbery, and realising it might be some time before she emerged, he went to the kitchen and made himself a fresh pot of tea, which he took out to the garden, along with a packet of biscuits and a cup with a saucer. He could think better with a hot drink inside him.

'I need to decide how to go about it,' he muttered to himself. 'It's no use just going into Bedford, and wandering about aimlessly.'

He wondered where he should start, then remembered: the river, that's where he'd go first.

When a short time later, Lottie came lumbering up the path, he quickly shut her in the kitchen. 'You behave yourself now!' he said through the door. 'I've no idea how long I'll be, but you've no need to worry. You've a bowl of water in there, and a small handful of biscuits. That's enough to keep you going, till I get back.'

In the hallway he grabbed his coat from the hook in case the weather turned unexpectedly nasty, as it often did.

'Good Lord!' Glancing at the wall clock he was astonished to see it was almost 5 p.m. But there was plenty of daylight left and the evening was most pleasant. All the same, now that his mind was made up, he needed to get there soon, or the day would be gone and he would be no further forward.

He felt good. With the sun's warmth on his face and a flicker of hope in his heart, he dared to believe that at long last, he might be able to bring that awful chapter in their lives to a satisfactory close.

CHAPTER NINE

J UDY LOVED TO look out at the world from her sitting-room window, and this evening was no exception. It had been a beautiful day, and now, just after 6 p.m., it promised to be an equally lovely evening.

The street was busy with men already making their way home from work and children playing. Enjoying the sunshine, they had congregated into little groups; girls playing hopscotch, others skipping, and occasionally the odd one running to meet her daddy as he turned the corner. A short distance away up the street, the boys whizzed about on their bicycles, kicked a football or loitered on the corner, to plan their next big adventure.

From the open window, Judy watched it all, and her heart was sore. Whenever she saw the children, laughing and playing, she recalled the time when she was a child, with loving parents, and a sister she could play with. But that was before.

She thought of another child, illegitimate, a precious creation despite her beginnings. She would remember that child for as long as she lived.

But it was all gone now. Gone for ever – along with any chance she might have had for a contented, normal life.

She let the memories flood in. She thought of her father and her family, and then she thought of that terrible night, when she was turned out of house and home. But she did not blame her mother, such a proud lady, always wary not to become the subject of gossip; her worst fears had been realised, and all because of her younger daughter.

Judy could understand why Norma had been so unforgiving. She could understand a great deal more, now that the years had flowed past. She knew what it was like to be ashamed, and to hit out. She knew what it was like to cry when you were alone at night, or to walk miles and miles, just to get away from the awfulness of what life had become.

She continued to watch the children a while longer, her pretty face uplifted in a smile as they turned to wave at her. She waved back, but it meant nothing really.

She did not know them, and they did not know her.

She was just a stranger at the window.

Closing the window, she turned the volume up on the Dansette record player. 'Lucky people!' she kept saying. 'Lucky, *lucky* people.'

When Phil arrived home, she was still curled up on the floor, listening to her records and unaware that he had come into the room. 'You look like a little pixie,' he told her. 'The prettiest, daintiest little pixie I've ever seen.' Reaching down, he grabbed her by the shoulders and bounced her into his arms. 'Well?'

Discreetly rubbing her shoulder where he had dug his fingernails into the flesh, she smiled up at him. 'Well, what?'

'Your hardworking hubby wants a kiss, that's what.' Grasping a hank of her long, untamed hair he jolted her head back and kissed her full on the mouth; a long, rough kiss that left her feeling bruised.

When she tried to draw away, he held her there. 'What's the hurry?'

'I've got your tea in the oven.' She could tell he'd been drinking. 'It's cottage pie . . . the way you like it, with plenty of onions and the mashed potatoes scooped into crispy little peaks.'

He laughed out loud. 'Forget all that,' he leered at her. 'I've

JOSEPHINE COX

got two other crispy little peaks in mind. Matter o' fact, it's all I've been thinking about.' Stripping off her blouse, he wrapped his hands around her breasts. '*This* is what I mean!' His two hands slid down to her buttocks. 'Soft warm skin between my fingers.'

Undoing her skirt, he let it slither to the floor, then stepped back to look her over. 'God, you're so beautiful!'

Licking his lips, he thrust her forward towards the bedroom. When she tried to protest, he grumbled, 'What's wrong with you! Had a man here already, have yer?'

'Stop it, Phil, you know very well I haven't.' She was used to his jealous suspicions.

He swung her round hard. 'I would kill you if you had – you know that, don't you?'

She nodded.

He shook her hard. 'HAVE YOU HAD A MAN IN HERE?'

'*No!*' Irritated, she shook him off. 'I've been here on my own all day, cleaning this pig-sty of a place, after the way you left it last night. I've asked you not to bring people in here, playing cards and drinking till all hours.' She took the opportunity to suggest, 'I should be out working, earning an honest wage, instead of being stuck in here bored out of my mind.'

'YOU'D BEST SHUT IT!' He took hold of her. 'The day I can't support you, I'll give up. Besides, I've told you before, whenever you've gone out to work, there's always been trouble.'

'Oh, and don't I know it.' She faced him full on. 'And who starts the trouble, eh? *You!* It's you who has this idea that I'm carrying on with every man who looks at me. You think I can't take care of myself, but I can. I really can!'

'I don't want my woman working. Folks will think we need your wages to manage, and I'm not having that. You don't need to work, not when you've got me, and don't try going behind my back because I'll know. I'll make sure no one will take you on ever again, not when I've finished with them.'

'You're a bully.'

He smiled at that. 'A bully, am I? Hmm, you seem to be getting very brave all of a sudden. What's brought this on, eh?' He prodded her in the chest with his finger. 'What have you been up to?'

'I already told you,' she answered warily. 'I've spent most of the day clearing up after your people.'

'Them "people", as you put it, are my friends, and I pay the rent on this flea-pit, so this is *my* gaff, and I'll have who I want in here, *when* I want. Got that, have you?'

Seeing how he was already making a fist, she nodded. 'Yes, Phil. I'm sorry.'

He smiled, a slow, sinister smile that made her flesh creep. 'That's my girl.' He stroked her face. 'Now, let's get on with the other business, shall we?'

Judy shrank inside; she knew exactly what he meant.

Phil Saunders' idea of lovemaking was not Judy's.

He took her without feeling. He broke her to him, in a most possessive and cruel way. Not for the first time, Judy wondered why she stayed with him. But then she realised: hard and brutal though he might be, Phil Saunders was all she had in the whole wide world. It was a shocking and sobering thought.

Later, with his carnal needs duly satisfied, he got out the booze. 'A toast to us!' He filled two glasses and handed her one. 'You and me . . . the best team ever.'

When she graciously refused, saying, 'I'll give it a miss, Phil. I'm not really in the mood for drinking . . .' he gave her a warning look that promised a beating, and so she succumbed, and hated him that little bit more.

As always, he drank to excess, then he slept and later, after wolfing down a plateful of reheated cottage pie followed by another generous measure of whisky, he told her gruffly, 'Get your coat on, we're off out.'

Judy protested. 'It's gone nine o'clock. I thought I might have a bath and an early night.' She was mentally and emotionally exhausted. Moreover, just now she did not like him enough to want his company. 'I'm really tired, Phil.'

'Too bad – I need you with me. Besides, if you're with me, I'll know exactly what you're up to, won't I?'

'When will you listen? I'm not "up to" anything!'

'So you say. The thing is, I've arranged to meet up with my pals at the pub, and I like showing you off. It makes 'em jealous.' Laughing, he slid an arm round her waist. 'Come on, Judy. Don't spoil my little bit of pleasure. Look, I promise we won't stay long. In fact, I might fancy an early night myself . . . if you get my meaning?'

Judy got his meaning only too well, and with a heavy heart, she made herself ready.

Having trudged the length and breadth of the river, Don stopped off at a café. The waitress was a dainty little thing with a wild mop of wavy hair that reminded him of Sammie. 'Tea, please,' he said, '. . . oh, and what sandwiches have you got?'

For the umpteenth time that day she went through the list. 'We've got cheese and onion, egg and cress, beef, pork, chicken and we've got ham with chutney. They all come with or without lettuce on white or brown bread.'

In spite of his aching feet, Don gave a little chuckle. 'I'm full up just listening to you.'

She gave him a bland stare.

Feeling somewhat embarrassed, he quickly moved on. 'I like the sound of that ham with chutney.'

She duly scribbled on her notepad. 'White or brown?'

'Er . . . white, please.'

'Toasted, or as is?'

'I didn't know you could toast chutney.'

'You can't. If you choose toasted, you'll get the chutney on the side.' She leaned on the table, gave an exaggerated sigh, and rolling her big eyes she demanded, 'Well, d'you want it or not?'

Trying desperately to stop from laughing, Don politely replied, 'Yes, please, I'll have it . . . toasted *without* the chutney.'

To which she gave him a shrivelling glance and swiftly departed, leaving Don pretending to stare out of the window, coughing into his hankie, when all the while he was creased up with laughter.

The toasted sandwich was, however, delicious and the tea was piping hot. 'I really enjoyed that,' he said at the counter, throwing a few coins into the 'tips' box.

'You're very welcome.' The young girl was nowhere to be seen, and in her place was a more mature woman of pleasant manner. 'We do our best to please.'

Don had to make a mention of it. 'Your daughter is very informative, isn't she? I mean, she recites that menu off by heart.'

'She does, yes, but she's not my daughter. She's a student at the secretarial college, working part-time to earn a few pounds.'

Leaning forward, she confided, 'She can be a bit . . . sharpish. Some of the customers have complained about her lack of respect towards them.' She kept glancing towards the door marked PRIVATE. 'She didn't say or do anything that upset you, did she?'

Don chuckled aloud. 'No, not a bit of it. In fact, I came in here feeling fed up and very weary, and the truth is, she cheered me up. I haven't laughed like that in a while.' He threw another coin into the 'tips' box. 'She earned that,' he grinned. 'Oh, and may I say, your ham sandwiches are a real treat.'

Pleased to see that he had put a smile on her face, Don was about to leave, but then he remembered something. 'I wonder if you might be able to help me?' Digging into his breast pocket he drew out the photograph of Judy. 'I don't suppose you've seen this young woman about, have you?'

Putting on her spectacles, she scrutinised the photograph.

'No, I'm sorry. We don't get many schoolgirls in here. Your granddaughter, is it?'

'Oh no, she isn't a schoolgirl, at least not now,' Don explained. 'She's my daughter, and this is the last photograph I have of her. She'll be in her thirties now. We lost touch. I was just hoping that someone might look at the photograph and it might jog a memory, that's all.'

The woman looked again. 'I'm sorry.' She took off her spectacles. 'She doesn't jog my memory at all.' A thought occurred to her. 'What makes you think she might be in these parts?'

'Just a feeling, that's all. She was born and raised near here, and somehow I can't imagine her moving too far away. Besides, she really loved the river. Every time we came into Bedford, she would persuade me to take her down to the river and she'd have to be dragged away.'

The memory was bittersweet. 'Truth is, if I'd let her, she would have set up home right there on the riverbank.'

'The thing is, your daughter is bound to have changed since her schooldays. All you can do is keep asking people until you get lucky.'

Don thanked her and set off for the town. It was becoming dark now, but he was a man on a mission, and didn't want to give up yet.

On his way to town, he stopped as many people as he came across. 'Does this photo remind you of a young woman you might have seen hereabouts?' The answer was always the same. 'Sorry, no.'

He was beginning to grow disheartened, when he saw a kindly-looking soul on the corner. 'Excuse me, would you please take a look at this picture,' he asked. 'Does the girl remind you of a young woman you might have seen?'

The woman looked hard at the picture, then she looked again. 'She's got beautiful hair. You don't often see long golden hair like that . . . just like a film star's, isn't it?' She looked at

Don, then took another glance at the photo. 'I'm not sure, but . . .'

Don grew excited. 'Oh, please! Any little piece of information . . . anything at all?'

'Well, I have seen a woman . . . early to mid-thirties, I'd say.'

'Where?' In his enthusiasm, Don grabbed her by the arm. 'Where did you see her?'

Startled, the woman backed away. 'Out and about.' She grew wary. 'I can't recall where, but I've definitely seen her. It was the hair that drew my attention – lovely hair, down to her waist it was, and wavy! She apologised. 'I'm sorry, but I can't remember exactly where it was that I saw her, although I'm always out and about town, so you might be looking in the right area.'

Truth was, she knew exactly where she had seen her, but she thought the man would be hurt if he knew the truth, and so she kept the knowledge to herself.

Don, however, could not let it go. 'The young woman you saw – did she seem well? Was she happy, do you think? Did you hear her laugh? Was she well-dressed, and did she have a teenager with her? Please think! How did she look, this young woman you saw?'

'I'm not sure, but I know there was no youngster with her. I would have noticed that. Like I said, it was the mop of golden hair that drew my attention.'

In fact, she recalled seeing the woman drunk and almost coming to blows with the rough-looking man who was her companion. But how could she relay that to this dear man? He was obviously in distress, clutching the photo of the girl as if it was the most precious thing in his life.

Loath to crush his hopes, she spoke kindly to him. 'Look, I know it's none of my business, but you look tired. Don't you think you should go home and forget all about the young woman? You may never find her.'

Before Don could reply, the sound of raised voices brought their attention to a group of people outside the Bedford Arms pub. 'It's dreadful, the carry-on outside these pubs of an evening!' The woman Don was talking to shook her head in disgust. 'No decent person can walk out these days, without being accosted by drunks and beggars. Something should be done about it. Lock them up, that's what I say!'

But Don wasn't listening any more because there, in the middle of the fracas, was a familiar figure. Her long, sun-kissed hair was unmistakable, and that certain way she hung her head when worried. Yes! It was definitely Judy. When she now began yelling and cursing, swinging her fists at the man, Don was shocked to the core.

'I'd best be off now.' Realising how Don had recognised the person he was searching for, the woman advised, 'Don't go over there.' She touched him on the arm. 'You won't find who you're looking for, not now, not after all these years, you won't.'

He turned to look at her, and when he saw the pity on her face he realised. 'You knew, didn't you?' he asked quietly. 'You knew exactly where you'd seen her, didn't you?'

The woman nodded. 'I thought she might be the one, but I was hoping for your sake that I might be wrong.' She saw how shock had seemed to make the old fellow shrink. 'Oh look, why don't you go home? Forget all this,' she urged him gently. 'Sometimes, however much you want to help your children, they still go their own way. It's not your fault.'

Don looked at her but said not a word.

Instead, he took a step forward, stretching his neck, so as to make sure that the young woman in the midst of all that arguing and fighting really was his daughter, Judy.

The woman walked away, leaving Don to witness a degrading scene. One he would have given his life not to see.

'BASTARD! I SAW YOU, OGLING MY WIFE! LOOK AT 'ER AGAIN AND I'LL BLACK YOUR BLOODY EYES!' Waving a clenched fist at the cowering man, Phil Saunders kept a tight grip on Judy.

'I don't know what you're talking about.' The man was

pinned down by two of Phil's mates. 'I never even looked in her direction.'

'What!' Seemingly plied with drink and ready for a fight, Judy had a plan. 'Are you saying you didn't fancy me? Well, I must say, that's a nice way to treat a lady!' She laughed out loud, a vulgar, ugly sound that echoed down the street. 'Let him go, Phil!' she screamed. 'He's not worth the bother!'

When suddenly one of the men pulled a knife and laid it across the man's throat, Judy screeched, 'Get away, the lot of you! I don't need any of you to fight my battles! I can fight my own!'

Surprising everyone by launching herself at the man, she knocked him aside and fought him to the ground. Rolling about on the pavement with him, and showing her suspenders and knickers she secretly thanked the Lord when the atmosphere relaxed and everyone erupted into laughter. 'That's my girl! Look at her go!' Phil yelled proudly.

While thumping at the terrified man and even grabbing a handful of hair on his head, Judy managed to whisper in his ear, 'Run for your life! I can't hold them off much longer. I've given you a chance . . . now go. GO!'

Hardly able to believe his ears, the man stared at her. He had thought she was drunk like the rest of them, but now he realised that she had her wits about her, and like himself, she feared for his safety.

As he took off down the street, the feel of a knife against his neck, and that young woman flinging herself on top of him was an experience he would never forget.

There was no doubt in his mind. She wasn't drunk, after all. She had seen how the thug was about to slice into him, and she had deliberately degraded herself to protect him.

In truth, that brave young woman had saved his life.

While the man was thanking the good Lord for Judy's intervention, Don, like the others, had witnessed an altogether different Judy. He had seen her yelling and leering, shamelessly baying for blood when the man was taken down. He had seen her claim that she could fight her own battles! Then she had launched herself at the man, wanting to hurt him, even kill him. When he ran away terrified, she had gone back, laughing and triumphant, falling straight into the arms of her husband, the one called 'Phil'.

Don had no doubts as to the nature of her lewd companion. Clearly the worse for drink, he was a thug pure and simple, jeering and goading the others on to hurt or maim, and there was Judy, a willing accomplice. Like Nancy had said, Judy truly must have been 'born bad'.

Half-blinded by tears, Don watched as a police car arrived and the officers inside it rounded everybody up and made them stand in a corner. He saw Judy, made to face the wall; he saw how the man called Phil reached out to take her by the hand and he heard her swear at the policeman when he snatched them apart.

Unable to watch any more, he turned away, broken and sickened by the events he'd witnessed.

In his head he could hear Nancy's warning words, and judging by the nature of the scene he had just witnessed, he had no doubts but that the rest of Nancy's cruel prophecy was also true.

Devastated, though relieved that he had not claimed her as his daughter, he started his journey home.

'She's gone,' he muttered to himself as he wended his way through the streets. 'The girl in the photo is gone. I have only one daughter now, and a family I love. If nothing else, I must be thankful for that.'

That young woman out there was not his daughter.

So now, he would live with happier memories, and pray that the young woman he had just seen might one day find a better life.

~

After questioning the bystanders, and also Pauline and Alan, Constable George Wearing had all the information he needed.

His treatment of Judy was stern but considerate. 'You should be ashamed of yourself,' he told her. 'What were you thinking of, getting mixed up with this rowdy lot? Have you no self-respect? No regard for your own safety?'

Deeply ashamed, Judy said, 'It won't happen again, Officer.' But she knew it would. That was the pattern of her life and try as she might, she could not seem to break it.

'If I do catch you brawling again, you'll be thrown in the cells and no mistake. You should think yourself lucky that no one was hurt, or it would have been an altogether different story.' The constable's manner was hard and officious.

Judy nodded.

'Now go home,' he concluded, 'before I change my mind and lock you up anyway!'

He watched her walk away, then turned to his partner who was still dealing with the troublemakers. 'This one was concealing a knife.' Showing the offensive weapon, PC Williams dropped it into a bag.

Williams looked at Phil. 'You got something to say, have you?'

Phil played the innocent. 'Not me, Officer. I was just coming out of the pub with my lady, and we walked right into it. I ain't done nothing wrong.'

'Mmm!' The constable took stock of Phil before turning to the others. 'That right, is it? He had nothing to do with what went on?'

Behind the officer's back, Phil gave the two men a silent warning not to drop him in it, or they would pay the price for it later.

'That's right, Constable.' The two ruffians nodded in unison. 'Him and his woman just walked into our argument.'

The officer returned his attention to Phil. He looked at him and for the briefest moment was tempted to cuff him and take him in anyway. But then he swiftly turned, nodded at his partner, and within minutes, the other two men were bundled into the car and driven away, leaving Phil standing there, feeling very pleased with himself.

A minute later, he was frantically searching for Judy. 'Judy! Where the hell are you? You can come out now . . . the coppers 'ave gone. Dammit, Judy, I'm in no mood for games.'

Alerted by all the shouting, Pauline and Alan appeared on the pub doorstep. 'Stop that racket, or you'll have the coppers back again!' Pauline said angrily. She'd had enough of Phil Saunders to last her a lifetime. Her uppermost concern was for Judy. 'What have you done with Judy?'

Phil swung round. 'Stupid cow. She's cleared off.'

Pushing his way forward, Alan reprimanded him. 'That's enough of the cursing. I should think she's gone home, and who could blame her, being quizzed by the police and all. It honestly beats me why you can never have a drink without always wanting to fight.'

'She was flirting with that bloke! I saw the way he was looking at her.'

Alan shook his head. 'According to you, she's flirting with every bloke that passes within a hundred yards of her. What's wrong with you, man?' He glanced about. 'Hey! They didn't cuff her, did they?'

Phil shook his head. 'No.'

'Well, there you are then. Like I said, she'll have gone home.'

Phil was having none of it. 'Not without me, she wouldn't.'

Growing frustrated, he bellowed, 'Judy, I mean it! If you don't come out right now, I'll leave you to it!'

He was greeted with an ominous silence.

Alan was not surprised. 'Like I say, she's probably had enough and gone home.' He turned to go back into the public bar, to look after his other customers.

The drunk man ignored him, cursing loudly at Judy, 'Right then, I'm off. So when you've finished sulking, you'd best make your way back . . . that's if I haven't locked you out!'

'Don't you dare lock her out!' Pauline knew what a nasty type he could be. 'You go on. I'll keep an eye out for her, make sure she gets home all right.'

Phil tried again softly coaxing. 'Judy, angel! I need you to come home right now.' His crude, low laughter spoke volumes. 'All that excitement's got me really worked up.'

From her hiding place, Judy understood his meaning all too well.

She felt ashamed and degraded; but she was not beaten. She didn't know why, or whether it was a figment of her imagination, but some tiny, nagging feeling inside was what stopped her from harming herself. A feeling of hope, that at some point her life had to change for the better.

Crouched in the alley beside the dustbins, she had sobbed until she could sob no more. Now though, she was defiant. 'Go away,' she whispered softly. 'Leave me alone.'

Disgruntled, Phil lurched into the night. 'I'll be waiting for you,' he shouted.

After watching him all the way down the street until she was truly satisfied that he had gone, Pauline went in search of Judy. 'I thought I might find you here,' she said, helping her up. 'I remember this place, from when you went missing before.'

The small, dark alcove tucked behind the bins was an ideal hiding place for a small person like Judy.

'Has he gone?' Judy held her breath.

Pauline assured her, 'He's gone all right. Look, stay with us tonight. I'll get word to Phil if you think he'll worry.'

Judy gave a scornful laugh. 'The only thing he'll worry about is himself!' she replied. 'But he'll be like a cat on hot bricks in case I've gone off with some man. If I don't show up soon, he'll be climbing the walls.'

'So you're going back tonight, is that what you're telling me?'

'I have to, or I'll pay the price when I do finally show up.'

'You don't have to do any such thing!' Concerned by Judy's submissive attitude, Pauline made a suggestion. 'Move in with us for a few weeks. Tell Phil you need time to breathe . . . time to work out what you want to do with your life.'

'No. I'm grateful for your offer, Pauline, but I can't do that.' Over these past years, Judy had come to know Phil Saunders better than anyone. She knew what he was capable of. 'He'll come after me. There'll be trouble. He won't ever give up until he gets me back.'

Linking arms, Pauline walked her back to the empty pub, where Alan was waiting anxiously. 'Let's get you inside,' he said. Taking hold of Judy, he took her into the back room, while Pauline locked the door behind them.

'Are you cold, m'dear?' Even though it was a mild evening, he could feel Judy trembling against him. 'Don't you worry, we'll soon have you right,' he promised. 'A cup of my hot choco-late works wonders.'

Having locked the outer doors, Pauline stood by the bar, watching the two of them amble along to the back room. 'Oh, Judy, love. How did it ever come to this?' It was times such as these, when she really feared for her friend.

While Alan went to make the drinks, Pauline tried once more to persuade Judy. 'At least stay the night with us, love. Give him a chance to calm down.'

'I'll be all right in a minute, then I'll go home. He'll be watching out for me.' Judy knew that if she didn't go back to Jackson Street, he would return to the Bedford Arms and break the place up to get at her. Just thinking about it made her sick to her stomach.

Seeing how pale and unhappy Judy looked, Pauline tried reasoning with her. 'I don't understand you,' she said. 'Why in God's name do you stay with him?'

In her heart Judy could find any number of reasons why she had stayed with him all this time; none of them good. When she now replied to Pauline's question, she gave only one answer. 'We're two of a kind, that's why.'

'Never!' Many times, Pauline had witnessed at first hand how kind and gentle Judy was. She had seen her with customers young and old, listening to their aches and woes, giving a sensitive cuddle here and there, and sometimes lifting their spirits by making them laugh.

When some time back an old regular had fallen ill, Judy visited her every day, sitting and talking with her, and running whatever errands were needed.

'You're a kind and lovely person, Judy,' Pauline told her now. 'You and Phil Saunders are like chalk and cheese. Everybody knows you would rather hurt yourself than hurt anyone else, so please, don't ever put yourself in the same class as that monster!'

'You don't know everything,' Judy told her. 'You don't know . . . what happened.' Her voice broke with emotion. 'I'm sorry,' she wept.

Sensing there was more to tell, Pauline asked quietly, 'What are you so sorry about, Judy? What's bothering you?'

Dismayed that she had almost revealed what she had tried all these years to forget, Judy gave a shaky smile. 'I'm sorry, because you and Alan are my only real friends in the whole world, and I'm such a nuisance to you both.'

'You are never a nuisance. Alan and I love you like family. We want to help, that's all.'

'I love you too,' Judy told her sincerely, 'but I need to deal with things myself. I really think I should go home now.'

Before Pauline could reply, the sound of loud snoring resonated through the room.

Startled, Judy and Pauline glanced across to where Alan was lying with his feet up on the arm of the sofa. His arms above his head, he was fast and hard asleep, mouth open and tongue rattling. Pauline tried hard not to laugh, but when Judy started giggling, she couldn't help herself. 'What am I gonna do with him, eh?' she chuckled.

'Should we get him to bed, or leave him there?' Judy asked.

'Leave the bugger there.' Pauline didn't think twice. 'Lazy article! If he thinks we're gonna bust our boilers carting him upstairs, he can think again! He didn't even make our hot chocolate, did he?' They laughed again.

Thankful for the timely intervention, Judy helped Pauline to cover him over and make him comfortable. 'We can sit and chat a while longer, if you like,' Pauline suggested. 'If you need to talk, that is?' She suspected Judy was keeping a secret, though what it could be, she had no idea.

An hour later, after much persuasion, Judy let Pauline show her to the guest room. 'You look really tired,' the landlady said, and yawned. 'One night away from your husband, just to get your thoughts together, won't hurt anyone – least of all you.'

It wasn't long before the pub fell quiet, save for Alan's loud rhythmic snoring. Having left him to sleep it off, Pauline settled in their bed alone.

Judy was in the spare room, but she was not asleep, nor was she in bed.

Folded in the deep wooden rocking chair in the corner, her mind was alive with all manner of thoughts and memories, of Fisher's Hill and Harry, and the way it was; and her heart was broken. 'Where are you, Harry?' she murmured. 'Why did you never come back for me?'

She turned her sorry gaze to the window, where the night skies were alive with shifting clouds, and for a long moment, she was mesmerised. 'I ruined it all, and now I have to face the consequences,' she told herself. 'My life will never be the same; no strong arms around me, no gentle talk and warm, loving glances.'

Closing her eyes, she could see Harry's face, feel his gaze on her, as though the two of them, so in love, was not so many years since, but only a moment ago. Wasn't it wonderful, she thought, how you could keep something in your heart forever, even though in the real world it was already gone.

She gave a deep, aching sigh, knowing in her heart and soul that she would never again know such love. 'I deserve to be unhappy,' she whispered to the skies. 'I should never have lied.

I should have been brave enough to tell him the truth, but I couldn't, and now I'm paying the price.'

She spent a while longer, thinking of the heartfelt vows she and Harry had exchanged. Vows that meant everything then, but that were based on deception. Her deception.

In spite of all that, her memories of the time with Harry were a precious lifeline to her. They were her shining light in the quiet, lonely darkness.

Above all else, the wonderful, heart-warming memories of Harry, kept her sane.

Getting undressed, she put on one of Pauline's nightgowns, then went into the bathroom and washed from head to toe. Pauline had brought in a bag of toiletries containing a toothbrush and toothpaste, and a brush to tame her thick, tangled hair.

Afterwards, feeling much better, she climbed into bed and was soon asleep – with Harry, and her beloved memories.

But then there was the other one! The one she so desperately needed to forget. The one who haunted her dreams night after night, giving her no peace.

Even now after all this time, the pain of it never went away.

In the early hours, Pauline awoke in a panic. 'What was that noise?' Turning to look beside her, she was surprised to see how Alan had made his way to bed at some time during the night. His snoring was as loud as ever.

Shaking her husband by the shoulder, she tried to wake him, and then she remembered. 'Judy!' In her state of semi-awareness, she had forgotten that Judy was in the house.

She listened again, and there it was: someone was crying!

Leaping out of bed, she went quickly along the landing. She inched open the door to Judy's room and peered in. 'Judy, it's me – Pauline. Are you all right?'

In the dimly-lit room, she could see Judy's small shape. She was still asleep, and obviously in distress, 'Harry, I need you! Don't leave me, I'm sorry . . . I'm so sorry.'

Pauline spoke softly to her, 'Judy, I'm here. Pauline's here.' Hurrying across the room, Pauline climbed onto the bed and took Judy in her arms; rocking her gently, 'Ssh! It's all right . . . I'm here . . . ssh.'

When Judy opened her eyes and saw Pauline there, all the fear and sadness welled over. Safe in her friend's loving arms, she sobbed as though she would never stop. 'I was bad,' she kept saying. 'I was bad and he left me . . . Harry left me.'

For what seemed an age, she cried and in between gave the tiniest insight into her most secret thoughts. 'I had to lie.' She said it over and over. *'I had to lie!'*

A short time later, when Judy finally succumbed to a deep, quiet slumber, Pauline made her way back to her own room and climbed into bed. She listened for a time, and when she was satisfied that Judy was resting easy, she settled herself beneath the eiderdown.

She was curious. Who was Harry? Was it someone Judy had once known and lost touch with? Certainly Judy had never spoken to her of anyone by that name.

Whoever he was, he had caught Judy's heart, until now he was invading her dreams. Where had he gone? Why had he left her, this Harry, whom Judy so loved?

Moreover, what did Judy mean when she claimed that she had had to lie. Who had she lied to? Was it this man called Harry? Or was it to someone else?

More importantly, what was this lie all about, and why was it haunting Judy in such a way?

Pauline got out of bed and sat in the chair, her thoughts straying back to Judy. Even though she had known her for some time, and loved her dearly, Pauline realised how little she really knew about Judy. Sadly, her dear friend was not one for confiding in others.

For just a moment back there, she had caught a glimpse of Judy's troubled mind, and it concerned her.

After a while, believing Judy to be soundly asleep, she climbed into bed and slid quietly between the sheets, 'Sleep well, Judy,' she murmured before closing her eyes.

Yet Judy's tearful words, and the heart-felt plea that Harry should forgive her, were too alive in her mind.

Now Pauline was the one who couldn't sleep.

CHAPTER TEN

A FEW HOURS LATER, when the morning sun came streaming in through the windows, Pauline woke with a start.

'Alan!' She gave her husband a shove with the sharp end of her elbow. 'Alan, are you awake?'

'No!'

'It's time to get up.'

Opening one eye, he winked at the bedside clock. 'Not yet.'

'What d'you mean, not yet! Look, it's seven o'clock already; time we were up and about!'

'You can be up and about if you like,' he rumbled. 'As for me, I'm here for at least another hour, and wild horses won't drag me out.'

'Oh, really? Well, if you're expecting *me* to do all the work while you laze in bed, you can think again.' She gave him another shove. 'Wake up, you bone-idle article. What's wrong with you?'

'Nothing's wrong with *me*!'

'So get your lazy backside out of bed.'

'No.'

'Why the devil not?' she demanded, flummoxed.

He looked up out of one eye, then grinned triumphantly. 'It's Sunday, you daft devil!'

Pauline had completely forgotten. 'Oh, right. Well, you get back to sleep for another hour or so. I'm off downstairs to make a drink.'

'Go on then, and don't come back.'

'What's that supposed to mean?'

'It means I'm tired, and you're aggravating me. It means I've already lost my precious sleep, on account of every time I close my eyes, there's you poking and prodding and threatening to shove a pillow down my throat because of a few gentle snores.'

'Oh, shut up! Don't be such a baby!' she groaned. 'Gentle snores indeed. Huh!'

'Bye!' waving his hand, he rolled over into her warm space. 'Just clear off and let a fella get some sleep.'

Grumbling and groaning, Pauline quickly dressed, brushed her hair and made her way to Judy's room.

There were no signs of their guest. The curtains were open and the bed was made, but Judy was nowhere to be seen.

Worried, Pauline made her way downstairs and there in the kitchen, pouring boiling water into a teapot, was Judy, looking more refreshed and with no sign of the upheaval in the night, apart from the faintest of shadows beneath her quiet, grey eyes.

'Morning, Pauline.' Judy had tried not to wake her two friends. 'I hope I didn't disturb you just now, when I came down?'

Pauline came across the room. 'No, you didn't. I just wondered where you were,' she said. 'I was worried in case you'd got up in the night and made your way back to *him*.' She made no effort to disguise her feelings towards Phil Saunders.

'Well, as you can see, I didn't go back.' Judy gestured for Pauline to sit. 'I will have to go back though. I'm surprised he isn't already battering on the front door.'

Taking the cup of tea offered, Pauline waited for Judy to sit at the table opposite her. 'I'm worried about you, pet,' she told her sincerely.

Judy shook her head. 'Don't be.'

For a few minutes they talked of this and that – laughing at Alan's snoring, and drinking their tea, both of them deliberately avoiding talk of the night's events until, after a while, Judy nervously approached the subject. 'Thank you, Pauline,' she said softly.

'What for?'

'You know what for.'

Pauline nodded. 'Do you want to talk about it?' she asked pointedly. 'I mean, *really* talk about it?'

For a moment it seemed as though Judy might confide in her, then she shook her head. 'No. Best not.'

'Okay.' Pauline wisely backed off. 'If that's what you want.' She sipped her tea and after a minute or so, said, 'I fancy a piece of toast – want some?'

'No, thanks all the same. I'll have my tea and then I'll make my way back, before Phil takes it into his head to cause any more trouble for you.' She added angrily, 'That's if he's not still blotto from last night.'

'It wouldn't surprise me at all.' Pauline recalled how totally out of his mind Phil had been. 'He knows how to make a fool of himself, that's for sure!'

While she talked she moved about, opening windows and making toast, adding an extra slice under the grill in case Judy changed her mind.

Then she came back to the table, where Judy appeared to be deep in thought. Sensing that she was going over last night's events in her mind, Pauline munched on her toast and gave Judy the time and quiet she obviously needed.

After a moment or two, Judy looked up. 'Pauline?'

'Mmm?' Pauline had a mouthful of hot toast.

'About last night.'

Pauline swallowed the remnants of her toast, 'What, you mean Phil getting drunk out of his mind?' she asked. 'Don't you worry about that. It's nothing new.'

Judy gave a sad little smile. 'Phil's drunk out of his mind most of the time, but I didn't mean that.' She paused, seemingly embarrassed. 'I mean, when you came to my room, I was dreaming, talking out loud.'

Pauline understood. 'It's all right,' she assured her. 'I didn't hear a thing, or if I did, I've already forgotten.'

Grateful for Pauline's integrity, Judy told her, 'You're a good friend.'

Having torn off another chunk of her toast, Pauline grunted acknowledgement.

Another few minutes passed, with Pauline chatting on about Alan and chuckling at how she had no idea why she'd put up with him all these years.

'You love him, that's why,' Judy told her. 'When you love somebody, you would do anything to be with them.' She had tried so hard not to think of Harry, but he was always there, in her mind and in her heart. So too, was her guilt.

Pauline knew she was thinking of the man called 'Harry' and she was curious. 'You talk as if you love somebody enough to do anything for him,' she remarked quietly. 'I don't believe it's Phil Saunders either.'

She did not pressure Judy, nor did it really matter whether the young woman answered her or not. All she wanted was for Judy to face her demons in the light of day. It was the only way forward.

So, she sipped her tea and waited.

In the background, the ticking of the wall clock seemed unusually loud, but then the silence between Judy and Pauline was thick and heavy. Having finished her short breakfast, Pauline went to the sink, where she rinsed out the cups.

Her mind was on Judy, and what she might be thinking right now. 'Is she thinking of the one called Harry, or is she thinking I should mind my own business?' Pauline asked herself.

Returning to the table, she began collecting up the sugar bowl and milk jug, and as she turned to walk away, she felt Judy's hand curl into hers. 'You want to know about Harry, don't you?' Judy asked.

Greatly relieved, Pauline acknowledged this with a nod. 'You need to talk about him, love. You need to share whatever it is that's hurting you.'

'I know you're right,' Judy sighed. 'Only, it's so difficult.'

Replacing the milk jug and sugar bowl, Pauline sat herself down. 'I'm here for you, Judy,' she said. 'All I want is to help you, and if you feel the need to talk, that's all to the good. But you don't have to tell me everything. You can tell me as much or as little as makes you feel easier. All I want is for you to face your nightmares, because if you don't, they will haunt you for ever.'

Judy heard what Pauline was saying and she knew that every word was true. She *did* need to face her nightmares. She needed so much for someone else to know what had really happened. She so much wanted to open that dark locked door inside her, and let the demons out.

To be rid of them once and for all.

She knew it would not be easy; all these years, whenever she thought she was ready to tell, she could never bring herself to do it.

That was not surprising, she thought sadly, for how could she ever tell the real truth to anyone else, when it was so ugly, she could not even deal with it herself.

Pauline's voice interrupted her thoughts. 'If you need to talk about it, now's the time.' She gave a little smile. 'Before Alan starts with the snoring again.'

As always, Pauline's wry sense of humour had broken the ice, and for a moment, Judy found herself actually laughing. But then as Irish Kathleen would say, 'after the laughter comes the tears,' and it was true, because now the tears were rolling down Judy's face. 'I do want to talk about it,' she told Pauline in a whisper. 'I just don't know how.'

Pauline knew then that there had been something very wrong in Judy's past life. 'Tell me about Harry,' she prompted, hoping that would be a good place to start. 'You obviously loved him very much?'

Judy took a deep breath. 'We were just kids, and yes, I *did* love him, more than I've ever loved anyone in my life. Oh, I know I married Phil, and that was unfair to us both, because the truth is, I've never stopped loving Harry. I never will.'

'So, who was he, this man you loved so much?'

'His name was Harry Blake. He lived down our street in Fisher's Hill, and he was my first real sweetheart. He was kind and thoughtful. Good-looking too!' She smiled, a wistful, beautiful smile. 'He was every girl's dream, and he chose me.'

Her voice broke with emotion. 'Out of all the girls he could have had, Harry chose *me*. We were so happy. We planned our lives together, and never a day went by when we didn't see each other. He was my man and I was his darling, and we were so much in love!'

For a moment she was quiet, remembering how it was, then in a soft voice she went on, 'Like two fools, we thought nothing could ever go wrong in our perfect little world.'

'But it did go wrong – is that what you're saying?' Pauline had seen the joy in Judy's face whenever she spoke Harry's name. She had also seen the pain, and what looked to her, like real fear.

Judy took her time in answering. For a while she lost herself in those blissful days when she and Harry were impossibly young and in love; when every sky was blue and every day was another wonderful adventure together.

'Judy?' Pauline quietly called her. 'Are you all right?'

Judy looked up. 'You asked me once if I had lost touch with my family.'

'I remember.' Pauline had never heard Judy talk of her parents or siblings. 'You said you had no family and I left it at that, but I must admit, I've always wondered.'

'I did have a family, once upon a time,' Judy enlightened her now. 'I had a mother and father and an older sister.'

Pauline was delighted that Judy was talking of things she had never discussed before. 'What happened to them?' she asked. Maybe the demons that haunted her, had to do with her family.

'They threw me out when I was fourteen.'

'*What?*'

Judy nodded. 'It didn't really matter, not then. Nothing did,' she said in a low voice.

'Did you ever see them again?'

Judy gave no answer.

'Did they ever try to find you?'

Judy shook her head.

'So, you don't know where they are now?' Pauline was baffled.

'I don't want to know!'

Shocked by Judy's hostility towards her family, Pauline asked gently, 'If you want to find them, I can help if you like.'

'NO!' Looking Pauline in the eye, Judy told her in a thick, harsh voice, 'I never want to see them again . . . *any* of them, as long as I live! They didn't want me then, and I don't want them now! They didn't look after me. They didn't care about me. To tell you the truth, I don't care whether they're alive or dead.'

'Don't upset yourself, pet.' Worried that Judy was growing agitated, Pauline assured her, 'It's all right if you don't want to see them ever again. Forget them. You have a new family now.'

Judy clenched her fists. 'Phil Saunders is *not* my family. He's bad . . . just like the others. I hate him! I hate him!'

'Hey!' Reaching out, Pauline took hold of her hand. 'I wasn't talking about Phil. I meant me, and Alan. We'll always be here for you, come what may. We love you like our own daughter.'

'I'm sorry,' Judy apologised. 'I've never really seen Phil as my family, but I can't blame him for the way he is. He knows I was never in love with him and he also knows that it was always Harry I wanted. *He* was going to be my family, then when he left, Phil just took over, and I was so desperate, I didn't really care.'

She dropped her gaze to the table and went on in a small voice: 'Phil knows I don't love him in that way. That's why he's so aggressive; why he follows my every move. He's afraid that Harry will come back and take me away.'

Pauline was horrified. 'Judy! You can't stay with a man just because you feel sorry for him. You can't throw your life away like that.'

Judy shrugged. 'I owe Phil a lot,' she told Pauline tonelessly. 'After Harry went, I fell apart.' Her voice became almost inaudible, as though she was talking to herself. 'I didn't know which way to turn, but then Phil rescued me, and now I have no choice but to stay with him.'

She gave Pauline a sad smile. 'Isn't it strange how nothing ever works out right?'

Pauline needed to understand. 'I can see how much you loved Harry,' she murmured. 'So what happened to drive you apart?'

'It was my fault,' Judy confessed. 'It was a bad thing I did. I spoiled it all.' She took a moment to compose herself. 'Harry left and I never saw him again.'

'What bad thing was it that split you and Harry apart?' Pauline enquired gently. 'You don't have to talk about it if you don't want to, but if it helps . . .'

Suddenly, Judy was out of the chair and hurrying across the room. 'I've got to go!' she said in a panic. As she went through the door, she called behind her, 'Thank you, Pauline. Thank you for having me.' The front door opened and closed – and Judy was gone.

Left alone, Pauline berated herself. 'Why didn't you just let her talk? Why did you have to keep pushing her?'

'Hmh!' A few minutes later, Alan entered the room. 'Talking to yourself is the first sign of madness they say.'

'What d'you mean?' she snapped.

'Take it easy! It's just that I heard you chuntering away to yourself as I came down the stairs.' He glanced about. 'I thought you might be talking to Judy, but now I see you were talking to yourself.'

Pauline's eyes swam with tears. 'Judy's gone,' she said.

'What d'you mean, she's gone?' He glanced towards the door, 'Why?'

'Does it matter?'

'But where's she gone?'

'Back to *him*, I expect.'

Alan poured himself a cup of tea and stood across the kitchen from her. 'Why would she do that? Especially after last night.' He gave an audible gasp. 'Did you see that thug with the knife, ready to slit that poor man's throat. And I'll tell you what . . .'

He had her attention now. 'What?'

'When Judy threw herself at the bloke, I reckon she did it to stop him from being killed.'

Like Alan, Pauline had seen that particular incident. 'I thought that too,' she said. 'I knew it wasn't like her to attack a man in such a vicious way.'

'So why didn't she stay with us a while longer? What made her go back to Saunders?'

Pauline leaned against the sink. 'I'm not sure, but I think it was something I said.' She remembered the question that had sent Judy running for the door: Do you want to talk about the 'bad thing?' That's what she had asked Judy, and obviously it was too difficult for her to talk about.

'Pauline?'

'Mmm?'

'What's wrong with Judy? Why does she hang about with thugs and bullies like that?'

'I don't know the truth of it, but I have a suspicion.'

'Oh, and what might that be?'

In her mind, Pauline went over the entire conversation between herself and Judy, and the more she thought about it, the more she was convinced. 'There's more to this than meets the eye,' she said thoughtfully. 'I think Judy is punishing herself.'

'That's ridiculous! What has that lovely girl got to punish herself for?'

Pauline looked up at him with a serious face. 'You are not to repeat a word of what I say now.'

'Shame on you.' Alan was offended. 'I've kept many a secret

told over the bar these past years. I think I can look after our Judy's interests, don't you?'

'I'm not sure what it is that troubles her,' Pauline confided, 'but something really bad must have happened a long time ago. It involves a young man called Harry, and Judy's hatred of her family, who she says she never wants to see again, as long as she lives.'

'Good grief! I didn't even know there was a young man called Harry in her past, let alone a family.' Alan was still unsure. 'So, for some reason she didn't want to talk about, you have a suspicion that she might be punishing herself?' He shook his head emphatically. 'Maybe it's just you reading more into it than there really is?'

'All I'm saying is, way back in Judy's past something happened to turn her young world upside down.'

The landlady was convinced it was not altogether because of Harry leaving, though that in itself had obviously been a real blow. 'Whatever it was, Judy still thinks about it. It's the real reason she went to Phil in the first place. It's why she stays with him, even though she has no real feelings for him.'

Alan was not convinced. 'There you go again.' He had seen it all before. 'You're letting your imagination run away with you, as usual.'

He recalled the time when Pauline was convinced that the previous owner of their pub had hanged himself in the cellar; he reminded her of it now. 'It's like the time you claimed that the previous landlord of this pub had hanged himself in the cellar. You said how you had an unsettling feeling every time you went down there. It "stank of death" was what you said.'

He laughed out loud. 'When that regular old codger told you the cellar had been used to hang raw meat as a favour to the butcher, you felt a right fool, didn't you, eh?'

In spite of herself, Pauline had to smile. 'I was right about the smell though, wasn't I?'

'So now, will you stop imagining there are monsters in Judy's past, and get her away from the monster she's with *now!*' Quietly chuckling, Alan sauntered away, leaving Pauline in a quandary.

She knew instinctively that there was more to Judy's story than she'd let on. The odd thing was, Pauline could bet a pound to a penny that this 'bad thing' Judy talked of had little to do with the boy called Harry. When Judy had talked of Harry, her face lit up, but when she had mentioned the 'bad thing', Pauline got the feeling that whatever had happened all those years ago was too disturbing and cruel for Judy to cope with.

Pauline wisely decided not to broach the subject with Judy again. Instead, she would wait for Judy to come to her.

She was not giving up though.

One way or another, however long it took, she would get to the bottom of whatever it was that still affected Judy so desperately.

It was the most beautiful evening.

Not too many miles from where Pauline was pondering on Judy's situation, Irish Kathleen was happily chatting away in her chair in the house on Fisher's Hill.

'I had the offer of a date with the coalman,' she was saying. 'Oh, he's not handsome nor is he young, but then he's a man after all, and I haven't had a date with a man for many a long year. I told him no though. I mean, what would I be doing with a fella? I've lost the habit of it, if you get my meaning.'

She looked up from her knitting. 'Oh, now will ye look at that!' She glanced about the room. 'So, where's he gone off to this time?' She had soon learned how restless Harry was. One minute he was here and the next he was gone, and here she was chattering to herself, like some silly old woman losing her marbles.

Putting down her knitting, she made her way to the kitchen. 'Harry, where the divil are ye?'

She glanced out the window, and there he was in the moonlight. 'Aw, Harry Boy.' She was sad for him. 'What is it that makes you so restless, me darlin'?' Like a cat on hot bricks he was forever on the move; he was here, then he was there, and then he was nowhere at all!

She remained at the window, careful not to let him see her if he suddenly turned round, but near enough so that she could keep an eye on him. 'God bless ye, Harry Blake. Yer good woman is gone to her Maker and there is no way on God's earth you can ever bring her back.'

Her kind old heart went out to him. 'I can't help ye,' she whispered. 'Nobody can. Oh, but you'll not rest . . . not until you come to terms with it all.'

She watched him pace the garden, then sit on the bench, then he was walking again, and now he was leaning on the fence, looking lost and alone, his face upturned to the skies.

She shook her head forlornly. 'Ah, you'll be missing your lovely wife so ye will,' she muttered. 'But I imagine there'll be someone else on your mind just now; someone you loved very deeply when you were just a boy.'

She cast her mind back. 'I miss her too. Sure, didn't I love that girl as though she was me very own? Soon after you went away though, Harry, it was like she disappeared off the face of the earth.' As did her entire family, she recalled.

Watching Harry now, she could hardly imagine what trauma he had suffered; back then when he was so young, and more recently, when his beloved wife was so tragically taken from him and young Tom.

'I wonder what the future has in store for you.' Leaning forward with a grunt, she collected her knitting. 'Already the world has turned time and again, taking your darling wife into the past. Sure, wouldn't it be a fine thing if the world has altogether done a complete turnabout, and the girl Judy, is destined to be your future?'

She chuckled to herself. 'Ah, but the Lord has a strange way of doing things, so He has.'

She stole another glance at Harry, alone in the dark with his deepest thoughts, and thought of the boy-child upstairs soundly sleeping. 'Harry's son,' she said, smiling, 'out of Sara.'

With much regret, Kathleen now recalled the last time she had spoken with Judy, and the secret they shared. A secret she had promised hand on heart never to divulge to a living soul. Thinking of it now, Kathleen's heart was sore. Oh, poor Judy! Such a terrible burden for a young girl. She paused in her knitting. 'I pray to God you took note of what I said,' she whispered, furtively glancing again to where Harry was standing. 'Oh, my darling girl . . . I hope you did the right thing in the end.'

On that day when Judy sobbed in her arms, she had given her love and comfort, and good sound advice. Whether Judy had acted on it, Kathleen never did find out.

So, being the wise old woman she was, and knowing she could do nothing more than she had already done, Kathleen left it all in the hands of the Master, and went quietly back to her knitting.

~

Unaware that she had been watching him, Harry remained by the fence, looking up at the skies and talking with Whoever was up there listening. 'I don't know what to do, or where to start,' he whispered. 'I try so hard to put her out of my mind, but I can't. I really can't!'

He shifted his gaze to the ground; thinking, remembering . . . and now he was talking again. 'It all ended badly, but I still love her . . . so very much.'

He gave a weary smile. 'But then you always knew that, didn't you, Sara . . . my precious love. You were the one who carried me through. The one who kept me sane all those years, and made me promise to come back here, to my roots. Now that you're gone, it's as if I've been cast adrift. I know now, how Judy must have felt. It was all wrong. We were just children. Too young, too reckless.'

For a time he was quiet, looking up at the skies and wondering if Judy was looking at those very same stars. 'Where is she?' he kept saying. 'Should I try and find her? Or should I leave her to the life she has now?'

Another moment of solitude, and then he made his way inside.

'Aw, there ye are, you rascal,' Irish Kathleen greeted him with a wide smile. 'Put the kettle on, will you, me darlin'? I'm that parched, me tongue is stuck to the roof of me mouth!'

Like the canny old soul she was, Kathleen made no mention of seeing him outside.

Harry had thought he was alone with his precious thoughts; and that was fine by her. Yes . . . fine and dandy, so it was.

PART THREE

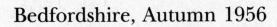

Bedfordshire, Autumn 1956

Strangers

CHAPTER ELEVEN

'FETCH IT, LOTTIE!' Throwing the stick into the canal, Don sat on the bank while the stocky, white bull terrier launched herself belly-first into the murky waters. He laughed at the dog's antics as she spun round and round, frantically searching for the stick. 'Look, there it is . . . right in front of your great big nose!'

Catching the stick between her huge jaws, the dog swam back. Struggling out of the water and up the bank, she dropped the stick at Don's feet, before shaking the excess water from her plump body and spraying him from head to toe.

'Whoa, you gormless bugger!' Scrambling to his feet, Don wiped himself down. 'Are you trying to drown me or what!'

In reply, the dog gave another almighty shake, and when Don ran for cover, she followed him at the gallop, thinking it was a game and giving a loud, excited bark.

Laughing, Don dug into his pocket and fed Lottie a biscuit treat. 'Well, at least we've stretched our legs and felt the sunshine on our backs, eh?' He looked up at the skies, noting the fluffy white clouds beginning to move in. 'We've been lucky with the weather all week, and we've still got a few hours of daylight yet,' he told her. 'Tomorrow night the family are back, so we'd best make the most of it, eh?'

When he settled himself on the fallen tree trunk, the bitch

fell against him, shifting and fidgeting until she was as close and as comfortable as she could get.

Don didn't mind; in fact, he welcomed her genuine affection.

Since the day he had gone into town and witnessed for himself the way his daughter had let herself be drawn into a life of violence and debauchery, he had been more than grateful for the company of this faithful old friend.

Cutting across the back ways to the little corner shop in Heath and Reach, he bought the basic necessities ready for the family's return: bread, butter, cornflakes, and a good helping of ham and cheese. 'Oh, and I'd best take a new jar of marmalade; the old one looked a bit worse for wear, so I threw it out. And I'll need a two-pound bag of dog biscuits, please.' He pointed to the sack spilling over with the bright colours and shapes of the biscuits that Lottie loved.

'So, is that it then?' The shopkeeper was a man of considerable proportions, with a friendly manner and a bright twinkly smile.

Don gave a firm nod of the head. 'It'll have do till Nancy comes home,' he answered. 'I've kept me and the old dog going all right, but I'm blowed if I know what else to get the family. I know young David likes his cornflakes, and that Sammie looks forward to her marmalade on toast, so there you have it. The milkman is going to leave three pints tomorrow.'

While the shopkeeper packed the goods into a bag, he chatted as always. 'So, the family have enjoyed their holiday then, have they?' Don's family were regular visitors, so he knew them well enough.

'I think so, yes,' Don informed him. 'Apparently they've had excellent weather and they've each done what they wanted. Me and the faithful mutt have wandered hill and dale and even been swimming in the canal, so it can't be bad, can it, eh?'

The younger man agreed. 'So, it was daughter, son-in-law and two children, was it?'

'That's it, yes.'

'Must be nice, having a grandson . . . especially as you don't have a son of your own, eh?'

'That's right, and he's a good lad, is our David.'

'Me and the missus, we had three daughters and one son, though I would have liked more children.' The shopkeeper smiled. 'At least we had three girls . . . all of them Daddy's little darlings.' He gave a sigh. 'I would have welcomed a dozen more just like them.'

'Just be grateful for what you've got.' Don was thinking of Judy. 'We don't always get what we want.'

'So were you disappointed? I mean, it *is* just the one daughter you have, isn't it?'

Taken aback by the other man's pointed question, Don took a moment to answer. When he did, it was with a forced smile. 'Just the one daughter, yes. But like I say, we don't always get what we want, do we?' With that he collected his brown carrier bag of groceries and took his leave.

'Good afternoon, then. Nice seeing you.' The shopkeeper was surprised when Don left so abruptly. 'Must have been something I said,' he muttered, closing the till with a clatter.

The bull terrier was excited to see Don emerge from the shop doorway. She could smell the ham. 'Come on, old lass.' Don untied her from the lamppost. 'Let's get off home, eh? We both need a bath, or the house will smell of canal water, and Nancy would not like that, would she, eh?' he chuckled. 'What! She'd be down on us like a ton of bricks and no mistake.'

No sooner had he got inside the kitchen than the telephone rang. 'Hello?' Dropping the groceries on the table, Don snatched up the receiver.

It was Sammie. 'Hello, Grandad, are you all right?' came her voice.

'Hello, love – yes, I'm fine. Me and Lottie have just got back from a long walk.' He told her how the dog went in after the stick and soaked him top to toe, '. . . shook herself all over me, the dopey mutt.'

When she laughed, he playfully chided her. 'Oh, go on – mock your poor old grandad. Never mind that I might get pneumonia.'

They chatted for a while, about the holiday, and how Uncle Mac and Rita were already on their way home, and that they would all be together for their last night. 'Uncle Mac said we're to put our glad rags on, because he's taking us out to dinner, as a thank you for looking after the house. We'll be home tomorrow though, Grandad.'

'So, you're being wined and dined, eh?' Don smiled. 'That's your Uncle Mac for you – nothing but the best, eh?'

'I wish you were coming with us though, Grandad.'

For a moment, Don thought he detected something in Sammie's voice, something not quite right. 'Is everything all right with you, my love?'

Sammie sounded brighter. ''Course! Why shouldn't it be?'

'I mean, you've not caught the sun or anything, have you? I hope your mother's keeping an eye on you.'

'Huh! Mother *ALWAYS* keeps an eye on me, fussing and fretting. She doesn't seem to understand that I'm old enough to look after myself.'

Now Don realised the problem. 'Oh, I see. So your mother's been laying down the law as usual, has she, and now the two of you are at loggerheads. So go on – tell me I'm wrong.'

'Not exactly, Grandad. Only she caught me chatting to this boy I met at the beach, and now she's watching me like a hawk.'

'Oh, I'm sure you've got it all out of proportion. She just doesn't want you getting in any trouble.' Judy came to mind, and his heart sank.

'I knew you'd say that.'

'Well, if it all gets too much, you can always call me and have a moan.'

'Sammie laughed, 'All right, I will!'

'Oh, and tell your mother she'll find her house all spic-and-span. I've not been partying or entertaining, and the dog hasn't chewed everything in sight. In fact, you tell her we've both been very well behaved.'

'I will, Grandad. Got to go now and put on those glad rags. Apparently, we're being taken somewhere really posh.'

'Ah well, only ever the best for your Uncle Mac.' Don was not surprised. 'It's very thoughtful of him, especially when he's only just got back.'

'That's what I told David, but you know what he's like.' Her voice dropped. 'David is always looking for a reason to dislike him. He says Uncle Mac is only taking us out to show off.' She gave a grunt of disapproval. 'I think he's just jealous!'

Don gave a little smile. There had been a time when even he had been jealous of his younger brother, but not any more. Not since he'd seen how hard Mac worked, and how many hours he put in.

He relayed that to Sammie now. 'Besides, your Uncle Mac enjoys treating people, especially family, and there is nothing wrong with that in my book. So, you tell David he's to enjoy the evening, and not to forget his manners. All right?'

'All right, Grandad. I'll tell him.'

'Have a good time then, and give my regards to everyone.'

'I will. Bye then, Grandad. Love you.'

'Love you too, Sammie. Bye, see you soon.'

Replacing the receiver, Don took a minute to consider his younger brother. 'Mac has done very well for himself,' he told the dog. 'But it didn't come easy. He always said he would be rich one day, and by God, he's kept to his word. Even as a kid he would work after school, running errands and what-ever else might earn him a pocket full of coins. All us other kids used to laugh at him, but we're the fools now, because here he is, all grown up and making money hand over fist, with a big grand house, a boat in the Mediterranean and a healthy bank balance, while the rest of us have little to show for all the years of slogging.'

He laughed out loud. 'If I'd let him show me a trick or two while we were kids, who knows? Even I might be a wealthy man now.'

In his mind he went back over the years. 'Funny how we were so different,' he muttered while unpacking the groceries. 'I'd be out them school gates and off to the woods, climbing trees and collecting conkers, or swimming in the canal, and there was young Mac, doing his deals and leaving the rest of us far behind.'

He nodded approvingly. 'Oh, yes! Whatever young David thinks of his Uncle Mac, he can't deny that hard work pays off.' He felt a rush of impatience with the boy. 'Matter of fact, it might do our David a world of good, if he was to take an example from his uncle.'

He chuckled, 'Especially when it comes to chasing girls instead of getting on with your school work. By! You would have never seen my brother chasing girls, oh no! Work first, play later, that was Mac's philosophy.'

Pausing in his task, he looked down at the dog, who was waiting for a biscuit, her whipcord tail wagging and her soulful bloodshot eyes fixed on Don's face.

Giving her a playful pat on the head, Don threw her a biscuit. 'We may never be rich, Lady Lottie,' he murmured, 'but y'know what? You and me over the fields and down at the canal today – I wouldn't swap that, not even if you were to offer me a heap of banknotes. Oh no!'

Though he regretted not having been successful in material matters, he had lived his fair share of joy and contentment, and felt not a shred of envy towards his younger brother. Instead, he felt a rush of sibling pride. 'The boy has done well! He deserves the best.'

Apart from his profound shock and sadness at Judy's downfall, he was mostly content with his lot. 'Best get this place shipshape.' He gave the dog another biscuit. 'Take it outside now,' he instructed, 'and don't you be dropping crumbs, or Nancy will have our guts for garters!'

~

Nancy was in a panic as usual. 'Honestly, Brian, we ought to be headed back to Mac's now. There's so much to do, what with all the clearing up and packing, and you know what Sammie's like when she's getting ready.'

Slapping the sun-tan lotion on her hands and face, she smothered her legs with it before tucking the bottle underneath the cushion. 'I swear, that girl believes the world revolves round her.' Phew! She couldn't believe the amazing weather they had had this week. One or two days had been hotter than July. They were all tanned and healthy-looking.

Lying beside her on his deck chair, Brian seemed not to have heard, or he had shut his ears as he had long ago learned to do when Nancy was on the rampage.

'Brian!'

'Yes?'

'Did you hear what I said?'

'Er . . . yes, and I totally agree with you.' He had not the slightest idea what she was talking about.

'Brian!'

'What now?'

She gave a loud tut. 'I swear, the world could be tumbling round your head and you wouldn't even notice.'

'What's wrong now?'

'Nothing – at least, nothing I can't handle.'

Thankful that he was let off the hook, he flicked the pages of his newspaper. 'Ah!' Arriving at the racing page, he scanned the list of runners in the four-thirty. 'Fair Play, eh?'

'Are you talking to me?' Nancy stared down at him.

'No.' He tapped the page with his finger. 'I was just talking to myself.'

'Huh!' She gave him a scornful glance. 'That's about right.'

Igoring her cynical comment, he concentrated on the horse's form. 'I think I'll put a couple of quid on Fair Play. It's won the last three times out, and was pipped at the post just last week.' Licking the end of his pencil, he put an asterisk beside the horse's name.

'Oh, for heaven's sake, is that all you can think of . . . horse-racing?'

'Ah well, you wouldn't say that if I won a fortune. You'd be up the high street, shopping for another holiday before I could say Jack Robinson!'

'You might be right,' she conceded with a little smile. 'But just now, I'm more concerned about getting us all back to the house. First we need to clean ourselves up, and then make sure the house is thoroughly clean before Mac and Rita get home.'

'Which won't be for at least another six hours.' Brian looked at his watch. 'It's just gone midday. They're not due home until after six. There's plenty of time, so stop panicking. Just enjoy the beautiful day – our *last* day remember – before we get back to the hustle and bustle of life at home.'

Nancy had to smile at that. 'Heath and Reach is hardly hustle and bustle, is it?'

'Stop nit-picking. You know very well what I mean – daily routines, driving to work, keeping to schedules. All that.' His smile fell away. He felt really down now. The reality of this wonderful, lazy holiday coming to an end had only just dawned on him.

Nancy had stopped listening. She was too busy keeping an eye on Sammie. At the far end of the beach, talking and laughing with a group of people her own age, Sammie was in her element. 'I do wish she wouldn't keep talking to strangers.'

'Who?' Shifting his sunglasses to the end of his nose, Brian followed his wife's concerned gaze. 'Oh, you mean Sammie? Oh, now look, Nancy, you're going to have to stop treating her like a little kid. She's a teenager. She likes to chat. Where's the harm in that, eh?'

'Don't you dare take her side on this!' She was still bristling from the other day when she and Sammie had strong words, about the very same subject. 'I was hoping you might back me up on this, but I should have known better than to count on any support from you.'

'I'm sorry, Nance, but I just don't happen to think Sammie will come to any harm talking to people of her own age. Especially when she's never out of our sight.'

'I see.' Turning away, Nancy lapsed into one of her famous silences.

'Oh, for heaven's sake, don't go all sulky on me!'

Putting her back to him, Nancy lay on her side.

'Nancy!'

She ignored him.

'Oh, right! So now you're not talking, eh? Well, that's just dandy, isn't it? All four of us, invited out to a special dinner in a special place, and my wife won't even talk to me. That's wonderful! Bloody wonderful!'

Nancy swung round. 'Stop that swearing and cursing.'

'Only if you stop the sulking.'

'So, do you want an ice cream, or not?'

'Are you offering?'

'I might be.'

'Are you paying?'

'If I have to.'

He grinned from ear to ear, the winner of round one. 'Go on then, I'll have a choc ice.'

'You'll get fat.'

'So there'll be more for you to cuddle, won't there?' He peeped at her. 'What are you having?'

'Same as you.'

'Don't you care if you get fat then?'

'Nope!'

'Well, neither do I.'

He watched her treading through the sand. 'Oh, Nancy, Nancy!' he groaned. 'When will you ever learn that Sammie is a young woman now. Keep crowding her the way you do, and we might lose her altogether.'

The very thought of that made his skin crawl. Sammie was his special person. She was what put the smile on his face and the spring in his step. His daughter could be unpredictable – deeply caring, yet fiercely argumentative, she was one of the most generous, loving creatures on God's earth, and Brian Wells was the proudest father alive.

A short time later, Nancy came back carrying the cornets, with the ice cream dripping over the backs of her hands, 'Quick!' Handing him his one, she then proceeded to wrap her tongue around the steady trickle of ice cream, meandering down the side of her cornet.

'Mmm!' Easing herself into the deck chair, she fished a hankie out of her bag and handed it to Brian. 'Look at the state of you,' she grinned. 'The chocolate is all round your face. You're worse than the kids!'

Brian called her attention to the string of donkeys travelling across the beach in front of them. 'Look there!' He pointed to the donkey at the back of the line, a great lump of a thing with huge sticky-up ears and a long tail that brushed the sand as it went along.

Shading her eyes with the palm of her hand, Nancy peered through the sunshine. 'It's our Sammie sitting on it!' Horrified, she stood up to make sure. 'Whatever does she think she's doing?'

'She's enjoying herself.' Brian drew her attention to their son, who was kicking a football about with a group of youths. 'David and Sammie are making the most of their last day, and so should we,' he advised. 'Leave them be for another hour or so. Then we'll pack up and head back, all right?'

His wife nodded. 'If you say so.'

There were times when she had to give in, albeit reluctantly, because as Brian frequently pointed out, David was more than capable of looking after himself, and Sammie would all too soon be leaving her childhood behind. It was a terrifying thought.

Nancy consoled herself with the idea that Sammie still had a way to go before she was a young woman, so, until then she meant to keep a firm hand on the girl, whether she liked it or not!

~

The plane was late landing. 'I'm not so sure I want to go out tonight now,' Rita said tiredly. She did not like airports as it was, let alone hanging about after luggage when they were already over an hour late. 'Can't you ring the family and explain?'

'I've already phoned them,' Mac told her. 'You saw me go off in search of a phone booth.'

Usually placid and non-argumentative, Rita came back with, 'Yes, but you only told them we would be late. You didn't ask them if they would mind staying in tonight and having fish and chips.'

Mac patiently reminded her, 'I wouldn't even dream of it! My brother's family have been good enough to take care of our property while we've been away. Don't you think the least we can do is take them out for a decent meal?'

His wife felt ashamed. 'Of course you're right. I'm sorry if I sounded ungrateful. It's just that I'm really tired and fed up. It's almost seven-thirty now, and there's still no sign of the luggage.'

Three-quarters of an hour later, they were actually on their way home. 'Feel better now, do you?' Mac asked.

'Yes, thank you.' Leaning back in her seat, Rita gave a sigh of relief. 'It's a good job you rang and changed the time of the restaurant booking.'

'It will still be a bit of a rush,' he reminded her. 'I've allowed half an hour for us to wash and change, and another fifteen minutes for the drive to the restaurant. Do you think you can manage that?'

'Of course.' Sometimes he had a way with him that made her feel inadequate. 'If *you* can manage it, then so can I.'

'Good girl!'

It was just as well he did not see the frustration on his wife's face.

~

'SAMMIE!' Nancy's voice sailed up the stairs. 'Aren't you ready yet . . . they'll be here before you know it!'

'I'll be down in a minute!'

'Oh, look!' When the car drew up outside the house, Nancy was frantic, 'SAMMIE! THEY'RE HERE!'

'All right, all right!' Giving her hair a final brush, Sammie stepped back to see herself in the mirror. 'I hope you don't let anyone down.' She had taken ages trying to control her wild hair, and even now it still looked scruffy to her. 'Don't forget, you need to be on your best behaviour!'

She wagged a finger at her image. 'This is the first time you've ever been to a posh restaurant.'

When Mac and Rita got out of the car, Brian came out of the house with David, waiting to give a helping hand with the luggage.

Rita was the first to thank them, for looking after the place. 'It means that Mac and I can really relax,' she said, 'knowing we've got family keeping an eye on things for us.'

A moment later they were in the house and up the stairs, with Rita rushing about, searching out a pair of shoes and a clean shirt for Mac. 'Your stuff is on the bed,' she told him. 'I'd best get myself washed and changed.' She then hurried off to the bathroom, leaving Mac to fend for himself.

In a remarkably short time, everyone was ready to leave – apart from Sammie. 'Where *is* that girl!' Nancy was exasperated. 'She has more time than anyone to get herself ready and she's always the last to show.'

When Sammie did finally come down the stairs, Mac was the one to voice what everyone else was thinking. 'My Lord!' He appraised her from head to toe; the calf-length blue fitted dress, and darker blue shoes with a heel. Her usually unruly hair was sleek and shining, the natural burnished curls teasing about her face and neck. She looked so grown-up.

'Oh Sammie, you look beautiful!' Rita smiled on Sammie with genuine affection. 'I can't believe you're the same girl,' she said.

'WOW!' David was well impressed. 'Is that really my little sister?'

Brian was equally proud. 'Who is this young woman?' he wanted to know.

Laughing, Sammie launched herself at him. 'I'm still your little girl!' she protested. 'Only I'm all dressed up to go out.' She had been so excited about the prospect of going to a 'posh' restaurant that she had even raided her savings for a new outfit.

Up until then, Nancy had said nothing. Seeing her daughter looking all grown-up had a strange, disturbing effect on her. 'I want you to go and change!' She said it almost without realising.

Like everyone else, Sammie was shocked. 'Why? What's wrong? Don't I look nice, Mum?'

Aware that everyone was hanging on her every word, Nancy mentally shook herself. 'Oh, I'm sorry, sweetheart,' she said. 'It's just that you took me by surprise. You look so . . . so . . .' Suddenly she was stumbling for words.

'So different?' Brian discreetly rescued his wife. 'I'll be the proudest man in the restaurant tonight.' He looked directly at Nancy. 'So now, shall we go?'

On the whole, the evening was a great success. Lovely venue, choice wine, good food and delightful company.

Everyone chatted and laughed; Mac was extremely entertaining, even though a little inebriated. Brian teased Sammie about riding the donkey; Rita had a little moan about the plane being late, and David relayed a few tales of scary exploits.

Nancy, however, was noticeably quiet, her gaze constantly straying to Sammie.

When in an unguarded moment she caught her mother looking at her in that certain way, Sammie asked teasingly, 'What's wrong, Mum? Have I got gravy on my chin or something?'

Nancy forced herself to laugh out loud. 'Keep waving that fork about and we'll *all* be covered in gravy!'

Nancy's well-chosen comment had the desired effect of shifting the focus from herself, and on to Sammie.

But there was no doubt about it, Nancy had been deeply affected by Sammie's appearance. She was no longer the impossibly mischievous tomboy. Her daughter was fast becoming an attractive, confident young woman, with strong ideas, and a powerful thirst for life's adventures.

There was something else too. Something Nancy had not noticed. Until tonight.

Try as she might to enjoy the evening, she was too deeply unnerved by the thoughts swimming through her head. For her, the evening was ruined, though she hid her fears as best she could.

'Well, do you want it or not, before my arm drops off?' Brian had been holding the wine bottle over her glass for a while, before Nancy realised.

'Oh, sorry! Yes, please.' She then astonished him by instructing, 'Fill it up, right to the very top.'

'That's not like you,' he remarked quietly. 'Half a glass is about your limit.'

'Not tonight,' she said with a smile. 'Tonight, I just might get tipsy.'

Brian laughed at the idea of his wife being tipsy. He could not even envisage it, though tonight there was something about

Nancy that was beginning to bother him. 'Are you all right?' he murmured.

She gave an impatient nod. 'I'm absolutely fine! I just want to make the best of our special evening out, that's all.'

Her explanation went only partway to satisfying him. He had no idea what it was that troubled Nancy, but there was definitely something. He knew her too well.

After a glass or two, everyone was merry. Uncle Mac was the life and soul of the party. David ate everyone else's leftovers, much to his father's disgust. Rita got giggly and started Sammie off, though not unduly, as the girl had stuck to one glass of red wine.

As for Brian, he found himself trying to keep up with the flow of conversation, while at the same time keeping a wary eye on Nancy, who to his thinking was too quiet, and not at all like her usual bossy self.

Nancy made a supreme effort to join in, but it was not easy.

Not when she had seen something that took her back over the years, *to a time she would rather forget.*

All too soon the evening was over and a much-inebriated Mac was shepherding them into the two taxis he had ordered. 'Squash up at the back,' he joked. Thrusting Rita in between Sammie and David, he clambered into the front seat.

Laughing and joking, and being altogether too loud, Mac entertained them all the way home, where they climbed out and made their way up the steps to the front door.

'Wait!' Frantically searching his pockets, Mac finally located his wallet and paid the fares, together with a handsome tip which put a big smile on the drivers' faces. That done, he scrambled up the front steps to be with the others.

'Who's got the key?' Rita had forgotten to bring her own, and now there followed a brief confusion, when Mac fell backwards down the steps, to be heroically rescued by Brian.

Producing the key from her purse, Nancy saved the day. 'Panic over,' she said and everyone poured into the house.

Everyone but Nancy that was.

Having drunk more than she was used to, she watched the others go inside, her worried gaze constantly returning to Sammie. 'I'm so sorry,' she whispered brokenly. 'I'm such a bad . . . *bad* person!'

Realising his wife had not followed them in, Brian returned outside to find her leaning over the railings, and sobbing her heart out.

'Hey!' Taking her into his arms, he rocked her gently back and forth. 'What's all this about, eh?'

'I'm sorry.' Nancy clung to him. 'I didn't mean it.'

Brian shook his head. 'What didn't you mean?'

'Nothing.'

'It's the wine, I guessed as much.' Brian had seen it all before. 'I knew it would affect you. It always does.'

Jumping at the excuse, Nancy quickly agreed. 'That's it!' She wagged a finger. 'You never should have let me drink wine. It doesn't agree with me.'

Brian groaned. 'How did I know I'd get the blame – as per usual?'

'Because it's your fault!' Wiping the palms of her hands over her face, she assured him, 'I'm fine now. Come on, let's get inside – see what everyone else is up to?'

Brian had other ideas. 'It's such a lovely evening, Nancy. Incredible weather for the time of year. Let's sit over by the summerhouse for a while, eh?'

'Why?' Nancy was not in the mood for small talk.

Slipping an arm around her waist, Brian explained, 'I just think it would be nice to end a great evening, sitting together away from the others, just you and me.'

'But *why*?'

Taking a deep sigh, Brian spoke softly. 'Because we never seem to have any time to ourselves. We've had the most marvellous holiday, and I'm grateful to Mac and Rita for that, but we've never once enjoyed each other's company without the children around us; or without being frantic when they're out of sight. The thing is, love, they're not babies any more. It won't be too long before they leave home for good, to set out on their own life adventures, and then it'll be just you and me.'

Without realising it, he had touched a raw nerve. 'Do you think I don't already know that?' she snapped, and reached for her hanky again.

'I wasn't meaning to upset you. It's just that, well, it's almost time to go home, where we'll have even less time for you and me. There'll be work, and the kids, and . . .' He hesitated.

'And *what?*'

Embarrassed, he looked away. 'It's just that I never get you to myself these days, and I miss you, Nancy. So very much.'

'Oh, I see.' Nancy was in the mood for a fight. 'You mean my *father*, don't you?' she demanded. 'You don't like it because I asked him to come and live with us after we lost Mum. Admit it! You want my father out of our house and the sooner the better. That's it, isn't it? That's what you're trying to say.'

Brian was shocked. 'Never. That is *not* what I'm saying, and you know it. I love your father as much as you and the kids do. Besides, it was *me* who suggested he should come and stay with us – or have you forgotten?'

'No, I haven't forgotten, but it sounds to me as though you're beginning to regret having suggested it in the first place.'

Angry, Brian took her by the shoulders. 'What the hell is wrong with you tonight?' he demanded. 'You've been acting strange all evening.'

'Nonsense.' His wife tried to wriggle away. 'You always did have a vivid imagination.'

Brian wasn't about to fall for that one. 'It has nothing to do with imagination and it has nothing to do with the wine you drank either. I saw you, Nancy! I saw your expression when you looked at Sammie. It was as if you'd never seen her before. As if you were looking at a stranger.'

'Now you really are talking nonsense!' Nancy snapped.

'Apart from that, you've hardly spoken a word to anyone all evening; then you asked me to fill your glass to the brim, even knowing how wine can affect you.'

He went on, 'Just a while ago I found you sobbing your heart out, and now, for some reason I can't even fathom, you seem to be hellbent on picking an argument with me!'

All evening he had seen her behaving out of character, and it worried him. 'As for accusing me of wanting to throw Don out of house and home . . . For crying out loud, Nancy, I think the world of him, and you know that. So why don't you tell me, what's *really* going on in that head of yours?'

Exasperated when she deliberately turned away, he swung her round to face him. 'I'm beginning to think there's something you know and I don't. So come on, out with it. What's going on?'

Aware that she had foolishly aroused his suspicions, Nancy quickly turned the tables on him, 'It's *you*! You've got me all confused, with your need to sit in the summer house, just the two of us. Then you moan about the kids always being round us, so where else would you have them be, eh? Roaming the streets, getting into trouble?'

Just as she had planned, her tirade put him on the defensive. 'Don't be silly, woman! It's just that we seem to have lost touch with each other. We never have time to sit and talk about us – you and me! It's always other people – family, neighbours, the woman in the corner shop or the man who sells papers on the market. Other people!'

When he thought he had got her attention, he went on more quietly, 'The truth is, Nancy, we seem to have lost our way. All I want is for you and me to get to know each other again . . . just to talk and be together without anyone bursting in on us, or demanding our time, or calling us away . . . stealing what time should be ours, so that in the end, there's nothing left for either of us.'

His voice grew soft and persuasive. 'I bet you can't even remember the last time I told you how much I love you?'

Nancy gave a small embarrassed laugh. 'Honestly, Brian, just listen to yourself! We're not two young people who need to keep telling each other things like that.'

'Oh, but you're wrong, Nancy. It's at our time of life, when the children are learning to flex their wings and time is running short, this is precisely when we need to let each other know our feelings.' He took hold of her hand. 'I want you to know that I do love you, Nancy. I always have and I always will.'

He smiled knowingly. 'In spite of the fact that you can be bossy and frightening at times.'

Humbled and somewhat flustered by his unusually sincere outburst, Nancy drew away from him. 'You're drunker than I thought!' she chided. 'We'd best go inside, before they wonder where we are.'

More sober now, and definitely in control, she marched up to the house, with Brian staring after her, forlorn and rejected. 'All right, girl, if that's the way you want it,' he mumbled, following behind. 'You can pretend all you like, but *I know* there's something different about you tonight. You've been too quiet, and just now when you flew at me in a temper, it wasn't me you were angry with, oh no. Seems to me, it was someone else who upset you tonight, and for some reason, you don't want me to find out – in case I start a skirmish, eh? Well, you needn't worry, because I'm not *that* drunk.'

Kicking out at a loose stone, he raised his voice to yell after her, 'And I'm not taking the blame either!'

~

In fact, there very nearly was a skirmish later on that night – but neither Brian nor Nancy had anything to do with it.

David and Sammie were in Sammie's room, chatting about the end of their holiday, and saying how they would have liked

217

to have stayed on a while longer. 'I'm sure if we asked to stay for another few days, nobody would object,' Sammie remarked. She couldn't remember now why she had been so reluctant to come on holiday. It had been brilliant!

David shook his head. 'No. I've had enough of the seaside. Anyway, I'm due back at work on Monday. How do you fancy a weekend in London instead, seeing the sights? Sam Martin's brother had his stag night there, and apparently it was the best night they've ever had in their lives.'

'Oh, whoopee-doo!' Sammie threw one of her pillows at his head. 'We'll have to get *you* married off, then we can all have a party. That's if we ever find a girl who'll have you!'

'You little monster!' Grabbing the other pillow, David threw it at her, then when she retaliated, the pillow fight really got underway, with a volley of screaming and shouting and laughter that reached the downstairs lounge, where the others were talking about boats and holidays.

'What the devil's going on up there!' Nancy was already on her feet and ready to run up the stairs, when Brian caught hold of her.

'They're just being high-spirited,' he said. 'They're just kids, burning off energy. That's all.'

When Nancy seemed determined to go and investigate, Mac stood up, albeit rather unsteadily. 'I'm the man of the house,' he declared stoutly. 'You lot talk among yourselves, while I sort the kids out.'

Before anyone could object, he was already headed for the stairs.

David heard the footsteps approach. 'Ssh. Somebody's coming!' In a minute he was out the door and back in his room, before Mac even got to the top of the stairs.

With his ear to the door, he heard his Uncle Mac knock on his sister's door. 'Sammie, it's Uncle Mac. Is everything all right in there?'

'Yes, thank you, Uncle Mac.'

'We thought we heard a lot of noise.'

'Oh, it must have been the radio. Sorry if it disturbed you. I've turned it off now.' There was a pause, then, 'Goodnight, Uncle Mac.'

'Goodnight, then. Sleep tight.'

David heard the conversation and was quietly chuckling to himself. '"I had the radio on, Uncle Mac".' He mocked Sammie's voice to perfection. '"Goodnight, Uncle Mac".'

He had to stop himself from laughing out loud.

Waiting until Mac's footsteps receded down the stairs, he then slunk out of the door.

As he came onto the landing, he was astonished to see that Uncle Mac had not gone downstairs, after all. Instead, he was half-crouched by the balustrade, stamping his feet in a manner that would suggest he was actually going further away, when in fact he had never left the spot.

Realising his intention, David smiled. You cunning old devil, he thought and shrank further back into the shadows. Trying to make Sammie believe you've gone down the stairs – until she starts with the 'radio' and then you'll be banging on the door again.

He quietly chuckled. 'You're more crafty than I gave you credit for!'

What he saw next wiped the smile off his face.

Unaware that David was watching from the shadows, Mac peeped over the balustrade, making sure there was no one on their way up. Satisfied that he was alone, he gingerly placed his hand on the doorknob to Sammie's room, and very carefully turned it, until the door inched open.

A furtive glance to right and left, then the man leaned forward, painstakingly pushing open the door, just enough for him to look inside and watch Samantha as she undressed for bed.

When he became visibly excited, licking his lips and shifting from one foot to the other, David was deeply shocked. He could hardly believe what his eyes were telling him.

Why was Uncle Mac still there? Why was he peeping into Sammie's room like that?

Suspicions were forming in his mind; dark, terrible suspicions that made his skin crawl. No! He had to be mistaken. But there in front of him was the truth – Uncle Mac, nervous and excited, like he had never seen him before. No, he had to be wrong! Uncle Mac would never do such a thing.

Making as much noise as he could, David came down the landing, whistling and calling, 'Uncle Mac! Oh, did the radio disturb you? I told Sammie she should turn it down, but she wouldn't listen.'

Flustered and shocked, Mac instantly shrank from the door. 'Oh, David! Er, yes, I was just waiting at the door to make sure she turned the darned thing off.' With the effects of drink still on him, he staggered drunkenly to the top of the stairs. 'Sounds as though she might have gone to bed now, so I dare say we won't hear any more of that tonight, eh?'

Going unsteadily down the stairs, he called back to David. 'Goodnight, lad.'

Still shaken by what he had witnessed, David mumbled back, 'Goodnight.'

Returning to Sammie's room, he softly tapped on the door.

Sammie called out, 'Who's there?'

'It's me! Can I come in for a minute?'

'What's wrong?' Sammie left the door open for him. 'I thought you'd be in bed asleep by now.'

'I don't feel tired, sis.' It was clear to David that she had just climbed out of bed; her robe looked like it had been thrown on, and her feet were bare.

'Uncle Mac was at the door, complaining about the noise.' Giggling, she threw herself onto the bed and swung her legs over the edge. 'I told him I was sorry to have disturbed them, but that it was the radio, which was now turned off.'

David already knew all that. 'Did you let him come in?'

''Course not!' she laughed. 'I was getting ready for bed.

Anyway, he was only there for a minute and then he went away.'

David wondered if should tell Sammie of his suspicions. But then if he did, what would he say – that Uncle Mac was peeping at her through the open door?

When he thought of it like that, it sounded ridiculous. After all, the very reason Uncle Mac had come upstairs was because of the noise, which she had told him was the radio. So wasn't it feasible that he should look in to make certain Sammie was not waiting to turn the radio back on, once his back was turned?

Besides, David wasn't sure if what he had thought to be Uncle Mac being excited or sinister, wasn't merely agitation at having reprimanded Sammie about the unacceptable noise.

He couldn't even be certain if Uncle Mac had seen anything untoward. What if Sammie was already in her bed and completely covered over? What if Mac really was just checking to see if everything was all right like he said?

David had partly convinced himself. 'Maybe I should run it by Dad?' he muttered aloud.

'Yeah, that sounds like a good idea,' Sammie declared.

David looked up. 'What are you talking about?'

Sammie groaned. 'I just said, telling Dad first, about a possible trip to London, sounds like a good idea to me. Then he can tell Mother, and maybe persuade her that we would come to no harm if she was to let us loose for a day. Then we could decide where to go and what to do.' While David was thinking of his suspicions about Uncle Mac, Sammie had been rattling on about the idea of going to London.

David gave a sigh of relief. 'Oh, right! Yea . . . or we could maybe go fishing, what do you think?'

Sammie didn't know *what* to think, 'I reckon you should make up your mind,' she grumbled. 'First we're going up in a hot-air balloon, then we're going to somewhere else. And now, it's fishing!'

Relieved to leave his suspicions behind and pick up on the conversation, David reminded her, 'Mother probably wouldn't let us go on our own anyway.'

Sammie was determined. 'We'll just have to *insist* then, won't we?'

'Oh, what! And start World War Three?'

'If needs be, *yes!*'

Something about Sammie's fighting attitude made David think. If he was to raise the matter of Uncle Mac peering in at Sammie's door, it might cause more trouble than it was worth. Or it would turn out to be something and nothing and he would end up with egg on his face.

He decided to let matters rest.

After all, he was probably overreacting. He reminded himself that Uncle Mac had obviously had too much to drink over dinner, and that he was probably fidgeting about because he was unable to remain steady on his feet.

Even though he had no particular liking for his uncle, there was no real evidence that Mac was harbouring bad thoughts towards Sammie, and why should he? They had always got on like a house on fire, even when David had tried so hard to turn Sammie against him; and that was probably out of petty jealousy. It riled him that Uncle Mac had always paid more attention to everyone else than he did to his nephew.

Yes, that was it! David told himself. It was nothing more than his own sibling jealousy, and that was the truth of it.

For the next little while, he and Sammie talked of certain things they'd like to do before getting back to normality.

The more brother and sister chatted, the more David became convinced that Uncle Mac was guilty of nothing worse than downing too many glasses of Bordeaux.

Even so, when he left, he made Sammie promise to lock the door.

His sister grinned. 'Why? Do you think Count Dracula is coming to snatch me away and suck my blood?'

'You've got a shockingly vivid imagination, do you know that?'

'And you're getting paranoid. Just like Mother!'

As he walked back to this room, David thought of what Sammie had said. 'God, I hope I'm *not* getting like Mother,' he muttered. 'When she sets her mind to it, she can be the most unreasonable, troublesome creature on God's earth. Sometimes I really pity Dad, having to put up with it.'

That settled the matter once and for all. 'Sammie is absolutely right! I'm getting paranoid and imagining things.'

After all, when it came right down to it, all he had seen was his uncle a bit worse for drink, impatient and irritated, because the noise had disturbed the adults downstairs.

He decided to put the whole matter behind him.

Mac though, found it far more difficult to forget the incident.

Restless into the early hours, he could not get the image of Sammie out of his mind. Until he looked inside the room and saw her just now, arms stretched up as she slid her nightie on, he had not fully appreciated how his delightful little niece was beginning to blossom into womanhood.

He had never considered Sammie to be beautiful, in the traditional way. Pretty, yes, and maybe with the *promise* of beauty, but not yet open to full bloom.

Lurking in him now was a carnal realisation of how deeply desirable she was. Seeing her like that had been truly disturbing. In a way that both shocked him and aroused his worst fears.

CHAPTER TWELVE

Harry looked at his young son, and his heart soared with pride. 'Tom Blake! I can't believe how grown-up you look in your school uniform,' he said, admiring the short dark trousers and knee-length socks, white shirt with blue tie, and the dark, peaked cap perched lopsided on Tom's head. When Kathleen had brought his son through to the kitchen just now, Harry had been close to tears.

Uppermost in his mind was Sara. 'Your mother would have been so proud of you, Tom.'

The boy's face lit up. 'Can Mammy see me?'

Holding back the emotion, Tom nodded. 'I like to think so,' he murmured, adding brightly, 'Don't you look smart!'

Tom nodded. 'Kathleen and me were out a long time and I tried all the other things on, but they were too big, and so she took me to another shop and we got this one,' he blurted out, then taking a long, invigorating breath, he stroked his blazer. 'I like this bit of my uniform best of all,' he announced decidedly.

Harry laughed. 'So do I,' he said.

'And so do I!' Kathleen had stayed back while father and son discussed the all-important subject of Tom's first day at school. Now though, she came forward and gave the boy a hug. 'How d'you feel then, Tom?' she asked stoutly.

Tom considered that for a moment, before stating boldly, 'I'm a bit nervous, bejaysus.'

He could not understand why both Harry and Kathleen burst out laughing. 'Oh dear me!' Kathleen protested, wiping her eyes. 'Sure, ye mustn't blaspheme like that.'

'What's blaspeem?'

'Blaspheme,' Kathleen corrected, 'is when you say a special person's name for no good reason.'

'Whose name did I say?'

Kathleen wished now that she had just let it go, but she explained anyway. 'The name of Jaysus,' she answered reverently. 'You must not say "Bejaysus".'

'*You* say it,' he reminded her, innocently repeating her words that very morning. 'You said it to Daddy. You said "Bejaysus, will you look and see how grown up the boy is" – that's what you said.'

Suppressing the laughter, Kathleen put her hands on the boy's shoulders, and in a very serious voice she informed him, 'Well, I'm very sorry, because I should not have done that.' She gave Harry a sideways wink. 'I can see I'll have to watch me tongue from now on.'

Harry agreed, though he could hardly hide the quiver in his voice as he mocked Kathleen. 'Oh sure, you will that,' he reprimanded, 'naughty article that you are.'

Tom flung his arms round Kathleen's neck. 'I still love you,' he said. 'And now I'm ready to go to school.'

'Right then.' Kathleen took him by the hand and walked with him to the car, where Harry bundled him inside. 'Now you be a good boy,' she said. 'You tell the teacher from me that she's got a little prince in her class, so she has.'

Tom's eyes opened like saucers. 'A little prince?' He drew in a huge breath. 'Oooh, Kathleen! Will I meet him?'

Kathleen gave him another hug. 'Aw, me darlin' boy, sure you've only to look in the mirror, so ye have.'

He pondered on that as his daddy got into the car and closed the door. Then he pondered on it as they pulled away, and when he waved cheerio to Kathleen, he was still pondering on her words. For the life of him though, he did not understand. How was he going to meet the prince if he looked in the mirror?

'All right, are you, son?' Harry thought him too quiet.

'Mmm.' The boy pondered a moment longer, then gave up and voiced a more important matter. 'Daddy?'

'Yes?'

'I wish Mammy was here.'

'I know you do, son.' Harry felt the boy's sadness. 'Sometimes, Tom, we want things we can never have. So, we just thank our lucky stars for the things we *do* have and we turn our minds to making other things happen in our lives. That way, we don't feel so bad any more.'

For a while, the boy was quiet. Then he leaned forward and touched Harry on the shoulder. 'Daddy?'

'Yes, son?'

'I'm glad I've got you, Daddy.'

Choked by a whole mingling of emotions, Harry pulled the car over to the kerb.

'Why have we stopped?' Tom wanted to know. 'Are we there already?'

'No, not yet.' Getting out of the car, Harry climbed into the back seat, where he took the boy into his arms and held him tight against him, his heart sore at the boy's childish innocence. 'I just wanted to hold you, and make sure that you know how very much you mean to me.'

Looking down into that small child's face, he felt oddly insignificant. 'You are the whole world to me, son,' he told the boy. 'You need never worry, because I'll always look after you. Just like Mammy wanted.'

'I'll look after you too, Daddy.'

'Not yet though, eh? Let's deal with one thing at a time. I'll get you to school and when school ends, Kathleen will be here to collect you. As I explained earlier, I've taken time off to bring you to school on your first day, and so I will have to work later tonight to make up for it.'

He brushed a stray lock of hair away from the boy's eyes. 'Like I say though, Kathleen will be here to take you home. Is that all right with you?'

Tom looked worried. 'Is Kathleen going to heaven like Mammy?'

Harry was shocked. 'Why do you say that?'

'She's going to the doctor. That's what Mammy did, and then she went away. I don't want Kathleen to go away.' His lips trembled.

'Ah, I see now.' Harry understood the boy's concern. 'When she told you she had to go to the doctor before she picks you up, she meant she was going to collect her tablets, that's all.'

'Why?'

'Because she has to watch her blood pressure.'

'Why?'

'Because when you get older, sometimes your body starts being a bit of a nuisance, and you need to take tablets to put it right. That's all it is, Tom. Nothing to worry about.'

The boy seemed relieved. 'I love Kathleen.'

'I know you do, son, and I love her too.'

'So, will you and Kathleen get married, and then she'll be my new mammy?'

Smiling, Harry had to look away. 'I don't think so, son.'

'Why not?'

'One day, you'll know why not.' Harry never failed to be touched by the boy's innocence, and the way children have of taking huge life-changes in their stride. 'Right now though, I'd best get you to school. We don't want you being late on your first day, do we, eh?'

Tom shook his head.

On arriving at the school, Harry took his son straight to the office. 'Oh, yes.' The secretary located Tom's name in her ledger. 'Tom Blake, first day.' Leaning over the desk, she smiled at him. 'Hello, young man. I'm called Miss Janet.'

'Hello, Miss Janet. I'm called Tom, and I'm five and a bit.'

Tom liked her straight off, with her round smiley face, bright lipstick and a ponytail of thick brown hair that swung when she turned her head.

'You can leave him with me now,' she told Harry. 'He'll be fine.'

So Harry said cheerio, and Tom frowned, but then Miss Janet took him by the hand and he went merrily away, though he did glance back once, as they went through the double doors to the assembly hall.

Harry waved, Tom smiled. The doors closed and he was gone.

Harry quickened his step along the corridors and down towards the outer doors. 'There you go, Sara.' Coming out into the fresh air he glanced up at the clear skies. 'Your little boy has started school. It's a great day for him, and we miss you so much.' He gave a sigh. 'He's growing so quickly, I expect it won't be too long before he'll be needing a new uniform.'

When the nostalgia began to creep in, he quickened his step, got into the car and was soon on his way to Jacobs' Emporium.

'Please don't be late collecting him, Kathleen,' Harry whispered as he slowed for the traffic-lights. 'He's bound to feel nervous after his first day.'

He felt confident that Kathleen would not be late though. Truth was, she had come to love young Tom as she might love her own child.

With that thought came another – so painful that he had to shut it out of his mind.

~

Judy was worried.

Having waved Phil off to work, she had bathed, shampooed, dried and brushed her hair and for the first time in ages, she had taken time to manicure her nails and pamper herself; not because she felt good, or because she wanted to make the most of herself but because a few days ago, her friend Pauline had wrenched a promise out of her.

Even now, with her two best dresses spread out across the bed, Judy continued to pace the floor in bare feet, agitated. Not sure what to do.

Throwing herself onto the dressing-table stool, she observed herself in the large oval mirror. Pauline was right. With the tip of her finger she traced the shadows underneath her eyes. She did look a mess! She noted the high cheekbones jutting out, and the sallow skin beneath, and she felt ashamed. 'You look old, and haggard. Who else but Phil would ever want you?' she murmured to herself.

Always in her mind and heart was the memory of her first love. '*Harry.*' Murmuring his name brought a sensation of pleasure; though there was also guilt and penance for what she had done to him – to them all.

'Where are you now, Harry?' she whispered. 'I wonder if you think of me now and then? Or have you managed to put me out of your mind for good and all? For your own sake, I hope you have.'

She heard herself saying it, but she didn't mean it, not for one second.

For a while longer she stared at herself in the mirror, before getting off the stool and pacing the floor again. 'No!' She punched her fists together. 'I *don't* want you to forget me! I need you to remember how it was between us. I need you to hold me in your heart till you draw your last breath! I want you to think of me, every time you feel down, and when you see a girl in the street who looks just a bit like me . . . think of me, Harry, like I think of you. What we had together was so special, you must never forget.'

A great longing came over her. She wished she had never been born. She wished with all her heart that she had not lied to Harry back then, when she was too young and too afraid of losing him. She so desperately wished that she had asked for his help instead.

So many times since that day, she had prayed for all the bad things to go away, but they never did. They never would, not for as long as she lived.

A kind of blinding rage coursed through her, towards life, and Phil, and even Harry, who she longed for every waking minute of every day. But he was gone. Here she was, lonely and desperate, and Harry was happy somewhere, with a new love and never a thought for her. The pain of it all was unbearable, and the rage all-consuming. 'Can you hear me?' Her voice rose to the rafters. 'Don't you dare forget me, Harry Blake! Don't you ever forget me!'

Grabbing the hairbrush, she threw it across the room. When it hit the wall with a resounding thud, she made no move to pick it up.

Inevitably, the tears began to fall. 'Love me, Harry,' she wept. 'Love me, because you loved me once . . . before you ever loved anyone else. You and me, Harry, we were meant to be. I loved you like I have never *ever* loved anyone in all my life. Oh, and love me, because like the fool I am, I threw it all away.' Sinking to the floor, she remained hunched against the wall. 'I'm so sorry. I was too young, and so afraid. Don't hate me for that.'

Emotionally spent, she sat quietly on the floor, allowing herself to go over that last scene with Harry, all those years ago. 'I remember how you looked, when I told you,' she whispered lovingly. 'I can still see the shock on your face.' She began to rock backwards and forwards. 'Harry Blake . . . Harry. My darling.'

Most of all, she remembered him walking away, his shoulders stooped, and his every step leaden and reluctant. Then afterwards, when she could no longer see him, she could still hear his footsteps going away into the distance, out of her life for always. Then the awful silence. Oh yes, she remembered that most of all.

'Was it really all those years ago?' she asked herself now. 'It seems like only yesterday.'

She took a deep breath and spoke from the heart. 'I hope

someone else has you now, Harry,' she murmured. 'I want you to be happy. I truly do.'

Scrambling up from the floor, she sat before the mirror. Taking up her make-up case, she applied a pinch of colour to her face, a smudge of mascara to disguise her tired eyes, and a soft pink lipstick that would lift the pallor of her face. Must be careful not to look like a cheap tart, she thought then gave a wry little laugh. 'Though Lord knows, I've earned the label over the years.'

While taking stock of herself, she looked down on her arms, at the jagged scars that told of her desperation after Harry was gone. Quickly now, she dabbed her finger into the jar of creamy foundation, tenderly stroking it into the marks, until they were hardly visible.

The jade-green dress was a good choice, with its long sleeves, little upright collar and fitted waist. Putting it on carefully, so as not to spoil her make-up, she then slipped her bare feet into the smart black shoes with slim heel and open toe.

Ready to face the world, and Pauline in particular, she stole a quick glance at herself in the mirror, thinking, I'd best be home before Phil gets back. He mustn't see me like this, or he's bound to think I've been with some other man.

She laughed, a wry, harsh sound, 'What other man would ever want me?'

Disillusioned, she grabbed her bag and hurried out the door.

As she came careering round the corner of Lord Street, the bus was already pulling in. Breaking into a run, she made it in the nick of time. Gasping and grumbling, she threw herself into the nearest seat. 'You're early!' she told the conductor, as he turned the handle of his machine and tore off her ticket.

'I'm not early.' The conductor was an old fella with a peaked cap and a runny nose. 'It's you that's late.'

Cuffing his nose with the edge of his sleeve, he chatted about this and that, and the fact that his wife had left him these past six years. 'Ran off with the bloody milkman of all people,' he grumbled. 'I wouldn't mind, but it's common knowledge how he's never been able to keep a woman, on account of his pecker's not up to scratch!'

With that he ambled away, leaving Judy collapsing with laughter the minute his back was turned.

After she'd composed herself, she concentrated on the reason for her errand, and wondered if Pauline would approve of the extra effort she had made with her appearance that morning.

She needn't have worried though, because Pauline was delighted.

When she saw Judy step off the bus, for one wonderful moment she saw the real Judy she had known was always there. Most times Phil preferred his wife without make-up, hiding her true loveliness behind frumpy clothes and a washed-out face. 'If you have a priceless diamond you don't flaunt it to the world, or they'll all be after it,' he once said.

Keeping Judy under wraps was his way of turning off any would-be admirers. That way he had her all to himself.

'My!' She looked at Judy and her happy smile said it all. 'Judy Saunders, you look a million dollars. Once we've been to the doctor's, I'll treat you to a bite to eat, and maybe even a new outfit.' Pauline had long wanted to dress Judy in nice clothes, but Phil was always there, watching, dictating.

When Judy's face fell at the mention of the doctor, Pauline felt the need to remind her of the real reason she was here. 'You need a pick-me-up, or some kind of tonic to put the twinkle back in your eyes,' she told Judy. 'You're still too thin and pale, even through all that make-up. Anybody else might not be able to notice, but I can.'

'I don't need to see a doctor,' Judy pleaded. 'I'll eat better – fruit and fresh stuff, and I'll make sure I go to bed earlier and not sit downstairs till all hours.' Going to bed meant having Phil all over her, and lately she had grown to loathe the very nearness of him.

'That's not good enough, my girl.' Pauline gave it to her

straight as always. 'I've heard it all before but this time, I'm not listening to you. First of all, the reason you don't eat like you should is because you're a bag of nerves. You're like a little bird picking and pecking, always waiting for Phil to have a go at you for something and nothing, and as for going to bed earlier, you know you won't, because the reason you stay downstairs is so he won't force himself on you. So don't you go giving me all that.'

She was adamant. 'You're not eating, and you're not sleeping. So no argument! I'm taking you to see the doctor and that's that.'

'But you just told me, I look great.'

'So you do.' Pauline was not letting her off that easily. 'I also said no one would ever know how pale and thin you are underneath all that paint and powder. *But I know!* So if you've made yourself up to fool me or the doctor, you can forget it. What's more, you made me a promise, and I mean to keep you to it. I don't want you fainting on me like that ever again.'

'I didn't faint,' Judy protested. 'I don't know what happened, but I did not faint!'

'Trust me, one minute there we were talking, then you went down like a ton of bricks, and for a good five minutes you were out to the world. You were still groggy, even after Alan and I got you through to the back room. So we're going to the doctor's as arranged, and no argument.'

Knowing how once Pauline had made up her mind, there was no changing it, Judy reluctantly agreed. All her make-up and pretty clothes had been in vain. She should have known. Pauline was not a woman who was easily fooled.

And neither was the doctor.

While Pauline remained in the waiting room, Judy was asked to go behind the screens, and partly undress.

On first meeting, Dr Morris could see little wrong with Judy, except maybe for her nervousness, though once he began his examination of her, he was more concerned. 'Are you a poor sleeper?'

'I suppose so, yes, Doctor.'

'Mmm.' He placed his stethoscope on various points across her back, listening and taking mental notes, then he was looking into her eyes, pulling the lower lids down, and now he examined her hands and nails, paying particular attention to the bases of her nails, which were unusually pale. 'Do you have a healthy appetite?' he asked.

From the answers she gave, he deduced that Judy neither ate nor slept well. He was also concerned that she flinched every time he was obliged to touch her.

He could not help but notice the scars about her arms; in spite of the fact that she had obviously tried to disguise them with make-up. It wasn't the first time he had seen self-inflicted wounds like this.

Examination over, he stepped back, 'Get dressed now, my dear. We'll have a chat when you're ready.'

When he left her there in the cubicle, Judy was visibly trembling. I should not have come here, she thought, frantically throwing on her clothes. I should never have listened to Pauline.

On emerging from the cubicle, Judy was asked to sit down. Sensing her nervousness, Dr Morris asked kindly, 'Do you mind if I call you,' he glanced at his notes, 'Judy, isn't it?'

Judy nodded. 'I don't mind.' All she wanted was to get out of there.

'Right then, Judy, let me give you the good news. Firstly, you appear to be in fair health, not given to any disease or illness that I can see.' Before she could speak, he went quickly on, 'although there are a few things I need to make you aware of.'

Taking off his spectacles, he laid them on the desk. 'I have to say, you do not weigh enough for your age and height. There is not an ounce of fat on your bones. More worryingly, you appear to be verging on being anaemic. Now this could be rectified by proper nutrition, enough sound sleep, and generally taking better care of yourself.'

'I will,' Judy was quick to assure him. 'From now on, I'll do what's necessary to take care of myself, I really will.' Hoping that was it, she gave a sigh of relief.

But Dr Morris was not yet done. 'There is one very important matter we have not yet discussed.' Reaching out to take hold of her hand, he pointed to the scars. 'Would you like to tell me about this?'

Judy was shocked. This was what she had been afraid of. When he concluded the examination without mentioning the scars, she assumed he had not noticed, especially after she'd gone to such pains to disguise them

'Well, Judy?' Releasing her hand, he waited.

Judy had never spoken of the scars to anyone – not to Pauline, not even to Phil when he asked her over and over, and had even grown violent when she refused to tell him.

Sensing her dilemma, the doctor nodded. 'It's all right,' he assured her. 'You don't have to talk about them if you don't want to.'

He began writing. 'I want you to follow this programme for two weeks, then I would like to see you again. I'm also prescribing a course of iron, to counteract the anaemia.'

'It was a long time ago.'

Judy's quiet statement caused him to stop writing and look up. He didn't speak. He simply waited for her to go on, though it seemed an age before she spoke again.

'There was . . . trouble.' She bit her lip, the fear like a huge presence inside her. 'I upset my family, and they threw me out.' Ashamed, she looked away.

Leaning back in his chair, the doctor silently willed her to go on.

'I was . . . very young. It was difficult. I caused a lot of trouble.' She could not bring herself to explain exactly what she meant by that. 'Afterwards,' she paused; it was almost as though she was back there, in that shocking situation, 'I couldn't be on my own any more, so I stayed with people of the streets. I went with anyone who would have me. One day,

I was all alone in this place, and I didn't want to live any longer.'

Wiping away the tears, she hid her face from him. 'It was not a nice place,' she revealed in a small voice. 'People had been in there. People like me, with nowhere else to go. The ceiling was hanging down, and some of the windows were broken . . . glass everywhere.'

Taking a moment to breathe deeply, she never once looked at the doctor. 'The people were long gone, but you could still feel them all around you. It was cold and dark . . . so dark.'

She shivered, feeling that same, bitter cold. For a moment it was as though the dark enveloped her. 'I found some long pieces of glass.' When, for the first time, she looked up at the doctor, her expression told its own sorry tale. 'You see, I had nothing at all. There was no one to care.' She shrugged her shoulders. 'I didn't want to go on.'

As she spoke, she felt strangely relieved. She wanted him to know how bad it had been; even though he could never understand.

'That night, someone found me – a tramp, I'm not really sure. They got me to hospital, where I was stitched up and kept in for a few days. They said I should talk to the welfare worker, but I begged them to send for my sister Nancy instead.'

The doctor had a thought. 'Was it your sister who made the appointment today?'

Judy shook her head. 'No.'

'So, did she come to you . . . your sister Nancy?'

Judy nodded. 'Yes. But then it was worse.' The memories were so vivid. 'I should never have asked her to help me!'

'Why do you say that?'

She almost told him, but then the enormity of it all stopped her from going on.

Horrified that she should have burdened the doctor with all of that, Judy suddenly clammed up. 'Thank you for seeing me,

Doctor Morris.' Getting up out of the chair, she told him sincerely, 'I really will try and look after myself better in future.'

Disturbed by her story, the kindly GP told her, 'It sounds like you've had a rough time of it. But you've come through whatever it was that set you off on the wrong foot.' His smile was encouraging. 'I had a friend once who used to say, "When you fall, the only thing to do is get up again".'

Judy smiled. 'He's right. But it isn't easy.'

'I know, but it can be done, if you really want it.'

When she gave no reply, he tore off the prescription and brought it round to her side of the desk. 'Certain things can haunt a person for ever,' he suggested gently. 'We might think we're in control of a situation, but often the situation is controlling us.'

Surprised, Judy looked up at him. That was right! She suddenly realised. That was it!

'I can see you know what I'm getting at,' he went on. 'If you don't seek help, you may never get over what it is that troubles you.' When he saw the tears threaten, he gave a slow, encouraging smile. 'All right, my dear. That's all I wanted to say.'

Handing her the prescription, he announced, 'The receptionist will make your next appointment for you now, before you go running off.'

Judy thanked him again, before going out to Reception, where she waited for her appointment.

As soon as they got outside, Pauline was eager to know how she had got on. 'Well, what did he say? And don't go skimming over the bits that you didn't like.'

Judy tutted. 'What makes you think there were bits I didn't like?'

'I know you, that's why. So, come on, what did he say?'

Judy relayed the conversation between herself and Dr Morris; although she kept back the bit regarding the scars on her arms, and the things she had confided in him. 'He wants to see me again in two weeks' time.'

'Good!' Pauline was pleased that at long last Judy was getting the expert guidance she desperately needed. 'Meantime, make sure you do as he's told you. Put on some weight, and get the colour back in your cheeks.'

Judy promised she would.

'I'll be watching you,' Pauline threatened. 'I'll be right behind you every step of the way – but not like Phil does, so don't worry!'

Feeling more relaxed now, Judy threaded her arm through the pub landlady's. 'It wasn't half as bad as I thought it would be.'

'Well, there you go, then. I told you it would be all right, but you always think the worst. Now that you know it's just you neglecting yourself, you can do something about it, can't you?'

Judy gave her a peck on the cheek. 'Thanks, Pauline. You're a good friend.'

'I know.'

Judy laughed out loud. With Pauline, what you saw was what you got.

They walked arm-in-arm as far as the bus stop, where Judy asked Pauline if she wanted to go to the café. 'Now that it's all over, I feel peckish,' she said. 'A cup of tea and a bit of cake would go down a real treat.'

'Sorry, Judy, I can't,' Pauline explained. 'We've got the brewers' man arriving in about half an hour and Alan will need me there. Look, you go and have your snack, and I'll see you later, eh?'

'I won't enjoy it half as much without you.' Judy had a thing about going out on her own. She wondered if it harked back to when she was just a slip of a girl roaming the streets, not knowing who or what might be waiting round every corner.

'You'll be absolutely fine,' Pauline told her, with a mischievous glint in her eye. 'If anybody nicks your cake, just you tell me, and I'll hunt the buggers down!'

Yet again, she had Judy laughing. 'All right then. Bye, Pauline. I'll see you later.'

Judy watched her get on the bus, before striding away in the direction of the High Street, where she meant to enjoy a much-needed cream cake, with a piping hot cup of tea, come what may.

Suddenly she found herself changing direction, walking down Midland Road and on towards the church. There was no particular reason why she should do that, because she had asked for sanctuary and forgiveness many times after what happened. Yet she had still not found the peace she craved.

Now though, she had a pressing urge to say thank you. For some inexplicable reason, she felt she had been given a second chance.

For a long time now, she had been thinking of leaving Phil and moving where he would never find her.

Maybe the time was nearer than she thought, and all she needed was strength and guidance from above.

Going in through those heavy doors was like entering a secret place. The first thing that struck her was the biting cold that went with yawning spaces and high ceilings. And the emptiness.

She knew about emptiness, because she had been in too many derelict places. In the church though, it was different. There was a welcoming atmosphere, whereas in her previous experience of empty places, there was nothing. No hope. No one to hear you. Just the clinging cold, and a crippling silence.

Making the sign of the cross, she went to the far side where the candles flickered beneath a statue of the Virgin Mary. Looking up at that gentle face, she told of her deep unhappiness, and of how she was married to a man she feared. 'I know I should leave him,' she prayed. 'I know I should have the strength to stand up to him, but I can't. You know I want to. But I'm afraid.'

Delving in her purse, she took out two coins and a small box of matches. Dropping the coins into the container beneath the shelf, she then collected a candle and placed it in the holder. Striking the match, she put the flame to the wick. She then returned to the main body of the church, where she located the nearest pew to the altar.

When she knelt, the cold of the timber struck through her knees and made her shiver. She bowed her head in reverence, before gazing up at the crucified body of Christ. 'I never meant to be bad,' she murmured. 'Nancy once told me that I was born bad, but I wasn't. How can anyone be born bad? You would never let that happen, would You?' Oh Lord, forgive me for the things I've done. Help me to be good.'

In the back of her mind, she could hear the doctor's kindly words: '*If you don't seek help, you may never get over what it is that troubles you.*' And she was troubled, more than anyone would ever understand.

There were things – bad things – that she had never related to anyone. Things that had ruined her childhood; awful things that would haunt her all her life.

In the beginning, they were not to do with Harry. They had happened long before Harry became her sweetheart. He never suspected, and she never talked of it to him. There was someone else, whose name she could not even speak, for if she did, it would make it all real again, and she had spent too many years trying to rid her mind of that name, that face, and what happened to her.

Yet in the silence of the church, with a unique presence of calm around her, she now opened her heart to the Almighty.

She told of when it all started. She explained how she felt lost and frightened, and when Harry came along, he was her saviour, and oh, how she had grown to love him.

Then it all went wrong. 'I lied because I didn't know what else to do,' she confessed to the figure on the cross. 'I thought it would be all right, but I didn't think things through. I wanted to be safe. I thought Harry would protect me, but he found out I lied, and he didn't understand . . . nobody did. I could never tell anyone the truth, not even Harry. It was all *my* fault – not Harry's.'

When it now came flooding back, she could hardly bear it. 'At one point, I wanted to tell Nancy everything. I needed to ask her help, but I knew she would blame me. Whenever anything went wrong, she *always* blamed me!'

The pictures in her mind told a sordid story. 'Nancy would never have believed me anyway.' Even so, Judy had a sneaking suspicion that Nancy already knew, but she could not be sure.

'I tried to tell her once, but she slapped me hard and told me to shut up.' Judy involuntarily put her hand up to her face. 'Why was she so angry?' Judy had always wondered about that.

She had suspected that her sister knew more than she was prepared to admit, but when Judy tried to confide in her, Nancy accused her of lying, and said that if she told anyone else, no one would ever believe her. She claimed that Judy must be crazy; that if she kept on saying things like that, she would be 'locked away in a madhouse'.

Now, when she recalled how it was, Judy felt a sense of panic. *Was* she mad? It was true, there had been times when she had doubted her own sanity. With Harry, she had proved herself to be both a liar and a cheap tramp, so maybe she was really mad.

'NO!' She could hear her own voice, echoing in that holy place. 'Nancy was wrong. I'm not *mad*.' Clenching her fist, she hit the rail so hard that pain shot through her fingers. 'She was right about one thing though. I *was* born bad, I know it now.'

She looked at the figure on the cross again, and it was someone else to blame. '*You* made me bad, and now You have to make me good.' Choking with emotion, she pleaded, 'I *need* help. I need to feel alive.' Her sobbing reverberated throughout the church.

Entering the church, the young couple were shocked to hear such distress.

When a few seconds later, a tender hand touched Judy on the shoulder, she was visibly startled. 'Ssh!' The young woman slid her arm about Judy's shoulders. 'I'm sure He will help you,' she promised.

Deeply ashamed and humiliated, Judy clambered up, and after whispering a garbled 'I should leave,' she ran, out through the door and across the car park, and hardly able to see for the tears flooding her eyes: she was fleeing down the street as though the very devil was on her heels.

Before she knew it, she was on the Boulevard, lost in a moving sea of shoppers. Nobody really noticed her. They were all too busy getting on with their own lives.

When Judy was too exhausted to go on, she sat on a bench and remained there for a while, broken and hurt, unable to believe that she had actually shouted in the church . . . may God forgive her.

After a time, she felt calmer, even thinking again of that pot of tea and cake. Slowly and tiredly, she began walking towards the High Street, and the little café opposite the bank. Nothing had changed though. The demons were still on her back, and Phil was there. He was always there!

Phil was her punishment.

CHAPTER THIRTEEN

Not too far away, having completed her shopping chores, Kathleen was headed for the Boulevard where she intended catching the bus back to Fisher's Hill. 'It won't be too long before I have to collect young Tom,' she said to herself. The thought of seeing him made her feel content.

Instinctively she found herself drawn to the young woman, a seemingly familiar slim figure, who was rushing towards the café.

'Good heavens above, it can't be!' She stopped and stared.

Judy? She craned her neck for a better look. No, that couldn't be her, she was far too thin.

All the same, curiosity made her turn and head for the café. She knew she'd not rest if she didn't find out.

A few minutes later, puffing and panting, Kathleen threw open the door of the café and ambled in. There was no sign of the young woman.

'Good day, and what might I get you?' The woman behind the counter looked to be in her forties, plump as a ripe apple, with a face to match.

Before Kathleen had even taken off her coat, she was right there, armed with a menu and in an irritatingly high-pitched voice, explaining the specials for the day. 'We've got homemade stew, meat pie and chips, a late breakfast with choice of sausage, bacon, egg and—'

'Bejaysus!' Kathleen stopped her short. 'Will ye let me get inside the door before you start gabbling on about sausage an' bacon and other such nonsense. Sure, all I want is a cuppa tea and a cream slice!'

The woman was taken aback. 'Oh madam, I'm very sorry. I thought—'

'Ah well, ye thought wrong, so ye did.' Taking off her coat, Kathleen threw it over the back of the chair. 'I'd like me tea good an' strong, with two sugars and the smallest drop o' milk.'

'Right away.' Already unnerved, the waitress recited as she went, 'Strong tea with two sugars and a wee drop o' milk. Cream slice to go with it. Got it!'

She had only just got to the counter when Kathleen caught up with her. 'Did ye see a young woman come in here?'

'When?'

'Only a few minutes back, just before me?'

'Er, a young woman . . . ?'

'Jaysus, Mary and Joseph, what's wrong with ye?' Weary from traipsing about the town, Kathleen was growing short on patience. 'Did you see a young woman come in, or did you not?'

'I've an idea she went straight to the toilet,' the woman answered timidly.

Kathleen gave a sigh of relief. 'Thank you. That's all I wanted to know.' Grateful for small mercies, she plodded back to her table and sat down, her gaze securely fixed on the toilet door.

It seemed for ever, when in fact it was only minutes before Judy came out, her head bent as she intently searched in her handbag.

Intrigued, Kathleen discreetly observed the young woman as she threaded her way in and out of the tables. There was something about her that touched a chord with Kathleen, but she wasn't altogether certain it was Judy, because this young woman was painfully thin and stooped at the shoulders, where Judy as a girl had been more shapely, and always carried herself upright.

Disappointed, Kathleen decided that she must have been

mistaken. Yet, there was something uniquely familiar about the woman . . . She wondered if she should call out or go over to her table, but then she worried that she might make a fool of herself.

It was when the young woman looked up that Kathleen's heart skipped a beat. Though the face was gaunt, and the soft grey eyes troubled, there was no doubt in Kathleen's mind that the young woman really was Judy.

Kathleen remembered looking into those same wonderful eyes many years ago, when Judy had turned to her for help, and she knew without a doubt that this woman was one and the same.

Judy!' Scrambling out of her chair, she hurried towards her. '*I* wasn't sure,' she was so excited she began gabbling, 'I thought it might be you, and then I thought it couldn't be . . . oh Judy! What have ye done to yerself? You're so thin! Oh Judy, me darlin', wherever have ye been all this time?'

When Judy heard her name being called out, her first thought was that Phil had paid someone to follow her. Convinced that she was in for another beating, she hardly dared look at the person crossing the room towards her. Instead she darted for the door, but Kathleen was there first and now she was saying things, and Judy was not afraid any more.

Judy felt the years rush away. In her mind, she was a frightened young girl, sitting in Kathleen's parlour, talking of Harry, and how he had gone away and left her with money for an abortion. Making no judgements, Kathleen had guided and comforted her. Judy realised then, as now, that she owed a great deal to this lovely, caring soul who had befriended her when there was no one else.

Back then, afraid and unsure, she had foolishly turned away, but she would not turn away this time, because more than ever, she desperately needed friends.

When Kathleen stood before her, tears twinkling in her eyes and arms open to enfold her, Judy fell into those warm, chubby arms and she felt that at long last, she was not alone any more.

'Oh, Kathleen,' she clung to her. 'I'm sorry.' She kept saying it over and over. 'I'm so sorry, Kathleen.' Kathleen led her back to the table, where the two of them sat down, although Kathleen could not let go of her hand. 'Judy, Judy.' She shook her head in disbelief. 'Sure it does me old heart good to see you again.'

Kathleen noted how gaunt and ill the young woman looked. 'I want you to tell me everything,' she requested sternly. 'I want to know where you went after you left me, and why you never got in touch. I need to know that you've been safe and well, and that everything is all right,' though she could see that Judy was extremely nervous, and not in the best of health.

In a fog of excitement and disbelief, it struck Judy how strange it was that just after she had been to the church and prayed for help, Kathleen should suddenly appear.

With emotions high, and her troubles still weighing her down, Judy wept openly without fear or shame.

For a time, unable to speak or even to look up, Judy held onto Kathleen's hand so tightly that the little woman could feel her fingers going numb. She made no comment, however. Instead she remained there, with Judy's hand in hers, and a comforting arm about her shoulders.

It was painfully obvious that Judy had been through hard times, and all Kathleen wanted now was to help her as best she could. If only Judy would let her.

From the counter the waitress watched this emotional reunion and she was made to wonder how the Irishwoman could be so downright grumpy one minute, and in the next so gentle and and caring. Just goes to show, she thought, and chose the biggest cream slice. A person may seem like a trouble-maker, but underneath lies a good, kind heart.

Her attitude towards Kathleen had changed from the minute she saw her take charge of the young woman who, judging by her sorry appearance, desperately needed someone to love her.

Filling the tray with Kathleen's order, the waitress instinctively included another pot of tea and a nourishing buttery teacake. 'I hope you don't mind, but I thought your friend might want something,' she told Kathleen as she placed the items on the table.

'That's very thoughtful of you,' Kathleen said with a smile. 'Is that all right with you, Judy? Or would you prefer something else?'

Judy shook her head. 'No, that's fine.' Smiling up at the waitress, she said quietly, 'Thank you so much.'

'You're very welcome, I'm sure.'

As the waitress went away, she thought how pretty Judy was. All it needs is a bit o' fat on them bones and a good meal down her, and she'd look quite attractive, she thought, and at that moment, she made a promise to herself. 'No more nibbling while I'm working. It's time *I* started taking more care of *my*self. When I get home tonight, I'm clearing out everything that's not good for me. I might keep hold of the old fella though.' She gave a naughty chuckle. 'He's still got his uses. Anyhow, they do say as how a little "energetic exercise" helps to get the weight off.'

What she had in mind had nothing to do with exercise and was more to do with slap and tickle, and the idea of it put a spring in her step.

Just then a young man entered the café, and not far behind him a couple arrived wanting a full meal, and soon the café began to fill, and she was run off her feet.

In the far corner, Kathleen and Judy remained deep in conversation.

Judy brought Kathleen up to date with what had gone on in her life. 'I'm so glad I came to see you that second time,' she told Kathleen. 'I will be forever grateful that you talked me out of having the abortion. I don't know how I could even have considered it in the first place.'

Kathleen nodded. 'You were afraid, that's all.' She glanced

about the room. 'I suppose the child is all grown-up and out at work?'

Judy discreetly changed the subject. 'Babies grow up and time marches on, Kathleen, you should know that,' was all she said. 'I mean, look how the years have flown away since I last saw you.'

Kathleen gave a slow, understanding nod of the head. 'Funny, I always forget how time flies.'

Secretly relieved that, for the moment, she had been able to move the conversation away from her child, Judy confessed. 'Oh well. Life hasn't exactly been a bed of roses, but I've managed to survive.'

Sensing that Judy was holding back on many truths, Kathleen gently chided her. 'Why did you never come back, as you said you would? When you and the family moved away, I had no idea where to look for you.'

She relived the experience. 'Time and again, I trawled the length and breadth of Bedford, Bletchley, and even Leighton Buzzard. I was so worried about you, Judy.'

The girl was silent for a moment, before telling her in a quiet voice, 'You were right.'

'What do you mean? In what way was I right?' But Judy seemed not to be listening. Instead she was constantly glancing at the door, as though expecting someone to walk in on her. 'What's up, love?'

'Mmm?' Swinging about, Judy apologised. 'Sorry, I was miles away.'

Kathleen recognised the signs. 'Is there a problem? Someone you're afraid of seeing?'

'No, of course not.' Judy now gave Kathleen her full attention. 'What makes you say that?'

'Just that you seem like a cat on hot bricks. If there is something wrong, I may be able to help, Judy. Remember that.'

'Thank you. Anyway, you were saying, you looked everywhere and couldn't find me?' Again she had her eyes on the door, agitatedly chewing her thumbnail.

'That's right. It was as though you had disappeared off the face of the earth – until, some long time afterwards, I heard different people saying that you and Phil Saunders had got married.'

Judy guessed what was going through Kathleen's mind. 'You disapprove, don't you?'

Kathleen denied it, even though it was true. It was obvious to her that Phil had always fancied Judy; he envied Harry because she preferred him. Moreover, there had been rumours about Phil's erratic behaviour, with the drinking and the fighting, and folks predicting that he would end up killing himself one day – or somebody else.

'I don't have the right to approve or disapprove,' she answered warily. 'It's just that . . . well, to be honest, I can't help but wonder if you let him persuade you into getting together, because Harry was gone and you were vulnerable. Someone like Phil Saunders might take advantage of the situation, that's all I'm saying.'

'Maybe you thought that if I couldn't have Harry, Phil was the next best thing. Is that it, Kathleen? Is that what you really thought?'

Kathleen was mortified. '*No*! No, I don't think that at all.'

Judy was instantly contrite. 'I'm sorry,' she said. 'I don't know what's wrong with me. I get so jumpy all the time.'

Kathleen had something else on her mind. 'If I ask you a question, will you be honest with me?'

'I hope so.' The way things were, Judy could promise nothing.

'Are you and Phil still together?'

'Yes.'

'Do you truly love him?' Kathleen rephrased that, because in truth she was sure that Judy had never loved Phil in the first place. 'What I mean is, are you happy?'

Judy's answer was deliberately vague. 'Why wouldn't I be? When Phil caught up with me, I was wild . . . completely out of control, sleeping in the streets or in the house of anyone who would have me.'

'You really should have come to me!' Kathleen was angry.

'I didn't think about that. You see, after Harry left, I didn't care whether I lived or died. Nothing was the same.' With tears in her eyes, she admitted, 'If Phil had not taken me under his wing, who knows where I might have ended up.'

Kathleen had something else playing on her mind.

'Did you tell him that the child was Harry's?' She was made to wonder how Phil Saunders had accepted the truth that Judy and Harry had made a child together. It was even more amazing to Kathleen that Phil would be prepared to raise a child that Harry and Judy had made as his own, simply to get Judy to marry him.

Kathleen apologised. 'I'm sorry. I don't mean to be nosey,' she assured her. 'It's just that, well, knowing how Phil used to be, with regards to you and Harry, so jealous, and always after stealing you away, I can't help but wonder how he took the news about the child, that's all.' Struggling with guilt, Judy took a moment to answer Kathleen's question. She had promised to be truthful and so she was; though she had not promised to tell the *whole* truth. She could never do that: not to Kathleen, not to anyone.

As though reading her thoughts, Kathleen addressed her in a whisper. 'Forget what I said, Judy. Sure, you don't have to tell me anything if you don't want to.'

'I do want to.' Here was a friend she had neglected for too long; someone who had helped her over the worst episode of her life and now, because she had not thought to confide in Kathleen before today, she was torn between truth and shame.

She quickly eased Kathleen's mind. 'There is absolutely nothing for you to concern yourself about. We're absolutely fine, both me and the child. It was difficult at first, but now everything has turned out all right.'

The older woman was relieved. 'Sure, that's all I needed to know,' she confirmed. 'I'll rest easier now, so I will.' Though she had never condoned it, Kathleen was beginning to understand more and more, why Harry had walked out. 'So, you really did know all along that Harry could have been prosecuted?'

Judy took a moment. 'Yes. I'm truly sorry.'

'At a time when he was still grieving for his parents?' Kathleen had never understood how someone as gentle and thoughtful as Judy, could hurt Harry in such a way.

Judy's guilt enveloped her. 'I knew all that, but at first it didn't seem to matter. I was desperate, Kathleen. I had no choice – I didn't know what to do. There was no one to help . . .'

Seeing the look on Kathleen's face, she realised she had said too much. 'I'm sorry. I know Harry was like a son to you, and I know I was wrong to do what I did, but it's done now, and I don't want to talk about it any more.' She was visibly trembling.

'Ssh!' Leaning forward, Kathleen took hold of Judy's two hands and made them be still. 'Look at me, love.'

Raising her head, Judy looked up at her.

'I just want to help, that's all,' Kathleen said very gently.

'I know, but you can't help. Nobody can.'

'Trust me, Judy. There is always help. All we have to do is look for it.'

Afraid, Judy grew silent.

Undeterred, Kathleen persisted, 'Just now, what did you mean when you said you had no choice, that you didn't know what to do, and that there was no one else?'

Judy was emphatic. 'I didn't mean anything! I was all mixed up, just like I was with Harry.'

Thankful that the other diners were busy with their own conversations and so were not aware of herself and Judy, Kathleen lowered her voice to a whisper. 'You said you would tell me the truth.'

'I have!'

'Please be honest with me, Judy. *Was there someone else involved?*' She hardly dare let herself think it. 'Tell me. Trust me.'

'Tell you what?' Judy was beginning to panic. 'I've told you all I can.'

'Well, I have the feeling you're holding back; that there *is* something else, something that you find hard to deal with, and that's why you were so desperate, why you needed help – *and* why there was no one there.'

Seeing the rush of tears to the wan young woman's eyes, her fears were confirmed. Instinctively, she cradled Judy's face with the palms of her hands, as she might do to a child. 'Putting the business of Harry aside for the minute. I reckon you were hurt long before that, and now I believe you can't get it out of your mind. Isn't that so, me darlin'?'

And then, when Judy remained silent, into Kathleen's fertile mind crept all manner of unthinkable things. 'Sure, I can't help you if you don't tell me.'

'There was nothing!' Having raised her voice, Judy was acutely aware of people looking. But the passing curiosity of strangers was nothing compared to the fear she had learned to live with all these years.

'Ssh now,' Kathleen calmed her. 'It's all right. I won't ask you again, me darlin'. Just know that I'm here, if you need a friend.'

Judy so desperately wanted to tell her everything, but the secret was too awful. She had promised herself long ago that she must never reveal it to a soul.

Kathleen had sensed enough, but not all of it. 'Like I say, I won't ask you again, but I hope you will come to me whenever you feel ready.' Although if the truth was what she suspected, it would have to be brought out into the open, and when that happened, there were bound to be serious repercussions.

Having composed herself, Judy confessed, 'All I wanted was for Harry to love me . . . as if we were husband and wife.' Cleverly twisting the truth in order to satisfy Kathleen's dangerous instincts, she went on convincingly, 'There was nothing else. I loved Harry too much, that's all.'

She felt deeply ashamed. She had told Kathleen the truth, just as she had promised – yet had left out a huge chunk of it.

What she had deliberately omitted was the reason *why* she needed Harry to make love to her; and she could never do that without hurting other people.

While Kathleen had convinced herself that Judy was not telling the entire truth, the girl was now saying: 'You know how much I loved Harry. I have never loved anyone else like that, and never will. Every minute of every day since he's been gone, I've missed him more than he could ever know.'

'So you're married to Phil, but you still love Harry, is that it?' Little did Judy know that Harry was now living with *her* – at the house in Fisher's Hill. Kathleen too had things to hide. Should she tell Judy? Kathleen wasn't sure.

Judy merely nodded, but the smile on her face told its own story.

'So why do you stay with Phil?' Kathleen burst out. 'Is it for the child's sake? Is it because you have nowhere else to go? Because if that *is* the reason, we can go back to your place and pack a few things right now. You can move in with me. Would you like that?' She would tell her about Harry – she would have to, now.

'I can't!' The stark realisation of what Phil would do if she ever walked out on him, made Judy tremble. 'Thank you all the same, Kathleen, but I can't do that.'

'Why not? What's to stop you? And besides, you just said yourself that you don't love Phil. It's Harry you love, isn't that right?'

'I've never loved Phil. It's always been Harry, right from the first.'

'Yet you're hellbent on staying with Phil. So, is it for the child's sake?'

'In a way, yes, I suppose it is.' That was true enough, because though she had deliberately kept Phil in the dark, he watched her every move, listened to her every conversation, and was never satisfied with anything she told him. Consequently, he still had it in him to wreak havoc, for her and others, and more importantly, for the child.

Judy could not let that happen, even if it meant that for the rest of her miserable life, she had to put up with Phil's jealousy and violence.

'Judy, please listen to me.' Kathleen had seen the girl's dilemma written in her face, and in the frantic way she was twisting her napkin round and round in her hands.

Having now got Judy's full attention, she went on, 'I've already promised not to ask what it is that you're holding back, and I will keep my promise. However, I do know there is something, and whatever it is, it will surely go on torturing you, unless you find the courage to speak out. You may feel there is nothing to be done about it, but there is always a way.'

She paused, allowing all of that to sink in, then went on, 'All I'm asking is that you think about what I'm saying, and when the day comes that you just can't live with it any more, you must come to me, and I promise hand on heart, I'll do all in my power to help you.'

She leaned forward to look into the girl's face, hoping that she might extract a promise. 'So, Judy me darlin', will you at least do that for me?'

Judy shook her head emphatically. 'No, I can't. I've already said too much.' She quickly went on to stress that she was content enough in the life she was leading. 'Me and Phil have been together a while now, and yes, we have our little tiffs, but they're no more serious than anyone else's,' she lied, 'so you're not to worry.'

The last thing she wanted was for Kathleen to get involved. She had learned to her cost what an unpredictable and violent man her husband was.

Choosing her words carefully, Kathleen now changed tack. 'If Harry was here right now,' she said quietly, 'what would you do?'

The mere thought of Harry made Judy's heart soar.

If Harry was here, she would run to him and plead for him to take her back, to forgive her. She would tell him how much she needed him, and that she would love him till her dying day. She would open her heart to him, and tell him how her life was a living hell, and that because of her, the child was gone for ever. She would admit that she was little more than a slave to Phil Saunders and how she didn't care what happened to her, because she was finished and worthless, and there was really no point in living any longer.

She would tell him things she had never told anyone else – the real reason why she had lied to him. She would hold nothing back; instead she would do what she should have done long ago . . . she would put her trust in Harry with all her heart and soul.

Yes! That's what she would do, and then she would throw herself on his mercy.

Kathleen's next words struck her to the heart.

'He came back, Judy,' Kathleen whispered. 'Harry came back, and now he's staying with me.'

Struck silent and hardly able to breathe, Judy reeled back in her chair.

She felt Kathleen's hand on hers, and heard the Irish voice soft and reassuring in her ear. 'Sure he's been through a terrible time lately,' she was saying. 'He has a son Tom, aged five, just started school.' And the last piece of information. 'As soon as he stepped out of the car, he was asking after you.'

Hardly able to believe what Kathleen was telling her, Judy's heart was pounding so fast, she thought it would burst right out of her chest.

'He's got a job at Jacobs' store, opposite the prison,' Kathleen went on. 'As soon as he can get sorted, he means to buy a place for himself and young Tom; he has the money from the sale of his own house, after . . .' She shook her head. 'Y'see, me darlin', Harry's wife passed on two months since. From what he tells me, she was poorly for a long time. There was nothing they could do for her.'

Moving on from that sorry business, she informed Judy,

'So there ye have it! After all this time, Harry Blake has come home to his roots. He means to build a new life for himself and young Tom. I told him he could stay with me for as long as he likes.' She smiled. 'He hasn't changed much. He's still as handsome as—'

She was amazed when Judy scrambled out of the seat and started gathering her bag and coat. 'I have to go!'

'Judy! What are you doing?' Desperate, Kathleen urged her to stay and talk. 'We have so much catching up to do, and now that Harry's back, you can maybe meet up. This is your chance to put matters right, Judy . . . you and Harry.'

She caught hold of the girl's arm. 'Please, me darlin' – won't you stay a wee while longer?'

Kathleen had always known these two people were meant for each other. 'What if I told you that Harry is riddled with guilt at having left you?' For a moment, she managed to keep Judy there. 'He still loves you,' she confided. 'Sure it's as plain as day, the man still has deep feelings for you. Make it right between you, Judy. Let him tell you what's in his heart, why don't ye?'

For a long moment it seemed as though Judy would consent to do just that. Then suddenly she was rushing away. 'I have to go,' she called back. 'I'll be in touch.'

She fled across the café and out the door, and was quickly gone from sight, leaving Kathleen stunned by Judy's reaction. 'I should never have told her,' she chided herself. Seeing the waitress approach, she began fumbling for her purse in order to pay the bill. 'Silly old fool that I am. It was too soon. Far too soon.'

The waitress was quickly by her side. 'Would you like anything else?'

Unsettled by Judy's rapid departure, Kathleen asked, 'Do you sell brandy?'

'Sorry, no, we don't have a licence to sell spirits.'

Kathleen groaned. 'Ah, well now, that's a great pity, so it is.'

'So, will there be anything else then?'

'Aye, go on with ye, I'll have another strong pot of tea . . . oh, and one o' them fine Bakewell tarts I saw behind the counter, thank you.'

Whenever she was upset or angry, she had a tendency to make for the sweet things. Besides, she was in no hurry to get to Tom's school. She had a great deal to think about.

The thing was . . . should she tell Harry that she had bumped into Judy? Or should she let sleeping dogs lie?

For the first time in an age, she searched her bag for that elusive little tin of brown snuff. Having found it, she then tapped the lid to loosen the snuff inside; she opened the lid, and with the tip of her finger and thumb, pinched out a wee helping of the brown stuff. Just as the waitress started her way over with the order, Kathleen quickly rammed the snuff up her nostrils, whereupon she began sneezing, fit to die.

'Oh my goodness.' The waitress was concerned. 'Would you like a glass of water?'

'No, I would not!' Kathleen could not even remember the last time she had drunk water. 'The tea will be fine,' she declared, with the discipline of a sergeant-major. 'I'll thank you not to offer me the water again, if ye don't mind.'

While the waitress went away with a smile on her face, Kathleen proceeded to pour out her tea, adding the usual minuscule drop of milk and four spoonfuls of sugar. After the first deep gulp of the soothing drink, she got to thinking.

'Those two should be together,' she decided. 'The question is, what is it that Judy is hiding? What is she so afraid to tell?'

Her thoughts turned to Phil. 'How can we be rid of that divil-man, Saunders?'

With Judy so adamant that she would not leave him, Kathleen could see only one way. 'We'll have to hit him over the head with a mallet.' Realising what she had said, she was now mortified. 'Oh, dear Lord above.' Frantically making the sign of the cross on herself, she groaned, 'The beast Beelzebub is already working his evil on me, so he is.'

Horrified at the prospect of a slow and merciless demise as her punishment, she took a huge bite out of her Bakewell tart and washed it down with a great gulp of tea – which had her coughing and choking again, and fighting to breathe.

Dutiful as ever, the waitress ran over with a glass of water. 'Take it away!' Kathleen wheezed. 'I'd rather choke than be poisoned, so I would!'

CHAPTER FOURTEEN

'I DO ENJOY the Sundays.' Harry had settled into Kathleen's cosy home as though he had never left it. 'I don't have to leap out of bed and rush off to work, trudging the streets in all weathers. It's good to take it easy and be with you and Tom.' He glanced out to the garden where Tom was playing. 'He loves it here,' Harry told Kathleen, 'and he loves you as much as I ever did.'

'Ah, well now.' Kathleen paused in her knitting. 'We all know why that is, don't we, eh?'

'We don't, but I'm sure you're about to tell me.' Harry so enjoyed these little banters between himself and Kathleen.

'It's because I make the best ginger biscuits in the world.' With her face beaming from ear to ear, she looked like a mischievous child.

Harry played along. 'You're absolutely right!' he exclaimed. 'That's what it is . . . the ginger biscuits.'

Folding her knitting, Kathleen laid it down and came to the kitchen window, from where Harry had been keeping an eye on Tom. 'I reckon he's got the makings of an athlete.' Harry gestured proudly to where Tom was leaping backwards and forwards over the flowerbed.

'Bejaysus! Will ye look at that!' It was not the first time Kathleen had seen Tom performing his 'athletic' skills; but never over her precious flowerbed. 'Sure, he'd best not flatten my dahlias,' she warned hands on hips, 'or he'll have the makings of a thick ear, so he will!'

Banging on the window she called Tom inside. 'Get in here, ye little divil.' She crooked a finger at him. 'I've a new batch o' ginger biscuits straight out the oven. If ye don't hurry, me and yer father will eat the lot.'

While Tom ran towards the cottage, the telephone rang inside, making Kathleen almost leap out of her skin. 'Damn thing always takes me unawares,' she complained, waddling over to the sideboard where she snatched up the receiver.

'Who is it and what d'ye want?' Kathleen had a way with words. 'He's right here, yes. You stay there and I'll get him.' Holding out the big black receiver, she nagged at Harry, 'Will ye hurry up, there's a man here, wanting to talk with ye.'

Smiling to himself, Harry duly thanked her and took the receiver. 'Hello, Harry Blake here.'

There followed a short conversation, during which Harry nodded and agreed, then disagreed, and when he brought the conversation to an end, it was with a heartfelt 'Thank you. We'll talk again next week, yes, sooner I'm able to.'

'Who might that be then?' Kathleen was never backwards in coming forwards. 'Sure it wasn't trouble, was it? Only I thought the man seemed a bit sharpish, so I did.'

Harry was glad to explain. 'No, that's just his way. He always sounds a bit miserable, but he's a good man, and an even better gardener.'

'A gardener, you say?' That puzzled her.

'You recall I told you I'd managed to find someone to tend Sara's little garden in the churchyard, in between me being able to get back and see to it?'

Kathleen nodded acknowledgement. 'Of course – yes, I remember. So is everything all right?'

'Apparently there was a bit of a problem with the cross and bird-droppings. He thinks it needs to be moved from under the trees.'

He relayed the gardener's conversation. When emotion took hold, he paused a moment to reflect, thinking it strange how at times Sara seemed so very close, and other times he found it difficult to even recall her face. He thanked the Lord for the years he had shared with her on this earth, but in the same heartbeat he was angry that she had been taken so young.

When Kathleen saw him struggling with his feelings, she deliberately diverted his attention by giving him a little shake of the arm. 'Just look at what yer budding athlete is doing now, the little tyke.'

Harry looked up to see Tom splashing about in the puddle left by the recent shower. Dancing and thumping his feet in the water, Tom was sending up huge showers of dirty water, which covered him from top to bottom.

Harry tapped on the window. 'Tom! That's enough!'

Excited and laughing, Tom glanced up.

'What d'you think you're doing?' Harry demanded, 'Inside . . . now!'

The minute Tom got inside the door, his legs and torso drenched from feet to chest, Kathleen grabbed hold of him. 'Will ye look at the state of you!' Wrenching off his shoes, she told him to 'Take off the wet shirt and trousers. I'll be away upstairs and get you some clean ones.' Grabbing a towel from the sink-top, she wrapped it round his head, before marching off, loudly tutting, and pretending to be angry.

'Did you have fun splashing about in the puddle?' Seeing it from the boy's point of view, Harry gave a conspiratorial wink. 'I used to do that too.'

'Is Kathleen angry with me for getting all wet?' Tom handed his sodden clothes to his daddy. 'She was tutting. She always tuts when she's angry.'

Taking the towel, Harry dried his son off. 'She's not really angry,' he promised. 'As for the tutting, she can make herself tut any time she likes, just to fool you.'

261

Tom felt better for that, and when Kathleen returned with clean shirt and trousers, he had a wide grin on his face.

'Oh, I see.' Hands on hips, she demanded, 'So, d'ye mind telling me what's so funny?'

'Nothing.' Tom straightened his face.

'So why were you grinning then, eh?'

'I wasn't grinning.'

Kathleen stared down at him with her fiercest expression. 'Sure, I might be old in the tooth, but I'm not without a pair of eyes. You were grinning, so ye were, and don't think I don't know why.'

'How do you know?' Tom feared that Kathleen might have heard him and Daddy talking.

Raising her eyebrows, she gave Tom a kind of half-wink. 'I think you were grinning, because you fancy you got one over on me, isn't that so?' She wagged a chubby finger. 'Now come on, own up to it . . . you thought you'd got one over on me, did you not?'

The boy took a minute to consider that, and bold as you like he told her, 'I'm sorry.'

'Right! There ye go. The very minute me back's turned, dragging me poor oul' bones up them stairs, fetching clean dry clothes so you won't catch your death, you go laughing and grinning and poking the fun at poor Kathleen. Shame on youse!'

'I'm sorry, Kathleen. I am.' Tom hoped she would not start tutting again.

Seeing the boy's contrite face, and, out of the corner of her eye, Harry trying not to smile, Kathleen burst out laughing. 'Yer a pair of mischievous divils, so ye are!' She handed Tom the clean clothes. 'Soonever you've got them on, you can help yourself to ginger biscuits in the pantry – no more than two, mind. There are others in this house who love the biscuits beside yerself.'

'Bet I could eat them *all* if I tried!'

'Aha.' Kathleen's finger was wagging fifteen to the dozen. 'You'll have me an' yer father to deal with if ye do.'

When Harry nodded agreement, Tom laughed out loud and the atmosphere was magic. 'Go on then young Tom, get and help yerself to a couple before I decide to put them up where you can't reach!'

While the lad was helping himself to lemonade and two plump, golden ginger biscuits, Kathleen managed to steal Harry away into the garden.

'I bumped into a certain someone yesterday,' she quietly confided. 'A certain someone you've been desperately trying to find.'

'Judy!' Shocked and delighted, Harry was laughing and hurting all at the same time. 'You saw *Judy*?'

Her name came so naturally to his mind, especially after years of living with it, and then these past weeks he had made all kinds of enquiries regarding her whereabouts, but at every turn his efforts had come to nothing. He had even casually mentioned her name at the houses on his rounds. Same result. No one seemed to have heard of her.

Excited and thrilled, he was hardly able to believe that Kathleen had actually seen her. The questions poured out in a fast and furious torrent. 'How is she? Is she well?' Then, the most important question of all: 'Is she happy and content, that's all I need to know.'

Wisely avoiding a direct answer, Kathleen informed him, 'We didn't spend too much time together, just a kind of passing re-acquaintance. Judy was in a rush. She didn't say much, but I'm afraid I told her she was far too thin, that she needed to eat more.' Pursing her lips in that comical way she had, Kathleen slowly shook her head. 'She has sadly neglected herself, if you ask me.'

'What else?' Harry was hungry for news of Judy. 'Are you saying she looks ill? What do you mean, she's neglected herself?'

'It's nothing to concern ourselves about, I'm sure,' she replied reassuringly. 'Young women these days have a tendency to eat like sparrows. Apparently they think it makes them look glamorous.'

Kathleen was loath to tell him of her very real fears for Judy. But there was one thing he had to know, so she now told him as gently as she could. 'It probably isn't what you want to hear, but Judy has been married . . . to Phil Saunders . . . for a good many years.'

When his face fell, she did not have the heart to relay her belief that Judy was trapped in a hellish marriage; and that she lived in fear of her husband.

Indeed, the last thing she dared tell Harry was that his child had not been aborted after all, but as far as she could tell through Judy's scant conversation, was being raised by none other than his old rival, Phil Saunders, who appeared to have been kept in complete ignorance of the fact that the child's father was Harry Blake.

Nor could she speak of the other matter that had constantly nagged at her since seeing Judy again. Something about the nervous manner in which she fidgeted and fretted served only to strengthen Kathleen's long-held beliefs.

After all these years, the old suspicions had returned with a vengeance. Just as before, Kathleen instinctively felt there was more to Judy's childhood troubles than the latter was prepared to admit.

It all made sense.

Moreover, Kathleen suspected that Judy's, deceiving Harry into taking their budding relationship that one step further, had had more to do with someone else than with Harry himself.

She recalled Judy's words. *'I was desperate . . . there was no one to help me.'*

While Tom tucked into his ginger biscuits, Harry and Kathleen chatted about Judy; with Harry wanting to know every little detail. 'Did she say how she and Phil got together?'

'No.'

'Or where she was living?'

'Not a word, and I didn't think to ask,' Kathleen informed him. 'We were just catching up on the years. By the time we got round to more personal things it was time for her to rush away.'

Harry wondered, 'Do you think she might have rushed away on purpose?'

Kathleen had the very same impression, but did not relay her concerns to Harry. 'Why would she do that?'

He shrugged. 'I don't know. I wasn't there.' A thought occurred to him. 'Did you tell her that I was back?'

'I did, yes.'

'So, was it *then* that she decided to rush away?'

Kathleen answered honestly. 'Come to think of it – yes, I do believe it was.'

'So, was she excited, or did it seem not to matter that I was back?'

Kathleen gave her answer carefully. 'When I told her, she fell quiet . . . sort of turning it over in her mind. And yes, I would say she did seem pleased that you were back.'

That put a smile on Harry's face. 'I wish I'd been there. These past weeks, I've tried so hard to discover her where-abouts, all to no avail. Oh, Kathleen! It would have been so good to see her again.'

His mood darkened. 'You do realise, don't you,' he murmured, 'Judy and I . . . well, we still have unfinished business.'

'I do know, yes.'

Harry's determination to track Judy down was heightened by Kathleen's news. 'I feel much more hopeful, now that we know she actually stayed in the area.'

'Ah, but we don't know that for certain, do we, eh?' Kathleen pointed out. 'She might live miles away. She might have made this one trip, to visit her childhood haunts. Maybe it was a goodbye trip. Maybe she never intends coming back. Have you thought of that?'

Kathleen's main worry just now was Judy, of course, and Phil Saunders, whom she considered to be a bad lot.

As boys growing up, Phil and Harry were always healthy rivals, in football, tree-climbing, racing and swimming. There was nothing they did not compete for, the two of them both wanting to be the best, the first or the strongest. Then, when they got older and girls became a serious prize, the rivalry moved up a notch.

Judy moved into the street and from the very first, it was Phil who went after her. But it was Harry she chose, and from that moment the rivalry between Harry and Phil took a darker turn.

Phil had always been a brash, troubled boy, resentful of Judy's choosing of Harry over him. So what now? What if the troublesome boy had turned into an even more troubled man? What if he and Harry ever met face to face, and he thought Harry was back to lay claim to his childhood sweetheart?'

Kathleen was troubled enough to relay her fears to Harry. 'You know how Phil always felt about Judy,' she reminded him. 'Constantly hanging around, following the pair of youse, spying on youse. Like a fox waiting to pounce.'

Harry smiled. 'Kathleen O'Leary! What an imagination you have,' he chided. 'Phil was a mate, that's all. Okay, I'll agree he had a thing for Judy, and yes, he did sometimes lurk about, but it didn't really mean anything, other than he was a bad loser.'

'No, it was more than that.' Kathleen needed to make him see. 'The trouble with you is, you're far too trusting – always have been.'

Harry remembered. 'Obviously, more so with Judy than with Phil,' he remarked cynically.

'There is a huge difference between Judy and Phil Saunders,' Kathleen told him firmly. 'Judy may have had reasons we don't as yet understand, while Phil Saunders was always a born villain, out to get whatever he wanted, in whichever way possible.'

Harry was struck by Kathleen's hostility. 'I thought you liked him back then,' he said. 'What's made you change your mind? Was it something Judy said?' He bent his head forward and lowered his voice. 'Kathleen, please. If Judy said anything to you about Phil, I'd like to know. Did she?'

Kathleen shook her head.

'So, is there anything that Judy discussed with you, and that you haven't spoken of – anything you think I should know?'

'Oh, bejaysus, will you stop firing questions at me!' Kathleen sensed that she might treading on dangerous ground. 'If Judy said something I believe you should know, I would tell you, wouldn't I?'

Harry took a long look at her. 'I hope so,' he said, his voice serious. 'I sincerely hope you would not take it on yourself to keep things from me; things that affect Judy; things that might give me a clearer picture as to her wellbeing.'

Thankfully, before Kathleen was made to give an answer, Tom came running up. 'They've all gone!' He looked pale, his mouth ringed in crumbs and his cheeks puffed out as though he had a whole batch of ginger biscuits in there.

'Good Lord above!' Kathleen was horrified. 'You've never eaten the entire lot of them, have you?'

Tom grinned and nodded, then he threw up all over the floor; causing panic. 'Harry, quick! The mop and bucket are out the back!'

Grabbing Tom in her arms, Kathleen rushed him to the sink where she turned him upside down and patted his back, until in a mangled heap, the rest of the biscuits shot out of his mouth.

There followed a flurry of activity and another bout of sickness, before Tom was bathed, put into his pyjamas and secured in the armchair with a blanket tucked round him. 'I can't believe he ate all the ginger biscuits.' Harry finished cleaning the floor and sat with his son, while Kathleen dialled the local doctor.

'Well, it was either Tom, or The Invisible Man!' Kathleen declared. 'And I can't see anybody else being sick around here, can you?'

She listened, then she answered, then she listened again.

'Yes, I've done all that; and now he's washed and wrapped up warm as we speak.'

After a moment she replaced the receiver, advising Harry, 'We're to watch for him sweating too much, or getting too hot. Keep him wrapped up and a bucket under his head, and let him have as much water as he can drink.'

'You are never to do that again,' Harry chided. 'Do you understand?'

Tom nodded. 'All right, Daddy.'

Kathleen tutted and tutted. 'And there was me, thinking I might have a fresh-baked ginger biscuit with my hot cocoa tonight.'

'I'm sorry, Kathleen,' Tom moaned. 'I'm really sorry.'

'So am I,' she said, giving him a big hug. 'But it doesn't really matter. All that matters is that you're feeling better. Okay?'

Tom gave her a bright, winning smile. 'Okay!'

Later, when Harry came down from taking Tom up to bed, he fell exhausted into the armchair. 'Now then, where were we?'

'We were talking about Judy,' Kathleen answered. 'But as far as I'm concerned, the conversation has run its course, simply because there is nothing more I can tell you.'

'Are you absolutely certain about that?' Harry was not altogether convinced.

'Sure, haven't I already said so?'

Harry leaned back in the chair to consider Kathleen's comments. Pondering for a time, he went back on their conversation repeatedly, before sitting up again to announce, 'I can't leave it there. I won't rest until I find her and talk with her. Like I said, the two of us still have unfinished business.'

In the light of Harry's rigid determination to track Judy down, Kathleen made no comment, but there was a certain little instinct that constantly nagged at her and would not go away. It had to do with Judy's obvious anxiety. This was certainly connected with Phil Saunders, and possibly something else – *or someone else* – though Kathleen could not be sure.

In truth, she had no way of knowing the whole story.

One thing was certain though.

The more she recalled her meeting with Judy, the more that little instinct tugged at her conscience.

Someone, at some time, had messed with Judy's peace of mind. Someone cruel and cowardly from way back – even before Phil Saunders.

Certainly someone other than Harry!

CHAPTER FIFTEEN

RITA ROBERTS WAS out in the garden pruning the roses late one Friday morning when Mac arrived home early. That makes a nice change, she thought. As always, she was pleased to see him. Snipping off a withered rose, she dropped it into the wheelbarrow. Most days he was late home, or else he had to go off somewhere for days on end.

Parking his new Mercedes at the top of the drive, Mac swung himself out of the car and came across to his wife.

'What's this?' she asked. 'You're early. I didn't expect you home till this evening.'

Giving her a peck on the cheek, he looked at the piles of rose-cuttings both in the barrow and on the ground. 'What are you doing out here?'

'What does it look like?' She gestured at the well-manicured roses, all cut back and ready for a new season. 'I'm taking out all the dead stuff.'

'I can see that for myself.' A flash of irritation. 'What I meant was, isn't doing that supposed to be part of the gardener's duties?'

'There's a problem.' Collecting the basket and sliding it over her arm, Rita smiled up at the skies. 'Besides, it's such a lovely day, I thought it would be nice to spend some time in the garden.'

When Mac began strolling away towards the house, she went

with him. 'So what is this problem?' he asked. 'And why should it mean that you have to go out and do *his* job?'

'Well, you know that Andy's wife is seven months pregnant, don't you?'

'Oh, right! So now he can't come and do what he's paid for, because his wife is seven months pregnant, is that the excuse he gave you?'

Rita hated it when he was in this kind of mood. 'Don't be like that, Mac,' she said. 'If you've had a hard week, it isn't my fault. You should delegate more. Taking everything on your own shoulders makes you difficult to live with at times.'

He had no answer to that, except to mumble a reluctant, 'Sorry, love. I'm just a bit fraught, that's all.'

He was angry with himself; angry at the driven world he lived and worked in; and he was more than angry at having shown that side of his character to his wife, who always went out of her way to make life easier for him. 'It has been an unusually heavy week, and I really am bushed.'

'Well, please don't take it out on me, Mac. It's upsetting.'

'All right! All right! I've said I'm sorry. So now can we start again, d'you think?'

Content with her place in his busy life, Rita loved him so much she would forgive him anything, and he knew it. 'You can relax now you're home,' she promised. 'If you give me a minute, I'll wash my hands and make you a sandwich and a coffee – strong and black just as you like it. Sorry, but I didn't know you'd be home early. Lunch won't be ready for another hour or so yet.'

'That's fine. My fault.' He went back to the matter in hand. 'So, what's all this about the gardener and his wife?'

Impatient, he began to stride on ahead, with Rita quickening her step to keep up.

'Like I said, his wife is seven months pregnant, and she was rushed to the hospital in the early hours . . . something isn't right, apparently. He rang about ten minutes since, to let me know.'

271

'Something gone wrong, eh?' Mac sympathised. 'I'm sorry about that, but no doubt everything will turn out all right, eh?'

'I hope so, yes.' One of her greatest regrets in life was not having children, and Mac so loved them. 'Anyway, with autumn just around the corner, I thought I'd take the opportunity to get outside. The thing is, I haven't done any gardening since you took Andy on, and I do miss it so.'

'If you want me to finish him, you've only got to say the word.'

'Good grief, no! That would be an awful thing to do. You know he only recently lost his driving job, and they had a really hard time for a while. In fact, that could be what's caused the trouble with the baby . . . maybe the upset was too much. Oh no, Mac! You can't even *think* of finishing him.'

'Oh, for heaven's sake, Rita, will you stop rabbiting on! It was just a suggestion, that's all, and besides, I've had enough nagging today to last me a lifetime!'

'Oh Mac, I'm sorry – really I am.' It made her feel bad when he was in a mood.

Shrugging his shoulders, he heaved a great sigh. 'No, it's me that should be sorry. I'm tired, that's all. It's been an exceptionally heavy week, what with taking on that new project on the seafront, and travelling miles to check up on other, ongoing projects. Today was tedious, catching up on paperwork, answering phone calls and contacting planning officials and such. When the phone wasn't ringing in my ear, the secretary was in and out of the office. "Do this . . . do that . . . Mr So-and-so called – it's urgent, he wants you to contact him" . . .'

Rita gave a little groan. 'Goodness, it makes me feel tired just *listening* to you.'

'So now you can understand why my head is all in a spin.'

Turning to look at her, he caught hold of her hand. 'Like you said, what I need is a strong cup of coffee, a long, lazy slouch in the armchair, then a good meal, and I'll be right as rain. Okay?'

She smiled. 'Okay.'

Once inside the house, Mac went upstairs to change out of his suit and into a pair of comfortable trousers and a short-sleeved linen shirt, while Rita busied herself making him a snack to tide him over before lunch.

'Rita! You know what?' All excited, Mac came rushing into the kitchen. 'I've had an idea.'

'Really? I thought you intended giving your brain a rest?' she joked.

Throwing himself into the chair, he reminded her, 'It's Friday.'

'Yes, dear, I do know that.'

'So, we have the entire weekend before us.'

'It would seem so, yes.'

'Right. So how would you like to go and see the family – Don, Nancy, Brian and the children?'

Rita was surprised. 'It's a long drive to Heath and Reach. I thought you needed to relax? Besides, it wasn't so long ago that we saw them.'

'True, but it's been a good while since I saw Don, and the Merc could do with a good long run.'

It would be so lovely to see Sammie again too, he thought . . . before the child was gone, and the woman emerged. Once that happened, the magic was never really the same.

Her attention caught by the idea of going away, Rita had a different suggestion. 'If you really want to go away, why don't we go back to Suffolk where we spent our first anniversary? We could stay at that lovely old manor house that was turned into a hotel. We always said we'd go back, but we never did. Oh Mac, it was so beautiful!'

For a long moment it was as though Mac was miles away in his mind, as he sat deep in thought, shoulders sunk and his two hands wringing one into the other.

'Mac! Did you hear what I said?'

He was visibly startled. 'Oh no! Er, yes, I did. And I have no wish to go back to Suffolk, at least not yet. It's just, I thought it might be nice to go and see my brother and his family. Oh, I know we can't stay there, because there isn't any room, but there is a suitable hotel just down the road in Leighton Buzzard. Still, if you don't want to come, I'll go on my own. It will do me good . . . blow the cobwebs away, if you know what I mean.'

The idea of him going away without her was unthinkable and hurtful to Rita. 'When did you want to go?'

'Now.' Clenching his fist, he stamped it on the table. 'I'll pack a bag, just enough for two nights, and I could be away down that drive before you know it.'

'All right then, but I'm coming with you.'

'You don't have to.' In fact, he was really looking forward to taking off on his own. Every day of his life he was surrounded by people, and though he was deeply fond of his wife and would always take care of her, she was not the most scintillating of company. Besides, there had been times when she had been positively jealous of him spending a quiet moment or two inno-cently chatting with Sammie.

He knew how badly his wife had wanted children and maybe she thought he was showing too much love to Don's grand-daughter. But Sammie was special. How you could not delight in her company?

He reassured Rita. 'Honestly, darling, if you're not too keen on coming, I won't mind. It'll only be for a couple of nights.'

'No, Mac! I want to come.' Having realised how serious he was, she began to panic. 'But what about lunch? It's already in the oven.'

He laughed out loud. 'Let's be wild, shall we?' he suggested. 'Let's just turn the oven off, and I'll throw it all in the bin.'

Rita was horrified. 'That's so wasteful.'

'So, let's be wasteful . . . just this once, eh?'

'Alright then. If you say so.'

She had never really understood him, she thought sadly. He was often unpredictable; his moods could be dark or light-hearted, and at other times – like now – he truly seemed a little mad.

Gulping down his coffee, Mac took a bite out of his sandwich before discarding it altogether. 'You go and pack us a few things,' he told his wife. 'I'll see to the oven and stuff.'

Infected by his enthusiasm, even Rita was beginning to get excited. 'I'll need to sort out my hair,' she said, ripping off the ribbon which had held it back. 'Oh, and I'd best leave a note for Peggy when she comes to clean.'

Mac wasn't sure about Peggy. 'Tell her to make sure she doesn't leave the back door open like she did last time. If it hadn't been for the gardener, we could have come home to find the place stripped to the bone! If you ask me, she's gettng too old to be cleaning this big house.'

'That's unfair.' Rita sprang to Peggy's defence. 'It was the first time she had ever left a door unlocked,' she argued, 'and she's *not* too old. In fact she's only four years older than me.'

'All right! If you want her, then keep her, but tell her she'll be for the chop if she ever does that sort of thing again. Now go and get yourself ready . . . go on!' Putting on the oven gloves he slid the tray of food out of the oven and for a moment the wonderful aroma of the plump cod chunks made his stomach roll with hunger. 'Sorry, but you've got to go!' With grim determination he marched them out to the bin, where he lifted the lid and tipped them all away.

That done, he returned to the kitchen and quickly tidied up, then he went from door to window through the downstairs, checking the locks and securing the place.

Going to the office, he sat at his desk, picked up the telephone receiver, and dialled his older brother.

The phone rang for so long that he began to get agitated; he couldn't cope with the idea that maybe the family had gone off somewhere. At the height of frustration, he was about to replace the receiver, when suddenly Don answered. 'Hello!'

'Don?' Mac smiled at the way Don always seemed to talk two

decibels louder when on the telephone; he wondered if maybe it had something to do with the fact that he was a tiny bit deaf. 'It's me – Mac.'

'Oh! Mac, how are you?'

'I'm better now it's Friday and the week's over. Honest to God, Don, it's been a nightmare of a week.'

'Well, there you go. That's what happens when your main aim in life is to make money.' Don chuckled. 'You'll never change, it's in your blood. You've always been a go-getter, and I've always been jealous as hell, but you've got it and I haven't, and I suppose that's the way of it. Still, while I'm content and settled, there's you still flogging away, making another pile, and when you've made your first million, you'll no doubt be looking for your second.'

Mac had to concede that, because it was true. He was born with a mission, and that mission was to make money, but right now, at this moment in time, he saw it as more of a curse than a blessing.

'You're right in one way,' he told Don, 'and you're wrong in another. First of all, after the taxman's done with me, I might make my first million. But at some point I definitely mean to retire.' He gave a wry little laugh. 'As you know, I've been saying that for the past four years.'

'Aw, don't go fretting about it.' Don was proud of his younger brother's achievements, but there were times when he did genuinely worry about him. 'I'm sure you'll know when the time is right to put your feet up. Just don't pop off before you get a chance to enjoy your money. It would be a crying shame to leave most of your hard-earned fortune to the Chancellor of the Exchequer!'

'Well, thanks for that little gem.' Mac gave a groan. 'I'll certainly bear it in mind.'

'Good. Now then, to what do I owe the pleasure of your call?'

'First of all, what about you and the family – are you all well?'

'So far as I know, yes.'

'What's that supposed to mean?'

'It means I can't speak for the others, but as we speak, Brian is outside trimming the hedges, with Lottie "helping" him, Nancy is out shopping, David is off somewhere with his new girlfriend, and Sammie . . . well, I'm not sure where she is, but I think she's upstairs in her room. So, all in all, the family are fine. I mean, you only saw them a week or so ago."

'So what's happening with college?'

'Colin who?'

'No!' Mac burst out laughing. '*College*, you daft old bugger. I thought David and Sammie were seriously thinking of going to *college*!'

'Oh, right. Sorry, this phone's playing up.' Don knew well enough that his hearing was not what it used to be, but would he admit it? Not in a million years!

'Anyway, as I was saying, David has day release to study at the local tech for his job qualifications. As for Sammie, as usual, she's caught up in a big argument with her mother. Nancy wants her to do a shorthand typing course and get an office job, but Sammie wants to relax a bit first – get out of the classroom and earn her keep some other way. With the pair of 'em being strong-minded and stubborn, it's a job to know who'll come out on top. Brian is saying nothing, and I for one, am keeping well out of it.'

'So, it's a case of wait and see, eh?'

'That's it. Anyway, what are you up to? And why the phone call? It's not often you manage to pick up the phone just for a chat.'

'I'm ringing to say that Rita and I have decided to take a little break.'

'Oh yes? Thought you'd just come back from holiday. Off to foreign parts again, are you?'

'Not exactly. We're coming down to see you and the family. I intend booking a room in the Swan Hotel in Leighton Buzzard. We stayed there once before, if you recall?'

There was a pause, then Don replied, surprised, 'You mean to say you two are coming here, to see us?'

'Well, that's the general idea. I've had a pig of a week and I've been a bit short-tempered with Rita, so I thought I'd take her away for a treat. Coming to see you will cheer her up no end. That's all right with you, isn't it?'

'Of course. Goes without saying we'll all be happy to see you both.'

They concluded the conversation, and while Mac was delighted to relay the gist of it to Rita, Don remained curious as to the reason for this sudden visit.

When he saw David and his girlfriend Patsy coming up the path, he anticipated his grandson's reaction. Sorry, lad; but I've a feeling you won't much like what I have to tell you, he thought. He was well aware of David's feelings towards Mac. For some reason, no matter how much Don sang his younger brother's praises, David had never taken to him. He had told Don once that his great-uncle gave him the creeps – then apologised for saying something so unpleasant about his grandad's brother.

Waiting for the two of them to get inside the door, Don greeted David with the news. 'Your Uncle Mac and Auntie Rita are coming to see us this weekend.'

David's face fell. 'Oh no!' The last person he wanted to see was his Uncle Mac. 'It wasn't all that long since we were at his house. What's he coming here for?'

Don made a face. 'Don't ask me. Maybe they just want to remind themselves of how the other half live.'

David was horrified. 'They're not *staying* with us, are they? They can't! There's not enough room.'

'No, they're not staying with us – though if they were, I would hope you could show just a little enthusiasm.' Don was none too pleased at David's remarks, especially in front of this young girl who had only recently been introduced to the family.

'I'm sorry, Grandad,' David said. 'I know Uncle Mac is your

brother and all. It's just that, well, he makes me feel . . .' finishing the sentence with a lame shrug of one shoulder.

'Putting aside the fact that Uncle Mac has never been anything but considerate towards you and this family,' Don said sternly, 'your Aunt Rita will be delighted to see you . . . you being her favourite and all.'

'I know.' David was suitably remorseful – though deep down he remained wary of his Uncle Mac, especially after that curious incident outside Sammie's bedroom. He had managed to convince himself that what he had witnessed had not been suspicious. It was not intentional. 'So if they're not staying here, where are they staying?'

'They've booked a room at the Swan Hotel.'

David felt the need to inform his girlfriend, 'Aunt Rita is a really sweet person. She never sees any wrong in anybody,' he grinned, 'especially me. Uncle Mac's all right too – a real high-flyer, he's wealthy and everything, and it's not that I don't like him.' He wasn't sure how to put his feelings into words. 'It's just, he makes me feel insignificant, if you know what I mean.'

Maybe it was petty jealousy. Maybe Mac was too much of an icon to live up to. Maybe he resented him being able to make piles of money while his own dad, Brian, found it hard to make ends meet.

Whatever the reason, try as he might, he could not warm to the man, not in any way, shape or form.

'I have an aunt like that.' Patsy was a sweet little thing with long blonde hair and baby-blue eyes. 'Auntie Barbara is tall and slim, and always looks amazing whatever she wears. I'll never look like that . . . ever. I'm too short and a bit plump.' She made a face. 'It's not her fault, but honestly, I can't stand the sight of her.'

David grinned, while Don laughed aloud. 'Out of the mouths of babes!' he said, with a knowing grin. In a minute, he decided, he would amble off into the front room, where he would settle himself down with the local paper.

'Well now, Mac and Rita coming to see us, eh? That's put the cat among the pigeons,' he chuckled. 'David wasn't at all happy about that. Nancy will be dead chuffed though. She'll be covered in smiles the whole time they're here. Brian will be pleased an' all. Like always, he'll be tapping Mac's brain, desperate to find the secret of how to make a million.'

Don had a sneaking suspicion that Brian was just the teeniest bit envious of Mac's success.

Ah, but then it's only natural for one man to be envious of another, he thought. He wouldn't be human otherwise, would he?

~

Just as Don had predicted, Nancy was thrilled to bits. 'Oh, that's wonderful!' Dropping her shopping bags on the kitchen table, she could hardly contain her delight. 'Funny thing, that,' she remarked thoughtfully. 'I was only thinking of them as I came up the drive.'

'Really?' Don teased her. 'Was that because you were missing the luxury of their grand house, and being spoiled by having a cleaner come in to clear up after you? Or maybe you got too used to being a lady of leisure, is that it?'

Nancy bristled. 'Don't be ridiculous. I'll have you know, it's none of those reasons. If anything, it's coming back here to you and your sorry sense of humour, that's what it is!'

Stung by her sharp tongue, Don backed off. 'Only joking, love,' he said hastily. 'Anyway, I'll be in the front room if you want me.'

While he hurriedly buried his head in the newspaper, Nancy muttered as she threw the groceries into the cupboard. 'Huh! Only joking, indeed! The very idea! Does he really think I need a big house and servants to keep me happy?' Secretly though, she couldn't help but wonder what it would be like to have anything she wanted; to click her fingers and be waited on, or to go on holiday anywhere in the world whenever the fancy took her. Oh, and to dine out if she didn't feel like slaving over making a meal. How great would that be?

'Hello, daydreamer.' Covered in brambles and leaves, with his heavy boots clattering on the tiled floor, Brian stumbled into the kitchen. 'Miles away, you were, and by the way you were stuffing that cabbage into the cupboard, I wasn't sure whether to come in or not.'

Nancy forced a smile. 'I didn't see you in the garden.'

He grinned amiably. 'You didn't see me, because I was grappling with a creeping clematis that had its tentacles round my neck. I could have been strangled and lying there for weeks before anyone found me!'

Nancy smiled. 'Don't be daft. Anyway, what do you want?'

'Oh, charming, I must say.' Brian thought he would never get used to her unpredictable moods. 'I saw you come up the road and I tell you what, you really timed it right, because I'm gasping for a cuppa.'

Fed up and tired, Nancy rounded on him. 'Before you come in here you'd best get outside and brush all that rubbish off. Oh, and get them filthy boots out of my kitchen. I'm not in the mood to be scrubbing the floor after you.'

The sight of an irritated Nancy advancing on him from across the kitchen sent Brian into a quick retreat. Racing out the door, he moved to a safe place where he brushed himself clean and stripped off his boots, which he placed very neatly side by side on the WELCOME doormat, before coming into the kitchen. 'Presentable now, am I?' he asked curtly. 'Does this suit the lady of the house?'

Still smarting from Don's teasing, she ranted at him, 'What's that supposed to mean?' Hands on hips and fire in her eyes, she looked a formidable sight. 'Are you insinuating I have ideas above my station, is that it? Because if it is, you can make your own tea, and cook your own meals. How would you like that, eh?'

Brian was shocked. 'Hey! Whatever's got into you? It was simply a cheeky remark to make you laugh, that's all.' Placing his two hands on her shoulders, he gently pushed her down into a chair. 'Look, you sit there and I'll make the tea. All right?'

Feeling unusually vulnerable, Nancy nodded. 'Yes, please, and I'm sorry to have yelled at you like that. It's just something Dad said, about me wanting to be a lady of leisure.'

Brian smiled at that. 'Oh, I see, and along comes thought-less Brian playing silly beggars. I don't imagine for one minute that your dad meant to upset you. You know what he's like. He teases, that's all.'

'I know. It's just, it's been a bad morning. I should never have gone into Leighton Buzzard. The shops were busy and the queues were never-ending. There was no crusty bread left in the baker's and all the pork and apple sausages were sold by the time I'd got round to the butcher's. My feet ache, my head's throbbing, and I feel really fed up.' She gave a long, noisy sigh. 'The thing is, when I got in the door I was ready for a good row and Dad kind of got in the way.'

'So, you don't really want to be a lady of leisure then?' Brian asked, the tiniest smile playing round his mouth. 'Don got it all wrong, did he – as usual?'

''Course I would like to be a lady of leisure.' Nancy playfully prodded him in the chest. 'What woman wouldn't like to live in a big house, or have servants, and be able to shop without counting the pennies?'

It was only when Brian lapsed into silence and drew away, that she realised how cruel her remark was. 'Oh, what a thought-less cow I am!' Throwing her arms round her husband's neck, she pulled him to her. 'There are more important things in life than having money in the bank and being pampered.'

'Such as?' Brian felt mortally wounded.

'Well, there's the love of a good man like yourself, and the fun of building a life together. Then there's the children.

I don't dare imagine what life would be like without the children, and you.'

Particularly the children, she thought proudly. Even though she said so herself, she had made an excellent job of raising them.

Their son David was intelligent and ambitious; a successful man in the making, much like his Uncle Mac. As for their daughter Sammie, well, she was Nancy's absolute pride and joy. Sammie was always straightforward and compassionate, and would fight to the death for what was right.

Nancy admired those qualities in her, though she would never admit it, not even if she had to walk over hot coals. She herself had never laid claim to having as warm a heart. Brian was more like Sammie . . . being able to forgive unconditionally. But sadly, Nancy was not made in the same mould. It was something she deeply regretted.

'You're right, Nance. We do have two wonderful kids.' Brian's familiar voice found its way into her thoughts. 'And yes, having a happy family life is worth more than gold.'

'That's it. We don't really need all the things that Rita and Mac have,' Nancy agreed, 'because we have something that they were never blessed with – children. Also, I've got you, Brian. A man who keeps us all safe and will always look after us; a man who loves me without condition, even though sometimes I don't deserve it.'

She paused, remembering the hard times and the worries that they had come through together. 'I know I don't often say it, but I do love you, Brian.'

When he now glanced up to look into her face, she planted a fleeting kiss on his forehead. 'You're a good man, Brian Wells.'

He held her for a moment. 'You'd best go and apologise to your dad,' he suggested.

'Dad can wait,' she answered. 'He's got his head in the racing paper, busy picking out his winners for this afternoon. No. The two of us are going to sit down together with a cup of tea and a slice of that Madeira cake I got from the baker's.' She gestured to the table. 'So go on then. Sit yourself down, before I change my mind. Your order is on its way, sir.' She gave a mock curtsy. 'But don't expect anything too fancy, not in this café!'

As always, Brian meekly did as he was told, encouraged by her words of appreciation for the energy and devotion he put into keeping this family fed, clothed and housed.

Without gratitude there would be no sense of accomplishment, and of late, he had been increasingly comparing his own achievements to those of Nancy's Uncle Mac. Not a very reassuring pastime, and one he would try his hardest to abandon.

The trouble was, Nancy's sour remarks about big houses, servants and being able to go anywhere she wanted in the world, had cut him deep. And though he knew in his heart it had not been meant in the way it was taken, the comments did hurt his sense of pride.

On hearing the news that Mac and Rita were coming to stay locally for a short break, Brian was less than thrilled.

'It'll do Uncle Mac a power of good to come down here,' Nancy said as she poured his tea. 'I'm not sure it's a healthy way to live, all that work and worry – not for Mac anyway. Rita simply enjoys the ride, reaping the rewards of Mac's hard work. It doesn't seem to worry her that she hardly ever sees him.'

Brian had thought of all that, and something else too. There was this one particular question that often popped into his head, as it did now. 'Do you think Mac ever has a little fling when he's away?' he asked.

Nancy was not unduly surprised at his question, because at times the same thought had crossed her mind too. 'I don't really know,' she answered, 'but I suppose it's likely. I mean, he's a red-blooded man, and he has got that kind of way with him that could have women fawning at his feet.'

Brian gave a wry little grin. 'Might I ask if that includes you?'

'Maybe the teeniest bit,' Nancy confessed. 'But it's not a physical attraction or anything like that. It's more a niece's admiration of her rich uncle's achievements. The thing is, I've grown up with Dad always singing his praises and it's kind of rubbed off, if you know what I mean.'

She laughed at the sorry look on her husband's face. 'Anyway, you've no need to worry, because firstly he's my uncle, and secondly even if he wasn't, he could never be my kind of man.'

'Oh, and why's that?'

'Because *you're* my kind of man. The first minute I saw you, I wanted you straight off. Nothing's changed on that score.'

'Well, thank you. I'm very pleased to hear it.' And he was. 'Coming back to Uncle Mac and other women,' Nancy went on, 'I reckon he might well have had a fling or two in his time.'

'Really? What makes you say that?'

'Well, let me ask you something.' She herself had noticed it time and again. 'I don't believe I've ever seen the two of them holding hands, or showing any signs of affection to each other. In fact, I don't think I've even seen them share a joke or laugh out loud with each other. Have you?'

Unlike Nancy, Brian had not really taken much notice, but now he was sure of it. 'Come to think of it, you're absolutely right,' he gave a naughty little chuckle, 'Ooh!' He said it again: 'Ooh!'

The smile on his face was positively wicked; until Nancy told him to grow up, and 'Get rid of that smug little grin!'

The conversation finished right there and a silence descended. All that could be heard was Brian slurping his tea while Nancy ate her cake, reflecting on the possibility of Uncle Mac, the 'cheat'. It was a curious observation. Cheating on Aunt Rita with another woman.

Whatever next!

CHAPTER SIXTEEN

I T WAS GONE teatime when Mac and his wife arrived.
Ushering Rita into the house before him, Mac greeted
everyone in sight, which did not include the youngsters, as they
and Patsy were all three upstairs in Judy's room. 'I've heard
Elvis Pelsey that often, I'm beginning to think it's *me* that's
headed for "Heartbreak Hotel".' Don was at the end of his
tether.

'It's Presley!' Nancy corrected him for the umpteenth time.
'Not Pelsey.'

Tutting and mumbling, Don made his way to the foot of the
stairs. 'I don't know how many times I've asked them to turn
that racket down! What with that and "Jailhouse Rock" . . .
Thoughtless, that's what they are.' He turned to address Rita
and Mac. 'Kids today, eh?'

'Aw, they're all right.' Mac could recall his own youth. 'When
kids start playing their music, they're in a world of their own.'

A bit riled, Don yelled up the stairs, *David! Sammie! Your
Uncle Mac and Aunt Rita are here! Are you coming down or what?'*

A moment later the music fell silent, then came the clattering of feet running down the stairs. David arrived with the
hint of a smile on his face and his girlfriend on his arm. 'For
us it's hello and goodbye, I'm afraid. We're just off out,' he
told everyone. 'We promised to meet up with some friends and
we're already half an hour late.'

'Hello, my love.' Rita gave him a hug. 'So, aren't you going to introduce us to this pretty girl then?'

Visibly embarrassed, David introduced Patsy to Rita, but when Mac stepped forward, the introduction was conducted more swiftly as David ushered his girlfriend towards the door. 'Sorry, but we'll have to rush or we'll be late.' A moment later they were hurrying down the garden path.

'Well, he's in a bit of a hurry, isn't he?' Mac said, rather put out.

'His girl seems a sweet young thing,' Rita commented.

From the kitchen window, Mac monitored David and the girl until they were out of sight. 'You're right,' he told Rita, 'Looks like young David's done all right for himself.'

As he turned, Sammie came into the kitchen; dressed in a swirly brown skirt and fitting white top, she had a ready smile on her face and a definite spring to her step. 'Hello again, you two,' she said, and hurried towards them.

Mac's face lit up at the sight of her. 'Ah, now here's the prettiest of them all.' Rushing forward, he gave her a long, affectionate bear-hug, at the same time vigorously rocking her from side to side and tousling her hair. 'How's my favourite girl then, eh?'

'I'm fine, thank you, Uncle Mac.' Sammie did not particularly care for those long bear-hugs, but then that was Uncle Mac's way. Over the years she had learned to live with it.

Rita was much more gentle. 'Oh Sammie, you look lovely, as always,' she said, offering a little kiss. 'We're only here for a couple of days – staying at the Swan in Leighton Buzzard. Mac's had a really busy time of it lately; he desperately needed this break.'

Sammie gladly returned the kiss. 'It's good to see you, Aunt Rita.'

'Oh, but I was so glad when Mac suggested coming here.' Rita glanced about. 'Where's your mum?'

'She's right here!' Bouncing in, Nancy explained how she

and Brian had been out the back. 'Discussing a complete re-organisation of the vegetable patch. Anyway, enough about that, it's good to see you.' After throwing herself into Mac's open arms, she then gave Rita a firm cuddle.

Brian shook hands with Mac and thanked him again for the use of his house while they were away. Mac told him enough said, and so Brian then gave Rita an energetic cuddle and the softest of kisses on the cheek, making her blush to her roots.

'Dad said you were coming to see us,' Brian addressed Mac. 'So – you decided to escape the rat-run for a while, did you?'

'Got it in one,' Mac answered. 'You either stay one foot ahead of it, or you go under. So, I decided to opt out for a couple of days . . . catch my breath, so to speak.'

Rita gave a kind of snort. 'Huh! In that case, why have you brought all that paperwork with you then? And what were those two long phone-calls you made at the hotel, the minute we got through the door?'

Mac seemed embarrassed. 'Ah, well now, I didn't say I was about to abandon my responsibilities altogether, love. Because if I did that, the sharks will have stripped me bare by the time I get back.'

'Come through into the sitting room,' Brian invited. 'If we ask Nancy nicely, she'll make us a pot of tea and perhaps rustle up a few little fancies.'

Nancy's voice cut in. 'Yes, you four kindly clear off into the sitting room, and I'll be along shortly.'

Mac felt a pang of disappointment. 'What about Sammie? Isn't she joining us?' Looking around, he realised she had gone.

''Fraid not. She's off to the village hall. The Parish Committee are putting a dance on and Sammie's been driving me crazy, wanting new shoes, a haircut and make-up. I told her, she doesn't need all that fanciness, because she's pretty enough as it is.'

'Quite right.' Mac had never thought Sammie would be a beauty in the traditional sense of the word, but there was something about her, with that wild blonde hair and a temperament to go with it. He, for one, thought she was very special.

'You don't mind, do you?' Sammie returned to say cheerio. 'Only it's gonna be great. Good music and plenty of dancing; I've been really looking forward to it.' Brought up by the sight of Mac's disappointed expression, she promised, 'Oh look, I'll go and tell them I'm not coming, if you like?'

'No, you can't do that,' Rita interrupted. 'Your mates want you there, so get off and enjoy yourself, my darling. After all, you're only young once.' She turned to Mac. 'Isn't that right?'

'Of course it is.' He winked at Sammie. 'Besides, how can you not go now, when you'll be the prettiest girl in the room? Rita's right. You get off and enjoy yourself.'

'Thank you, Uncle Mac. See you both soon. Bye!'

'Right then.' Brian began ushering them along. 'Let's go to the sitting room, shall we?'

Everyone agreed, and the two women set the table in there with tea, cakes and chunky ham sandwiches. Everyone was completely at ease – with maybe the exception of Rita – who always found it difficult to relax in other people's houses; even with relatives.

'You know what?' Don glanced about. 'How about breaking open those two bottles of wine I hid in the kitchen cabinet?'

'Yes!' everyone yelled in unison – even Rita – and so the wine was dutifully produced, with five best glasses, and a corkscrew.

A few minutes later, warmed by their first glass of a rich Bordeaux, they chatted about this and that, yet beneath the surface was the same old question that always arose whenever they got together.

Rita raised the subject now. 'I don't suppose you've heard from Judy, have you?' she asked nervously, her cheeks rosy from the wine. 'I mean . . . has she been in touch at all?'

Nancy positively bristled. 'We've heard nothing,' she answered with a stiff smile.

'Which is just as well, in the light of recent circumstances,' Don added.

'What circumstances?' Mac wanted to know.

'Best forgotten!' That was Don.

'Really?' When Mac caught Nancy giving her father a curious glance, he would not be silenced. 'What's happened? Have you heard something? Is she all right?'

In a quiet, aching voice and knowing that once Mac had the bit between his teeth, he would not let it go, Don told him a half-truth. 'We heard she'd gone completely off the rails – boozing, keeping company with men of a certain kind – that sort of thing.'

Rita was shocked. 'Oh, dearie me. Poor Judy.'

'Poor Judy nothing!' Nancy exclaimed. 'We all knew which way she was headed.'

'It's best if we don't discuss her,' Don said wisely. 'Water under the bridge and all that.'

Very slightly intoxicated, Rita could not accept that – and when she now voiced her opinion, it was totally out of character. 'Judy was never really a bad girl. I always thought she was such a lovely little thing . . . so kind and considerate.'

'Well, you were wrong, weren't you?' Mac patted her on the back of the hand. 'She may have been a sweet little girl once, but not any more. People change,' he said forcefully. 'They change, and often there is nothing anyone can do.'

Close to tears and made more emotional by the wine, Rita went on to make matters a good deal worse. 'Don't you ever regret throwing her out?' she asked of Don. 'If you had let her stay and helped her through that terrible time, don't you think it might have all turned out better?'

'Rita!' Mac shook his head, furious. 'Don't interfere! It's none of our business.'

'Oh dear, I am so sorry!' His wife was mortified. 'Mac's right. I am interfering . . . please, just forget what I said.'

Don, however, decided to lay the ghost of his lost daughter

once and for all. 'You've no need to apologise,' he said gently. 'The truth is, it was not just rumours we heard about Judy. I actually saw her with my own eyes, drunk on the streets, and actually engaged in a vicious fight. She was with another drunken person – a man who, according to certain quarters, is a brute of questionable reputation.'

'Good Lord!' Mac was shocked. 'And she was actually fighting, was she? I mean, it wasn't just him attacking her, was it?'

'No, I saw the whole thing. She was every bit as aggressive as he was.' Don gave a sad little smile. 'From my understanding of the situation and a certain remark I overheard, it was more than likely that the two of them were man and wife.'

'Well, I never.' Looking from one to the other, Mac shook his head. 'I swear, I would never have believed it of her.'

'Well, you should believe it,' Nancy announced cynically, 'because it's all true, every word of it. My father didn't want to tell me at first, but I knew something was wrong and I got it out of him. Like you, I was shocked – though of course, we never mentioned it to the children. As far as their Aunt Judy is concerned, they know little or nothing about her. As for myself, I had a sister once, long, long ago but now she might as well be dead.'

Reaching out, she took hold of Don's hand. 'This family has gone through hell and back because of her; my father particularly. As you can imagine, it was not easy for him to turn her out onto the streets all those years ago, and now he's having to deal with this new information, which only serves to remind us of her true character. Judy was born bad, or she would have got herself together and be living a decent life. Instead, she chooses to live like some crazed animal in the cesspits.'

Mac was shocked. 'That's a bit strong, isn't it?'

Straightening her back, Nancy looked him in the eye, telling him earnestly, 'Judy was my sister once, but for what she's done to this family, I will hate her for the rest of my life.'

Following Nancy's outburst the silence in the room was thick

291

and ominous, with Brian remaining quiet, mainly because he had not been as close to Judy's untimely exit as were Nancy and Don; though he had been made aware of it soon after, and he acknowledged the shame and upset which had fallen on the family. Now, the very last thing he wanted was to be drawn into the fracas.

'I should never have asked about her.' In the wake of Nancy's outburst, poor Rita was truly devastated.

Don now spoke quietly. 'You asked if I regretted throwing Judy out on the streets.'

'Oh, but I didn't mean it . . . I should never . . .' She faltered when Don put up a staying hand. 'It's all right, Rita,' he assured her. 'You are still family, and you have a right to ask questions.'

He went on, 'The answer is yes, I did feel regret – of course I did, and pain, and guilt; and in a way I still do, even after I've seen for myself what she's become. For a long time, I fought with my conscience about Judy. Where was she? What kind of life was our little girl leading? Was she safe and happy? Was the child all right? Day and night the questions riddled my brain until I thought I might go crazy.'

He paused, before resoundly concluding, 'In fact, my conscience troubled me so much, that when the family recently went to stay at your house, I used the time they were away to go looking for her.'

The memory of what he saw that day was still hard to take in. He thought of the girl he had put out of her house; that small lonely schoolgirl going away down the street, looking back at him with disbelief in her eyes; that child he had so cherished, and yet when she needed him, he had joined with her mother, to close the door in her face.

For what was left of his life, he would never be able to think about that, without his heart breaking.

When the emotion threatened to overwhelm him, he bowed his head and cleared his throat, before looking up to see them all waiting. 'Like I say, I went out searching for her. But I was not prepared for what I found.'

In his mind he could see the woman Judy had become; unkempt, so drunk she could hardly stand, and physically fighting with that man in the street. 'The thing is, what I saw convinced me I had done the right thing in turning Judy away. As Nancy so aptly put it, Judy must have been born bad, because there has been nothing of this kind in our family before or since.'

Mac was the first to speak. 'I'm sorry you had to find her in that way.'

Don nodded. 'So am I, but at least it became apparent to me that Judy was living the life she wanted; that she could never have found contentment in living an ordinary life, within an ordinary family.'

He sighed heavily. 'She's chosen her way, and we don't need to worry about her any more. In fact, after what I witnessed, from this day on, I do not want her name mentioned in this house.'

He looked across at Brian, who had been unusually quiet. 'If that's all right with the man of the house, of course. Brian, what do you say?'

His son-in-law nodded. 'I was never as close to the situation as you and Nancy,' he claimed, 'but I understand how you must both feel about Judy. I realise the pain she's caused, and to tell you the truth, I don't think I would ever want our children to know the true history of their Aunt Judy. So yes, I'm happy to go along with you and Nancy on this.'

He raised his glass. 'Here's to putting the past behind us, and looking to the future.'

Everyone drank to that; although some had more reason to suffer a pang of conscience than others.

Afterwards they talked of all things interesting and personal. They laughed when Don told comical stories of himself and the dog, who pricked up her ears when she heard her name and yawned hugely – a terrifying sight. Then they commended Brian on his recent promotion; albeit rather a modest one.

Yet, even though her name was not mentioned again, the

atmosphere was tainted by the previous discussion about Judy, so much so that Mac and Rita made their excuses rather too soon. 'Got to unpack the suitcase,' Rita apologised, 'before the clothes are creased beyond redemption.'

Mac suggested, 'We've got the weekend before us though, so maybe we could all go somewhere exciting, eh? What d'you say? Let's think about it and I'll call you in the morning.'

They said their goodbyes and together with Brian and Nancy, Don waved them off. He then hobbled off into the back garden; the only place he was allowed to have a puff of his trusty old pipe.

Nancy's shrill voice followed him, 'Uncle Mac said he would ring in the morning,' she yelled. '. . . and he will! You'll see.'

'Really.' Under his breath he was chattering and grumbling to himself, 'I'll bet my next week's baccy allowance, we won't hear another word from either of 'em, until they're back home.'

Putting distance between himself and the family, Mac drove on to Leighton Buzzard. Mentally reflecting on the unsettling conversation, he confessed to his wife, 'I must say, that business about Judy made me feel really uncomfortable.'

The same sentiments were running through Rita's mind. 'I thought Nancy's outburst was awful!' she said. 'So full of hatred and self-righteousness – and against her own sister too. It seems no one will ever be able to forgive poor Judy.'

'Ah, but can you blame them?' Mac asked now. 'By the sounds of it, she brought it all down on herself.'

'I don't see how that could be,' Rita argued. 'Judy was only a child – barely fourteen. A girl can't get pregnant on her own . . . Some man was involved, that's for sure. And why would she never let on who the father was, eh? I mean, if she'd had the courage to name him, she could have saved herself a whole heap of trouble.'

'Maybe she was protecting the man.'

'But why would she want to do that?'

'*I* don't know, do I?' Manoeuvring the car round a bend, Mac suggested, 'Maybe she loved him and didn't want to get him into trouble. You do realise he would have been put away – for having intercourse with a minor and all that.'

'There could be another reason,' Rita said slowly.

'And what's that then?'

'Maybe he forced himself on her, and then threatened her with all kinds of trouble if she ever told. Maybe Judy was too terrified to give his name.'

'Now you're getting melodramatic.'

'Think about it, Mac.' She had the bit between her teeth now. 'If the man really did force himself on her, he was obviously wicked enough to hurt her worse if she ever told on him. That's why she couldn't tell. That's partly why the family threw her out – not only because she was with child, but because she would not give his name. So they had no choice but to think she was every bit as bad as him.'

Mac was shocked. 'I never knew you had such a criminal mind,' he said with a low chuckle. 'You should have been a detective.'

Rita smiled. 'Oh sorry, I did get a bit carried away there, but I was only wondering what kind of man would have relations with a minor, get her pregnant and then leave her to take all the blame. He must have known how her family would react when they found out she was expecting – that they might not stand by her, but throw her out of house and home . . . disown her.'

Mac had an answer for that too. 'Maybe she never even told him, until it was too late and she had already told the family.'

'Maybe she never told him at all.' Rita could barely imagine what Judy must have suffered. 'All the same, if and when she *did* tell him, he should have come forward.' Her mind was made up. 'As far as I'm concerned, whoever he is, he's not only wicked, but a downright coward into the bargain.'

'Maybe he and Judy made a pact,' Mac argued. 'Maybe he persuaded her that if she told, he would go to jail and that the shock to his family would be devastating.'

'That would have served him right too.' Rita was unrelenting. 'They would have seen what a monster he was, to have taken advantage of a young girl.' Rightly or wrongly, she was on Judy's side. 'Going to jail would have been too good for him. He should have been shot, that's what I say!'

'Whoa!' Mac smiled. 'That's a bit strong, coming from you.'

With her judgement slightly affected by the wine, Rita was not about to let the subject go. 'Mac?'

'Yes?'

'Who do *you* think it was?' she asked. 'Who could have been so wicked as to put a fourteen-year-old girl in the family way, and then leave her to suffer the consequences?'

Mac cast his mind back. 'From what I can remember, Nancy was convinced that the person responsible was that lad Harry Blake. You remember his parents died tragically, and Irish Kathleen gave him a home. According to Nancy, that was when Judy and Harry became sweethearts.'

But his wife was having none of it. 'I know that was what Nancy claimed, but I should have thought Harry Blake was too busy grieving for his parents to think about much else. Anyway, he wasn't that much older than Judy, was he? Only by three or four years.'

Mac gave a smutty chuckle. 'Old enough though, eh?'

'There's no need to be vulgar!' snapped Rita. 'I don't care what any of you say, I never really believed it was him. The boy seemed decent enough, and besides, he really cared for Judy. They were best mates, always looking out for each other. Harry would never have done anything to hurt her.'

'Whatever you say, my dear.' Growing irritated by her constant probing, Mac had already moved on in his thinking. 'Where do you think Don found Judy?' he asked. 'Was it somewhere local, d'you think?'

'I have no idea,' Rita replied. 'But I'm pleased that he at least made the effort to track her down. You know, I always thought it was too harsh a punishment for little Judy. Mind you, I understand it was Judy's *mother* who actually kicked her out, and not Don himself.'

'Ah well, I've never been surprised about that. You know what Norma was like . . . too full of herself, what with her fancy ideas and tendency to look down on other folks. Nancy takes after her.'

Rita chuckled about that. 'She does come over a bit primadonna sometimes, but I do believe Don and Brian, and particularly Sammie, manage to keep her in line.'

Mac smiled. 'Young Sammie is a strong-minded girl,' he said, 'but in a different way from her mother. Sammie is softer, more balanced, with a much happier disposition. It's only when she knows she's right, that she digs her heels in.' He laughed out loud. 'I dare say she and Nancy find themselves at loggerheads more often than not.'

'Do you think she's pretty?'

'Who – Nancy?'

'No, silly! I mean Sammie. Do you think she's pretty?'

'That's an odd question.'

'I know, but *do* you?'

'I'm not sure. She's not what you'd call beautiful, and maybe pretty isn't the right description either. Sammie is more . . . striking?' He searched for the right word. 'More . . . Oh what's the word?'

'Alive?'

'Yes, you're right, that's it. Sammie is more alive than pretty.' He turned to smile at her. 'Why do you ask?'

Rita shrugged. 'No particular reason.'

There was a moment of quiet before she spoke again. 'Mac?'

'Mmm?'

'Where do *you* think Judy is?'

'Who knows? Mind you, after what Don saw, it does seem as

though she's got herself well and truly mixed up with some undesirables; though I reckon she can handle herself by now.'

'Should we look for her, do you think?'

Mac shook his head. 'Good God, no! Brian was right. Best let sleeping dogs lie, eh?'

He momentarily toyed with the idea though; initially finding it attractive, then eventually rejecting it, not least because finding Judy would rake up the past and all that went with it.

He now addressed Rita with a certain authority. 'I'm sorry, love, but it is not our place to interfere. The best thing is to put that chapter of their lives well and truly behind us.'

'But that's not fair on Judy.'

Mac wanted the conversation ended. 'Enough now! You're taking my mind off the road,' he complained. 'Besides, the family want it over and done with, and we should respect their wishes.'

'What!' Astonished, Rita laughed in his face. 'Since when have *you* ever respected anyone's wishes?'

'Ah, but this is different,' he responded sternly. 'It's family, so let's put an end to it now, eh?'

'It was you who started it, saying how that business with Judy had left you feeling uncomfortable,' Rita argued.

'Yes, well, now I'm ending it. Come on, Rita. After all, it really is none of our business.'

What was done was done, and as far as he was concerned, the shameful incident with Judy was best forgotten – and the sooner the better.

Reluctantly, Rita complied with his instructions as always; though in this instance, she was not happy to leave it there.

Somewhere in the back of her mind, and in view of what Don had told them, she had a sneaking suspicion that poor Judy still needed rescuing, just as much as she did all those years ago.

PART FOUR

~

Fisher's Hill, Autumn 1956

Dangerous Love

CHAPTER SEVENTEEN

Harry was at his wits' end. 'I don't understand how anyone could simply disappear like that!' Seated at the kitchen table, head in hands, he talked his way through the previous week. 'I've almost gone through the soles of my shoes looking for her,' he told Kathleen. 'I've been to the Central Library to check if her name is on the loans' register, and I've worried the girl at the council office, but they sent me away with all this nonsense about the right to a person's privacy. I got shown nothing, except the door.'

'So no luck anywhere then?'

'None at all. I've spent hours hanging about the Boulevard, hoping I might catch sight of her getting on and off buses, until even the drivers got curious. I was worried in case they thought I might be a bad lot, so I told them why I was there, so now would you believe it – *they're* even keeping an eye out for her.'

Kathleen laughed, that joyful sound that never failed to put a smile on everyone's face. 'Sure it's a wonder they didn't call the authorities and have ye thrown in jail for loitering.'

'Not funny,' Harry chided, though he did have the whisper of a smile curling the corners of his mouth.

Kathleen apologised. 'I wonder if I did right, now, to tell you about me bumping into her,' she said. 'Because here's you, tramping the streets and asking anyone who'll stop, to help ye find her.' Little did either of them know of the similar venture of Don Roberts, nor of its unsavoury ending.

'I'm glad you told me, because now at least I know she isn't all that far away.' His voice dropped to a whisper. 'I *am* meant to find her, I know I am.'

Kathleen was proud that he should care so much about the girl he had left behind, especially when it all ended on a bad note. 'Ye know what, me darlin'?'

Harry looked up. 'What?'

'You're right to keep on searching, so ye are.' She paused, taking in that sad face with the magnetic dark eyes and that certain look of helplessness men get when they feel out of their depth. 'Don't you worry now,' she said kindly. 'I've a feelin' in me water, it won't be too long afore ye find the wee girlie.'

Reaching forward, Harry planted a kiss on her chubby face. 'Thanks for that,' he said with a broad smile. 'That's all the encouragement I need.'

She folded her arms. 'So, where else did ye look then?'

'Everywhere!' he groaned. 'If the boss should ever find out I've been misusing working time, I'll be out on my ear.'

'Aw, away with ye! I'm sure you haven't taken much of your work time, and even if you had, you've no doubt made it up in your lunch hour. Anyways, it's not as though you're on set hours – unless you're actually based in the store. So far as I know, you've been late home four nights in the past week, and you've started early twice. So, don't you worry. The old rogue won't care how ye juggle the hours, so long as you get the job done and fetch back his tally money.'

'All absolutely true,' Harry agreed, amused.

'Right then, so now go on . . . you were saying?'

'Well, let me think. I've asked everyone and anyone, and all with no luck. I've also made enquiries about Phil Saunders, also without any luck.'

Kathleen warned him, 'Sure I don't know if it's wise, bandying that divil's name about. From what little information

I've managed to gather on the way he is these days, he is not an article you want to mess with.'

Before he could ask the question, she informed him, 'I already told you, I did *not* manage to get an address out of Judy at the time.' She waved her hand in the air. 'So, what next?'

'That's it really. I've pounded the streets and asked a thousand questions. I even sat in that little café where you said you met up with her; I was there for over an hour until tea was coming out my ears and the waitress seemed ready to call the police.' He gave a huge sigh. 'I know what you already told me, but think hard, Kathleen. Are you absolutely certain that Judy did not even give a hint as to where she and Saunders live?'

Kathleen shook her head. 'Not in the slightest, no she did not.'

Harry had to pose the next question. 'You *would* tell me, wouldn't you?'

'Bless you, me boy, why would I *not* tell you? Sure I'd *have* to tell ye, if only to keep you out of them boozers, and stop ye from loitering in public places. Bejaysus! It's a blessing you weren't already arrested, so it is.'

Kathleen did not mind him quizzing her again, because she fully understood his anxiety where Judy was concerned. Moreover, she so wanted him to find Judy. That way, the couple could talk through their problems past and present, and get things out into the open. The harsh fact that Judy was already married meant yet another barrier between any future for them, but maybe the marriage was already rotten to the core and the time was right for it to end.

There were other considerations too – Phil Saunders, for one; Kathleen suspected he was a nasty piece of work. Then there was the fact that Harry was still reeling from recent events, and was now gently bringing his son through the same trauma. On top of which he was presently settling into new employment, and was also determined to find a home for himself and the boy.

Kathleen had already mentioned how delighted she would be to have him and young Tom stay with her for ever, though she knew that was unlikely to happen. Harry Blake had been a fine, strong-minded boy, and now he had shown himself to be a man of strength and independence.

He had taken some devastating knocks of late, but Kathleen had seen how he was now ready to forge his way in the world, and she could not be more proud than if he was her own son.

'I know you've things to discuss with Judy when you find her,' Kathleen told him now. 'I have no doubt whatsoever that ye *will* find her, but when you do, I want you to promise me that you'll be careful.'

Harry was intrigued. 'Why careful?'

'Think about it,' she urged. 'Go back to when you were all young, and Phil Saunders set his cap at Judy, even when he knew she was seeing you. Right from the start, when the three of youse came to this very house one afternoon, I noticed how that young divil could not take his eyes off her.'

Harry understood what she was saying, but tried to calm her fears. 'He fancied himself that was all.'

'No. He was totally besotted. When you disappeared, he made a beeline straight for her – would not leave her be, not even for a minute. Then when she went away and her family with her, he was like a lost dog, standing outside where they'd lived and pacing the street as though expecting her to turn up any minute.'

Harry was shocked. 'I never knew that.' He had always seen Phil Saunders as a strange one, and they had clashed many times, but what Kathleen was telling him now, made him seem like someone unhinged.

'Well, o' course you weren't to know,' she went on. 'You were gone from the area; you and Judy both.'

'So, are you saying that I might be causing trouble for Judy if I was to seek her out? Do you think Phil would give her a hard time for talking to me – that is, if I ever did meet up with her?' Harry's heart sank. 'Be honest with me, Kathleen. Do you want me to give up looking for her, because I have to tell you now, I cannot! Come what may, *I have to find her*!'

Kathleen pondered on his words for a moment. She knew well enough that whatever she said, Harry would not be deterred from searching for Judy, and that his sole aim was to speak with her and make peace over the way they had parted. Come what may, she knew he would turn heaven and earth upside down until he had Judy standing right before him.

'No, o' course I'm not saying to give it up,' she answered emphatically. 'All I'm saying is this . . . if he should catch the two of youse even *talking* together, he would be so insanely jealous, there's no saying what he might do.'

'You think I can't handle him?' Harry's fists clenched by his side as he declared, 'The truth is, if I ever find out that he has hurt one single hair on Judy's head, I swear to God, I would have to swing for him!'

That was exactly what Kathleen was afraid of. 'No, lad. That's fighting talk and you don't want that. You must think of Judy – she is his wife, don't forget. You also have to think of your son, and even yourself. Phil Saunders is the kind of man who would sneak up on you one dark night and mow you down from behind. When you find Judy, you must say what you came to say, and let that be an end to it. Not by word nor deed should you give that man any cause to take against you.'

She pleaded with him. 'I need your promise on that.'

When Harry was slow to respond, she asked again. 'Harry – for the love of God, will ye promise me – for the sake of everyone, including Judy – that you will not goad that villain in any way whatsoever?'

Seeing how distressed she was becoming, Harry said, 'All right, I promise, no fighting talk. I'll just find her, make up for what happened back then, and . . .'

For some inexplicable reason, he could promise no more than that, except to assure Kathleen, 'You're not to concern yourself about Saunders. He won't cause trouble. He has no reason to. I know Judy is wed to him, and I will respect that.'

He took a moment to dwell on Judy's situation and his own part in it. 'Yes, I will respect that . . . *as long as he respects her*!'

Surprised at his last comment, Kathleen wanted to know, 'Why would ye say a thing like that? Why would he *not* respect her? Have ye heard something untoward? Or did ye discover some bad thing concerning the man himself?' Her hands went to her hips and there she stood, like a little battleship. 'Well, did you?'

'I've heard nothing with regards to him,' he replied, 'except what you yourself told me a little while ago.'

Kathleen wished now that she had kept her mouth shut. There was something else though, and she was thankful she had not relayed it to Harry. It happened on the day she and Judy met.

Kathleen had not forgotten how, even when she and Judy were deep in conversation, Judy kept glancing at the café door. It was painfully obvious that she was highly nervous of something – or someone.

'Right then.' Harry pushed his chair back. 'I'd best be off now. Saturday is always a busy time, and today we have a one-day sale to get shot of old stock. Jacobs is expecting a record turnout, so we've all been asked to come in an hour earlier.'

'A sale, eh?' Kathleen's old eyes lit up. 'Sure I've a mind to pop along and see what ye have in the way of mantelpiece runners.' She pointed out the frayed ends of the runner over the fire-range. 'Would you believe, the one in the sitting room is even worse!' she exclaimed.

'You'd best come along and have a rummage,' Harry suggested. 'I'm sure there are all kinds of bits and bobs in the bargain tubs.'

'I will, that I will.' Kathleen was beside herself at the thought of a new runner for each of her mantelpieces. 'I'll fetch Tom with me an' all,' she told him. 'I've already promised to buy him a new pair of Wellington boots. The old ones are far too small, and there are lots of puddles to splash in.'

Going to the stairs she called the boy. 'Tom!' Her voice sailed to the rafters. 'Your daddy's away just now. If you want to say cheerio, you'd best shake a leg and get yerself down here! Some time now would be good!'

Almost immediately, there was the familiar patter of little feet running, and even before Kathleen got back to the kitchen, Tom was throwing himself into Harry's arms. 'Daddy! Daddy! Kathleen says she's taking me for some new wellies.'

'New wellies, eh?' Harry feigned amazement. 'My word! It seems like only yesterday that I bought you a brand new pair.'

'But now Kathleen says they're too small, and my feet will be all crossed and twisted if I have to wear them, so she's getting me a new pair, so she is!'

Harry and Kathleen grinned at that. 'Sure, you have a son who thinks he's Irish, so ye have!' She gave her infectious laugh, until all three of them were in uproar. 'So she is,' Tom kept saying. 'So she is!'

Harry swept him up and gave him an almighty hug. 'You'd best behave yourself, my boy – although on second thoughts, you could do worse than take after Kathleen.'

He set the boy down on his feet again. 'I want you to do just as she tells you, and don't let go of her hand when you're out.'

'Oh, no. I'm not a baby, Daddy. I go to school and everything. Why does everybody make me hold their hand all the time?' Tom made a face. When would his Daddy realise that he was all grown up?

Harry replied in a serious voice, 'Look, Tom, nobody's saying you're a baby, far from it. The reason I'm asking you to hold Kathleen's hand is for *her* sake, not yours.'

The child looked puzzled. 'Why does Kathleen need me to hold *her* hand?'

Harry gave an aside wink at Kathleen who was wagging a finger at him. 'Go on then,' she urged wickedly. 'Tell the boy, why don't ye?'

'Y'see, son,' Harry went on, 'when people get old, they forget things, and sometimes they even forget where they are. Then they get lost altogether.'

Tom frowned. 'Kathleen won't get lost though, will she?' He was almost sure about that, especially when she was standing right behind them, tutting and making a face. Everybody knew that when Kathleen tutted, she was always right, and he had never known her to get lost at all.

'No, son. Kathleen won't get lost,' Harry assured him, 'especially if you're holding her hand. That way, you'll always know where she is, won't you?'

Tom had a question for Kathleen. 'Will you get lost?'

She made a woeful face. 'I nearly got lost once before, so yes, I suppose I might get lost again, especially if no one was holding my hand.'

'Oh.' Tom was taken aback by her answer. 'So if I hold your hand, you won't get lost then?'

'Absolutely not!'

'Okay.' Tom offered his face to Harry for a kiss, which he got twice over. 'I don't want Kathleen to get lost, Daddy, so don't worry. I won't mind holding her hand.'

'Good boy. So now I can go to work without worrying, eh?'

Before he prepared to leave, Harry got another cuddle from Tom, and a swift crafty kick in the shins from Kathleen. 'Thank you for telling him how it is,' she declared sweetly, 'that I'm a poor old thing who can't go down the street without getting lost. Sure it's a miracle to have a grand lad like Tom, to show me the way home.'

'Bye, Daddy.' Tom and Kathleen walked him to the car, with Harry pretending to limp, until Kathleen gave him a sly shove and nearly sent him headfirst into the gutter. 'Oh, dearie me!' she told Tom. 'Did you see yer poor old daddy? He lost his footing and nearly fell over, so he did. He must be getting old, don't ye think?'

Tom gave a child-groan. 'I can't hold *his* hand as well,' he complained, ''cause I need to hold yours, don't I?'

'You certainly do or I might get lost and we wouldn't want that . . .' she raised her voice to a suitable level, 'WOULD WE HARRY?'

Harry gave a cheeky wink, 'We might!' he chuckled, 'if you keep shouting at me like that.'

He climbed into the car and started the engine, 'Bye, you two. See you later, eh?'

'Now, come on you,' she told Tom, as they waved goodbye to Harry. 'Something wants washing, so it does.'

'What wants washing?' Tom was curious.

'Face, hands, neck and ears,' Kathleen grinned, 'and who d'ye think they belong to?'

'TOM!' He clapped his hands excitedly. 'They belong to Tom!'

'That's absolutely right.' She took a firm hold of him. 'So let's get on with it then. The sooner you're all clean and shining, the sooner we're off to the shops for them bright new Wellingtons.' She looked down as he skipped his way up the path. 'So, is that all right with you then, Tom?'

'It is!' He ran on ahead. 'SO IT IS!' he called behind him, and when Kathleen took off after him, puffing and panting, and threatening to report him to the fairies for daring to mock the Irish, the joyous little fellow laughed until he ached.

For the next few minutes it was all screaming and yelling, until a shiny face appeared from the depths of the towel. 'Good grief!' Kathleen declared in a shaky voice. 'Who's this little fella here? Sure I've never seen him before. Get out of my house at once . . . go on with ye! Sure, if ye don't get out of me house, I'll call on Tom. He'll soon be rid of ye, so he will!'

Giggling, Tom protested. 'It's me!' he cried out loud. *'It's Tom!'*

'Tom, y'say?' Kathleen took a step backwards. 'That's not my Tom, no, it's not. Never in a million years.' She peered at him, then she closed one eye to peer closer, then the other, until at last she cried with relief, 'Bejaysus, so it is! Will ye look at that! Sure, I never would have known it was you.'

Tom couldn't stop laughing, until she tickled him under the arms and he ran away with her giving chase.

When she eventually caught him, she first gave him a stern talking to for running off, then she cuddled him good and proper.

On the way down to the sitting room, he held her hand. 'Sure I'm not likely to get lost in me own house, am I?' she declared.

'So, don't you want me to hold your hand?' He felt disappointed, especially after promising his daddy.

'Well, o' course I do. It's grand, so it is.'

So, with her smiling and him in charge, she allowed him to hold her hand all the way into the sitting room. 'Are you all right now, Kathleen?' he asked.

'Right as rain, and thank you.'

'Listen a minute, Kathleen.'

'I'm listening, my love.'

'W-well . . .' he stuttered nervously, 'I can't hold your hand *all* the time. I'm too little.'

'Ah sure, I understand so I do, and I have an idea.'

Tom's eyes grew like saucers. 'Is it a secret?'

She took a deep breath. How to phrase her words so as not make him feel worthless, that was the problem. 'Let me see . . . ah yes, that's it. A special secret, just between the two of us.'

Lowering her head, Kathleen spoke softly, in a conspiratorial manner. 'Look now, Tom, shall we make a deal between the two of us, right here and now?'

Taking on her secretive manner, he leaned towards her, asking in a furtive whisper, 'How can we do that?'

Kathleen peered from right to left and again over his head,

before continuing in a whisper, 'Well now, Tom. When we're in the house or the garden, we won't worry too much about holding hands.' She paused momentarily, to have another furtive peek about. 'But when we're out in the streets or crossing the road, we'd best do as yer daddy says. So then, Tom, do you think that's a good deal?'

Before answering, Tom also had a peek about; he adored Kathleen and he loved their secret. 'Yes!' he whispered. 'It's good, yes.'

Groaning, Kathleen stood up to straighten her old bones. 'You're a wise old man in the making, Tom Blake. But we've made a wonderful deal so we have, and I'm very pleased.'

'Yeah!' Tom felt very proud of himself, and especially proud of Kathleen, who knew how to fix everything.

Kathleen ruffled his hair. 'That's you done with,' she declared, 'so now I'll be away and make the beds while you play with your Dinky cars, Okay?'

Tom was so happy, he could not help jumping on the spot.

'Okay, Kathleen!' and off he went to find his box of cars, leaving Kathleen to watch the happy little soul skipping away, and her old heart bursting with love for that brave little fella who had found a forever place in her affections.

'Ah, sure ye're a lovely little fella, so ye are,' she whispered. 'Never you fear, me darlin', ye're daddy and me will always take care of you.'

Feeling content with her lot, she went away to make the beds.

Not a million miles away in Jackson Street, Judy was busy clearing away the breakfast things. While Kathleen's home was cosy and inviting, however, the house where Judy and Phil lived was jaded and worn. Most of the furniture was second-hand, on account of Phil claiming that he did not have money to waste on new stuff.

In the beginning, Judy had stood her ground and managed to secure a new dressing-table and bed, and a smart sideboard for the sitting room. The sofa though was already past its best when they bought it; the brown cloth covering was rubbed bald and in the corner where Phil normally slouched to nap, there was a distinct hole which seemed to grow larger and deeper by the day.

That's where she found him now, stretched out on the sofa snoring like a pig. 'Phil.' She gave him a gentle prod with the end of the hoover. 'Wake up.'

Arms flailing, he sat bolt upright. 'Stupid bitch!' Rubbing his eyes, he demanded, 'What the hell's wrong with you?'

Instinctively taking a step back, Judy explained, 'I need to hoover underneath the sofa, and I have to tip it backwards. I've done all the other jobs and left this till last because I knew you were tired. Only I'd like to finish off now.'

'Oh, would you now?' Swinging himself up to a sitting position, he stroked her leg, pushing with the palm of his hand all the way up to her thigh. 'So, what's the big hurry?'

As always when he touched her, she began to tremble inside. 'No reason, only I had a mind to go into town and see how much their sofas were.' She gestured towards the kitchen. 'I was just looking at the local paper and Jacobs have a sale on. They're getting rid of old stock. Some of the stuff is going for less than half. I thought if I got down there early, I might be able to get a cheap sofa.' And if there was half a chance, she might see Harry. That would be so wonderful.

'What!' Clambering to his feet he laughed spitefully in her face. 'Why would we need a new sofa?' He began bouncing up and down. 'There's still a few good years left in this one.'

Hoping he was not about to be difficult, Judy pointed to the sagging area where he had lain. 'Well, for one thing that hole is getting bigger, and the pattern has rubbed off the cloth everywhere else. It's a mess, and I'm ashamed of it. Please, Phil . . . can't I just get a new one?'

'Oh, I see. Just like that – we go out and spend a chunk of *my* hard-earned money, to pay for something we don't need and don't want. Have you lost your mind or what?' As it happened, Phil had a nice little stash put away from his thefts at work. He and the big Scot, McArthy, had covered their tracks well.

Judy knew the signs. When he was in one of his argumentative moods, there was no reasoning with him. 'I know how hard you have to work for your money,' she admitted, 'but if you could agree this once, it would be money well spent. Take a good look at the sofa, Phil, and you'll see it's way past its prime. Your mate gave it to us after he bought his wife a new one, and that was years ago. I'll admit it's served us well, but we need to be rid of it now, before it falls apart.'

'It won't fall apart. It's made of wood, and likely to survive longer than the two of us put together.'

Detesting the nearness of him and realising that she had lost the argument, Judy turned away. 'All right, Phil, it doesn't matter.'

'Hey! Not so quick.' Gripping her by the shoulders, he spun her round to face him, his face wreathed in a smile, the kind of smile that spelled trouble. 'That's not very nice, is it . . . turning your back on me like that? Especially when you woke me out of a deep sleep.'

'Sorry.'

His face crumpled in disgust. 'Why must you always be sorry?'

She took a moment, before replying in a small voice, 'I don't know, really. I suppose I'm always sorry, because . . .' She wanted to say she was sorry because she hated herself for kowtowing to him; and that she hated him for making her afraid; and because he had made her little more than a prisoner, keeping her to himself, and now she had no friends and no one else to turn to. She wanted to tell him how desperately unhappy she was, and that if she had anywhere else to go, she would leave him here and now.

More than anything else, she longed to tell him that every minute of every day she ached with regret, for being so naïve and trusting in saying yes, when he asked her to marry him.

She was desperately sorry, because he had turned out to be a bully and a brute. She was sorry that every time he took her to himself, it was with a degree of sadistic savagery that only made her loathing of him all the greater.

All of that and more, she wanted to shout from the rootftops, but she did not have the courage to face the pain and punishment that would surely follow.

Slowly but surely, Phil Saunders had turned her into a recluse, a frightened, cowardly creature who continued to put up with him and his domineering ways, because over the years he had systematically taken all the fight out of her.

That was the sad list of reasons why she was 'sorry' – but she would never dare say it out loud. Not if she wanted to go on living.

Checking her need to yell at him, she gave him a quiet, studied answer. 'I'm sorry because you won't let me go out to work, so I can help bring in some money, to get more of the things we need.'

As soon as she said it, she knew she had made a mistake; her comments were like a red rag to a bull. 'Phil, I only meant—'

'I know what you meant!' He pushed his face close to hers, the spittle flying out of his mouth as he raised his voice. '*Liar!* What you really meant was, you don't think I bring home enough money. You resent me going for a pint on a Friday night, don't you? Admit it! I'm right, aren't I?' Taking hold of her, he shook her hard. 'ADMIT IT!'

'No, Phil. I didn't mean that at all.'

There was no let-up. 'You're a barefaced liar! You sulk when I have a pint or a bet on the horses, and you hate me talking to other women. You whine all the time about how we never go anywhere, that you never have enough money for this or

314

that, and now you're nagging to go out to work, so's you can eye up other men and get them into your knickers. That's it, isn't it? I SAID, ISN'T IT?'

'No, I would never do that . . . you know I would never do that.'

'LYING COW! I know what you're up to. Don't think I haven't seen you looking at other men when you've been out with me. Time and again, I've had to forcefully claim what's rightfully mine, because you would rather give it to some other man. And look at you now, eh? Not satisfied with what I provide, you're after spending my hard-earned money on a sofa, when we already have a perfectly good one right here. What do you take me for, eh? WHAT THE DEVIL ARE YOU TRYING TO DO TO ME?'

Dreading what was bound to follow, Judy began trembling. 'I'm sorry, Phil.'

'Oh, there you go again, with the "Sorry, Phil",' he mimicked. 'Well, I'm sorry too. Sorry that you can't live peaceably with me, and sorry that you feel I'm not looking after you as a man should.'

He threw her aside. 'You make me sick!'

As she went to claw her way up from the floor, he pushed her down with the knuckle-end of his fist. 'If you think I will ever let you go out to work, you'd better think again. Your place is here in this house, keeping it clean, having my meal ready when I come home from work, and giving me comfort when-ever I need it. You're my wife! It's my right. You're supposed to understand that, for pity's sake.'

Hunched on the floor, she merely nodded at his every word. Right now, there was nothing left to say, nothing in her heart to give him.

'Oh, so now it's the silent treatment, is it?' Stooping, he stared her in the face. 'What's your little game, eh? What are you up to?'

'I'm not up to anything!' Angry and frustrated, and regardless of what the punishment might be, she found herself yelling back. 'I've told you before, I'm not a liar and I don't make eyes at other men. All I want is to work and earn money so we can have a new sofa, and curtains. Maybe we could even afford to go on a holiday, or just spend one day at the beach. Or just for once when I see something I like – a pair of shoes or a dress – how lovely it would be to go in and buy it, instead of grovelling to you for money and then waiting until you're good and ready to give it. Don't you see? I could take that burden from your shoulders, if I went out to work.'

Mentally and emotionally drained, she finished lamely, 'Besides, I get so lonely staying in this place. There's no one to talk to. The thing is, Phil, I need to be with other people. I find myself doing little things twice over, like wiping down the table, hoovering, or going round the furniture with the polish, and sometimes when I'm really lonely, I might walk down to see Pauline.'

After keeping the news to herself for too long, she now confessed, 'Pauline has offered me a job. Nothing much and it won't pay a fortune. It's just now and then, helping behind the bar, or cleaning the tables, or whatever else I want to do.'

'Oh, did she now?' With an animal-like growl, Phil flattened the palm of his hand and brought it hard across the side of her face, with such force that she fell into the wall. 'So! The pair of you have been plotting, have you? Well, you can tell her from me, your place is here, at home where you belong!'

Grabbing a hank of her hair he jolted her up, roughly steadying her when she seemed to slump in his arms. 'Did you hear that? Shall I say it again? *I will never let you work behind a bar . . . with men leering at you.*'

Digging his fingertips under her chin he forced her to look at him, his face a picture of evil as he promised in a harsh whisper, 'I'd rather finish you here and now, than let you do that.'

316

Throwing her down again, he watched her for what seemed an age, his face dripping with sweat and his fists clenching and unclenching as he fought with his demons. Mesmerised, he watched the blood from her nose trickling onto the frayed cloth beneath her head. He saw her squirming and sobbing, and his heart was hard like iron.

As though in a trance he began swaying. 'Whore!' He said it over and over again. 'You whore . . .'

When, growing silent, she peered up at him, his moment of lunacy began to subside.

'Oh, my Judy.' He fell to his knees and stroked her face, holding her as she began to tremble uncontrollably, her arms folded across her head as though ready to fend off possible blows.

'Judy.' He wrapped his two arms about her, crying out when she flinched with pain. 'Ssh. I won't hurt you no more, but it's *your* fault! You made me angry, talking like that. You know I can't let you go to work, and yet you still keep on and on about it. You're playing with my head, Judy.'

Closing his eyes, he gave a small cry of anguish. 'You ought not to do that.'

One minute he was talking to her as he might talk to a child, and in the next he was sobbing uncontrollably. 'I love you so much . . . oh, my sweet girl, I can't stand the thought of any other man touching you!'

When his grip tightened she tried her best to fight him off, but his manic strength was too much; his big, muscular arms were like an iron band around her chest, so much so that her fear of suffocation was very real.

Now he was pulling her up, with such incredible ease, she could have been a rag doll. 'It's all right . . . ssh, Judy. Ssh.'

With immense love and care he took her to the bathroom, where he washed her face and combed her hair, and Judy merely stood and let him do it, for if she were to complain, it would mean another beating.

So she was the 'good little girl' again; a role she had learned well, while trapped in a vicious circle of love and hatred.

Afterwards, knowing what he planned, she pleaded with him, 'Leave me now, Phil, I don't want to . . . Please, I hurt too much.' Smiling, he carried her into the bedroom, where he laid her down in the gentlest manner and then, without any thought for her, he furiously and viciously gratified himself, while at the same time professing his love.

'Don't fight me, Judy,' he warned. 'I need you.'

Time and again he murmured in her ear, 'You belong to me, now and for always.'

When he was satisfied, he sat back on his haunches, smiling down on her tearful face. 'Look at me!' He slid his hand beneath her face and tenderly but deliberately shifted her head so she was facing him, though she did not look at him. Instead she turned her gaze to the wall.

'Judy, look at me.'

She kept her eyes averted. To look at him would defile her all over again.

'Hmh! Sulking again,' he mumbled, climbing off the bed. 'Get yourself ready now,' he instructed in a matter-of fact voice. 'I've decided to let you have your sofa. So hurry up, there's a good girl. It'll be your fault if we're too late for the sale.'

'I thought you had a game of darts down the pub this afternoon?' Judy crossed her fingers behind her back. 'You told me you had some kind of competition coming up and you needed to get in plenty of practice. I really don't mind.' She was desperate. 'I can always take Pauline to look at the sofa.'

He laughed at that. 'You don't think I'd let *her* go with you, do you?' he asked. 'Especially after she had the nerve to offer you a job.'

'It was me that asked her.'

Astonished, he swung round. 'You never said that! You said she offered you a job – that's what you said.'

'Well, it was a bit of both really, but it doesn't matter now, does it?'

'Too right. The idea was a non-starter from the off.'

Judy tried another tack. After meeting Kathleen, she had hatched a secret plan, but it had plainly backfired, and this time it was not herself she feared for; it was Harry. 'You're right, Phil. You're always right.' Flattery usually did the trick.

'Right about what?'

'About the sofa being good for a while longer yet.'

She had been all kinds of a fool to think he might agree to her going alone.

Reaching out, he pulled her effortlessly to the edge of the bed, grabbed her legs and swung her round until her feet touched the floor. 'Don't argue with me!' he warned. 'I've told you, my mind is made up. I want you to have a new sofa. Now do as I ask, and get ready. Or do I have to get cross with you again?'

Without another word he snatched up the clothes he had so wantonly thrown aside, then he went into the bathroom and washed.

When he was dressed, he stood by the door until she got off the bed and made her way towards the bathroom. 'Good girl.' Pleased that he had won the day, he stepped aside to let her pass. 'I knew you'd see it my way in the end.'

While Judy set about getting ready, he took a deep breath and congratulated himself on his authority. 'Women, eh?' He chuckled to himself. 'They have to know who's boss, or they'll make your life a downright, bloody misery.'

Digging into his pocket, he took out a packet of cigarettes. Inside the packet there were two matches rolled up in a tissue. He took one out, struck it on the sole of his shoe, and lit the cigarette. He then sucked in a long deep mouthful, which he blew out in a series of perfectly formed rings. He watched the rings float and wobble and finally dissipate altogether, then laughed out loud. 'You haven't lost it, Phil m' lad,' he chortled. 'You still haven't lost it.'

A few moments later, Judy emerged. She had done her best to hide the weals and marks on her face and neck, but however much cream and powder she had plastered on, the faint shadows of his brutality were still there.

Cupping her chin between his finger and thumb, he turned her head this way and that. 'I can still see the bruises. Can't you disguise them a bit better than that?'

'No.' In truth she didn't care if the whole world was to see them, but not Harry. She did not want Harry to know how low she had sunk.

Almost as though he had read her thoughts he said quietly, 'Sit down.'

'Why?'

'Because I said so, and because we don't want everyone seeing your poor little face.' He gave her a shove towards the dressing-table stool. 'Sit down . . . now!'

Judy argued that she had done her level best to hide the marks, but as always he believed he knew better. 'Sit!' Thrusting her into the chair, he went to the bathroom, returning a moment later with her cosmetics bag. 'I could do a better job than you, with gloves on and my eyes shut.' Throwing open the bag, he tipped the contents onto the bed. 'Now then, let me see. What have we got here?'

After meticulously tending her face to disguise the results of his wicked handiwork, he replaced the cream and powder, together with the dark foundation she rarely used, and which she had meant to throw out. 'Now, look in the mirror.'

Judy noted how he had plastered a thick coat of foundation over her skin, then with a layer of powder on top he had managed to disguise the damage; though in the process he had made her look like a tart off the streets. 'It's too thick,' she objected. 'You've put too much on. I look hideous!'

'Nonsense.' He kissed the back of her neck. 'Not to me you

don't, and it doesn't matter what other men think. Now shift yourself. You've kicked up a great fuss about wanting this sofa, so let's get on with it. I've got better things to be doing with my time than hanging about in shops.'

'Honestly, Phil, I know how you love your darts, so why not let me go on my own?' she offered. 'I promise I'll go straight there and straight back.'

His answer was to shove her across the room and out the door. 'Thought you'd got me there, did you, eh?' he chuckled. 'Hoped I was about to turn you loose, did you?'

'I'm only trying to be fair to us both,' she protested. 'You could go to your darts practice, and it would be really nice if I could choose the sofa myself. If you come along, you'll only argue with me over colour and such. In the end we'll probably get something you choose, and I won't like it. Please, Phil. I'll be better off on my own. Besides, I know exactly what I'm looking for.'

'The darts practice can wait,' he answered slyly. 'Besides, with you wandering about and my money burning a hole in your pocket, who knows what you might get up to. Look – I'm coming with you, and that's an end to it. After all, I need to make sure you keep your eyes on the sofas, and not on any man that might take a fancy to you.'

'I have no interest in other men, you know that.' Yet, always at the back of her mind and part of the reason she wanted to go to Jacobs' Emporium, was the news that Kathleen had given her; the unbelievable, wonderful news that Harry was working there.

In her deepest heart, she desperately wanted to see him.

Having noticed the advert for the sale, she had thought to use the old sofa as her excuse for going there. All she wanted was to maybe just catch sight of him – just to see him again, with her own eyes. To see how he had turned out; whether he still bore any resemblance to that wonderful, good-looking boy she had fallen in love with, and whom she had never stopped loving through every minute of every day since he'd been gone.

Every time Phil used and hurt her while making what he termed as 'love', the only way she could get through it, was to imagine it was Harry holding her; Harry with his mouth on hers; Harry who was whispering in her ear.

But then, the Harry she had known would hold her more gently. He would not bruise her lips with his hard, spiteful kisses, and if he whispered in her ear it would be with soft, loving words, not filthy innuendoes and promises of the perverted things Phil planned to do to her.

Her heart was aching with the need to see Harry again, but her head was telling her that the worst thing that could happen was for Harry and Phil to come face to face, and now that her plan had gone wrong, she was caught in a trap.

Trying every which way to worm out of it, she suggested now, 'Maybe we'd best leave it for another day, eh? I'm not feeling so well. Like I said, there will always be other sales, and other places we can try.'

Bringing her to a halt, he gave her a suspicious look. 'What are you up to?'

'For pity's sake, Phil! How many times do you want me to say it? I'm not up to anything!' If only he knew what was really on her mind, she thought.

He grinned. 'All right, I believe you, but thousands wouldn't.' He slid his arms round her waist. 'Now, let's go and choose this damned sofa, and then maybe a man can get a bit of peace round here, eh?'

Outside, Judy climbed into the car, while Phil walked round to the driver's side. In the rear-view mirror she saw him stop to talk with a neighbour; a man some years younger than Phil who loved to party, rolling home legless at all hours of the day and night. 'Another pea out of the same rotten pod,' she muttered.

She could hear them laughing, and her hatred of Phil Saunders was never more alive than it was in that moment.

'I have to leave you,' she whispered. 'Somehow, I have to find the courage to go where you will never find me.'

Over the years she had said that same thing time and again. But here she still was, and here she would probably stay. I expect you'll kill me one day, she thought, resigned. One terrible day, or in the middle of the night, when you're out of your mind, you'll go too far, and you will kill me.

Right now though, with her life stretching out before her like a grim punishment, the prospect of leaving this world did not seem so terrible.

CHAPTER EIGHTEEN

A MY'S FAMILIAR GIGGLE echoed through the store. 'Harry Blake! That's the biggest piece of cake I have ever seen. Are you trying to get me fat or what?' Taking a sizeable bite out of the huge slice of Victoria sponge, she licked the cream off her lips. 'Mmm. That is so scrumptious!'

She offered Harry a bite, but he graciously refused. 'Kathleen has gone completely mad about baking,' he said. 'There's more cake in her pantry than I've ever seen in one place, and she truly expects me and Tom to finish off the lot.'

'Good old Kathleen, eh?' Spluttering crumbs of cake as she spoke, Amy went on, 'My mam could not bake a cake to save her life, and neither can I.'

'I asked Kathleen to cut an extra big piece because it's your birthday today,' Harry explained.

Suddenly, Amy looked up and there was Kathleen herself. 'Ooh, look! Here's the very woman, and she's brought your son to see you.' She recognised Kathleen and Tom from the previous time they had come to the store.

Quickly wiping the cream from her face, Amy smiled as they approached. 'Your cake is delicious – thank you so much.' She grinned down at Tom. 'Who's a clever Kathleen, eh?' she asked in a baby voice. 'I bet you couldn't bake a cake like this.'

'Yes, I could,' he declared, puffing out his little chest. 'I made a biscuit at school with green icing and pink buttons and everything.'

'That's true,' Harry said. 'What's more, it tasted wonderful.' He and Kathleen exchanged glances, with Kathleen smiling at his tender lies.

Breaking away from Kathleen, Tom ran straight into his daddy's arms. 'Hello, Daddy!' He planted the sloppiest kiss on Harry's face. 'Kathleen wants a new table-runny, so we have to go shopping, and we need to get some shiny black wellies for me.'

While Harry and his son continued to chat a moment longer, Phil Saunders was ushering Judy in through the front door. 'You didn't tell me they were selling records and LPs at half price.' His attention was drawn to the long table, heaving with sheet music, gramophones and records of all types. 'You go and look at the sofas,' he suggested, striding away, 'while I see if there's anything here that takes my fancy.' He liked to give the impression that he had an educated knowledge of music, when apart from being tone-deaf, he had no real interest in it.

Left alone by the door, Judy looked around; she was worried in case Harry was here, and even more worried that he might not be. Now, when she heard male laughter and saw him throwing the small boy in the air, making him squeal with delight, her heart leaped. Oh, my God! she thought. It really *is* him!

A great sense of joy swept through her. She felt nervous and excited all at the same time. Tears filled her eyes as her senses drank in the man that was Harry, the man who had been her first sweetheart, love for whom she had always carried deep in her heart, through thick and thin.

She was aching to speak with him, yet fearing the consequences if she did. She wanted to call his name and run to him, to hear his voice and look in his eyes, but then she saw Phil and the bubble burst. Bending forward to examine a cabinet-mounted gramophone, he had no concept of her dilemma, nor of the fact that his deadliest enemy, Harry Blake, was standing just a short distance from him.

Judy was grateful to have his attention diverted onto something else. Her emotions torn in every direction, she stood there for what seemed an age, delighting in watching Harry with his son. 'Oh, Harry!' she whispered. 'So many times I prayed you might come and find me, but you never did.'

She could not blame him for that. 'You're here now though; all grown up into an amazing man, with a son of your own. Where have you been all these years?' She had so many questions, so much she wanted to tell him, with a heart full of love and a need for him to take her in his arms and hold her there, where she could never be hurt again.

Look at you, she thought. Look at how you've turned out. The sigh she gave was from deep down. You're close enough for me to touch, and yet I mustn't. I daren't.

Recalling the manner in which they had parted, another thought crossed her mind. *Would you even want me to?*

Afraid he might suddenly glance up and see her there, she wanted to move away, to get Phil and herself as far from here as possible. But her feet seemed glued to the floor, and her whole being cried out for Harry to see her, to want her, to help her be strong. Like a schoolgirl, she wanted him to sweep her off her feet and carry her away.

'Silly fool, Judy!' she chided herself softly. 'You had your chance and you threw it away. It's too late now. No good will come of wanting what you can't have.'

She forced herself to face the truth. Thanks to her lies, Harry Blake had been lost to her a long time ago. But then, she reminded herself, it was not altogether her fault.

Someone else must carry the blame.

Someone who betrayed her trust. Someone she would loathe and despise for as long as she lived.

While she was watching Harry, she saw Phil out of the corner of her eye. Horrified to see him heading straight to the counter where Harry was saying cheerio to Tom and Kathleen, she waved her arm to catch his attention.

To her immense relief, her husband turned and saw her. Shifting direction, he made his way towards her. Knowing he would follow, Judy went at full stride in the other direction, towards the furniture display.

'What the devil are you playing at?' he demanded, coming alongside. 'Where are you off to now? Don't tell me you've been standing by the door all the time I was gone.'

'I was just looking about,' Judy replied casually. 'Seeing what was on offer.' She glanced at the box in his hand. 'Found something interesting, have you?' She guessed he would not come back with records or other music paraphernalia.

'It's a camera,' he answered. 'A real bargain.'

'You've already got a camera,' she reminded him.

He was instantly prickly. 'What? So now you're telling me I'm only allowed one camera?'

She knew he was trying to draw her into another argument. 'You can have as many cameras as you please,' she said tiredly. 'It's none of my business.'

'Too right it's none of your business. Besides which, it's my money, so I can buy whatever I please. You need to remember that.'

It was on the tip of her tongue to say she was sorry, but she stopped herself. She was *not* sorry. She was sick to her stomach of his petty sniping and bad temper. It was odd, but seeing Harry again seemed to have given her a certain strength of mind; a fleeting reason to believe in herself.

Phil drew her attention to the sofas. 'I like this one,' he said, seeing a cheaply-priced sofa with thin material and flimsy legs. He lowered himself into it. 'It's comfy enough,' he stated, 'and cheap into the bargain. We'll take this one.'

Judy wasn't listening. Her attention had involuntarily strayed to where Harry was now tending a customer. Lingering on,

Kathleen was chatting to Amy, while at the same time pulling up Tom's bedraggled socks.

'Hey!' Phil called for her attention. 'Are you listening to me or what?'

Startled, Judy quickly sat down beside him. 'I was just looking,' she said, 'seeing if there were other sofas.'

'No need for that,' he declared confidently. 'Not now I've found this one. I reckon it's exactly what we want.'

Judy stood up. 'It's not what *I* want though, Phil.'

'Why not?' He gave her a curious look. 'Go on then, what's wrong with it?'

'It's cheap and nasty and it won't wear well, so before too long you'll be having to buy another, but if you don't mind wasting good hard-earned money, that's up to you. It's your wages, after all.' As he loved to remind her. 'Besides, the colour is too much like the old one.'

Dark reddish, with brown undertones, it seemed to suck in the light. 'I thought it would be nice to have something bright and cheerful for a change.' While she spoke she was conscious of Harry being in the same room, and every time Phil looked away for a brief moment, she snatched that moment to peek at Harry.

Married to one and loving another. What a mess I've made of my life, she thought.

Astonishingly, and because he knew Judy was right that it would not last five minutes, Phil offered grudgingly, 'All right then, choose another, but remember I'm not made of money, so don't get carried away. Oh, and be quick about it. I've got things to do.'

Easing himself up from the sofa, he dug out a cigarette from his pocket and hung it on the end of his lips. Having located a match in his other pocket, he strode off. 'Get a move on!' he commanded her. 'I'll be outside. Come and find me when you're done.'

Once he was safely out of sight, Judy moved to a quiet corner, from where she could see Harry quite clearly. Just to look at his face and see him smile, gave her a warm, safe feeling.

She watched him shake hands with a customer, and then saw the customer go over to the counter where the girl assistant dealt with the payment of his purchase.

She then saw Harry go to a bunch of balloons advertising the sale; he carefully broke one off and handed it to his little boy, who was so excited he started running in circles with it.

While Harry went away to help a young couple who were after a set of curtains, she saw Kathleen walk into the department, Tom following behind her, flying his balloon and having great fun swinging it about in the air.

Careful not to let Kathleen see her, Judy shrank back into the corner. She thought Harry's son was a credit to him, blessed with his daddy's strong capable build, and a face carved with good looks and character. While she continued to watch him, she thought of her own child, and was racked with guilt.

The nearer Kathleen and Tom got, the more nervous she felt. As soon as they were gone past, she meant to leave the store and tell Phil she could not find a sofa she liked.

From her hiding-place, she heard Kathleen talking to the boy, and felt guilty that she had been too much of a coward to step out and greet that delightful old friend.

The decision to leave was taken out of her hands when suddenly the balloon came floating by, and above the sound of young Tom's distressed cries, Kathleen's familiar voice carried through the air. 'Don't you worry, I'll find it, so I will. Now then, stop that awful noise and tell me . . . where did it fly off to?'

When the balloon landed on a shelf above Judy's head, and realising she was bound to be discovered, Judy caught hold of the string and stepped out, just as Kathleen rounded the corner.

The Irish woman was flabbergasted. 'Well, I never!' She laughed with delight. 'Sure, if it isn't the girl herself.' Stretching out her chubby arms, she clasped Judy in a firm embrace. 'Oh, me little darlin', it's lovely to see you, so it is.' Holding her at arm's length, she smiled into Judy's eyes.

'It's lovely to see you too,' Judy replied, and that was the absolute truth.

But Kathleen gave no answer, for she had seen something that alarmed her. 'What have ye done to yer pretty face? Sure it's looking a bit bruised – have you had a mishap of sorts, pet?' All manner of suspicions ran through her mind.

Taken aback by Kathleen's remark, Judy retreated into the shadows. 'It's nothing,' she lied, 'I tried out some new face powder and it's caused my skin to go a bit blotchy, that's all, but the blotches have almost gone now, thank goodness.'

Visibly shaking, she handed the balloon to Tom, who had been hopping up and down impatiently. 'There you are, sweet-heart.' Then she mumbled to Kathleen, 'I've been looking at sofas but they don't have what I want, so I'd best be off now.'

Afraid that she had frightened Judy away with her comment about her bruised face, Kathleen took her by the hand. 'You're not here just for a sofa, are you?' she asked caringly.

'Why do you say that?'

Kathleen gave a wink. 'You came here to get a peek at Harry, did you not?' Her quick smile was encouraging.

Judy had an urge to deny it, but instead she nodded. 'Just a peek,' she whispered. 'Nothing more.'

From across the room where Harry was just finishing with the couple, he was surprised to see that Kathleen and Tom were still in the store. 'Can you deal with these customers?' he murmured to Amy. 'They've decided on the curtains that are out on display.'

'Right away,' Amy said, and to the customers: 'We're not allowed to get the curtains down off display, so while we're waiting for one of the men to fetch some from the warehouse, would you like a cup of tea?'

Harry was straining his eyes to see who Kathleen was talking to. There was something about the slim young woman with the shoulder-length fair hair . . . Somewhere in his deepest memory, an image emerged, of a girl named Judy.

He dismissed the feeling as ridiculous, but it was deeply unnerving.

The truth began to dawn on him when Kathleen turned to look at him in a particular way, with a proud little grin on her face that said, 'Look who I've found – it's our Judy, come to see you.'

At first he dared not let himself believe it. 'It can't be!' he whispered. But somehow, he knew it was her. He just knew! And every nerve in his body was screaming with excitement, and terror. 'Judy?' he murmured. Her name fell so easily from his lips.

Almost in a daze, he started towards her.

As he came nearer, her smile wrapped itself around him, until he could hardly breathe. Observing her, he took in every little detail. She had changed, and yet she was the same. Slightly taller and slimmer, she seemed so delicate, and he did not know what he would say to her.

Judy stood motionless, watching him, loving him, and willing him towards her. Then she glanced at the door. Remembering what Phil had done to her face, she began to panic. There was bad blood between Phil and Harry, and there was no telling what a madman like Phil would do if he saw her talking to the 'enemy'.

'Tell Harry I'll see him again – sometime,' she told Kathleen. 'I have to go.' In a lower voice she confided, 'Phil's waiting outside.'

Thankful that Harry was suddenly intercepted by another customer, Judy hurried towards the exit.

Harry saw her, and quickly excused himself from the customer. 'Wait! Judy!'

Already on his way back inside, Phil heard someone call Judy's name and hurried to see who it was. As he came in through the door, Judy crossed his path. 'Let's go!' She tried to sound calm, but she was in a state of panic. 'The sofas are all the same,' she gabbled. 'Cheap and nasty. We'd best go elsewhere, or stick with the one we've got for now.'

Suspicious, he grabbed her by the shoulders. 'Just now, I heard a man call your name. Who was it, eh?'

'It was the salesman – he saw me looking at the sofas. You know what they're like . . . they won't let you escape if they can help it.' She managed a nervous little laugh. 'You were right anyway, Phil. We really don't need a new sofa.'

'LIAR!' Incensed, he blocked her way. 'I've never known a salesman who would call out like that, and how does he know you by your first name? Something's not right here.'

'Listen to me, Phil. You're imagining things.'

He gave her a spiteful shove towards the car. 'In the car – now!' When she still hesitated, he leered at her. 'Unless you want trouble?'

Hoping that if she got into the car, he would go with her, Judy nodded, 'All right! Let's go home. We should never have come here.' Then realising his intention to go back inside the store, she was panic-stricken. 'Phil! Leave it!'

His words echoed back to her. 'I've told you! Stay where you are!'

Inside the store, Harry was quizzing Kathleen, who was using every ploy possible to waylay him, to keep him from following Judy outside. 'You've got it wrong,' she insisted. 'That was a young woman I met in the doctor's surgery last week . . . she was just asking after my health.'

She was not in the habit of lying, but she dreaded the outcome if Phil and Harry ever crossed swords. When they were young there had been a healthy rivalry between them. Now the stakes were higher, and if Harry should see those badly-disguised bruises on Judy's face, he would want to know who was responsible. Kathleen though, had her own suspicions.

Her attention was caught by the man now entering the store. Thickset, with a hostile manner about him, she suspected it could be Phil Saunders. There was a certain familiarity about him.

To her horror, he stood for a minute, hands on hips, his black eyes scouring the room. At one point, he actually glanced at her and Harry . . . then at the child, and now again at Harry.

For a moment Kathleen held her breath, but then to her great relief, he turned away. It seemed he had not recognised either her or Harry – probably because Harry had his back to him. She was immensely grateful for that.

Saunders might have left at that point, had it not been for Amy's shrill voice, which carried the length of the showroom. 'Harry! Have you a minute?' He was so intent on questioning Kathleen, that she called him twice. *'Harry!'*

That was when Phil Saunders' entire body seemed to expand. Stretching himself to his full height, he looked at Amy, then he followed her gaze until his attention was brought first to Kathleen, and then to the man she was talking to.

At first he wasn't sure, but then he smiled. 'My God! Harry Blake, of all people.' The smile slid away as he followed Harry back to the counter.

Because of the boy, Kathleen kept her distance for the moment; her lips muttering a prayer that commonsense would prevail and there would be no bitter confrontation.

Aware that Judy had come back inside, she waved her over. 'Don't interfere,' she warned. 'Let them talk. There are things they need to get off their chest and I suppose now is as good a time as any.'

Judy was paranoid. 'You don't know what he's like. Phil has been known to carry a knife, and he's not afraid to use it!'

When she made to run forward, Kathleen held her back. 'Harry is no fool,' she informed Judy. 'Sure, he's been through the war and is well able to take care of himself.' Though right now, she too was afraid of the outcome between these two old rivals.

Harry recognised Phil instantly; the same shock of hair, the same piercing, hostile gaze, and the swagger that identified him now, as it did then. Arrogant as ever, Phil Saunders had not changed over the years.

Thrusting himself between Harry and Amy, Saunders addressed Harry in a hard voice. 'Well, well! I never thought to see you again, not after you ran off with your tail between your legs.'

Realising that the other man was merely goading him, Harry asked, 'What d'you want, Saunders?'

Phil stared at him, his face twisted with loathing. 'I think you and me had best have a little word. Just so there won't be any misunderstandings.'

'I've got no wish to talk with you,' Harry informed him coldly. 'I think you'd better go.'

Saunders persisted. 'We can talk here, or we can talk in private. I don't much care one way or the other.'

'I don't think you heard me right. I said, I think you had better go.'

'Make me!'

Surprised by Phil Saunders' sudden arrival, Harry suspected that for obvious reasons, Kathleen had deliberately misled him, and that the woman he had seen really *was* Judy.

He now glanced at Kathleen and, sensing real trouble, he made a subtle, sideways gesture with his head. Kathleen nodded. Taking Judy and Tom along she left the store.

Satisfied, Harry returned his attention to Saunders. 'The same old Phil – ready to fight the world,' he said. 'Go on, then. Say what you've come to say, then get out.' Most of the customers had come and gone, and though there was a couple still browsing, they were far enough away not to hear the heated exchange between Harry and Saunders.

Addressing Amy, Harry asked, 'Amy, I wonder if you could please see to the customers?'

'Sure.' Aware of the tension, she did not need asking twice.

'Huh. Quite the big boss-man, aren't we, eh?' When Saunders

prodded his finger into Harry's chest, Harry caught hold of his hand and gripped it so tight that Saunders could neither open his fist nor escape the other man's iron-fast grip. 'Bastard! Let go . . . damn you!'

Harry had something to say first. 'It seems to me there are things on your mind that you want to share. Things from the past, maybe?'

'How right you are, Blake.' Pulling hard to release his hand from Harry's grip, Phil warned, 'You'd best watch your back, because I'm on to you.'

Harry shook his head. 'Like I said . . . always ready to fight the world. Well, you listen to me, Saunders. I'm sure neither of us needs trouble, so unless you intend being difficult, I suggest you say what's on your mind. After that, you can make yourself scarce.'

Releasing Saunders, he remained alert, knowing from old that this man was dangerously unpredictable. Many times in the past, he and Saunders had clashed, and each time the latter had backed off. But he was older now, and judging by his current mood, much more aggressive; he obviously had old scores to settle.

Discreetly rubbing the life back into his numbed hand, Saunders launched straight into the attack. 'I want to know what's going on here!' he demanded. 'And don't try telling me there's nothing because I know damned well there is. Why else was Judy so insistent on coming here, pretending to want a new sofa, and not being too keen on having me along?'

Harry shrugged. 'It seems to me you'll have to answer that one yourself.'

'She knew *you* were here, that's why. You forget, Blake, I'm nobody's fool. Admit it . . . you and she are up to something!'

'You always were a distrustful devil.' When it now seemed that Saunders was about to argue, Harry pre-empted him. 'For your information, I have not spoken to Judy since the day I left, and you know how many years ago that is.'

He gave a quiet smile. 'So! You actually believe that Judy would cheat on you, do you? That sounds to me like you're not too sure of your woman. You and Judy are together, so she obviously loves you. Or does she?'

Incensed by Harry's cynical remarks, Saunders took a step forward, his manic eyes boring into Harry's face. 'As far as me and Judy are concerned, you are history! You're no threat to me or my marriage, and I don't know why I ever imagined you could be.'

Suppressing the instinct to knock him off his feet, Harry would not be drawn. 'Right, is that it then?'

Enraged by Harry's controlled manner, Saunders thrust his face close. 'You lost! D'you hear me, Blake? *You lost!* Judy is mine now! She is *my* wife, and she loves *me*, and remember this: I'll kill any man who tries to take her from me.' He paused, staring at Harry,

Harry got his message all right. 'The trouble with you, Saunders,' he pointed out, 'is that you can't let go of the past. You can't believe that Judy chose me over you, and it still riles you to think about it.'

'Oh, you'd like to think so, wouldn't you, eh?' Raring to fight but cautioned by Harry's strong build and that quiet controlled manner, Saunders was so fired up, he appeared to be hopping on the spot. 'You're wrong, Blake, and you know it. Look how your ridiculous little fling came to nothing in the end. Judy didn't want you . . . she wanted me. ME – PHIL SAUNDERS! A better man than you will ever be. I would never desert her, but you did. And that's just fine by me, 'cause your loss was my gain, so to speak.'

Saunders continued to gloat. 'I expect you're sorry now though.' He attacked Harry where it hurt most. 'It's plain to me that you obviously don't understand women. They're a strange breed. Where we men can use 'em and chuck 'em and not think twice about it, a woman is different. She has feelings for a man; deep, strong feelings that make her want to be with him night and day.'

'Is that so?' Harry was determined not to let the other man see how he was beginning to rile him.

'Well, you wouldn't know, would you?' Saunders believed he now had the upper hand. 'I do, because I know how Judy feels about me. So there it is.' He shrugged his shoulders. 'Either a woman has feelings for you, or she doesn't, and Judy decided I was the one she wanted. Unfortunately, where you were concerned, Judy never really had any feelings at all.'

He gave a hideous grin. 'After all, with you gone, she didn't waste much time before she picked up with me.'

Harry let that bitter comment wash over him. Aware that Amy was returning, he addressed Saunders in a calm and quiet manner. 'You've had your say. Now get out.'

As he turned away, Saunders grabbed him by the arm. 'I'm not done yet, matey.'

Harry looked at Saunders, then glanced at the heavy hand across his arm. 'I wouldn't do that if I were you,' he said meaningfully.

Seeing a certain gleam in Harry's eye, Saunders swiftly moved away. 'You listen to me, Blake, and listen good,' he growled. 'If I find out you've been anywhere near my wife, I swear I'll have you good and proper. You won't know where or when, but I'll be there, and I will have you.'

Harry stared him out. 'I hear you, Saunders,' he acknowledged. 'So now that you've got that off your chest, you can make yourself scarce, either under your own steam, or with a bit of help. Which way will it be?'

The other man stood for a moment, his face contorted with rage and his fists tight by his side. He wanted Harry dead and buried. He wanted him off the scene altogether. But there was time enough, he thought cunningly. Time, and opportunity enough.

For now, Phil Saunders had one more card up his sleeve.

Lowering his voice almost to a whisper, he confided in Harry, 'Don't think I don't know the real reason why you ran out on her. Judy told me. She tells me everything. That's why she'll tell me what's been going on between the two of you.'

He giggled like a maniac. 'Oh yes, she'll tell me all right, don't you worry about that.'

With his last, sly comment, Saunders turned round and hurried away before Harry could question him further.

Saunders thought he had been very clever. Tell a man you know his secret and he'll worry that you really do know something! he thought triumphantly and congratulated himself on having the last laugh over his old enemy.

Cut to the heart, Harry watched him go, all manner of questions racing through his shattered mind.

Did Judy actually tell Phil that Harry left because she had deceived him and was with child and that regardless of his love for her, their relationship was irretrievably damaged by that deception?

If Judy had confided all that, had she also told him about the abortion? And if he knew that, why hadn't Saunders made more of it? Why had he let it go so easily, when he could have goaded Harry far more viciously than he had done so far?

Harry suspected Saunders was merely fishing with his throwaway comment. Or was he holding back, to keep the information for another time?

In spite of his misgivings, and because the alternative was too awful to consider, Harry made himself believe that Judy would never have told Saunders what had really happened between the two of them.

'Sick in the head,' he concluded. 'That's what he is.'

Outside in the car, Judy saw her husband striding towards her, and her heart sank; she prepared herself for the worst.

When he climbed into the car she was astonished to see that he was actually grinning to himself. 'That's unsettled him,' he boasted. 'That's got him wondering what I know that he doesn't.'

In the blink of an eye his mood changed and the darkness was on him again. Turning slowly, he looked at Judy, his eyes boring into hers. 'So, my pretty.' His voice had that meanness she had come to fear. 'What have you been up to?'

Judy shook her head. 'Nothing. Why do you say that?'

'You and Blake,' he said. 'The two of you laughing at me behind my back.'

'NO!'

'That's why you wanted to come here. That's why you didn't want me along, because you've been meeting up. He's had you, hasn't he?'

'NO! I would never do that.'

'Why not? You did it before. When I offered you everything, you chose him.'

'That was a long time ago, Phil, but I chose you in the end. I said yes when you asked me to marry you. That should tell you something, shouldn't it?'

'All it tells me is that you only latched onto me, because he deserted you.'

'No, Phil! It was more than two years after he'd gone. I was over him,' she lied. 'I wanted *you*. When you asked me to marry you, I was thrilled, you know that.'

For a long, unsettling moment, he stared at her, then in a kind of whisper, he demanded to know, 'There's something that still puzzles me.'

'What is it?' She was grateful that he seemed more curious than angry.

'Why did Blake leave you, and in such a hurry? One minute he was here, and the next he was gone – and nobody knew where.'

When she hesitated, he asked again, in a harsher voice, 'Well? Cat got your tongue?'

Made nervous by his persistent questioning, Judy answered, 'He went to join up. What's so strange about that? He left because . . . well, because I told him I didn't want him; that I didn't love him any more.' The last thing she wanted was for Phil to know the truth; that she had been pregnant, and the reason Harry left was because she had deceived him – not because she wanted to, but because she could see no other way.

'You might as well know. I've been doing my sums,' he revealed.

'Doing your sums?' She never knew what he would say or do next.

He rounded on her. 'Don't come the innocent with me! Do you think I'm stupid? As far as I can make out, you were still only fourteen when you and Blake were together.' He looked at her in a way that really unnerved her. 'Why did you let everybody think you were sixteen?'

Judy went on the defensive. 'No reason.'

'So, if you and he were at it, Blake broke the law. He should be in jail.' And he would be the one to turn him in, he thought.

Judy's stomach turned. She knew without a doubt that her husband would go to the authorities. It would suit him down to the ground to get Harry put away. 'We were not "at it" as you say.'

'Am I supposed to believe that?'

'Of course. It wasn't that kind of relationship. I was just a kid. We were just going out together, that's all.'

'So, are you saying I was the first?'

'Yes, because you were.'

He paused, biting his lip, deep in thought. 'I never really gave it a thought until now. Maybe I should have.'

Judy's mind was spinning. 'Think about it, Phil,' she suggested. 'You know how that first time with you was very difficult. Remember how painful it was for me.'

He paused again. 'There was a drop of blood on the carpet, I remember that.' He peeked at her out of the corner of his eye. 'So he never touched you in that way?'

'No! I just told you.' Because of the circumstances, she had deceived Phil, and he was conceited enough to believe he was the first, but he was not. As far as she was concerned, Harry was still her one true love to this day.

The only reason she had agreed to marry Phil was to hide many dark truths, and to feel safe so she would never be hurt again.

Because of that, she had held out on Phil right up until the wedding night, when he had been so hungry for her, he took her right there on the bedroom carpet.

Taken unawares as she came out of the bathroom, she had instinctively resisted his vicious attack. That was the reason for the blood. That was when she realised what a terrible mistake she had made.

That was when the past came flooding back with all its horrors.

Her present ordeal was not yet over, for now he had started the engine and was roaring away, demanding over and over, 'You'd best tell me what you and Blake have been up to – and don't give me no lies! Not if you know what's good for you.'

He was relentless. 'I'll deal with you first. Blake will keep, for now.'

He sounded so calm, but Judy knew from experience, that this was when he was at his most dangerous. Over the years she had learned to read his moods, and right now, he was more crazy than she had ever seen him.

Inside the store, Mr Jacobs had emerged from his office, in time to hear the last exchange between Saunders and Harry.

'Is there some kind of issue between you and that man?' he asked sternly.

Harry confirmed. 'There was – years ago.'

'And now?'

Harry looked at him, but said nothing.

'I see.' Jacobs was not best pleased. 'I will not tolerate trouble in my store. If you and that man have a grudge, you must keep it outside these walls. If you don't, then I shall simply have to let you go.'

Harry nodded. 'I understand.'

'So tell me, Harry – do I need to be worried?'

'No,' Harry assured him. 'You have no need to worry.'

'Good!' Crossing to Amy, Jacobs asked her to bring him the sales figures and a mug of strong coffee.

Compiling the figures for the day's sales, Amy took the paperwork up to the office, where Bernie Jacobs spread them out on his desk. 'So what do you think then, Amy? Did we do well today?'

'It's been really busy,' she replied. 'Best sale yet, if you ask me.'

'Thank you. Oh, and would you remind the salesmen about the office meeting . . . eight-thirty tomorrow? I know I'm bringing them in early for a Sunday, but I want them all here on time, raring to go, and full of ideas for the Christmas promotion.'

'Yes, sir.'

'That's all for now, Amy.' He looked up at the wall clock. 'It's almost five o'clock. Tell the others it's time to lock up. Then they can go. I'll see them in the morning, eight-thirty sharp.'

Amy delivered his instructions.

Half an hour later, after the monies were counted, bagged and duly delivered to the safe in Jacobs' office, the salesmen left one after the other, until only Harry remained, leaning on the counter, his thoughts miles away – on Judy, and the thug she had married.

He wondered if that was his fault. Whether after he had left, Phil had moved in like the predator he was, and Judy turned to him because she had no one else.

If that was the case, then he had to carry some of the responsibility. Unless, of course, it was right what Saunders said – that Judy had never really loved him, and that she was glad to be with Phil instead.

He could see Judy in his mind; the way she had been then

and the way she was now. She still had that magical loveliness, he thought.

Through all the years, he had loved Judy as much as he did in the beginning. All this time, he had carried a picture in his mind of the small, quiet person who had stolen his heart.

Was Saunders right? Was it true that she had never really loved him? Thinking about the way it was between himself and Judy, Harry found the man's claim hard to believe. But then he reminded himself of other times when Judy had seemed cold, even hostile towards him, before becoming clinging, almost like a frightened little child. He always comforted her when she was like that. But he never understood, and Judy would not discuss the reason for her moods.

Yes! Now he came to think of it, there had been times when he thought she did not really love him at all. He angrily dismissed the thoughts. His deeper instinct told him that Judy loved him, as much as he loved her.

Sometimes though, she had been distant . . . and kind of sad.

'Hey! Penny for them?' Amy's shrill voice startled him.

He looked up. 'Sorry, Amy, I was miles away.'

'Yeah, I could see that. It's a good job the others have gone, because you were talking to yourself – something about Saunders and Judy.'

Harry was shocked. 'God! Was I really talking out loud?'

'Well, more like muttering.' Curious, she asked, 'Is there something wrong? Was it that man – a nasty piece of work, I thought. I saw how agitated he was getting.'

'It was just a shock to see him,' Harry explained. 'He was an old acquaintance from way back. There was an argument that was never settled, and which he can't seem to let go of.' Harry felt able to confide in Amy, at least to some extent. 'He was someone I never thought, or hoped, to see again.'

'Oh, right. Like that, was it?' Reaching underneath the counter, the girl withdrew a packet of Wrigley's spearmint chewing gum. 'Want one?'

Harry shook his head. 'Thanks all the same, but it'll only end up sticking itself somewhere on my jacket.'

'Okay.' Rolling a strip of gum into her mouth, she mumbled, 'That bloke, the one you haven't seen for ages?'

'Saunders,' he answered. 'His name is Phil Saunders – not a man you'd want to get mixed up with.'

'I gathered that.'

'Why?' He did not think she had heard Saunders' threats.

'I dunno.' She replaced the packet of chewing-gum in the drawer. 'I've got a feeling I've seen him before.'

'What?' Harry sat up straight. 'Where did you see him?' He was excited that she might know where he and Judy lived.

'Is he a mate?' Amy asked. 'Thought you didn't like him.'

Harry gave a wry little smile. 'Not so's you'd know.' Impatient, he pushed for an answer. 'Amy, think! Where did you see him?'

Amy cast her mind back. 'He was coming out of some pub in Bedford town centre – blind drunk, he was – fighting-mad and cursing at passers-by. He got into a fight and somebody called the police; they took him away in a Black Maria.'

Her eyes were popping out of her head. 'Cor, if you ask me, he's a right bad lot! That's why I was surprised when I saw you and him talking together. I didn't think you were the type to mix with a bloke like that.'

'Amy?' Harry had another question. 'I don't suppose there's any chance you'd know where he lives, would you?'

'Not bloody likely!'

'Okay, so has he ever been here, in this store before – apart from today?'

Amy shook her head. 'Not that I recall, and if he had, I'm sure I'd remember.' She cringed. 'Not only is he a loud-mouthed thug, he even looks like one!' She made a face. 'Ugly bugger, ain't he?'

'Look, Amy, it's important that you help me here.'

'I *am* helping you,' she groaned. 'Matter o' fact you're beginning to get on my nerves! It's my birthday, remember, and me mum's making me a special tea. I want to push off soon.'

'Do you think he might be a home-buyer?' Harry asked. 'Maybe he hardly ever comes into the shop, but just buys from the catalogue and then pays the tallyman?'

Amy wasn't sure about that. 'We don't have many customers who just buy from the catalogue,' she said. 'Not unless they live miles away and can't get in, but that's not usual.'

He had to try. 'Could you not take a peek at the register?' he pleaded. 'Phil Saunders . . . his wife's name is Judy.' It really angered him to say that. She had always been Judy Roberts to him, and now she was Judy Saunders. It riled him, to think she had taken that thug's name.

'Why didn't you just ask him for his address when he was here?' Amy was puzzled.

'I've got my reasons. Please, Amy, just take a peek at the register.'

While Harry kept an eye out for Mr Jacobs coming down, Amy went through the list in the company register. 'He's not in here,' she said, slamming the ledger shut, 'but I've a feeling Len keeps a separate, more personal register, of valued clients and all that. You never know, this Saunders bloke might be in there.'

'Len hasn't been in today, has he?'

Amy shook her head. 'Nope. He had four days' holiday long overdue.'

Harry bit his lip. 'When will he be back?'

Amy counted on her fingers. 'Day after tomorrow.'

'Does he keep the ledger here, in the office maybe?'

Pursing her lips, Amy thought for a minute. 'Nope, he takes it home. Matter o' fact, I don't think anyone's ever seen inside Len's ledger. He keeps it close to his chest.'

Making big eyes, she leaned forward, whispering as though sharing a secret. 'Maybe he's an axe-murderer. Oooh! Maybe it's a list of them that he's killed.'

Harry had to smile. 'Will you give over, and tell me how I'm supposed to find out Saunders' address?'

'Well, I don't know, do I? Who d'you think I am – Rosie of the Globe?'

Harry laughed out loud. 'Who the devil is Rosie of the Globe when she's at home?'

'She's the old gypsy on Yarmouth Pier . . . read my hand once. Said I was gonna marry a handsome man with a fortune.' She winked at Harry. 'That wouldn't be you, would it?'

'No, not unless you count a good head of hair and a wage that only lasts Friday to Friday.'

'Naw!' She made a face. 'It can't be you then.' More's the pity, she thought.

She gave a long, shivering sigh. 'Trouble is, while I'm waiting for this handsome rich fella to come and rescue me, I'm getting older and uglier. So, by the time he turns up, he won't give me a second glance.' She giggled mischievously. 'That's when I'll come after you.'

'What!' Harry feigned indignation. 'Do you think I'll settle for some ugly old woman who only wants me for second best? I don't think so!' He led her back to what was urgent. 'That pub you mentioned?'

'Yeah, what about it?'

'Can you remember the name of it?'

'I'm not sure.' She twirled the strands of her hair, as she did when thinking hard. 'I don't know,' she admitted, 'but I can tell you whereabouts it is.'

'Wonderful!' Harry listened while she outlined the directions, '. . . onto the Boulevard and it's right there in front of you,' she finished.

By the time they parted company, Harry felt a whole lot better for having discovered the place where Saunders went to drink. Moreover, seeing Judy with his own eyes was so gratifying.

From where he was, she looked just as lovely as ever – older, yes of course, and maybe too skinny – but a wonderful, heart-warming sight nevertheless.

CHAPTER NINETEEN

WHEN WORK WAS done, Harry's first instinct was to go straight to the pub and ask questions, but then he thought of Kathleen, and how she and Tom had both seen the argument with Saunders. 'I should go home first,' he murmured. 'Put their minds at rest.'

He was uneasy, itching to discover more about Saunders: where he worked, where he lived, how he and Judy got on together. Was it an idyllic marriage? Did he treat her well, or was she unhappy?

When all was said and done, she had tied herself to a bully like Saunders, though somehow Harry could not let himself believe that she actually loved him. But then for whatever reason, she had married him.

His fears for Judy were very real. After all, Saunders had come at him like a bull at a gate, convinced that he and Judy were having some sort of affair. So, if he could tackle another man like that, what was he really capable of? Would he treat Judy with the same contempt? Would he hurt her? Was he right now, at this very minute, torturing her with his warped and unfounded suspicions?

If he could only discover where she lived, he would at least be able to keep a watchful eye on Judy.

He glanced at his watch. It was ten past five. The pubs wouldn't be open yet. Besides, he didn't want to make too many waves. It would only call attention to himself. It was best if he went in as a customer, and got casually chatting to the barmaid. That way, people would not be so wary of him, and he might then pick up more information.

So he turned the car towards Fisher's Hill and home, where he would spend some time playing with Tom, chat with Kathleen about events, then head back to Bedford and find the pub Amy had described in such detail.

~

The journey home did not take too long. It being a Saturday, most people were relaxing over tea, until either they got ready for the pub or the flicks, or even a twirl on the dance floor at the local Palais.

As for Harry, he had made his plans for the evening, and was looking forward to the chase.

'Daddy! Daddy!' Tom was watching for him. The minute Harry was parked and on his way up the garden path, Tom came rushing out of the house, to run straight into his arms. 'Whoa!' Harry laughed as he caught the boy and raised him high. 'You'll have us both upside down in the bushes if you're not careful.'

Tom was so excited he couldn't stop talking. 'I'm sorry, Daddy, my balloon popped. I've been waiting to tell you. Kathleen said I could sit at the window and watch. I saw you coming up the street. We've got tea ready, and I've got my Wellington boots and everything!'

'So, where's Kathleen?'

'In the kitchen. I told her you were here, and she said she won't be a minute.' He whispered in Harry's ear. 'Kathleen's made jelly, but I'm not supposed to tell you because it's a secret.'

'Okay. I won't tell, don't worry.' Kathleen always did make the most wonderful jelly, he thought, licking his lips.

At the door he put the boy on the floor. 'Go and tell Kathleen

I'm home,' he said, chuckling contentedly when his son went off at the run.

He heard Tom yelling as he ran, 'Daddy's here! Kathleen, Daddy's here!' Then in a lower voice, 'I never told him about the jelly.'

In the kitchen Kathleen had to smile to herself. 'So, you never told him about the jelly, did you?' she said, as he came rushing in through the door. 'Sure you might as well have, the way you're yelling and shouting!'

She came out to greet Harry, and though she did not mention the day's incident with Phil Saunders, or her own observation regarding Judy and the bruises, each knew they had to talk, and plan, and look for the best way forward – but not in front of Tom, and not until they had eaten.

'I expect you're famished, are you?' She set the table with a pot of tea, two cups, milk and sugar, with a glass of Kia-Ora for Tom.

'It's fish pie, chips and cauliflower.' She grinned. 'Oh, and we've got raspberry jelly with fruit for afterwards.'

'Sounds perfect!' Harry declared. 'Just what the doctor ordered.'

Thrilled to have his daddy home, Tom went into a long excited explanation of how 'Mr Butterworth from the post office said if we keep eating all the fish there'll be none left in the sea. He told Kathleen he never eats fish, but he likes a crab now and then. Kathleen told him a crab bit her toe once when she went to Blackpool, and it really hurt.'

He made a grimace. 'I don't want a crab to bite my toe, Daddy. I just want to watch them swimming. Can we? Can we watch the crabs swimming?'

'I don't see why we can't go crabbing one day. Yes, if that's what you want, that's what we'll do.' Harry finished his cup of tea and poured another, while topping up Kathleen's at the same time. 'In fact,' he went on, 'a day at the seaside might do us all good, but not just yet, son. Soon though. When I've got time to spare.'

A few minutes later, dinner was served.

'You're an excellent cook,' Harry congratulated Kathleen. 'Trouble is, me and Tom will be fat as elephants if you keep feeding us like this.'

'So you'll not be wanting jelly and fruit afterwards then?' Kathleen winked aside at Tom.

'Hey, I never said that!' Harry exclaimed. 'I'll just have to walk a bit faster on the rounds and work it off.'

'Ah, so you're back on the rounds soon then, are ye?'

Harry nodded. 'Next Friday, or so I'm told.'

'You prefer that to being inside, don't you?'

'I do, yes, but we've got one man down with the flu, and another away on holiday. The sale was already scheduled, and it was every hand to the deck, so to speak.'

His quiet smile spoke volumes. 'If I hadn't been inside today, I would never have seen Judy.'

Tom was intrigued. 'Is that the lady Kathleen was talking to? I like her, she's nice. She found my balloon.'

He had more important things on his mind. 'I'd like some more jelly,' he piped up. Having already served him a whole dishful, Kathleen was not so sure.

'Maybe just a little taste,' she said. 'We don't want you having a tummy upset, now do we, eh?'

Tom thought a little was better than nothing at all. 'All right then, yes.' Impatient, he began bumping up and down in his chair.

'So you want some more then?'

Tom nodded his head.

'What was that?' Kathleen wanted the 'magic' word. 'I didn't hear you?'

'Yes, I'd like more jelly.'

This time Harry pulled him up. 'And what do you say?'

Tom had a think. He had told them he wanted more jelly already; and he did what Kathleen wanted and said he would have just a little bit. So, what else should he say? 'Oh, I know.'

He giggled. 'I forgot, sorry, Kathleen. *Please* may I have some more jelly?'

'Why, o' course ye can.' She gave him a swift cuddle. 'Jelly coming up.' Off she went to dish him out just the smallest portion.

Later, Kathleen cleared the table, with Harry's help.

'It was so good to see Judy today,' Harry confided. 'Was she well, d'you think? Did she say much? Is everything all right between her and Saunders?'

'Why do you ask that?' Kathleen had still not mentioned the bruises on Judy's face. She wondered if Harry had seen them, after all. But then from that distance, it was hardly likely.

'No particular reason,' Harry answered. 'It's just that I would never have put her and Saunders together, never in a million years.'

Kathleen had little to say until the cutlery and dishes were in the sink and the table-cloth neatly folded.

When she saw Tom yawning, she decided, 'Right, me boy. It's an early night for you. You've had an exciting day, and you look bushed, so ye do.' Taking him by the hand, she led him to Harry. 'A kiss for your daddy, a quick bath and pyjamas, then into bed.'

She was right about him being bushed. Soonever the boy was washed and dried and in his pyjamas, she put him to bed. Even before she got to the door, he was fast asleep. 'Aw, bless yer little cotton socks,' she murmured. 'You're just a babe, so ye are.' Blowing him a kiss, she softly closed the door.

On arriving downstairs, she was amazed to see the dishes all washed and put away. 'Well, I never.' The smile on her face went from ear to ear. 'That's wonderful. Thank you, Harry, but you shouldn't have.'

'It's the least I could do,' he replied. 'Tom and I would be in a poor situation if it wasn't for you.'

'Well, now you can go and sit down,' she ordered. 'I'll make us a fresh brew and then I'll join you. I have an idea there's something on yer mind that won't wait.' She peeked at him through bright little eyes. 'Am I right?'

Harry nodded. 'You are, as usual.'

'So, it's to do with Judy, is it?'

'Right again.'

'Do like I said, and make yourself comfortable while I brew the tea, then we'll talk. Young Tom's out to the world, so it'll be just the two of us.'

When Harry went away, deep in thought, Kathleen made the tea, which she then carried through to the sitting room. 'Here we . . .' She stopped in her tracks. Harry was nowhere to be seen, 'Harry?' When there was no answer, she called again, 'HARRY?'

Still no answer.

'Where the devil's he gone?' She wandered from room to room, and still there was no sign of him.

She set the tray down and went to the window, where she looked out, and there he was at the bottom of the garden, leaning over the fence and looking up to the skies.

Saddened by that lonely, troubled figure, she wondered where it would all end. 'What's gonna become of yer, eh?' She was concerned that having seen Judy, he might have detected her deep unhappiness, just as she had done.

For a few minutes she stayed by the window, watching as he leaned on the fence, head bent and looking as though he had the whole world on his back.

After a while, she collected the tray and went out to the garden, where she set the tray down on the little wooden table. She called him over. 'This tea will be stone-cold if it's left much longer!' she chided, 'I thought you had things you wanted to discuss?'

Harry turned and looked at her, then he nodded, and now he was on his way over, 'Sorry, Kathleen,' he apologised, 'how long have you been there?'

'Long enough,' she said, 'Now come and sit down, and tell me what's bothering ye?'

While he talked, she poured the tea, and when she took a sip of it, she made a miserable face. 'Whoo! It's mashed in the pot, so it is!'

Harry took a sip of his own. 'Tastes all right to me,' he said. 'Thank you, Kathleen, this is a lovely way to round off the evening.'

'So, what's on your mind?' she wanted to know. 'All through dinner you were listening to Tom and talking to me, and sure ye weren't even with us at all. You were someplace else . . . back there with Judy, I shouldn't wonder.'

He nodded. 'Are you ever wrong?'

'More often than not.' She laughed. 'More times than I care to remember.'

Harry fell silent for a moment, and during that tense moment, Kathleen sipped on her lukewarm tea, and waited.

After a while Harry spoke. 'It was amazing, seeing Judy today,' he told her. 'I'm still shaking inside. Oh, I knew straight off it was her. She has a way with her – the way she stands, the way she holds her head slightly to one side as though considering something. How was she, Kathleen? *Really*, I mean, and don't just tell me what you think I want to hear.'

'Well now, let me see,' Kathleen answered carefully. 'She seemed all right, I suppose, but . . .'

Harry prompted her. 'But what?'

Kathleen took a deep invigorating breath. 'Don't get all riled up now, but I'm not altogether sure she's happy. But then, I can't be sure she's not.' Winking knowingly, she went on, 'She's always held her cards very close to her chest, so she has.' She distinctly remembered Judy being that way as a young girl.

'You both saw him, didn't you,' Harry prompted, 'wanting to settle things with his fists? Accusing me of seeing Judy behind his back.' He gritted his teeth. 'I should have taken him outside and thrashed him!'

'Oh, aye? And what would Judy have thought to that, eh? Moreover, what would it have solved?'

Harry shook his head. 'Nothing, but it might have given me some satisfaction.'

'He hasn't changed then?'

'No. If anything, he's got worse. The thing is, Kathleen, I'm concerned that he might be taking out his temper on Judy. He's such a big brute, and she looked so fragile.'

Judy's image washed through his senses. 'It all seems so long ago, and yet it was like only yesterday . . .' He began to reminisce in his mind. 'I can't get over the fact that I've actually seen her,' he said with a fleeting grin. 'Except she looked so vulnerable. What if Saunders *is* making her life a misery? What if he's going at her like he went at me?'

Seeing how agitated he was, Kathleen calmed him down. 'Now stop that,' she warned. 'Getting all worked up won't solve a bally thing.'

'Did she happen to tell you where they lived?' he asked.

'No.'

'Or whether she was happy?'

'No.'

'Does she intend seeing you again?'

'She didn't say, and I let her be the judge of that. It's never wise to force things.'

Harry was both hurt and puzzled. 'There were things Saunders taunted me with – about me deserting Judy and all that awful business. He said Judy went to him; that she never wanted me. It was him she wanted all the time, that's what he said.'

Kathleen tutted. 'What utter tosh!' she exclaimed. 'The man is deluded, so he is. To my dying day, I will never understand why she ever agreed to marry that monster in the first place. It's almost as though she didn't care what happened to her after you were gone.'

'How long after I was gone did she go to him, I wonder?'

Kathleen shrugged. 'Who knows? All I know is that she never once mentioned him to me. Then some two years after you left, a neighbour told me she and Saunders were wed. Sure, I don't rightly know whether they meant Judy and Saunders had only just got wed, or if they'd wed some time ago. I was so thrown by the news, I just wanted to get home and think about it.'

She loudly tutted and tutted. 'Married to that ne'er-do-well! Whatever was she thinking?'

Harry too, was deeply unsettled. 'I have to find her, Kathleen,' he said. 'I need to know she is safe.'

Kathleen understood, but: 'Is it wise to interfere though?'

Looking at it from both sides, the little Irishwoman could see the pitfalls. 'If Judy was unhappy, or being ill-treated, I think she would have confided in me when we met; and the very fact that she did not, leads me to believe one of three things. Firstly that she thinks it is none of our business; secondly that she does not want to draw us into it or thirdly, that she's capable of handling it herself.'

She finished with a possibility that Harry found difficult to accept. 'On the other hand, she and Saunders might be getting along reasonably well, as married couples go.'

The truth was, while trying to put Harry's mind at rest, Kathleen herself had much the same concerns as Harry.

'Maybe it's best left alone?' she wondered aloud. 'To my thinking, Judy must be all right with him, or she would have said. Think about it, Harry. If she needed help, she knows where you are. She knows where *I* am, and I've already told her she is more than welcome here any time she wants. So far, she has not taken me up on it. So, tell me, what are we to make of that?'

'She could be afraid.' Harry could not let it go. 'He might have threatened her in some way – doesn't want her to have friends, maybe. He's always been a bit crazy, we know that.'

'Yes, that's true – But have you thought of the possibility that she might really love him; that she's put her past life behind her and feels the need to settle down? Have you thought of that, Harry?'

'Of course I have, but I just can't make myself believe she's in love with him.'

'Is that not your manly pride talking?'

'No. I'm saying she's too gentle to love a man who is so cruel and brutish, a man who would rather fight than talk. A man who has no compassion for anything or anyone – including his wife.'

Detecting his pain, Kathleen smiled on him, in that sincere way she had. 'You still love her, don't you, Harry?'

Unable to speak, he merely nodded.

'Maybe that's it,' she said. 'Maybe you love her so much, you can't stand any other man being with her – especially if that other man is your old arch-enemy?'

Harry knew it was more than that. 'There is something going on between Judy and him,' he said. 'Something bad is happening, and Judy is caught right in the middle of it. She's in danger, Kathleen, I know it. I can feel it!' Scrambling out of his seat, he began pacing the floor. 'I have to find her!' he declared urgently.

'Ah sure – and how do you propose to do that?' Kathleen was really concerned for him. 'Judy has deliberately refrained from giving me any insight as to how things are between her and Saunders, or why she wed him in the first place. I'm like you; I can't imagine she can be in love with him. She has not mentioned where she lives, nor has she has taken me up on my invitation to come and see me here.'

'So doesn't that tell you something?' Walking over to Kathleen, he leaned forward and looked into her eyes. 'Think about it. Does that sound like the Judy we know? Does it even sound like any other person who's just met up with an old friend again? No, it does not! It sounds like a frightened woman, trying to hide the truth. I've given it endless thought, and I'm sure there are bad things going on.'

'You think he's beating her up, don't you?'

He began pacing again. 'Yes.' He didn't really know what else to think. 'Something in the back of my mind keeps telling me that she needs us. Judy is a frightened woman, I just know it.'

Seated at the little table, Kathleen was thinking, about whether he might be right in what he felt. After all, she had seen the bruises on Judy's face. When Tom's balloon floated off and Judy stepped out of the corner with it, she had a feeling that Judy had been hiding there.

Then, when she mentioned the marks on her face, Judy seemed embarrassed, even afraid. She had been too quick to say it was some new powder she'd been trying. Firstly, Judy did not seem a person to use much make-up, and secondly, Kathleen did not know of any face powder that would do such a thing.

But why would she lie?

Though Kathleen herself had misgivings, she had no wish to fuel Harry's concerns. But she had to ask herself; what caused the marks on Judy's face, and why was she hiding in the corner? Was she there merely to steal a look at Harry? Or had she come to ask for help and lost her courage in the moment? Either way Kathleen was convinced that, for some reason she had not yet fathomed, Judy was afraid to be seen.

Before she could talk with her she was gone, like a will-o-the-wisp. She scurried away, just like she did in that café on the High Street. Did something frighten her off? It was odd, how just then Saunders showed up.

From that very first meeting with Judy in the High Street, Kathleen had her suspicions, though she had tried to convince herself she was being silly, that if Judy had problems then she would surely confide in her old friend.

One thing Kathleen was thankful for, and that was the fact that Harry had not seen the bruises on Judy's face. If he had, he would surely have got the truth out of her – and then there might well have been serious repercussions.

Should she tell Harry about the bruises, and to hell with the consequences? she fretted.

Back came the answer. NO!

'There's something I haven't told you,' Harry said suddenly, interrupting her train of thought. When he explained his findings, she began to understand why he was so desperately worried. He told her how Amy had seen Saunders drunk and abusive outside a pub in Bedford Town. 'She said he was fighting-mad and like a crazy man, hitting out at passers-by and creating havoc in the street. The police were called, and they took him away.'

Though the news was alarming, Kathleen was not surprised. 'He was always a bit crazy,' she commented, 'but it doesn't mean to say he's hurting Judy, does it?'

'I don't know about that,' Harry declared. 'If he can make trouble with strangers in the street, and want to fight me for what happened all those years ago, who's to say he wouldn't take his frustrations out on Judy?

'Think about it, Kathleen!' he urged. 'If he's harbouring suspicions about me and Judy, it stands to reason he must be tackling Judy about it, and if he is, do you really think she's able to stand up to him, like I did?'

Kathleen had to admit he could be right. 'All I'm saying is, don't jump to conclusions. He might be totally different with Judy. He must love her, after all. Sure he's wanted her since you were all in your teens.'

'He only ever wanted her because he couldn't have her.' Harry was sure of it. 'Anyway, about this pub . . . Amy said I can't miss it. It's the nearest one to the Boulevard.'

Oh, dear Lord. Harry would be off creating mayhem if she didn't put a stop to it, Kathleen thought. Swiftly, she devised a plan. 'Oh dear me!' She leaped up as though she'd had a fright.

'What is it?' Now it was Harry's turn to be worried. 'What on earth is wrong?'

'Good heavens above – I completely forgot.' She scrambled

out of the chair and grabbed her coat. 'I promised to go and see Lorna Smith – you know, my dear friend who lives in Woburn Sands. What with everything, I've been sadly neglecting her of late. I bumped into her husband yesterday and he told me she'd been very ill – that she would really love me to pay a visit. I promised faithfully that I would.' She looked up at the mantel-piece clock. 'Look at that, I'm late already.'

Harry was sympathetic. 'Oh, Kathleen, you must go.' In a softer voice he murmured to himself, 'Shame. I really needed to go into Bedford, to that pub, but it can't be helped.'

Kathleen had sensed that was his intent. It was why she had devised the plan. 'Oh, of course,' she said as she heard his quiet murmurings. 'The pub. You needed to speak with the landlord, didn't you?'

She meekly laid her coat over the chair and sat down again. Remembering to put on a sad little face, she told him in a sorry voice, 'Oh look, Harry. You go, me darlin'. I can see Lorna tomorrow. She'll understand, I'm sure.' She completed the picture by picking up her knitting and started to work on the pattern.

Ashamed, Harry would have none of it. 'No, you go and see your old friend. The pub can wait until tomorrow.'

'It's Sunday tomorrow,' she reminded him. 'They'll be closed.'

'I know, but thinking about it, that might be the best time. If I go mid-morning, I'm sure there'll be someone there. Besides, they'll be so busy tonight, they won't have time to talk to me, even if I do go. Yes, tomorrow will be best. You go and see your friend,' he instructed firmly. 'Tom might still be awake. We'll run you to the bus stop.'

'All right then, I'll go, if you really don't mind. But there is no need to run me to the bus stop. Sure, it's only at the end of the street and the walk will do me good. Besides, I imagine Tom is fast asleep by now.'

Harry collected her coat and held it out for her. 'If you want me to come and pick you up, give me a ring,' he said. 'Tom won't mind if I get him out of bed. In fact, it'll be a treat for him.'

'Right, well, I'd best get off,' she told him. 'There's a bus leaves the bottom of the street in about ten minutes – goes straight through to Woburn Sands.' She collected her bag. 'I'll see youse two later.'

The walk to the bus stop took no more than eight minutes. As she turned the corner, her poor old legs were beginning to ache, so she was more than grateful to see the bus pulling in. Clambering aboard, she found herself a cosy seat by the window. With her plan already in place, and thankful that, for now at least, she had managed to stop Harry from pursuing Phil Saunders' whereabouts, she took out a pen and paper and, recalling the detailed instructions Amy had given to Harry, she wrote them all down.

When the conductor came along to collect her fare, she paid for her ticket into Bedford. 'There you are, my beauty!' he said. Handing her the ticket, he gave her a wink that made her blush.

'Don't you be making eyes at me, young man.' Wagging a finger at him, she couldn't help but smile. 'I'm old enough to be your grandma, so I am.'

'Ah, but it's the eyes,' he sighed. 'You've got the prettiest, sparkly eyes. My grandmama was hairy and miserable. You're a beauty queen compared to her.'

With a mental picture of his grandmother in mind, Kathleen chuckled to herself.

Amy didn't know the name of the pub, but it was in the centre of Bedford town, directly opposite the Boulevard. She remembered that much at least, and if Harry could find it, then so could she.

She had been so busy perfecting her plan that she had not realised how quickly the time had passed.

'Bedford town centre!' The bus was slowing down and the conductor was shouting, 'End of the line! Everybody off!'

As she made her way down the bus the conductor gave her another wink. 'Bye, sweetheart,' he said. 'See you on the way back, will we?'

'You might,' she answered, winking back mischievously, 'if you play your cards right.'

As she went away down the street she could hear him laughing out loud. 'You little beauty!' he shouted. 'I reckon you and me might have a future together!'

She was still laughing to herself as she left the Boulevard.

Being Saturday night, the place was heaving with people. Digging out her spectacles from her bag, Kathleen glanced at her untidy scribbles. 'Opposite the Boulevard,' she mumbled. 'The pub is opposite the Boulevard.' Looking about, all she could see were shops, people and buses. 'Which way?' she asked herself. 'Right, left or straight on?'

She waylaid a passer-by, a young fella with a miserable face, but when he smiled as he did now, his whole face lit up. 'There's only one pub that I can think of that's close enough to the Boulevard, and that's the Bedford Arms. But it's not opposite like you said. It's a five-minute walk that way . . . towards the river.' He pointed to the far end of the Boulevard. 'Go through there, turn right and keep going . . . onto the High Street, then over the river bridge. You can't miss it.'

Kathleen thanked him and set off.

Ten minutes later, she came onto the High Street. 'Him and his five-minute walk!' she tutted. 'That might be the case if you're young and fit, and got legs up to your elbows, but it won't do for an old 'un like me.'

She noticed the bus stop. 'That's where I'll get the bus home,' she decided. 'It'll save me old legs, so it will.'

Then, just as the young man had promised, there in front of her was the Bedford Arms.

With renewed vigour she made her way there, pushing the door open rather shyly. There, perched on stools by the bar, a group of men were talking and drinking, with the occasional burst of laughter. But from what she could see, there was no one behind the bar.

'Excuse me.' She tapped the nearest man on the shoulder. 'Do you happen to know where the landlord is?'

Before he could answer, a head popped up from behind the bar. 'I expect you'll be wanting my husband.'

Lifting out two crates of lemonade Pauline plonked them down with a grunt. 'I'm afraid he's locked in the cellar,' she teased. 'When he misbehaves I shut him away until he cools down.'

Realising that Kathleen was not a regular customer, she apologised. 'Sorry about that,' she said. 'Me and my warped sense of humour. Can I help?'

'I need to speak with the landlord.' With everyone now looking in her direction, the little Irishwoman felt decidedly uncomfortable.

'He's busy at the minute,' Pauline informed her. 'You can wait if you like, but he's changing the barrels and that might take some time. Or if you'd rather, you can talk to me.'

She grew curious. 'So, what's it about?' The men had stopped, listening to them.

Kathleen leaned forward. 'It's a bit . . . delicate.' She had no intention of airing Harry's business all over the place. Moreover, for all she knew, any one of these men might be Saunders' best mate.

'Delicate, eh?' Pauline was even more curious now. 'If you'd rather, we can go in the back room?' Then she made an offer Kathleen could not refuse. 'It'll take me just two minutes to put the kettle on, then we can talk over a nice cuppa tea. What d'you say to that, eh?'

After the walk from the Boulevard, Kathleen's legs were aching, and she was that thirsty, her tongue was stuck to the roof of her mouth. 'Oh, go on then!' Besides, it might be a good thing to discuss such things with a woman, she decided.

'Keep an eye on things, would you, Jack?' Addressing one

of the men in the group, Pauline waved a dishcloth at him. 'While you're at it, you can run this over the bar.'

'Oh aye?' He was a kindly shrimp of a man, but when he spoke his voice was so thick and deep it seemed to rattle the walls. 'You can think again, lady!' he declared, shaking his head. 'I don't use a dishcloth at home, and I'm not about to start now; I've got a wife for that kinda stuff. But I'll watch the bar, though I'll need paying, mind. So, what are you offering?'

'Half a pint?' Pauline bargained.

'A couple . . . one now and another afore I leave?'

'One now, and that's an end to it.'

'You're a hard taskmaster.'

'That's why I'm in business and you're not.'

'Cheeky bugger.' He was smiling though, and totally unfazed by her comment. 'A pint, a quick cuddle, an' the boss will never know.'

'Hey! I'm the boss and don't you forget it!'

While Kathleen laughed at their playful banter, Pauline pulled the man a pint and put it on the bar before him. 'Paid in full,' she declared.

'All right, if you say so. Go on then. Clear off and see to that lovely lady, and don't worry, I won't raid the booze while you're gone.'

Kathleen followed Pauline into the back, pleasantly surprised at the cosy room, with its pretty floral curtains and thick handsome rugs. The furniture was old wood and leather, and when Katheen sat in the armchair, she thought how wonderfully comfortable it was.

'I'm sorry to bother you,' she said as Pauline busied herself in the adjoining kitchen, making tea and such, 'only I had to come and talk to someone, because I'm worried about a certain situation with regards to Judy Saunders – Roberts as was.' She might have explained further, but Pauline came rushing in from the kitchen, a look of horror on her face.

'Judy!' Putting a cup of tea and a saucer of biscuits on the arm of Kathleen's chair, she threw herself into the chair opposite. 'What's happened? Where is she? What the devil has he been up to now? I've told her . . . time and again I've warned her – get away from him!'

Kathleen could not get a word in.

'I told her!' Pauline fumed and fretted. '"One of these days he'll hurt you real bad", but will she listen? No! She's too afraid to stand up to him, that's the trouble.'

Believing Judy to be lying somewhere badly hurt, she was panic-stricken.

'She's not in any trouble,' Kathleen calmed her. 'At least, not so far as I know.'

Pauline almost collapsed with relief. 'Ooh, thank God for that! You had me going there,' she said. 'I'm sorry, but I've been so worried about her of late, I never know what to think.'

Kathleen persuaded her, 'If you get yourself a cup of your own tea and calm down, I'll tell you why I'm here.'

Pauline was in and out of the kitchen in minutes, talking as she went, asking questions. 'So, who are you, and why are you here?' she asked, seating herself opposite.

Firstly, Kathleen introduced herself. 'It isn't altogether to do with Judy,' she explained, 'although she is at the root of it all.' She needed to know. 'Tell me, do you know anything of Judy's past?'

'A bit.' Pauline was intrigued. 'She does tend to keep things to herself though. Why do you ask?'

'Has she ever told you about her first love?'

'Harry Blake,' Pauline said immediately. 'Once she starts on him, you can't stop her. Her first love was Harry Blake. She thinks of him all the time. When it's just the two of us together, she hardly ever talks about anything else.'

'Do you know what happened between them?' Kathleen asked.

Pauline paused to consider the question. 'Well, she told me that Harry went away when they were young – said that it was all her fault, and that she never saw him again. She didn't explain what had happened, or why he went away.'

She gazed down at the floor. 'I know she cries a lot when she talks about him.'

Kathleen knew she must be careful what she revealed. After all, this woman was a stranger to her. How could she be sure she was trustworthy?

'You said it was not altogether to do with Judy,' Pauline reminded her, 'but that you needed help. What exactly did you mean by that?'

Kathleen answered a question with a question. 'First of all, I need to know that I can trust you to keep what I have to say to yourself.'

'You have my word. Judy is a very dear friend. Me and Alan, my husband, we look out for her. She is very gentle in her ways, very hard on herself at times, while Phil gets . . .'

She cautioned herself. Like Kathleen, she was not sure of her ground with this stranger, however homely she might appear. 'Well, he can be difficult, put it like that.'

Growing more confident, Kathleen told her the whole story of the ongoing rivalry between Harry and Phil Saunders. 'When they were younger, they each wanted Judy, but it was Harry she fell in love with . . . Harry she wanted. Phil was bitter about it; dangerously jealous. Then Harry went away – he joined up – and soon after that, so did Judy and her family. For a long time I heard nothing from either of them. Then Harry rang me from out of the blue. To cut a long story short, he suffered a terrible tragedy and I took him in, along with his young son, Tom.'

Pauline could tell that Kathleen had a kind manner. 'That was a lovely thing to do,' she said.

'It was as much for me as for them,' she confessed. 'Harry was always like family to me. Now though, he's heard that Judy is married, and he also knows that Phil Saunders is as crazy as ever, fighting in the streets, causing trouble and getting himself arrested. There are also rumours that he served time for assault.' She had learned as much from listening to gossip, though was wise enough not to convey it to Harry.

Pauline anticipated what was coming. 'So, now that Harry's back, and he knows that Judy is married to Phil Saunders, he's worried, is that it?' From what Judy had told her of Harry, Pauline was not surprised. 'Has he seen either of them?' she asked. 'Has he contacted them?'

Kathleen sighed. 'Judy went to the place where Harry works. They saw each other fleetingly, though as yet they haven't spoken. When Judy realised he had recognised her, she ran away. Saunders was there too. It was a difficult situation. When Judy ran away, I suspect it was because she was afraid that Saunders might see Harry and make something out of nothing. She seemed really frightened.'

'So what did Harry do?'

'Saunders went after Harry – accused him and Judy of having an affair. Harry saw him off, then Saunders took Judy away and now Harry suspects he's taking it out on her. He means to find out where they live and now he's got a lead from one of the girls at the store. She says she saw Phil Saunders drunk and violent, accosting people in the street outside this very pub.'

Pauline remembered. 'Yes, that's right. It must have been the night he was arrested,' she said. 'This stranger called in for a pint; he made a play for Judy and Phil was already drunk out of his mind. Alan had already stopped serving him – he offered to take him home, but Phil was having none of it. He stormed down the street after the man, and was beating the hell out of him when Alan caught up. Someone called the police. When they arrived he started beating them up too! Crazy, he was. Out of his mind.'

She looked downcast. 'I really don't know how Judy puts up

with him. I've a sneaking suspicion that he hits her, but she denies it. Sometimes, when I know he's in one of his dark moods, I make every excuse to keep Judy here. But she always goes back to him – says it's not right that she should put on me. For heaven's sake, she's got no one else. I would do anything for that girl.'

Containing her anger, she told Kathleen, 'I tell you here and now, Harry is not the only one desperately worried about Judy.'

Satisfied that they were all on the same side, Kathleen informed her, 'I'm here to ask something of you. Harry knows the whereabouts of this pub. He would have been here now, but I managed to bamboozle him into thinking I had an urgent errand.'

'So, what does he intend to do?'

'He intends to find out from you where Phil Saunders and Judy are living. Once he's got that information, he will go round there and have it out with Saunders. He won't rest until he makes absolutely certain that Judy is safe and content.'

'Wouldn't it be a good thing to let Harry know where they are?' Pauline asked innocently. 'If Harry was to give Saunders a damned good thrashing, it might be just what he needs.'

Kathleen was horrified. 'You're not listening to me! Saunders hates Harry with a vengeance. If the two of them ever get together, there will be murder. I know what I'm saying . . . I saw the way it was when they were younger. When Phil looked at Harry in the store, I saw the murderous expression on his face. If Harry turns up on his doorstep, I'm worried what might happen.'

She was also concerned that 'Much as Harry means well and he needs to make sure Judy is all right, we neither of us want it to be Judy who pays the price.'

Pauline was only now beginning to see the full picture. 'I understand what you're saying, but are we worrying for nothing? We might suspect that Saunders lashes out at Judy, but we don't really know, do we? Every time I've questioned her, she clams up or denies it emphatically.'

Kathleen was not convinced. 'Like I say, I had not seen or heard from Judy in years, then a few days ago, I accidentally bumped into her in town. There was something about her that shook me to my roots. She didn't say she was unhappy, or that Phil Saunders was making her life a misery, but there was something in her eyes, in the way she sat, nervous as a little bird, watching the door as though someone or something would come in and carry her off.'

She also recalled more recently, 'At the store she was the same – highly nervous, constantly fidgeting, ready to flee.'

She had made her case, and now she desperately needed Pauline to agree. 'If you give Harry the address and he goes there, I'm afraid of what might happen. We both know Saunders is unpredictable. If it all ends in violence, it could be Judy herself who gets hurt. Or worse!'

'I hear what you're saying.' Pauline was convinced that Harry was the only hope for Judy, but not through violence, because in the end no good would come of it.

'It would be wonderful if Judy was to see sense and leave Phil of her own accord, but I know she won't,' she told Kathleen now. 'The thing is, Phil would commit murder rather than let her leave, and she knows that. When she realised what Phil was like, she vowed to leave him, but then he fooled her into thinking he would change, so she stayed. The years passed, and she lost heart. Bit by bit, he's taken away her freedom, and her independence.'

Kathleen was devastated at the extent to which he had ruined Judy's life. 'It seems to me as though he's taken control of her,' she mused. 'We have to help her, but Harry going in with all guns blazing is not the answer. Maybe you could give me Judy's address, let me speak with her?'

'She won't listen.' Pauline had tried. 'That nasty piece of work has her exactly where he wants her – under his thumb.

He won't even allow her to go out to work. He prefers her to stay in the house while he's away working or playing, or knocking some poor bloke senseless. Judy has so little self-worth she doesn't really care any more – about him, about herself or even about whether she lives or dies. I've tried, Kathleen . . . I've really tried.'

Her voice broke. 'Sorry! Just tell me what you want me to do, and I'll do it.'

As Kathleen set out her plans, she made a remark that shocked the younger woman to her very roots. 'It goes without saying that the child must be considered in all of this, but if it's done carefully, no one will come to any harm.'

When Pauline sat bolt upright in her chair, a look of confusion on her face, Kathleen naturally assumed it was all to do with Judy's difficult situation, and the overall discussion. It never occurred to her that Pauline knew nothing of the child.

Pauline was stunned. *What* child? she thought. In all their deepest conversations, Judy had never mentioned a child.

Pauline searched her mind, recalling how, on the rare occasions when they were out together, Judy would look longingly at a child in the street, or sometimes become tearful for no reason.

Pauline had assumed that it was because of Saunders, and the hold he had over her.

While Kathleen chatted on, Pauline wondered if Judy had borne a child to Harry, and maybe the child had died.

Maybe that was the deep sadness that Judy found hard to live with.

Pauline looked up at Kathleen. 'Can I ask you something?' she ventured. 'About the child?'

Kathleen nodded. 'Of course.'

'Did she have the child with Saunders . . . or is Harry the father?'

Kathleen was instantly on the defensive. 'Are you saying Judy never spoke with you about it?' In truth, she was not altogether surprised.

'I'm sorry.' Pauline got the strongest feeling that she had strayed over dangerous ground. 'I was just wondering, that's all.'

Kathleen was cautious. 'I think it best if you ask Judy that question,' she answered kindly.

She was not too concerned by Pauline's curiosity. She simply assumed that Judy might have found it too delicate a matter to discuss with anyone, for many reasons – not the least of which was Saunders. And of course the child itself, together with the shocking fact that if it had not been for Kathleen dissuading her, Judy was in such distress that she might well have had the baby aborted.

Pauline began to understand. If the child was Harry's and it had been stillborn, then obviously Kathleen had no idea that it had not survived. Obviously Judy had never disclosed the truth, not to anyone. Maybe she found it far too painful to talk about, especially to the lovely Kathleen, and more especially to Pauline, with Saunders ever close; always watching and listening.

Kathleen abruptly changed the subject. 'First of all, like I said, we must keep Saunders and Harry apart – at least until I can talk to Judy and make her see that Harry still loves and wants her.'

For now, the only thing they needed to concentrate on, she said, was getting Saunders out of Judy's life for good. 'If my plan is going to work, it all has to be done quietly, without Phil knowing until it's too late.' For that, I need you to give me Judy's address,' she reminded Pauline. 'Then when Harry comes here – which he will – don't tell him anything! Whatever you do, *please* do not tell him where to find Saunders. Speak to your husband. Let him know what's going on. Ask him not to let out any information with regard to Judy, or Saunders. Will you do that for me? Will you give me a chance to get Judy away from that madman, without blood being spilled?'

Pauline was in full agreement. 'It seems to me that Harry is exactly what Judy needs, though if I'm honest, I don't think she'll go with you.'

'We'll see.' Although, in view of what she had already learned, and having personally now witnessed Judy's nervous nature, Kathleen was not altogether confident.

'I hope you understand what you might be letting yourself in for,' Pauline warned her. 'If Saunders ever found out you were trying to take his wife from him, there's no telling what he might do.'

She gave Kathleen her absolute promise. 'Rest assured though. If Harry does turn up here, he will get nothing from us.'

A few minutes later, Alan poked his head round the door. The two women informed him of what was happening, and he readily agreed with everything they asked of him. 'Phil Saunders?' He gave a little smile. 'Never heard of him!'

A short time later he insisted on driving Kathleen home, though when they got to the end of the lane, she asked him to drop her off there. 'Best if I walk the rest of the way,' she said. 'When Harry comes into the pub, sure I don't want him knowing I've been anywhere near you or your good wife.'

She waved at him as he drove away, calling, 'Thank you for everything.'

As she approached the house, she felt so much lighter of heart. 'I'm sorry, Harry, me darlin',' she whispered. 'I've scuppered your plans, so I have.' She saw him through the window, pacing back and forth as he did when troubled. 'Sure, it's the only way.'

~

The following day, just as Kathleen had predicted, Harry came into the pub at lunchtime and introduced himself. 'I'm Harry Blake. Sorry to intrude, only I'm looking to find a man by the name of Phil Saunders. His wife is called Judy. I'm told you might know their whereabouts?'

While he spoke, Pauline quietly took stock of him. Judy had described him so many times, and now here, standing before her in the flesh, was the man himself . . . Harry Blake, Judy's first love, and judging by what Judy had confided, he was also her last.

Pauline thought him to be a fine, handsome fellow, and as Kathleen had informed her, he was built like someone who could take care of himself. She assumed he had been in the Army and fought during the war, not like Phil who had been an 'Erk' or mechanic for the RAF and had escaped action.

'I'm sorry,' she lied, 'I know most of my customers, but I don't recollect anyone of that name.'

Harry was devastated. 'Please? Think hard. He's a stocky man with darkish hair and a quick temper. Apparently he got in trouble with the police, right outside this pub.'

Pauline laughed. 'We get a lot of trouble outside the pub,' she informed him. 'Like I say, I can't recall anyone by the name of Phil Saunders. Sorry.'

Harry was not about to give up so easily. 'Is there anyone else here who might have heard of him?' he enquired.

Pauline gave a good performance. 'Hang on a minute,' she said, 'I'll ask.'

Going to the door beside the optics leading to their private quarters, she called inside, 'Alan! Can you come here a minute?'

When Alan appeared, Harry asked him the same question. 'Do you know where I might find a man called Phil Saunders? I'm told he frequents this pub. His wife's name is Judy.'

Alan pretended to think, then shook his head decisively. 'Never heard of him,' he shrugged. 'Sorry, mate.'

When Harry went away, visibly disheartened, the two of them watched him from the window.

'It's a bloody shame.' Alan hated the lying. 'He looks like a decent sort. I so wanted to tell him that we *did* know Saunders

– and where he lives. I feel like a louse, turning him away like that.'

Pauline, however, felt as though they were being cruel to be kind. 'That man loves Judy from way back. You've seen her face when she talks about him. According to Kathleen, there's been bad blood between Harry and Saunders these many years. If Harry goes bursting in there, wanting to take Judy away, all hell will be let loose, with that lass caught up in the middle of it.'

'You're right,' Alan conceded. 'I know exactly what I would do if someone was looking to take you.' He gave her a cuddle. 'But then you have a man who adores you, with or without your bad temper and sloppy ways.'

'Hey!' She pushed him away. 'Watch it, matey.' Then she returned him to the subject at hand. 'You do realise that Kathleen is determined to get Judy away from Saunders.'

'Yes, I could see that.'

'I'm hoping she might succeed where I've failed,' Pauline sighed. 'I am worried though. We both know what Phil Saunders is capable of.'

Alan nodded. 'I've been wondering whether we should call the police and let them deal with it.'

'And tell them what?' Pauline was realistic. 'That he adores Judy with every bone in his body; or that he goes out to work in order to keep her? Should we tell them all that, and then say we're concerned for Judy, and that we suspect he beats her?'

'Maybe they'll question her,' Alan suggested. 'They'll know then, won't they?'

'They won't know because she won't tell them the truth. Saunders will be there, looking over her shoulder; he'll have his arm round her; he'll smile and be the perfect husband. You know as well as I do, that Judy will deny everything; she'll agree with whatever he says, because he'll be right there, listening to her every word. And when the police have gone because they have no evidence, he'll threaten her . . . probably thrash her within an inch of her life. So, you tell me, husband of mine . . . what good will it do to bring in the coppers?'

'All right! All right! I see what you mean. But I don't like the idea of that lovely Kathleen going there on her own. I reckon it might be a good idea if I went along with her. What d'you think?'

'I think you would be doing exactly what Kathleen does not want – otherwise she would let Harry go. The plan is to quietly persuade Judy to come away with her old friend, and take time to recover; to build up her confidence, and to let Harry and that darling woman take care of her.'

Having made her point, she finished, 'Kathleen's idea has every chance of working. At least it can't do any harm.' She reminded her husband, 'You've heard Judy speak of her with affection; so you know that if she'll listen to anyone, it would be Kathleen.'

'I know all that,' Alan replied. 'I know she has Judy's inter-ests at heart, but Saunders is a sick man. Before he would let Judy go, he'd finish her, and likely himself too.'

With that sobering thought they each returned to their chores.

Pauline chose not to tell Alan about the child whom Kathleen had mentioned. After learning about this, she now felt able to see the wider picture.

She firmly believed that the loss of the child could have played a big part in Judy losing her confidence, and making bad decisions with regard to her future. The shock of Harry leaving, and then dealing with their child being stillborn and with no one to confide in, would affect anyone deeply, let alone a young girl.

'Poor kid!' Pauline murmured. 'No wonder she turned herself over to the first person who promised her love and care. Unfortunately for her, this happened to be Saunders, a man with neither heart nor scruples. A man who saw a weak and wounded girl that he could bully and control, and treat as a punchbag whenever the fancy took him.'

And because she thought she deserved it, Judy had not cared enough to protect herself.

'Hey now.' Alan's voice gentled into her mind. 'Don't go fretting, love. Maybe Kathleen really can get through to her where we have not been able to, eh?'

Pauline nodded. 'I hope so,' she whispered. 'Oh Alan, I do hope so.'

~

Early on the Monday morning, as Harry was getting ready for work, Kathleen's phone rang. 'Answer that, will you, Harry,' she called from the kitchen. 'Sure, I've no idea who that could be this time o' the morning.'

She overheard the gist of the conversation. Harry sounded upset.

'Oh, I'm very sorry to hear that, Mrs Sparrow. Please give him my best wishes for a speedy recovery. Look, I think I'd better come down and sort things out myself. Could I meet you at the church this afternoon?'

He fell silent for a time, listening earnestly to what was being said, before replying, 'Oh, I'd say early to mid-afternoon, all being well. Yes, I've got your number, I'll stop off and tele-phone you. Thanks very much for letting me know so soon. Goodbye, Mrs Sparrow.'

'Is everything all right?' Kathleen ambled in from the kitchen.

'There's been an accident,' Harry informed her. 'Poor Mr Sparrow, the gardener who looks after Sara's grave in Weymouth, has broken his hip. That was Mrs Sparrow, his wife, on the phone. He's in hospital, apparently, and won't be fit for work again for some considerable time. She says he tripped over his spade, but I wouldn't mind betting that a bottle of whisky came into it somewhere!'

Both he and Kathleen chuckled before Harry went on, 'I shall have to drive down there and sort things out. I can tidy up the grave and find someone else to look after it for us.' Part of him longed to be with Sara again; another part was gripped with a pain too deep for telling.

'Don't worry about Tom,' Kathleen offered. 'I'll take him to school as usual, so I will. I'll have him here when you get back . . . but it won't be tonight, I shouldn't think. Or will it?'

Harry thanked her profusely. 'I know you would look after Tom,' he said, 'but I was wondering – should I take him with me to visit his mother's grave? He'll lose a day from school, but I'll try and make sure I get everything sorted, so we can make our way back tonight. It's a long day's driving, but I'd rather we spent the night here.'

When Harry made his call through to Amy, she assured him that, 'Mr Jacobs will understand. Besides, it'll be quiet today. It always is after the big sale.'

When he replaced the receiver, he found Tom had come into the room, dressed in his school uniform and ready for breakfast.

Harry collected the boy into his arms and sat down at the table. 'I have to go back to where we used to live. The man who looks after Mammy's garden has hurt his leg and can't do it for a while.'

Tom was suddenly bright-eyed and wide awake. 'Can I come too? Please, Daddy, I want to come and see Mammy's garden!'

Harry held him close. 'That's what I was about to tell you . . . that you could either go to school, or come with me to take some flowers for Mammy.'

'Take some flowers for Mammy! Yes please, Daddy.'

An hour later, after Tom had been fed and washed and changed into his smart little trousers and jacket, the two of them set off. 'Don't you worry!' Kathleen called. 'I'll be sure and call the school, so I will.'

When they were gone from sight, she shed a little tear. 'Well now, doesn't the house feel awful empty without them.' She gazed round her much-loved home, then wiped her eyes. 'Now stop yer silly blubbering and get this house cleared up, she scolded herself. 'The pair of them will be back soon enough and sure, doesn't this give you a chance to have a grand tidy-up. Men – they are the very devil at making a mess!'

CHAPTER TWENTY

A T NINE-THIRTY ON that same Monday morning, Sammie was in her room packing her bag, while downstairs Nancy and Don were caught up in a heated argument. 'What the devil does Mac think he's playing at?' Don demanded. 'Can't you see what he's up to? What right has he to interfere anyway!'

Don was beside himself. 'My granddaughter should be going off to college to learn a skill, not taking off to live with *them*! For heaven's sake, Nancy, talk some sense into her!'

Frustrated, Nancy had given up. 'I've tried until I'm blue in the face, but she's too pig-headed to listen. Why will she always go the opposite way to what we want? I'm sorry, Dad, but the plain truth is, she's beyond me. I can't argue with her any more. As of now, I'm washing my hands of her. Let her go to Mac's; let her earn a living in the big wide world. Let her realise how hard life can be. If she wants to work in some dreary office, let her get on with it. Because I for one am past caring!'

'Good.' Sammie appeared at the door. 'Because I'm fed up with everybody telling me what to do.' Advancing into the room she looked from one to the other, her gaze resting on Nancy. 'I'm sorry, Mum,' she told her sincerely. 'I don't have a burning ambition to rule the world. And it's high time I moved out of home for a while. I know I cause a lot of rows. All I want is to earn a living and make a life for myself. Is that so very wrong?'

While Nancy looked away, too upset to reply, Don stepped forward.

'Yes, it's your life to do with as you please, but don't you think it might have been more courteous, at the very least, to discuss these plans with your parents first?'

'Maybe,' she conceded, 'but to be honest I thought you would all talk me out of it, and my mind was made up. Oh look, Grandad, I may be wrong, I know that, but for now, I just want to see what it's like in the outside world and have my own money.'

'So you keep saying. But for pity's sake, Sammie, why does it have to be with Mac?'

Somewhat taken aback by her grandfather's question, Sammie shrugged her shoulders. 'Why not?'

'Because, well . . . Mac is family. I thought your whole argument was that you wanted to get away from family. I thought you wanted to be independent?'

'I do! But it makes sense, don't you think? Uncle Mac has built a thriving business; he's wealthy and shrewd, and he'll not only teach me, but he'll give me somewhere to live, and pay me a decent wage as well.'

She glanced across at Nancy, who was seated on the sofa, her face turned away. 'Honestly, Mother, I never meant to upset you – or anyone else, come to that.'

Nancy kept her face averted. 'Oh, do what you please. You will anyway.'

'Can we make a bargain then?'

Suddenly, Nancy was on her feet and glaring at her. 'What nonsense are you talking now?'

'It's not nonsense!' Sammie protested. 'If you and Dad let me go to Uncle Mac for one year, without kicking up a fuss, I promise I'll consider going to college next year.'

This was not enough for Nancy. 'Sorry, that won't do. It's no good you just considering it,' she said. 'I want you to give me your solemn promise now.'

'But what if I'm doing really well with Uncle Mac?' the girl wanted to know. 'What if I'm happy, and making a name for myself in his company? Surely you wouldn't want me to give it up?'

'Promise me, Sammie!' Nancy would not give an inch. 'Even if you're flying high and he's offered you your own office and given you a secretary, it will not hurt you to go to college. That way you will always have something to back you up. Everybody knows, you can never go wrong with solid qualifications.' Then, seeing her daughter's obdurate face, she flounced out of the room, her final words echoing behind her. 'That's the deal. Take it or leave it.'

Sammie shouted after her, 'That's not fair! You can't have it all your own way, Mother. I deserve some say in my own future!'

The anger slid away and a sadness washed over her. 'Why is she so hard on me, Grandad?' she asked, the tears flowing down her face. 'It's almost as though she doesn't want me to do well with Uncle Mac.'

'Oh, sweetheart, it's only because she wants you to have good qualifications, so if anything goes wrong in the future, you will stand a good chance of securing a decent position.'

'That's what David said,' Sammie revealed. 'We had a real row last night, and now it's Mum's turn to have a go at me.' Looking at him through tear-filled eyes, she said, 'You're not even happy for me – I can tell.'

Don felt the need to justify himself. 'All I want is for you to be happy,' he said. 'The thing is, your Uncle Mac works eighteen hours a day, six days a week. On the seventh day, he sits in his office at home, phoning and scribbling, and planning this and that. Rita says she feels like a widow most of the time; he thinks, dreams and lives his work.'

He held the girl close. 'That's not much of a life, is it? None of us want that for you.'

'But it won't be like that.'

Don shook his head. 'Like I say . . . it's your life, my darling.' But oh, how they would all miss her. He secretly hoped she would decide to stay at home.

Sammie found her mother in the garden, smoking a cigarette and striding the lawn like a crazy woman, backwards and forwards, backwards and forwards. 'What now?' she snapped as Sammie caught up with her. 'More arguments, is it?'

'No, Mother. I want us to be friends,' Sammie assured her. 'I don't want us to part like this.' She shivered; it was a chilly, rainy day.

'So, you still intend going to your Uncle Mac's then?'

Sammie nodded.

'Right then.' Pushing the girl aside, Nancy told her, 'It's obvious you don't give a damn about anyone else. As far as I can see, there is nothing more to say.' With that she strode off back into the house and slammed the kitchen door.

A quarter of an hour later, right on the dot, Mac drove up in his car; surprised to see Sammie sitting outside on the wall, with her suitcase on the ground beside her. Getting out of the car he came across to her.

'Are you all right?' he asked.

'Yes, Uncle Mac, I'm fine.' Sammie handed him the case. 'Can we go?'

Mac was perplexed. 'Well, yes, we can go, but where is everybody? What are you doing out here?'

When she looked away, he groaned. 'Oh, I see. There's been a row. Somebody doesn't think you should be coming to work for me, eh?'

'Please, Uncle Mac, let's just go.'

Mac stood his ground. 'Is it your grandad?' he asked in a stern voice. 'Has Don been trying to persuade you not to come away with me?'

'Not just Grandad,' she informed him. 'Mother and David too. I managed to talk Dad round. He gave me his blessing and fifty pounds before he went to work, and he and Mum are having a row about it. The others are all nagging me to stay here and do a course at college.'

'And what have you said?'

'I just said it was my life and I can do whatever I like.'

'Oh, Sammie, that was a bit strong. After all, you're still very young. Well, seventeen seems young to me.'

'Please, Uncle Mac. My mind is made up. I want to work this year and then next year I can think about whether I want to go to college and get some qualifications. I am just so sick of being in a classroom.'

'And if I don't take you on, you'll still go out to work?'

'Yes, come hell or high water.'

'Then I've got no choice,' he conceded. 'I have to take you on.' Taking her case, he put it in the boot. 'You wait in the car,' he said. 'I need to speak with your mother.'

Nancy was waiting at the door as he came up the steps. 'You're taking her then?' She stood, formidable, arms folded and a stony look on her face.

'She gave me no choice,' he revealed. 'If I don't take her on, she'll get work elsewhere, that's what she said. To my mind, it's best if she comes to me and Rita, rather than be let loose in the big wide world, don't you think?'

'She should be going to college,' Nancy said obstinately. 'That's what I want for her.'

'I'll look after her, I promise.'

She stared at him with a hard expression. 'You better had,' she warned.

'Don't worry, I will.'

At that moment, Don came to the door. 'You managed to persuade her then, did you?' he asked his brother.

For a moment, the two men looked at each other, and there was a palpable tension between them that Nancy had not seen before.

It was a moment before Mac spoke and when he did, it was with caution. 'I'll make sure she comes to no harm,' he told Don. 'You have my word on that.'

'You make sure you keep it!' Don warned. 'We'll come up regularly, to make sure everything is all right.'

'And you'll be very welcome.' Mac turned to go back to the car. Time was getting on and he wanted to be back in Lytham as soon as possible.

Both Don and Nancy waved to Sammie as the car drove off, with Sammie calling out, 'I'll be okay, Mum . . . I'll telephone you!' before winding up the window.

'We'll be waiting for your call!' Don shouted, and Sammie waved until she could not see them any more.

'I'm glad you two made friends before she left,' Don remarked as they went back inside. 'I don't like to see you at each other's throats.'

Calmer now, Nancy laughed a little sadly. It was an emotional moment for her, seeing her daughter leave home. Things would never be quite the same again. 'You'll be disappointed if you think we'll never argue again,' she said, chokily. 'Didn't you know . . . Sammie and I were born to torment each other.'

When Nancy disappeared into the kitchen, Don stood before the window, watching the tail end of the car as it turned the corner. 'Don't think I don't know what you're up to,' he muttered as the car went from sight. 'Don't underestimate me, Mac. I'm nobody's fool!'

Having cleared the breakfast things from the kitchen, Nancy went to her bedroom, where she was like a cat on hot bricks. First she was looking out the window, then she was sitting on the bed, and now she was pacing back and forth across the carpet.

Going to the dressing-table, she sat on the stool and observed herself in the mirror, noticing how the fine lines on her face had deepened into the beginning of wrinkles. 'You're looking your age,' she muttered sadly. 'One day, when you're old and ugly, the things you should have done and never did, will come back to haunt you.'

She sat there for what seemed an age, before returning downstairs. Don was in the garden, gently swinging back and forth on the tree-swing, smoking his pipe, and absent-mindedly throwing an old ball around for Lottie.

Hesitating for just a moment, Nancy went across and sat beside him. 'Sammie will be all right, won't she, Dad?'

He put his arm round her, 'We all know she can be stubborn as a mule...much like yourself.' He drew her close, '...but deep down she's a sensible girl.'

For a time, father and daughter sat together, gently swinging back and forth, deep in thought, until Nancy spoke. 'It's so hard, seeing Sammie going away like that. It seems like only yesterday she was just a little girl at school.'

'I know.' He understood. 'But life goes on, as they say.'

'Dad?'

'Yes, love?'

'I know I can be difficult at times,' she confided. 'I'm bad-tempered and argumentative, and I hate myself for it, but I love you all, I really do. I just couldn't bear it if this family fell apart.'

'Now you're being silly. In fact, if only to put your mind at rest, I was thinking maybe we should all go and see Sammie this coming weekend. Make sure she's settled in okay.' His voice stiffened. 'We need to satisfy ourselves that she's being taken good care of.'

Surprisingly, and because she wanted Sammie to see that she really was trying, Nancy disagreed. 'Best not. It would only aggravate her. She would think we can't trust her.'

'Mm. Maybe you're right. I'll go along with whatever you say.' Don grinned. 'On this occasion anyway.'

There was a long pause before Nancy spoke again. 'Do you think we're being punished?'

Putting his feet to the ground, Don promptly stopped the swing. 'Punished? Whatever for?'

'For Judy,' she replied in a low voice. 'For doing what we did to her.'

Don became very agitated. 'We did nothing to her!'

Knocking his pipe out on the arm of the swing, he reminded Nancy, 'You know as well as I do, the lass brought it on herself. She ended up in the family way, when she was little more than a child. We loved her and took care of her, and that was how she repaid us.'

He remembered it as if it was yesterday; it still hurt. 'There was a time when I convinced myself that it wasn't altogether her fault, much like you are doing now. I blamed everyone but her. I even blamed myself for not being a proper father. I went looking for her – spent weeks wandering around, until I gave up.'

He shuddered. 'What I saw that night in Bedford recently shocked me to my roots. I knew then that she must have badness in her; that whatever we did, she would have gone wrong anyway. I saw the devil in her that night. It made me realise she was beyond saving! I could not believe what she'd made of herself – little more than a woman of the streets, she was. Drunk out of her mind, and fighting like an alley-cat with some man.'

He let slip something he had not divulged up until now. 'You never knew it, but I went back again, hoping I might have been too quick in jumping to conclusions; that maybe it wasn't Judy I saw after all. Maybe there was a riotous party, and she just got caught up with the revellers.'

His voice was almost inaudible, as though he was talking to himself. 'I saw that same man she had been with, and I followed him to Jackson Street. Judy was there. I saw him go inside. I watched them through the window. The light was on and the curtains were open. Almost as soon as he got through the door they were arguing. The man was shouting and bawling . . . it was bedlam! He hit her, and then she gave herself to him. It was disgraceful. I couldn't stay. I was sick to my stomach.'

He shook his head as though in disbelief. 'I never went back.' His face hardened. 'That woman was not my daughter. She was not the Judy we knew. She was bold and cheap. A stranger to me.'

As though realising he was thinking aloud, he spun round to tell her, 'So don't you ever punish yourself over the sister you once had. She's gone. The Judy we knew does not exist any more.'

'I never knew you went back,' she said. 'Why didn't you tell us?'

'No need really. It was just to satisfy myself that I really did see Judy at her worst, and that I hadn't imagined it.' He made a gruff noise from the depths of his throat. 'I did not imagine it though. I saw how she had turned out, and now I never want to see her, or hear of her again.'

'I do understand what you're saying,' Nancy was quick to acknowledge. 'It's just that, well . . . sometimes I wonder about her. Why did she turn out like that? When we were girls together, she was good to be with. She was kind and lovely, and so funny, she made me laugh. And then she changed – became secretive and sullen. I just couldn't get though to her any more.'

Blocking out the good memories, she asked, 'What made her go bad? Why did she turn out wild and wanton like that? We were always a respectable family, and she spoiled it all. She made it impossible for us to stay in the neighbourhood. We had to move away, and it was all Judy's fault.'

'Let it go, Nancy.'

But his elder daughter couldn't. 'One minute she was a happy girl, looking forward to the future, and then she was all moody and quiet, and so aggressive, she frightened me. I just don't understand why!'

Standing up from the swing, Don told her firmly, 'I said I never wanted to hear her name again! I mean it, Nancy. I thought we agreed?'

Nancy patted the seat beside her. 'Come and sit down, Dad,' she said. 'I'm sorry. It's just . . . well, seeing Sammie going out of our lives like that, it just seems like the family is falling apart all over again.'

'Nonsense.' He sat down again. 'What happened to Judy was

a totally different matter. I can't see that ever happening again. Trust me, Nancy, this family is as strong as ever. It's just that Sammie is growing up. She's flexing her wings, that's all.'

Nancy nodded. Deep down she knew he was right, but she still felt uneasy, afraid. 'I suppose it's just that when a bird flies its nest, the nest seems that much emptier, doesn't it?' she asked.

'That's exactly right. That's all it is.'

'Do you think Sammie will ever come back home?'

'Maybe not for ever, because that wouldn't be right – but even birds that have flown come back to the nest sometimes.'

They spent a few more minutes swinging together and talking, until Nancy decided on something. 'I've got to go,' she said.

'Go where?' Don objected. 'You can spare a few more minutes with your old dad, and your old dog, can't you?'

Nancy was already on her way to the house. 'Maybe later!' she said over her shoulder. 'Shan't be too long.'

She ran into the house and on up the stairs, and in her bedroom she grew both excited and troubled. 'Got to do it.' She drew her shoes out from the wardrobe. 'I have to see her,' she muttered feverishly. 'I have to talk with her.'

Don was making his way back to the house when he saw her. 'So you're off out then?' He strolled across to the car. 'When you get back, how d'you fancy taking the dog for a walk, eh? Blow away the cobwebs, so to speak. Being as you've got yourself all wound up over Sammie, I reckon it'll take your mind off things.' Lottie barked loudly, as if to agree, and they both chuckled. Nancy leaned forwards to pet the dog's huge, blunt head.

'Thanks, Dad. I won't be long.'

'Take care then, love.'

'And you.' She felt ashamed, knowing she was doing something he would not approve of. 'I'll be quick as I can.'

'Where are you off to?'

She pretended not to hear him. 'Bye then.'

Don waved her off. 'I don't know, old lass.' He talked to the dog as they ambled back. 'We've been deserted again.' He shook his head, gave a sigh, and followed Lottie to the kitchen, where he set about making himself a pot of tea. 'She's promised to take us out for that walk when she gets back,' he advised the elderly bull terrier. 'We shall just have to settle for that.'

While the dog munched her biscuits, Don sat back in his chair, sipping his tea and enjoying a couple of biscuits of his own, out of the biscuit barrel. 'It don't matter who comes or goes, this family is rock-solid,' he declared, dipping a Rich Tea finger in the brew and cursing when it disintegrated.

Kathleen was weary. Having spent some considerable time knocking and getting no response, she stooped to the letter-box, at the entrance to the flat in Jackson Street, opened it up and shouted through the slit. 'Judy, will ye please talk to me, sweetheart. Sure, I only want to help.'

No answer.

'Judy, I know you're in there so will ye open the door. Please me darlin'. Open the door for the love of God!'

Still no answer.

Wondering what to do next, Kathleen hoisted herself up and leaned against the wall. 'I know she's in there,' she muttered to herself. 'Somehow or another, I have to make her answer, so I do!'

Weary and cold, she tried once more. 'Judy, listen to me. I know how unhappy you are, and I want to help! Open the door and come home with me, Judy, and we'll sort it out.'

The house was quiet. Kathleen could hear no sign of movement, though she had an instinct that Judy was listening to her every word.

'All right, me darlin'.' She leaned forward, opened the letter-box yet again and put her mouth close, her voice quieter, more persuasive. 'Harry loves ye, so he does. We want to take care of you and the child. We have an idea of what's going on here, and Harry wants to help. I have to say, he was all for coming down here and sorting things out, but I thought it best if I got here first . . . just you and me, and no one else. Open the door, me darlin'. Please!'

Silence!

Weary but undeterred, Kathleen went on, 'It isn't your fault. Phil Saunders is a dangerous man. He won't stop till he has you so frightened of him, you will never be able to escape. This is your chance to be rid of him once and for all. Listen to me, Judy. Let Harry take care of you and the child. We love you. Harry has never stopped loving you.'

Pausing a moment, she listened. 'I know you can hear me,' she said. 'I'm sure I saw you at the window when I came earlier. I'm here to help you, Judy. You must believe that.'

The silence was unbearable.

Wiping her two hands over her face, Kathleen murmured, 'I'm worn out. Me old legs ache, and I'm shivering like a good 'un. You're in there, I know you are. Why won't you answer me?'

Growing angry, she tried again. 'That's it! If you won't let me help, there is nothing I can do. I've begged and pleaded, and you just ignore me!'

The anger subsided. 'Oh, come on, me darlin'! Please won't you open the door? Trust me. You know I would never lie to you, or do anything that might hurt you. If you come out now, we'll go and collect the child, wherever it is. We'll all go back to my house and when Harry comes home, we'll decide what to do. We won't let Saunders get his hands on you again. Sure, neither of us will ever let that happen.'

For one fleeting moment, she imagined she heard a noise. When the silence fell again, she gave it her last shot. 'I can hear you in there,' she said through the letter-box. 'Judy, be sensible. Let's go back home to mine, where *he* will never find you. That's all I'm asking of you. We won't let him hurt either of you again. He won't even know where we are. Oh Judy, please! Why will you not listen to me?'

The silence deepened. 'That's it!' Kathleen had had enough. 'I'm away now! Are you listening?'

Still nothing.

'I'll be back, lady, make no mistake about it! I intend coming back, tomorrow and the day after, and the day after that – in fact, every day until you open this door! D'ye hear me? I won't give up. One way or another, I mean to put an end to this situation, once and for all!'

When the rain started pouring down, and her pleas still drew no response, she bent her head to the letter-box again, 'I love you,' she whispered, 'Harry loves you too. I want you to know that, my darling.'

Drawing her scarf further over her head, the little Irishwoman put up her coat collar, and went away down the steps.

Across the road, Nancy remained in her car. She had been there just long enough to hear Kathleen threaten to *put an end to this situation once and for all!*

She had a fleeting suspicion that she had seen the woman before, but focusing on the more important issues, she dismissed the idea. What on earth had Judy done, to make her so angry? She recalled how her father had described Judy as being violent; fighting in the street with a crazy-drunk man.

She must have done something terrible to make that woman hammer on her door like that, she reasoned. Had she stolen from her? Did she break into her house and threaten her? Did Judy and that crazy-drunk man attack her husband?

Another horrific possibility rose to mind. 'My God! What if Judy's taken to recruiting women and girls into prostitution?' she breathed. Maybe that woman's daughter or granddaughter was part of it, and that was why the woman was so desperate. Because of the depths to which Judy had apparently sunk, Nancy thought it was not beyond the realms of possibility.

She waited a while, watching, wondering.

After a few minutes her decision was made. 'It was a mistake to come here,' she told herself. 'Dad was right. Judy is the bad apple in the barrel . . . rotten right through.'

Having only been there a few minutes with the engine running, she slammed into gear and raced off down the street. 'I had to try,' she said aloud. 'But I won't try again.'

Inside the house, Judy remained crouched behind the sitting-room door; she reached for the beer bottle beside her and took a long, deep swig. The liquid helped her forget. It dulled her senses.

She began to shiver with cold, then she was giggling. 'He's won,' she shouted at the top of her voice. 'Phil Saunders always wins!'

She took another swig, then pulled herself up to the letter-box and peeked out. 'She's gone away,' she whispered sadly, as though talking to someone beside her. 'Kathleen's gone away.'

Then followed the heart-breaking sobbing. 'I couldn't even tell her,' she cried brokenly. 'How could I tell her about the baby? How could I tell her I didn't have a child?' She began shouting. 'THERE IS NO CHILD, KATHLEEN! NO CHILD! IT'S GONE! DID YOU HEAR ME? THE CHILD IS GONE!'

She rolled herself into the corner, where she curled up into a little nothing, sobbing as though she would never stop. Then suddenly she was quiet; a deathly, awful quiet.

Steadying herself, she looked around – at the old sofa that still adorned the room, and the curtains, so grim and dusty they shut out the light. The room looked just like she felt. It was cold and empty, dark with sadness. Dead, just like her.

But she didn't care. Why should she?

With a supreme effort, she dragged herself to the bedroom, where she managed to pull herself onto the bed, and there she lay, out to the world, a lost and lonely young woman who carried the weight of the world on her small shoulders.

Racked with guilt, and plagued by shocking secrets she could never tell, she dared not let anyone else share the burden she carried.

~

Walking up the path to her little house, Katheen could not get Judy out of her mind. 'She was there, I know it,' she said aloud. 'Why would she not answer the door?'

Putting her key in the lock, she had an idea. 'She has to show herself sometime. Maybe the best thing is to leave it till the afternoon.' She decided to give it a try; even if it took several days to worm Judy out, it would be more than worth it in the end.

As she came into the sitting room, the sound of the telephone made her almost leap out of her skin. 'Blessed thing!' She had never really got used to it. Gingerly lifting the receiver off its cradle, she asked nervously, 'Hello. Who is it, please?'

'It's me.' Harry's voice came through. 'Is everything all right?'

'Oh, Harry! Yes, yes, everything is fine. How lovely to hear your voice.' She chose not to tell him about her unsuccessful escapade. 'So, what's happening?'

She listened a while longer. 'Oh, I see. Yes, very well, I'll see you then. Take care of yourselves and please give Tom a cuddle for me. Bye, love. Drive carefully.'

She replaced the receiver, then she took off her damp coat and went to make herself a cup of tea.

While seated at the kitchen table, her thoughts went back to Judy. 'I can't leave you with that man,' she murmured. 'I'm so afraid for you, Judy.' She took another sip of her tea. 'It's a blessing that Harry won't be home until late. That way he can't be out looking for Saunders. It means I've got a bit more time to get you away from that bad bugger.'

She gasped at her use of bad language. 'Oh! Kathleen O'Leary!' She quickly made the sign of the cross on herself. 'May you be forgiven.'

As for Saunders . . . what would he do when he found Judy gone, she wondered? 'When we manage to get her away, we'd best be sure we don't say too much about it to anyone outside the family. Walls have ears,' she muttered fearfully.

From what she had seen and heard, it was obvious that Saunders looked on Judy as his property, bought and paid for.

'Phil Saunders was a bad boy,' she murmured, 'and now that he's all grown up, it seems he's turned out to be a bad man.'

She lifted her cup to her mouth, took a long invigorating sip, then another, before she put the cup down.

Going into the sitting room, she fell into a chair and kicked her shoes off, groaning, 'Oh, that's lovely.'

Within few minutes, she was hard and fast asleep.

On a rare day, she truly felt her age. And whichever way you looked at it, today had been a long and tiring one.

Later in the day, some hours after Katheen had gone, Phil Saunders turned into the street.

'Evening, Phil.' The man was both a mate and a neighbour. 'What you been up to then, eh?' Striding alongside him, the man gave a knowing wink.

'What the devil d'you think I've been up to?' Phil snapped back irritably. 'I've been working my arse off as usual. Why? What have *you* been doing? Rummaging about in the rubbish tips, same as always?'

'Don't knock it, matey,' the man replied with a wag of the finger. 'You can find good stuff if you know where to look.'

'Yes? Well, I'm not into all that.'

'Yer must be into something though, what with folks hammering on your door, threatening all and sundry!' The words were hardly out of his mouth than Phil had him by the throat.

'What are you saying? Who was hammering on my door?' he demanded.

Struggling against the iron grip that held him, the man told him in snatches, 'Some woman . . . shouting for Judy . . . to come home with her.'

'You said she was threatening all and sundry. What did you mean by that?'

'Well, I heard her saying that she would be back with a vengeance.'

'Oh, did she now?'

'A feisty old biddy, she was.'

'Go on then. What was she like, this woman?' Saunders gave him a shaking.

'I dunno. Oldish woman . . . sounded Irish, or Scottish – I'm not sure.'

'Oldish woman, eh?' Throwing him aside, Saunders got to thinking. 'What else did she say exactly?'

'She were yelling "Open the door and come home with me, Judy, and we'll sort it out".'

'Who's we?'

'How would I know?'

'What else did she say?'

The man shrugged. 'Dunno. I was on my way out – that's all I heard. Now will you let me go!'

'Irish, you say?'

'Sounded like it.'

'An *old* woman?'

'Yeah, but not old or bent, nothing like that.'

'What was she wearing?'

'Bloody hell, Phil, I can't remember every little detail.' The man wished he had never spoken.

Saunders pinned him by the ears. *'What was she wearing, damn it!'*

In pain, the man struggled to remember. 'Er . . . a coat – kinda tweedy, if you know what I mean. Oh, and she had a headscarf on – blue, I think. And that's all I can remember, I swear!'

Satisfied, Saunders let him loose. 'Now bugger off. There'll be a pint for you in the pub on Friday. Okay?'

Thankful to have been released, the man gave a quick nod, though he had no intention of getting too pally with Phil Saunders again, not after this.

What the man had told him repeatedly played on Saunders' mind. When he let himself into the house, he knew straight away that she'd been drinking. 'Judy! Where are you?' He slammed the door shut. 'You drunken slut! You've been at the booze again, I can smell it! Judy? JUDY!'

It wasn't too long before he found her, stretched out on the bed like a rag doll. 'Get up, idle bitch!' Taking her by the arms, he dragged her into the bathroom where he slung her over the bath and turned the cold tap on her. When she began struggling and shouting, he threw her roughly to the floor. 'Get yourself together, woman! You've got some talking to do.'

While Judy shook herself awake, he went to the kitchen to make himself a cup of tea. 'Slag!' he kept saying. 'If she's entertaining that bastard, I'll swing for the pair of 'em!'

Feeling like death warmed up, Judy set about making herself look decent. Kathleen had called round, she remembered. She wanted to take her away. She said something about the child. I didn't tell her, Judy thought. I should have told her.

The tears were never far away. 'I didn't mean to send her away, but she can't know,' Judy sobbed. 'Nobody can ever know!' The thought of it made her feel physically ill.

When she came into the kitchen, Saunders was rummaging through the cupboard. 'Where's my dinner?' he demanded. He threw a tin of luncheon meat across the kitchen, where it clattered against the wall. 'I'm a working man, damn it, I deserve to be looked after!'

When she made no response, he strode across the room, grabbed her by the hair and swung her to him. 'I hear you've had a visitor,' he whispered into her ear. 'No lies now. I'm not in the mood for lies.'

Trapped by his manic strength, and with his voice reverberating in her ear, Judy went into a spasm of shivering.

'Stop that!' He shook her hard. 'This visitor . . . who was she?'

Judy took a deep breath. 'I don't know what you're talking about.'

'Liar!' Throwing her aside, he watched her crumple against the chair; heard the dull sound as wood collided with bones, and he laughed. 'Can't even stand up,' he chuckled. 'What use are you, eh?'

He observed that small heap of humanity, broken and used, and he was filled with contempt. 'Get up,' he ordered, and when she was slow in moving, he yelled louder, 'Get up, damn it, or you'll feel the weight of me boot!'

He watched while she struggled up, and when she was standing on her own two feet, he lunged at her. Gripping her by the arms, he pulled her close. 'The woman,' he hissed. 'Who was she?'

Shaking her head, Judy closed her eyes, expecting the worst; waiting for his fist to jar her body.

When he laughed out loud, she was shocked.

'No matter,' he said casually. 'I know who she is. And I know why she was here.' When Judy opened her eyes to look at him, he told her softly, 'I saw her that day at the store . . . you were talking with her. Your boyfriend Harry was there, as I'm sure you remember.'

Fear struck Judy's heart. He knew! He knew about Kathleen, so what else did he know?

'It didn't mean anything,' she said shakily. 'She's an old friend, that's all.'

'Oh, I know well enough who she is,' he reminded her. 'Or have you forgotten we all grew up in Fisher's Hill . . . you, me, Harry Blake – and your old friend, Kathleen O'Leary!'

'We were just talking!' The fear showed in her voice. 'I didn't know she would be there.'

'Did you know Blake would be there?'

Judy shook her head.

'I asked you a question!'

Before she could think what to say, he told her wickedly, 'It doesn't matter anyway.' He smiled into her face – a certain evil smile that she had come to know so well. 'I have a plan,' he whispered. 'A plan that will put paid to your precious Harry Blake.'

She knew what monstrous things he was capable of. 'What plan?' she asked nervously.

'Oh, I see!' He moved away. 'So now you're talking to me, eh? You take a beating, but you can't take the idea of anything happening to your beloved Harry. Is that what he is, eh? Your beloved?'

When she remained silent, the smile fell away and his eyes grew cold and hard. 'We'll soon put paid to that; you and me, and my clever little plan. You'll know soon enough what it is, because you'll be the one to help me.'

'I'm not helping you to hurt anyone – especially Harry, because he's done nothing wrong.'

The mantelpiece clock ticked noisily in the background as he continued to stare at her, his mind fevered with jealousy, and his hands twitching at his sides. He wanted to punish her for being so bold, but especially for defying him, in coming to Harry Blake's defence.

He had to be careful though. His plan would not work if she was marked in any way. He had to keep her looking good, so she would carry out her part well.

Realising that she would never take part in his scheme if she thought it would part her and Harry forever, he had to think hard as to how he could get her on his side.

'I won't help you!' she was saying, 'I mean it, Phil! I won't help you to hurt anyone!'

'You *will* help me!'

When he came too close, she shrank into herself.

'You and Blake. Have you been seeing each other?'

'No.'

'Liar! You went to the store because you knew he was there. You made it clear you didn't want me along, and then when you knew I meant to come with you, you changed your mind and said you didn't want to go, after all. You were meeting him, weren't you? Tell me the truth!'

'No! I was not meeting him, and that's the truth.'

'I don't believe you.'

'I can't help that, because I'm telling you that's the truth. I was not meeting up with Harry. I have never met up with him. Up to me going to Jacobs' Emporium, I hadn't seen or heard from Harry Blake for nearly eighteen years.'

She sounded sincere, as though she really was telling the truth, but Phil knew she had seen Harry that day, accidentally or otherwise, and he sensed, like a jealous man does, that Harry Blake desperately wanted her back.

'If Blake was to ask you to leave me for him, what would you say?' Before she could answer he gripped her by the arms until she winced. 'Be very careful, my love. I'll know if you're hiding something.'

For a long moment, Judy said nothing. She knew he was up to no good. She knew that if she said the things that were in her heart, her husband would finish her there and then, so she played it carefully.

'Firstly, he would not ask me to leave you. Why should he? I've never given him any encouragement. And secondly, I'm your wife. My place is here with you.'

He smiled that certain smile. 'Just as I thought, you can't even give me a straight answer. I was right! I said I would know if you were hiding something.'

With a gentleness that made her afraid, he led her to the sofa, where he sat her down. He then sat beside her. 'I know you're wondering what my little plan is,' he said. 'I need you to listen carefully, because I'm about to outline it in detail.'

Which he did, taking her through every step, every word, the time and place, and her part in it.

When it was done he sat back, pleased with himself. 'So, what d'you reckon to it, eh?' he asked gleefully. 'A good plan, don't you think, and nobody gets hurt. Well, maybe just a little, eh?'

He saw how the blood had drained from Judy's face and he was beside himself with satisfaction. 'Tomorrow,' he instructed. 'Do it tomorrow, or you know what will happen, and I can promise you it will not be pretty.'

That night, greatly excited, he took her with such force that she felt only loathing for him; and for herself. Afterwards, while he was sleeping, she ran a bath and lay down in it, until her skin dried and wrinkled and the water trickled away through the drains. She wanted to do away with herself. She even took his razor from the shelf and held it to her already scarred arms.

But then she thought of what might happen if she did go through with it. Harry would find out the truth, and he would go after Saunders with a blind vengeance. There would be blood spilled, and she would be responsible!

Realising she had little choice, she crept into bed, and quietly sobbed herself to sleep.

Phil heard her, and smiled. She'll help me, he thought. She won't let me down.

He took a moment to savour his victory, then he turned over to sleep. A satisfied man, in more ways than one.

~

Many miles away, down in Weymouth, Harry had a lot to think about, including Judy, but for the moment he had to keep her to the back of his mind.

Having placed the fresh flowers in Sara's little garden, he opened his heart to her. 'I went back like you said,' he told her. 'You were right. I found comfort, and a certain peace in my homeland.'

He explained the present situation. 'I haven't found me and

Tom a permanent home yet, but I've got a job, and we're all right for now. Irish Kathleen took us in, as you knew she would.'

Looking about, he saw Tom at the far end of the church-yard, chasing a stray cat. 'Don't wander too far, Tom,' he called.

'I won't, Daddy!'

He returned to his conversation. 'Tom gets on so well with Kathleen, but he misses you. He doesn't cry as much now, but I know he still hurts for you. We both do.' He choked back the emotion. 'You were such a wise and beautiful soul,' he smiled wistfully. 'Life really does have a way of going forwards, and like you said, we must go with it and do the best we can.'

At that moment, the breeze heightened and with the church being high up on the hill, the force was that much stronger.

'It's getting chilly now.' He pulled up the collar of his over-coat. 'I've done what I came to do, my sweet. I had a talk with poor old Roland Sparrow's wife, and his mate Arthur is going to tend your garden for us.'

The knowledge that her resting-place would be kept beau-tiful had come as a great comfort to him. 'For now though, I need to see the priest. After that, if I'm to get home in time to get Tom a good night's sleep, I'd best make tracks. We won't have to stay the night after all.'

He lingered a moment longer. 'I saw her,' he revealed. 'I saw Judy like you wanted, only things are not good with her. She was so thin, and sad-looking. She's married now, to an old rival of mine by the name of Phil Saunders, a real bad lot.'

He thought of Judy, and Saunders, and the anger boiled in him. 'I promise I won't do anything that I shouldn't,' he said. 'Only I don't believe she's at all happy. I think she needs help, and I'm not sure quite how to deal with it.'

Taking a moment to think of Sara and the way it was between them, he smiled. 'You would know what to do,' he whispered. 'If you have any influence up there, I know you will try and help her. If you can.'

A little prayer, a kiss over her name, and then he went after Tom. 'Tom! We need to go now.'

A happy little fellow, thankfully fast recovering from recent events, Tom came running. He stooped to place his little bunch of wild flowers on the grave, then hugged his mammy's name for the second time. 'I hope you like it in heaven,' he told her. 'Love you, Mammy. Got to go now.'

Holding Harry's hand, he went along the path and into the church, where the priest was replenishing the candles.

'Ah, Harry, there you are!' said Father Connor.

The priest offered Tom the chance to put the candles in the tray. 'Do you think you could do it without breaking any?' he asked, and Tom puffed out his little chest. 'Daddy says I'm worth ten men,' he declared, and both men had to smile.

'Right then, meladdo.' Father Connor put the candles in Tom's reach. 'Let's see what you can do.'

Like two old friends, the men sat side by side in the pew. 'Has everything gone well with the new arrangements?' Father Connor wanted to know.

Harry explained that everything was fine, that Sara would be well looked after by Arthur, Roland's friend, until the former was back on his feet. 'It's a worry off my mind,' he finished.

Father Connor gave him a sideways look. 'You have some-thing else on your mind, don't you?' he said. 'Something you want to share with me.'

Harry nodded. 'I'm not sure what to do,' he said, and went on to explain his history with regards to Judy. 'I know she's unhappy. I could see it in her face.'

'And you say Sara advised you to go back there?'

'She did.' Harry wanted to find a way to explain. 'I met Sara a couple of years after I was demobbed. She knew all about my past, including Judy. I was an orphan, when a wonderful lady called Kathleen O'Leary, a neighbour in Fisher's Hill, took me under her wing. Judy and her family had recently moved into the street and right from the first I was drawn to her; she was such a sweet and lovely girl. Quiet, so shy.' He smiled at the memory.

'You loved her, didn't you?'

'Oh, yes.' Harry felt it strongly even now. 'I adored her.'

'And you love her still, yes?'

'I don't think I ever stopped loving her.'

The priest could read it all in Harry's expression. He saw the love – a powerful thing – and he saw the pain. 'Did something go wrong?'

Harry hesitated. 'At first, being with Judy was indescribable,' he recalled. 'I was never happier than when we were together. No matter what went on around us, we had each other, and the world was ours.'

He paused again. The memories had darkened.

'Go on, Harry,' the priest gently urged. 'Tell me what you came to tell me.'

Harry took a deep breath. 'It was all so wonderful, and then it went horribly wrong. Judy led me into a situation that should never have happened. She deceived me. I was really thrown. It wasn't like the Judy I knew and loved.' Thinking about it now was too painful.

He went on, going over it all in his mind. 'It had to end. Afterwards I felt bad about the way it finished. All I could think of, was that she had lied to me. There was no trust left between us, so I walked away . . . just walked away.'

Ever since that day, he had wondered how it might have been if he had stayed, though always at the back of his mind was the question: if Judy had lied to him about her age, what else had she lied about?

He concluded the story. 'I came here after the war to Weymouth to visit an old Army friend, met Sara, and stayed. I never saw Judy again, until after Sara was taken from me.'

'You've had a lot to deal with,' Father Connor acknowledged. 'The untimely death of your parents, then losing Judy, fighting during the war, being in constant danger, and more recently, losing Sara. You may not think it just now,' he said gently, 'but you have been blessed in other ways. You have a strong heart, good health, and you have a wonderful son.'

'I do know that,' Harry said sombrely. 'I also have my adopted mother back, and I'm home, where Sara so much wanted me to be. When she was ill, and all hope was lost, she was the one who made me promise that I would go back, and she was right . . .'

He did not finish what was on his mind, though Father Connor finished it for him: '. . . if it wasn't for Judy?'

Harry nodded. 'I'm not sure what to do, Father. I feel in my heart that she's in desperate trouble. After I left, she went through a lot of bad stuff. Her family disowned her. Apparently, she went a bit wild, then she got married to a known trouble-maker. By all accounts he's been in jail for violence. There are rumours that he beats Judy, but I don't know for certain.'

He recalled the incident like it was only a moment ago. 'All I know is what I saw that day when she came to the store where I work in Bedford. She was so pale and waiflike, and when she looked across at me, it was as though she was crying out for help.'

He confessed, 'I want to get her away from him, but I'm not sure if that's the right thing. Since I've been down here, I've been asking myself: if he really is beating her, why doesn't she leave him?'

'Are you asking my advice?' Father Connor could see Harry's dilemma.

'I would welcome some advice, yes, Father.'

After a moment's consideration, Father Connor outlined his thoughts. 'Firstly, I think Sara was very wise to send you back to your roots. To my mind, it was the right thing to do. It's very plain to see you have never stopped loving this girl, Judy. Oh, and that's not to say you didn't love Sara. I know you did.'

'Oh, yes! Sara was the saving of me and I loved her for many reasons.' But it was a different kind of love. 'Sara was beautiful in every way,' he said, 'and I will never stop loving her.'

He turned to ask the priest, 'I expect you think that's a strange thing to say, being that I love Judy as well?'

'No,' Father Connor said gently. 'There are many kinds of love. There is the love of a parent, a friend, or a child. Then there is the love of a partner, a deep abiding love that protects and holds and keeps you safe; a love that shares and gives, a comfortable love that will always be cherished.'

He concentrated his gaze on Harry. 'If we're very blessed, there is that one, amazing love. It takes hold of your heart, it opens a world of emotions, it awakens your every sense . . . entwines itself into every fibre of your being, almost as though you're living and breathing it. Some people will never know such a love. Others will live their every moment, holding it in their hearts, until that heart stops beating and then maybe, for all we know, it may even transcend life itself.' He smiled. 'I've heard some people describe it as having a soulmate.'

He looked at the cross above the altar. 'A priest might say it's the love for the Almighty. In your case, it's Judy. Through your very real love for Sara, for your son and the life you built here, through all your trials, Judy never left you.'

His amazing words touched Harry deeply. He felt the truth of them, and he accepted it had been and would always be that way. Judy really was his soulmate. He had only had to look at her that one time in the store and he knew her every thought. He felt her deep unhappiness and her need of him.

'I don't know what to do,' he whispered now. 'I'm so lost.'

'So, what do you *think* you should do?'

'I'm not sure.' Harry had agonised over it. 'Judy is a married woman. What right do I have to interfere? Should I let Judy decide, or should I help her as best I can?'

'Has the young woman actually asked for your help?'

'No, not in so many words.' Harry tried to justify his concern. 'She doesn't need to ask. I can tell she's in distress. I have a bad feeling about it. Phil Saunders was always paranoid about Judy. He even stalked her when Judy and I first got together.

He threatened me all the time. I'm concerned that he might assume that Judy and I are meeting up for old time's sake.'

'And are you meeting up?'

'No!' Harry assured him. 'I'll admit it did cross my mind to find out how she was, but no! I saw her just the once at the store. I didn't even talk to her. One minute she was there, and then she was gone.'

'Do you think she came to see you?'

Harry smiled. 'I thought about that. I hoped she had, but she didn't stay, so I can't be sure.' He searched for an answer. 'I can't forget how sad she looked,' he said softly. 'She was much thinner than I remember, and there was something about her that worried me – I mean *really* worried me.'

'I see.' The older man understood. 'And she never came back?'

'No. She never did.' He turned to look into the priest's eyes. 'What should I do, Father?'

Father Connor looked up towards the altar. He bent his head in silent thought, and then he spoke to Harry. 'Follow your conscience,' he told him. 'That's what you should do.'

He then softly got up and left.

Harry watched him leave. Father Connor did not look back. Where Harry Blake was concerned, his work was done.

It was very late at night when Harry arrived home. He parked the car outside the house on Fisher's Hill.

Kathleen came out to greet him. 'It's good to see you back safe and sound,' she cried, throwing her arms about him. 'I thought you would never get here, and where's the boy?' Going to the back of the car, she called his name. 'Tom! It's Kathleen, wanting a cuddle!'

Tom's weary face appeared at the window. 'I'm tired,' he yawned. 'I fell asleep.'

'Ah, the poor wee soul,' she sighed. 'He's asleep on his feet, so he is.'

Harry swung the boy into his arms. 'He's not the only one,' he said. 'I've never seen so much traffic! We got stuck behind a lorry for ten miles, then a tractor turned out of a lane and kept us dawdling for another half an hour.'

Kathleen was sympathetic. 'Sure, it's no wonder the pair of youse look done in.'

'Then, when we finally did get underway, Tom decided he wanted the toilet, and we had to find a café. I thought that while we were there with still a way to go, we might as well get something to eat, so that made us even later.'

He gave a guilty look. 'Mind you, I was starving hungry too, so it wasn't Tom's fault. Anyway, we're here now, so once I've put this young man to bed, you can tell me all the news.'

'There isn't much to tell,' she informed him as they went inside.

'Well then, I'll tell you *my* news,' he replied.

After Tom gave her a cuddle and a kiss goodnight, Kathleen went into the kitchen to make a drink, while Harry put the boy to bed.

'Best not tell him I went to see Judy,' she muttered as she went about her work. 'Not that it did me any good, because either she wasn't there, or she did not want to talk to me. I've done all I can, and I can't do no more,' she chatted on. 'The thing is, how do I stop Harry from going round there?'

'Hey! Talking to yourself is bad news,' Harry chuckled as he entered the kitchen. 'What's that all about?'

'Aw, take no notice of me. 'Tis simply an old woman's ramblings. I'm just so pleased you're back safe and well, so I am.'

Kathleen wisely moved the conversation on. 'Now then, Harry me darlin', what have you got to tell me?' Plonking the two cups of steaming hot tea onto the table, she drew out a chair and sat opposite him. 'Did it all go as you wanted? Is everything all right down there?'

Harry calmed her down. 'Hang on a minute,' he laughed. 'Let me get through the door.'

'It's good news, I can tell,' Kathleen said. 'You've got a smile a mile wide on your face.'

'You're right,' he informed her. 'It is good news. Mr Sparrow is on the mend, and his mate Arthur is a thoroughly decent man. My Sara will be safe in their hands.'

Kathleen was thrilled. 'Aw, that really is good news. Now what about young Tom? He didn't get upset at going back there, did he?'

Harry shook his head. 'Not a bit of it. He talked to Sara as though she had never gone away. I think he doesn't altogether understand. There was one point when he went very quiet. I thought we might have tears but when I told him his mammy could hear what he had to tell her, he seemed to get over it. He told her about you, and the house, and how he likes his new school. Yes, he's doing fine. I'm really proud of the little fella.'

Kathleen was greatly relieved. 'Did ye go back to your old house?'

'No,' Harry said quietly. That would have been too upsetting.'

'You seem to have been gone an awful long time.'

'The travelling took such an age. Then we went to the hospital to visit Roland, and met Arthur, and later Mrs Sparrow. Tom and I got more flowers and we spent quite a while with Sara.'

He wasn't really sure if he should tell her about the priest.

She seemed to sense he was holding something back. 'Sure, half a tale is worse than no tale at all' she commented.

He laughed. 'Kathleen O'Leary! You're too canny for your own good,' he joked.

'So, what else then?'

'I saw the priest, Father Connor. He was there for us, when we lost Sara.'

'I see.'

'He gave me some good advice.'

'Concerning what?'

'Concerning Judy . . . and the way things are.' Harry looked down as he recalled Father Connor's wise words. 'He said there are many ways to love someone. You can love a parent, or a child, or a partner . . . all very different kinds of love. He said he knew I loved Sara deeply, but that I had also been blessed with another, more powerful kind of love.' He felt it now, in his bones and in his being.

'Go on, Harry.'

'He said some people called it the love you have for a soulmate. It is a kind of love, different from any other. It winds its way into your soul, and fills your senses; it touches every fibre of your being, and you will never forget it until your heart stops beating, and maybe even beyond that.'

Having told, he fell silent, thinking how wondrous it seemed. Yet in his deepest heart he knew what Father Connor was saying, for he had lived with Judy's love inside him, for all these many long years.

Kathleen also fell silent.

She too had known that other kind of love; with her husband, taken from her just when she needed him the most. Yet he was never far away. As Father Connor had told Harry, a love like that is in your blood for evermore. She still felt her husband's presence, every moment of every day and night; keeping her safe, watching over her and inspiring confidence whenever she began to doubt herself.

'Father Connor is a wise man,' she said softly. 'Every word he says is true. If you are fortunate enough to find your soulmate, then you really are blessed.' She guessed where all that had come from. 'You told him, didn't you?' she urged. 'You told him about Judy, how much you loved and missed her.'

'I told him everything,' Harry confessed. 'How very much we had loved each other right from the start, then how certain things happened and I had to leave.'

'Did you tell him you were worried that Judy might be in danger?'

'Well, I told him what kind of man Saunders was, and that I had seen Judy from a distance and was concerned for her.'

Then doubts overrode his instinct. 'The thing is, Kathleen, I've had time to think. What if I'm wrong? What if I'm jumping to conclusions? I don't know for sure that she's being knocked about, and she hasn't said that she is. Judy hasn't asked me for help, has she? Saunders is still the hard man he's always been, that's clear enough, and there's been talk that he ill-treats Judy, and because of it, maybe I've been too quick to think the worst. I love Judy, I always have, so am I using any excuse to get her back – is that what's happening? After all, Judy willingly married Phil Saunders, so it follows that she must think a great deal of him. So, however much I love her, do I really have the right to track them down and go barging in heavy-handed?'

Kathleen took a moment to dwell on his words. 'When you put it like that . . .'

'I do! We have to look at the cold facts, Kathleen. It's all we have – except for idle tittle-tattle from people who might have their own grudge against Saunders. I know from experience he can be a nasty piece of work, but then I might be the same if some old boyfriend turned up out of the blue and was trying to move in on my wife.'

The more he examined the situation, the more Harry wondered about his own motives. He desperately wanted Judy back in his life, and that was the truth, but was his love for her colouring his judgement?

'It might be a different matter if Judy had come to me for help, but the very fact that she has not should be enough to tell me two things. Firstly, that she is in no danger, and secondly, no matter what I feel for her, I should keep my distance. And what about her family? If Saunders was hurting Judy, surely they would deal with it?'

Kathleen had not thought of that. It was strange though,

how Judy had not even mentioned her family that day at the café.

For a long moment they were quiet in thought, remembering Judy's family, her mother and father, and sister Nancy. They recalled what a close family they had been.

'You're right,' Kathleen remarked thoughtfully. 'They kept themselves very much to themselves. As I recall, the mother was a formidable character, but the father seemed kindly enough – and the older sister . . . what was her name? Noreen?'

The name escaped her for the moment. Then 'Nancy – that was it, I remember how she and Judy often used to walk down the street talking and laughing together.'

She agreed with Harry. 'Yes, you're right. If Judy was in trouble, I'm sure they would have stepped in, her being the younger and all.' But then, as Kathleen reminded herself, there was the business of Judy being with child, and soon after Harry had joined up, the Roberts family had left Fisher's Hill. It was strange, how they were here one minute and gone the next.

Returning the subject to Harry, she asked, 'When you spoke to the priest, did he have any advice for you?'

Harry drew in a long, deep sigh. 'He told me to follow my conscience, and I've been thinking about that all the way home.'

'And . . . ?'

'If Saunders really does beat her, I can't help but ask myself why Judy doesn't leave him. She knows I'm here now; she knows she only has to ask, and I'll move heaven and earth to make sure she's safe.'

'So, what do you intend doing?'

Harry had decided. 'To stand back for a while, and not go hot-headedly looking for Saunders. I shall watch and wait, keep my eyes and ears peeled, and if I see her again, I'll look into her eyes and I'll know if she's in trouble.'

Of one thing he was adamant. 'If Judy really is in danger, I'll have her away from him, whatever it takes! Until then, I mean to tread carefully. One way or another, I intend getting to the truth; only I won't be so much a bull at a gate.'

Kathleen was torn two ways. Unlike Harry, she had looked into Judy's eyes that day at the café, and she was close enough to see the sadness there; although in truth Judy had never once said she was being ill-treated. Nor did she run Saunders down or ask for help,

'I'm glad you've decided to take a step back,' she said, considering. 'I've been thinking myself that it might all be moving too fast. After all, what we think we know is mostly hearsay and gossip, and maybe a part of it has come about simply because she's married to a monster like Saunders.'

She was ever conscious of what Pauline had to say, and her fears were still very real. But, like Harry said just now, how could they be sure – unless Judy herself confirmed it?

'If I can just get to Judy, I'll be able to find out the truth,' she promised. 'Once we know how the land lies, we can decide what to do.'

In spite of falling in line with Harry's thinking to a certain extent, Kathleen decided that she would pay Judy another visit, but not until the heat had died down. So she would go back to Jackson Street – not today or tomorrow, but soon.

If it turned out that the rumours were true and Judy really was in danger, then the priority was the same as before. To get Judy away to safety.

While they talked and planned, with Judy at the heart of their conversation, neither Kathleen nor Harry could have foreseen how events were already moving on.

Much faster and more dangerously than either of them could ever have anticipated.

PART FIVE

~

Bedfordshire, Late Autumn 1956

The Price of Sin

CHAPTER TWENTY-ONE

T HAT NIGHT, AFTER Phil had told her his secret plan, and of her part in it, Judy had cried herself to sleep. She woke to find Phil standing by the bed, looking down on her with a smirk on his face. 'Time to get up, my beauty,' he said. 'You and I have a busy day ahead, don't we, sweetheart?'

He gave a wide smile. 'I've taken the morning off,' he announced. 'I called in, told them I'd been awake all night with a stomach upset and would be in later . . . when I felt a bit better.'

Making no comment, Judy glanced at him with hatred.

He gave the bed a vicious kick. 'Did you hear what I said, bitch? It's time to get up!'

Snatching at the eiderdown, he pulled it off her and threw it across the room, leaving her shivering. Just as he was about to grab her by the ankles, she rolled to the other side of the bed and clambered out.

'That's it,' he chuckled. 'Wasn't all that bad, was it, eh?'

As she passed by him he took hold of her arm and drew her to him, real close, his face almost touching hers. 'You haven't forgotten what you need to do, have you?'

Unable to look at him, she shook her head.

'Answer me! *Have you forgotten what we planned?*'

This time she answered, her voice quiet, filled with loathing. 'No, I haven't forgotten.'

'Get on with it then, and make sure you do it properly. Or you know what will happen, don't you?'

She stared him out. 'They should never have let you out of prison.'

'Ah, but they did, and it's just as well I had somebody watching you. Goodness me! You could have got miles away, if I hadn't been clever enough to keep tabs on you.'

When she tried to walk on, he caught her by the face and squeezing his fingers either side of her chin, he forced her mouth open and gave her a long, sickening kiss; then he thrust her aside. 'You should remember, Judy my love: you belong to me. I would never allow any other man to take what's mine, especially Harry Blake! That's why it's so important that you do the job right today. Understand?'

When Judy tightened her lips, he bellowed, 'DO YOU UNDERSTAND?' so loudly that she almost leaped out of her skin.

'Yes, I understand.'

'Good girl.' Turning her about, he raised his boot and kicked her in the small of her back, sending her towards the dresser, which thankfully broke her fall. 'Oh dear, silly me, I almost forgot.' Crossing the room, he stood her up and brushed her down. 'We don't want to mark you,' he said mockingly. 'Mustn't do anything to make him suspicious.'

He glanced at the clock on the bedside table. 'Lazy cow!' He gave her a disapproving glance. 'It's already gone nine. You've got a couple of hours to make yourself look good. After that, you'd best get to it. Oh, and in case you're wondering why I'm taking the morning off work, it's because I mean to deliver you there safely, to make sure you don't chicken out. Oh, I'd love to be there to see his face, but I can't afford to hang about. I don't want to lose my job, not with you to keep and clothe.'

He grinned broadly. 'No matter. I can look forward to hearing all about it when I get home.'

He followed her into the bathroom. 'I fancy sausage, mash and mushy peas for my tea . . . oh, and get the fat sausages, not the thin ones that curl into a ball when you fry them. The fat sausages swell and split.' He licked his lips. 'I like it when all the goodness oozes out and clings to the skin.'

The images made him feel hungry. 'And I want the peas well mushed, not hard like they were last time. Are you listening to me?'

Judy had never hated anyone in her life the way she hated him; not even the other one. The one who had ruined her life for ever.

Sometimes she wished she had the black heart of a murderer, because then she would kill them both.

Phil Saunders.

And the other one!

He watched her bathe, his avaricious eyes following every small, perfect curve of her body. He noted the bruises still covering her back and smiled. She was his woman, and every man should know it.

The bruises were his mark, his brand; delivered with passion.

Preening himself, he went to the kitchen where he made tea and afterwards sat sipping it with great delicacy, like some dear old woman savouring the flavour; though he was savouring not the flavour, but the act about to be perfomed by Judy. An act of vengeance to rid him of Harry Blake once and forever.

As always, Judy took her time bathing. She let the water go cold then she filled the tub again, with water as hot as she could stand it. She soaped and scrubbed every inch of her body with a kind of fever, desperate to rid herself of his smell, his touch, in every crease and crevice he had caressed.

She could hear him downstairs in the kitchen chuntering to himself, sometimes laughing, sometimes cursing. 'You'll never know what's hit you, Harry Boy!' he addressed some unseen figure. 'This is *my* day; *my* woman! And it's the end of your dreams. You're done, Harry, my old friend, d'you hear me? What makes it all the better is that it's your old sweetheart who's teaching you the lesson you so badly need. I don't even have to lift a finger. Oh yes! You're done, all right. Once and for all!'

Raising his dainty cup to his mouth, he took a good long sip.

Afterwards, his laughter echoed through the house – hard and manic, like the man himself.

Judy took a while to do as he instructed, and when she finally emerged, her pretty face looking more beautiful than he could ever remember, Phil Saunders was taken aback. 'Gawd Almighty!' He gawped her up and down. 'Judy Saunders, my angel, you look like a million dollars.'

Then his mood changed and he became black with anger. 'Why do you never take that kind o' trouble for me, eh? What the devil are you playing at?'

Judy stood her ground, secure in the knowledge that if he wanted her to do what had been asked of her, she had to leave this house looking the best she had ever looked. 'You said to doll myself up, didn't you?'

'Well, yeah, but I mean . . . look at you!' His eyes were popping out of his head. In the black dress with the sweetheart neckline and those pink shoes with the black bow, she looked like a film star. Her fair hair shone like spun silk, falling in waves about her face and neck, and her grey eyes shone like a child's, clear and innocent. 'I've never seen you like this before.'

The questions poured out. 'How much did that bloody dress cost, and where did you learn to do your hair like that? Oh, and the make-up . . . the shoes. Where did you get the money to pay for all that?'

Judy calmly explained, 'The shoes and dress have been in the wardrobe ever since we got married. I never wore them because the only place you ever took me to was the pub. I did my hair myself, and the make-up I copied out of a magazine I found in a neighbour's rubbish bin. So you see, I didn't have to spend one single penny.'

He had no answer for that.

Instead he pushed past her and went into the bedroom, where he opened a drawer and reached inside. When he came back out, he kept his hands behind his back. 'Close your eyes,' he ordered.

'Why?' Again she was not afraid; he would not hurt her now. He needed her to look good for the awful thing she had to do.

'Stop asking damned questions, and close your eyes!'

Judy closed her eyes. When she felt his breath on her shoulder, she began to object, thinking he wanted to take her again. 'No, we can't,' she said, cringing in disgust. 'I'll be all messed up, and then—'

'Shut your mouth and keep your eyes closed.'

He struck her from behind, and she spun round, horrified when he brandished a handgun in her face. 'Oh, my God!' She had never actually seen a gun before, but there was no mistaking it. 'What d'you think you're doing? Where did you get it?' She backed off; believing this was some kind of crazy game, devised by his warped mind. 'Put the gun away, Phil.' She spoke softly. 'Put it away, please . . . before you kill somebody.' In a rush of madness, she hoped it would be her.

'Shut up and sit down!' he told her, and she did.

Waving the gun in her face, he then stroked the barrel down her neck, laughing hideously when she flinched.

'If you mean to kill me, then do it!' she screamed. 'GO ON! DO IT, I DON'T CARE!' At least if he shot her dead she would not have to carry out his wicked plan on Harry.

'Oh dear me, is that what you think?' he asked with big innocent eyes. 'You think I've got you all dolled up like that so's I can shoot you dead? Oh no, my little sweet, this is insurance, in case you chicken out on my scheme to be rid of Blake. So, if you're thinking of backing out, I've got this little number to finish him off. I'll tell the police you did it . . . that you shot him because he was worrying the life out of you.'

He rolled his eyes in frustration. 'Oh, silly me, I forgot. Yes, I'll tell them you shot him in self-defence, and then you shot yourself. Oh, they'll believe me. Make no mistake about that.'

He bent to whisper softly in her ear. 'Y'see, my pretty, if you don't do what I ask, that tells me you still have feelings for him. It means you lied to me all along. It means you've been seeing him, and that he's touched you.'

Straightening up, he concluded, 'It means you are soiled goods, and I would rather see you dead alongside him, than touch you again.'

Judy had no doubts but that he would carry out his threat. 'Where did you get the gun?' she wanted to know.

He tapped his nose. 'That's for me to know and you to find out,' he said cunningly. 'You forget, I know the right people. They're always about . . . hiding in the dark with the rats and rubbish. I could have had Blake put away a millon times over, but I didn't want to do that. D'you know why? Because I'd be far more satisfied if it was you that got rid of him. That way, I know you really don't care for him; or that you do, but you're prepared to sacrifice him for me.' He grinned. 'I like that idea. It makes me feel good.'

All the time he was speaking, he waved the gun about, first at himself then at Judy, and now he was holding it straight at her head, looking down the sights at the fear in her eyes.

'Put the gun away, Phil, please?'

'And if I don't?'

'Then I won't do what you asked.'

'Ah, but you weren't listening, were you? I said if you chicken out, I've got to finish the job myself, and I won't be too merciful.'

He pointed the gun at her legs. 'First I'll shoot him in the knees.' He raised the gun to her middle. 'Then in the guts . . . oh, you'd be amazed – blood everywhere!'

Now he was aiming at her head. 'It will be a terrible way to go,' he warned. 'More painful than you could ever imagine.'

He came closer, stooping to her level until he was eyeball to eyeball with her. 'First I'd make him scream for mercy. Then you. But there's no need for all that. Not when you could be rid of him easily and quietly. So, you will do it, won't you?'

She nodded. 'I'll do it – not for me, but for him.' She looked her husband hard in the face. 'But I'll never forgive you, not as long as I live.'

He laughed. 'Am I supposed to worry about that?' he sneered. 'I've always known you didn't love me . . . not like you loved him. But it doesn't matter, does it, because I'm the one who put the ring on your finger, I'm the one who snuggles up to you in bed, and I'm the one who makes sure you never stray far away.'

He seemed to tremble with excitement. 'And it'll be me, who one day will bury you deep, bring you flowers and cry over your grave. You see how it is, my sweet. You are my property, and that's the truth of it.'

When she made no comment, he merely smiled. 'You look good enough to eat,' he said, ogling her. 'I like the fact that you've taken a great deal of trouble with yourself, even if it is to please another man.' He giggled. 'You're like a delicious sweet; we offer it to him, and then we snatch it away. Yes, I like that.' Chucking her under the chin, he bent forward as though to kiss her, then turned smartly about and walked away.

He pointed at the clock. 'Ten minutes past eleven already. My, how time does fly.' Spinning about, he ordered her, 'Get your coat on. Time to go!'

A few moments later they were on their way towards Bedford centre, then on to Jacobs' Emporium, where Harry was busy clearing his desk, ready for when Len got back and they would begin their rounds.

~

'What time did Len say he'd be back?' Harry stopped Amy as she whizzed past his desk.

Amy looked up at the big wall-clock; it was eleven-thirty. 'He won't be back now until the afternoon,' she informed him. 'He said if he wasn't back in the store by eleven-thirty, he wouldn't be back until half one.'

'He didn't tell *me* that. He said to be ready for half past eleven, that we had more customers to sign on.'

'My fault,' Amy informed him sheepishly. 'He asked me to let you know and I completely forgot. Jakey wanted me to go into town for some—'

Harry stopped her. 'Don't worry, it's okay.' He looked at his clean desk and groaned. 'Because I thought I'd be going out on the rounds, I've filed everything away. I don't really want to be hanging about for an hour and a half, waiting for Len to turn up.'

He had an idea. 'I might as well start the round on my own. I know all the established customers, so I'll call on them. We can sign up the new ones, after Len catches up with me.'

Amy tried to discourage him. She was adamant. 'He would not thank you for it. You know what he's like if anyone trespasses on his territory.' She went away chuckling. 'He wouldn't want you moving in on any of his special ladies, now would he?'

'Behave yourself!' Harry was keeping an eye on Len for that very reason, but Amy seemed to know all about it.

'Take an early lunch,' she suggested.

'I'm not all that hungry.' Kathleen was very generous with her fried breakfasts. 'I can either open the files and get my paperwork out again, or I could give the warehousemen a hand, shifting that new load.' He patted his stomach. 'I could do with the exercise.'

'Ah, but then Mr Jacobs wouldn't like that,' Amy informed him. 'He has this policy, each man trained to excel in his own job, and no swapping over.'

'You're a killjoy, you know that?'

'And you should go for lunch. By the time you get back, Len will be here.'

Harry was still contemplating what to do, as Phil Saunders drew up at the end of the street. 'Right! Make sure you do it proper.' He watched Judy climb out of the car. 'Don't let me down.' He opened the glove compartment to give her a sight of the gun. 'I meant what I said.'

Judy nodded. She knew he would not hesitate at murder if necessary.

Saunders watched her walk down the street. He saw her pause at the entrance to the store, and breathed a sigh of relief when she walked inside. He smiled. 'Good girl!'

He waited a moment, then drove slowly by; thrilled to see how she was actually inside the store and heading towards the desk. 'She'll do it,' he gloated. 'She knows what will happen if she doesn't.'

Amy saw her first. Having brought Harry a cup of tea, she put it down on his desk, and looked towards the entrance, at the young woman coming their way. She recognised her as the same young woman who had stood at the back of the store that day, talking to Harry's friend Kathleen. Today, however, there was something different about her. The last time she was here, she had been quite plain in her appearance. Now, she seemed to be dressed for some special occasion.

'You make a great cup of tea, Amy, I'll give you that,' Harry said. Noting the expression on her face, he turned to see who or what had caught her interest.

He saw the young woman standing halfway down the store, just standing there, looking straight ahead, almost like someone in a dream.

'Judy?' Her name fell from his lips like something precious. Was it really her?

When she looked straight at him, with that familiar, wistful smile, he got out of his chair, his heart beating like a crazy thing. *Judy!*' The mere act of saying her name gave him comfort.

Looking on, from one to the other, Amy was in no doubt but that these two were deeply in love. It shone from their faces, lit up their eyes, and she could sense the powerful link, a force-field between them. 'There's that couple looking at the carpets,' she muttered, backing away. 'I think they were wanting some advice . . .'

Approaching Judy, Harry cleared his throat nervously. 'You look lovelier than ever,' he said shyly. 'I really didn't think to see you again so soon.'

For a moment Judy looked up at him, drinking in his features, and blossoming in the aura of his tall, confident stance. Oh, how she loved him, had always loved him and would for ever.

She forgot why she was there. She wanted to throw her arms around him and ask him to take her away from this dark place.

Yet she knew what would happen if she did that.

What became of her was of no consequence; in fact, it might be a mercy if Phil were to kill her. Harry though had done nothing to merit such a fate – and what of his child, already without a mother? Little Tom would suffer the same fate as his daddy all over again: he would be orphaned. Judy could not let that happen.

Then there was Kathleen to consider. It would destroy that old dear friend, if Harry's life was snuffed out by a madman like Phil Saunders.

'I think we should talk,' she suggested softly, '. . . but not here. Somewhere quiet, just the two of us.'

Harry agreed readily. 'That would be wonderful. I'll go and tell Amy.' He smiled. 'She's already been nagging at me to take my lunch break.'

Judy watched him walk up to the desk; she saw the quick exchange between him and Amy, with Amy occasionally peeking at her, and the shame of her errand made her feel like a Judas.

In a minute he was back, sliding his arm in hers, as though it was the most natural thing in the world. For Judy it was some-thing she had longed for.

Leading her to the entrance, he beamed down on her and gently squeezed her hand. 'You're right,' he said. 'We do need to talk. There so much I want to ask you . . . if that's all right?'

Judy told him it was, though as they came out of the store, her heart sank, for there was Phil, parked at the corner, watching every move she made.

Alarmed, she quickly looked away, allowing Harry to lead her down the street and round the corner, where they emerged into the High Street. 'So, where did you want to go?' he asked. 'There's the River Hotel; I'm told they have a great restaurant.' He felt like a kid on his first date, hardly able to believe that Judy had actually come looking for him. 'I'm sure they'll find us a table,' he speculated.

Judy graciously declined; she wasn't used to fancy places and she had an idea that neither was Harry. 'I'd rather go to that little café just up by the Boulevard.'

Harry was happy with that, as he pinched himself into believing he was really holding Judy, and they were actually going on a date – well, a kind of date.

It was then that he began to wonder. Why had she come to the store? What did she want to talk about, and why was she dressed to kill?

Somehow, it was not like her, and if his instincts were true, she was in a strange mood. As they made their way to the café, she kept looking back, then quickening her step, and when suddenly she lapsed into a deep silence, his curiosity was greatly heightened.

But then he thought she might be nervous, just as he was. After all, it had been many a long year since he and Judy had walked down the street together, and it was just amazing!

The café Judy had chosen was the very same where she and Kathleen had met, and when the waitress showed them to the table, it was also the very same where she had sat and lied to her dear old friend. How fitting to the occasion, Judy thought cynically.

They placed their order – ham sandwiches and a pot of tea

for two – and while the waitress was dealing with that, Harry concentrated on Judy. By now, he could tell there was something very wrong. 'What is it, my love?' he asked tenderly. 'What's wrong?'

For a moment she said nothing. Instead she toyed with the end of the tablecloth, before looking up with a bright smile. 'What makes you think there's something wrong?' she asked in a brittle voice.

'I don't know . . . it's just that you seem so nervous. I'm not sure what to think.' He asked her outright: 'Why did you come to the store, looking for me? What is it you need to talk about?'

Peering out of the window, she saw Phil's car parked across the street, and she knew that time was running out.

Her soft grey eyes swept over Harry, as she etched his face into her mind for all time; that strong face full of character and goodness, and her love was tenfold. 'Will you do something for me?' she whispered.

'Anything.' He struggled to understand; he knew she was troubled. 'What is it you want me to do?'

Judy leaned forward. *'Kiss me!'*

'What?' Excitement rippled through his senses.

'Kiss me,' she urged, 'like you used to when we were sweethearts.'

Reaching up to place his hands either side of her face, he leaned to her and smiled; a moment just to be sure, then he covered her soft lips with his, and kissed her long and tenderly, his senses in chaos.

As he reluctantly drew back, the waitress returned with their order, which she placed before them. 'I hope you like chutney on your ham,' she remarked, 'because that's how we make the sandwiches.'

There were a few awkward moments when they pretended to eat their food and talk of days gone by, until Harry asked quietly, 'Can I kiss you again?' He was disappointed when Judy answered, 'Best not.'

Embarrassed and confused, Harry chatted on, 'So much has happened over the years, but I never forgot you. I got married, to a wonderful woman called Sara. Right from the first I told her about you, and she understood. After she died, someone else told me how we can love in so many different ways, but we never forget that special love – the kind you and I had.'

Stretching out his two hands, he cupped her slender fingers in his. 'I loved Sara from that first day, but you were always there . . . my special love. She knew that, and as I said, she understood.'

Judy envied her. 'She must have been a wonderful person.'

'She was. She did not deserve to suffer as she did, and then to leave us.' Swallowing back the tears, he asked Judy again: 'What was it you wanted to talk about?' He had been amazed when she asked him to kiss her and hardly dared to go on: 'Is it about you and me? Is there a chance we might get back together?'

When she looked down, he feared he might have gone too far too soon. 'I'm sorry. Forgive me if I've overstepped the mark.'

There were so many pertinent questions he had to ask. 'Are you happy with Phil, Judy? Does he take care of you? Does he treat you right?'

For one agonising moment she was tempted to tell him the truth; that Phil was a maniac, that he beat her into submission and made her life a living hell. She wanted to tell Harry how she had often thought to take her life, because of Phil; and that she missed Harry, every waking minute.

She wanted to scream from the rooftops that she was here to do something she wished with all her heart she did not have to do, but that if she did not do it, Harry would be murdered, and so would she, but that she cared nothing for herself. She cared only for Harry, and the son who would be orphaned.

Sensing danger, she looked towards the door; there was no one there. Then she glanced into the far corner of the café, and there he was; Phil Saunders, dark and shadowy, like evil itself.

She saw him take the gun from his pocket and lay it on his leg, where only she could see it.

Judy knew the message he was sending, and she was so afraid, she could hardly breathe.

Seeing that gun had galvanised her intent. She thought of Harry and his son, and she decided that it would be better for Harry to have his heart broken than to be murdered.

'Judy?' Harry gently brought her to her senses. 'You didn't answer me.'

'Phil takes great care of me,' she lied, averting her gaze. 'He makes sure I never go without, and in spite of his reputation, he's so tender and loving.' She made a supreme effort at a happy smile. 'We love each other so much, Harry. I'm such a lucky woman to have a man like Phil.'

Harry was struck to the heart. After that soul-kiss, he had not expected this. He was devastated, yet at the same time relieved that his darling Judy was not being ill-treated.

'It seems as though he's changed then?' he said rather shakily. He swallowed hard. 'I'm pleased, really I am.' He gave a half-smile, but felt physically sick. 'When I saw you at the store just now, I imagined all kinds of things – that he was beating you, that he was taking it out on you because of me. I don't blame him for threatening me at the store. He must have thought I was chasing after you, that I wanted you back.' The words spilled out, but what he really wanted to say, remained unsaid.

Judy leaned forward, her voice so quiet it was almost inaudible. 'And do you, Harry? Do you want me back?'

Harry looked into her dove-grey eyes and for one incredible, wonderful moment, he was lost. 'I won't lie,' he whispered. 'I still love you. To have you back would complete my life.'

Mortified, he then backed away. 'Oh, I'm sorry, I should never have said that. I was wrong even to think it. I let my love for you colour my judgement. I badly misjudged Phil Saunders. I listened to gossip and I wanted to believe it. I'm sorry.'

Judy choked back the emotion. 'Please don't be sorry.' Out of the corner of her eye she saw Phil Saunders; he was here to remind her of a purpose – one which she must carry out or face the consequences.

Turning her attention to Harry, she raised her voice. 'To tell you the truth, I've never forgiven you, Harry. You left me when I desperately needed you. My life was ruined for a long time because of you. When Phil found me, I was living on the streets, caring for nothing and no one, not even bothered if I lived or died.'

She was out of the chair now, hands spread on the table and shouting at him. '*You* did that to me, Harry! I will never forgive you for running away like you did.'

Harry was shocked to his roots. One minute she was soft and gentle, the Judy he knew, and now she was behaving more like Phil Saunders! 'What the hell is wrong with you, Judy?' he appealed to her. 'Have you forgotten the truth of what happened back then? It wasn't like you just said, and you know it.'

Aware that the waitress was watching, he tried to persuade Judy to sit down, so they could discuss this calmly and quietly, like civilised people, but she would have none of it, and so he reminded her again. 'You deceived me, Judy. You let me believe something that wasn't true; something that could so easily have had me sent to jail, but it wasn't just that. It was you, and the way you lied – that's what I couldn't live with.' He remembered how it had been; he recalled how Judy was at the time. 'You were behaving strangely,' he recalled 'much as you're behaving now. It was as if something had happened to change you. What was it, Judy, because it certainly wasn't me!'

'Hah! Now you're trying to shift the blame. It *was* you who ran off, you who deserted me.' She deliberately kept her voice loud.

'No, Judy, you were different. There *was* something, and you wouldn't even talk to me about it. Then you lied, and not long after that, you dropped the bombshell. I left because you lied to me. You were even prepared to see me jailed.' He shook his head. 'What kind of love is that? You didn't love me then, and you don't love me now, so tell me, Judy . . . what game are you playing?'

'Enough, Harry!' She had to stop him there, before he revealed too much. She had never told Phil Saunders about there having been a child, when Harry left. If Phil knew that, it would be yet another stick to beat her with. 'Why did you come back here?' she deliberately taunted him. 'Yes, you're right – I never did love you. I used you, that's all. Now I wish I had never clapped eyes on you. I never want to see you again. I want you out of my life, for good. Do you hear what I'm saying? Do you, Harry?'

The look of disbelief and pain on his face was tearing her apart. She had to end it quickly, before her resolve collapsed and she poured out the truth to him.

Stunned by her cruel outburst, Harry could only wonder if she had lost her mind.

She insisted, 'I need to hear you say it, Harry Blake! I need you to tell me that you will never bother me again.'

He took a moment, then 'If that's what you want,' he replied firmly. 'You have my word, you will never see or hear from me again.' He was broken by her admission that she had never loved him.

That, above all else, had touched him deep.

'I'm glad you've got the message!' She spoke with conviction.

Throwing the chair back so hard that it fell over, she ran out of the café and away down the street, the tears blinding her as she ran. 'I'm sorry . . . I didn't want to hurt you like that. Forgive me! I love you, Harry! I didn't know what else to do!'

Running into the alley, she threw herself on the ground and sobbed until her heart might break.

A moment later *he* was there, filling the alley with his

presence, praising her. 'You did well.' Saunders had delighted in her performance. 'I never knew you could be so cruel,' he said.

'I've had a good master.' Judy couldn't even look at him. 'Go away, Phil. Leave me be.'

'Get up!'

She ignored him.

'I said . . . GET UP!'

When she continued to ignore him, he grabbed her by the hair and yanked her up. 'I've decided not to work today,' he informed her as he marched her to the car. 'You and me need to have a word. I heard snatches of you and him in there . . . some of which needs explaining. But not yet. It's been such an exciting day, I've a thirst on me like an elephant. So, while I'm enjoying a few well-earned bevvies, you've got time to think about what was said in there, because when we get back, I'll be asking questions.' He turned to stare at her. 'I'll know if you're telling me the truth.'

At the car he opened the door and threw her inside, slamming the door shut behind her.

Judy said nothing during the drive. Crippled inside by what she had done to Harry, she slowly came to realise how little her life meant, and that if she didn't make a stand, it would go on getting ever smaller, until the day when she either ended it, or it was ended for her.

She could hear Phil Saunders laughing and talking beside her, and occasionally he would touch her knee, but she seemed far removed from it all. She felt different, as though she was changing inside.

Just now, when Harry had kissed her, it seemed to breathe life back into her sorry soul. That warm, familiar feel of his mouth on hers was a beautiful, strangely healing experience. And when he wrapped his strong, gentle hands around hers, she had felt a resurgence of the strength she believed she had lost for ever. It was still there! Tears of happiness welled in her eyes. *The old Judy was still there!*

For a fleeting moment she felt real joy and pride; something precious that she had not felt since a child – or maybe it was a sense of innocence. What had happened was not her fault. She promised herself now: *the bad thing was not her fault.* The feeling of relief from this powerful revelation was indescribable. It changed everything.

'We'll stop off at the Bedford Arms.' His voice was invasive. 'I feel like celebrating.'

Alan was outside sweeping the pavement. 'Hello!' Surprised to see them, he asked Phil, 'Why aren't you at work?'

Saunders was a practised liar. 'Had a bit of a tummy bug,' he answered, climbing out of the car. 'Thought a pint might settle it.'

Alan swept the fallen leaves into a corner. 'You'd best come inside then.'

Going straight to the bar, Saunders ordered two pints for himself. 'Line 'em up,' he told Alan. 'The first one won't touch the sides. Anyway, I reckon I'll be here for a while . . . got things to celebrate.' His laughter echoed through the snug. 'It ain't often you rid yourself of an enemy without even lifting a finger, is it, eh?'

Alan had long ago given up trying to understand this man. 'If you say so,' he replied. 'Look, I'd best get back outside . . . finish my sweeping and keep an eye out. I could be had up for letting you drink out of hours. You do know that, don't you?'

'Don't worry, I'll not tell,' Phil smirked. 'That'd be like killing the golden goose.' He glanced around. 'Hey! Where's Judy gone?'

'Into the back for a cuppa with Pauline – talking women's stuff, I expect.'

'Hmm.' Losing interest, Phil picked up his pint and tipped half of it down his throat. Licking his lips, he leaned his elbows on the bar and belched. 'Bugger your cuppa. This is the life,' he chuckled. 'Beats working any day.'

Pauline was glad to see Judy. 'Hiya, sunshine,' she called as

Judy came in. 'So what's going on then?' She had been ironing for almost an hour when she saw the car drive up.

'Why isn't Phil at work?' She was curious. 'And where have you been, all done up like that?' She observed the dirty marks and scuffs on Judy's best dress. 'You obviously went somewhere special, and then it all went wrong. So, how did your clothes get spoiled?' She glanced at Judy's feet and was shocked. 'For pity's sake, love, look! Your foot's bleeding . . . and where's your shoe?'

Horrified, she put the iron down and switched it off. 'It's *him*, isn't it?' She made a sour face. 'What's that bastard gone and done now, eh?' You'd best tell me, Judy, or I swear I'll go out there and raise holy hell!'

Judy had kept her composure up to now, but seeing Pauline's genuine concern, she could hold out no longer. Her face crumpled and the tears she had tried so hard to keep back flowed down her face.

'Help me, Pauline,' she whispered brokenly. 'Please help me.' As two comforting arms held her tight, Judy sobbed like a child. 'I had to do it,' she kept saying. 'I had to do it.'

'Hey, come on, now.' Pauline knelt on the floor beside her. 'I can't help you, sweetheart,' she said tenderly, 'not unless you tell me what's on your mind.'

Judy looked into that kindly face and she knew she could trust her. 'I did a bad thing today,' she said. 'I didn't want to do it, but *he* made me.'

'What did he make you do? Tell me!' Pauline urged. 'You must not be afraid of him any more. He's sick in his mind, you must know that.' She held Judy tight. 'You're such a sweet little thing. Somewhere you took a wrong turn. What happened to you, Judy? Why do you think so little of yourself? What in God's name made you marry a man like that?'

Judy drew herself away, wanting to tell Pauline everything, but afraid to; always afraid. So many innocent people would be hurt. She didn't want that. She never wanted that.

She forced herself to look back over her life, to when it all started; that downward slide into a trap that was designed by Phil Saunders.

When she was just a child she was happy and loved, and her life was perfect; until one day, when she was badly damaged by someone she trusted. Then her whole world fell apart. There was no more love. No more trust. There would never be again, from that day to this.

All the way back there, in her teenage years; that was the start of it all. And there was no one she dared tell.

Then Harry was there; Harry whom she so adored, and whom she deceived. She could not tell him the awful truth. So when she found out the consequences of that badness, she lied to Harry, and as he so rightly claimed, she risked him being sent to prison. For that, she would never forgive herself.

Having let the young woman sob herself quiet, Pauline offered, 'Let's get you cleaned up. Change into a pair of my shoes, since we're the same size, and then we'll go somewhere, just you and me.'

Taking hold of Judy's shoulders, she gently pushed her back until they were face to face. Observing the tear-stained grey eyes, Pauline felt a surge of compassion.

'Whatever it takes, I'll help you put it right,' she promised her. 'Don't be afraid.'

A short time later, Judy was washed and tidied up, and comfortable in Pauline's black low-heeled shoes. 'I can't wear them tall things you favour,' Pauline laughed when Judy shrank another inch. 'Besides, I'm tall enough as it is.'

Interrupting their conversation, his voice slurred with booze, Saunders called from the bar. 'What are you two doing in there? I'm ready for the off. Judy! We're away now. Say goodbye to Pauline.'

The two women looked at each other. 'Tell him no,' Pauline advised. 'Tell him I'm taking you out shopping or something.'

She was disappointed when Judy shook her head.

'Oh, Judy! I thought we'd settled all that . . . you running at his every command.' She confronted Judy. 'I'm worried about you, love. I need you to confide in me, so's we can put right whatever's haunting you. I'm here to help you. Phil Saunders is a bully, and I'm so afraid he might hurt you badly one day. Listen to me, please, Judy. You don't have to do anything he says. And you must not be afraid. It's what he feeds on.'

Pauline was puzzled when Judy stared at her for what seemed an age; looking at her yet not looking at her, as though she was turning something over in her mind. 'I have to go now,' she said softly, almost to herself. 'You mustn't worry, Pauline.'

'*Judy!* WHERE THE HELL ARE YOU? MUST I COME IN AND GET YOU?' His voice grated on their conversation yet again.

Pauline yelled back, '*You'd better not come barging in here, matey . . . not unless you want a frying-pan across your scrawny neck!*' she warned. '*I'll have you know, these are our private quarters!*'

Judy slid her two arms round the older woman's neck. 'It's all right,' she whispered. 'I promise, I won't be afraid any more.'

Finally, after being trodden down by years of guilt and submission, that core of courage, once lost inside her, was beginning to re-emerge.

As he drove her to the home she had come to detest, she could hear Phil Saunders talking and swearing, and calling her all the filthy names he could lay his tongue to. She thought it strange, how he did not matter any more; she wasn't even aware of what he was grumbling about. Nor did she notice the dangerous way he drove, swerving and speeding and almost knocking the teatime paper-boy off his bike.

All she could think of was the distraught look on Harry's face when she said all those terrible things to him.

It made her realise how low she had sunk. It brought home to her just how much of a hold Saunders had got on her, and how he manipulated her, sometimes without her even knowing it.

JOSEPHINE COX

How could he say he loved her, when he treated her like a dog, a whore, and a servant to be ordered here and there; doing things that pleased him; sending her on errands that not only made her as bad a liar as he was, but also degraded her sense of decency?

The more she thought about it, the more angry she got: a cold, hard anger that was born out of desperation, and a controlled loathing of this creature she had married.

This time though, Phil Saunders had gone too far. He had overstepped the line; belittled her, made her attack someone who had only ever loved her. Harry was a wonderful man whom she had used for her own purposes, and now she had used him again – because Phil Saunders had made her.

She thought about that. Phil had made her lie to Harry, made her hurt him and use him, just as she had done all those years before. Her act of treachery had sent Harry away then, and it would do the same again. *If she let it!*

Suddenly, she knew what she must do, and she would do it without any hesitation.

It was time for Saunders to pay the price.

Time and again, fight after fight, she had always lost to him; but not this time. This time, it was Saunders who had lost!

Her mind was made up. She felt an incredible sense of relief. Whatever price she had to pay, she would pay it gladly.

There would be no turning back.

~

Amy was concerned. 'Good grief! You look like death warmed up,' she exclaimed as Harry returned to the store. 'Are you ill, or what?'

'No, I'm fine, Amy, thanks.' But he was not fine. He was in shock; devastated by all those dreadful things Judy had said; things that weren't even true. Judy knew how it had been, yet she shifted all the blame onto him. How could she do that?

He had a feeling there was more to it than met the eye. Judy had been different somehow. She was all right one minute, and then she seemed to go crazy. He had nearly gone after her, but decided it would only make things worse. And anyway, more importantly, he had promised to leave her alone.

He cast his mind back. That's exactly how it was back then, he recalled. We were talking, making plans, and then she went for me like a tiger, claws out, saying I'd taken advantage of her when she was only fourteen, and now her life was in tatters and she would never forgive me.

He had been deeply disturbed by her lies then, and now he had that same feeling. I always thought there was more to it than she would admit, he thought now. But what about today? Where had all *that* vicious anger come from? And why?

When Amy came back from the office, Harry quickly composed himself. 'I was just wondering where Len had got to?'

Amy chuckled. 'Wonder no longer, because he's up in the office as we speak. He'll be down in a minute and ready to go. Okay, Harry? Will that do you?'

'Thanks, Amy.' He returned her smile. 'I'm ready to leave right now. I could do with blowing away the cobwebs.'

Amy worried about him. He was not the same Harry Blake who had left the store just a short time ago, smiling and chatting with that pretty blonde woman. She couldn't help but wonder what had gone on between the two of them, to make him seem so down.

In no time at all, Harry and Len were on their way to the first call. 'What a morning I've had!' Len complained all the way. 'Dealing with suppliers, pacifying creditors and extracting money from bad payers.' Blowing his face out in a great sigh, he went on. 'This is the part of the day I like best. Chatting to the ordinary customer on the ground . . . my ladies of the back streets.' One in particular, he thought excitedly.

When Harry made no comment he asked in a mock grumpy

voice, 'Cat got your tongue? Somebody rattled your cage, have they?'

Harry gave no answer. This was between himself and Judy. It was not up for discussion.

When Len chose to start at the back end of his route, Harry was curious. 'Why the change in routine?'

Len tapped his nose. 'You'll see soon enough,' he told him slyly.

In order to complete the round as quickly as possible, they went off in separate directions. They had each visited several houses between them, before they met up again. 'We might as well leave the car here,' Len decided. 'I've a very special call to make,' he confided. 'I'll tell you all about it when we meet up afterwards.'

They were only a few yards from their next port of call down Jackson Street, when they heard the argument. 'Oh, my.' Len looked up at number 16. 'That couple are at it again!'

There was a crash, like something heavy being thrown, and then a scream, and what sounded eerily like a gunshot, 'Bloody hell!' Len turned white. 'Was that what I thought it was?' Then he shrugged. 'No, it couldn't have been. It must have been a car backfiring . . . they sound like that, don't they?'

Quickening his steps, he ushered Harry along with him. 'Best make ourselves scarce,' he muttered. 'The last thing we need is to get caught up in that kinda trouble!' Almost running, he physically dragged Harry down the street.

Suddenly, two incidents happened in quick succession. A van came hurtling round the corner, screeching on two wheels; at the same time the front door of number 16 was flung open and a woman came stumbling down the steps, a river of blood flowing down her face. She was crying, panic-stricken; hardly able to see as she set off across the road.

Both men saw instantly what was about to happen. It was only when Harry looked again at the woman that he began to realise, it was Judy. Harry began running back to her. 'JUDY!' There was a scream and a thud and the woman was thrown high into the air. 'Oh my God!' With his lungs almost bursting, Harry ran like the wind until he fell on his knees to take her in his arms, his voice shaking with terror. 'Judy . . . Judy, look at me . . .' Oh, dear God, NO! 'I've got you, my love, I've got you!' He yelled out, 'Somebody get an ambulance!'

Grey with shock, Len assured him quietly, 'Somebody's already called them.' A neighbour had seen it all. Len looked across to where the driver of the van had been thrown out of the vehicle. 'I reckon he's had it,' he muttered. 'The poor sod didn't stand a chance.

After hitting Judy, the driver had been thrown out, and the careering van had trapped him against the house wall. Lolling across the mound of broken bricks and shattered metal, he looked like a discarded doll, head twisted and arms thrown forward.

While Len sat on the steps, head bent and his whole body trembling, Harry talked to Judy, telling her he loved her, promising how they would be all right. He would take care of her, he vowed. She couldn't die, because there were so many things they had to do . . . a life they had to live.

He kissed her mouth, and he stroked her face, warm and sticky with blood. He rocked her in his arms, and still she made no move.

'Where's the ambulance! For God's sake, Len! Why isn't it here!'

'It's on its way,' Len assured him again. 'It's on its way, mate.' He glanced at Judy and wondered who she was, and how Harry came to know her. But it didn't really matter anyway, because she was gone. Her and the driver both.

In that moment, the tallyman made a vow: he would never mess around with women again, but would stick to his long-suffering wife. No, Len thought, if this was what passion led to, he would do it strictly by the book in future.

Inside the house, Phil Saunders lay on the floor of the sitting room, his head against the fender, a trickle of blood spreading a pattern on the arm of his shirt; but he was not dead.

YOU CAN'T KILL EVIL.

CHAPTER TWENTY-TWO

Nancy was up the ladder in the bathroom when the phone rang. 'Get that, would you, Dad?'

When the phone continued to ring, she called again. 'DAD! Answer the phone, would you, please?' The curtain she had been hanging fell to the floor.

Cursing and clambering down the ladder, she left the curtain where it was and ran downstairs to answer the phone. 'Yes?' she snapped.

For a moment she listened, her face opening with shock as Harry related what had happened to her sister, Judy.

With the receiver still in her hand, she stood a moment, letting the message sink in, rubbing the palm of her hand over her face, and muttering to herself, 'I should have helped her. She needed me to be there for her. Oh Judy, I've been so selfish.' She knew how it had been. She had known all along. Some things are so painful, you tend to shut them out of your mind.

Unaware of the call, Don ambled in. 'I'll strangle that blessed cat from next door,' he was grumbling. 'It's been digging up my vegetable patch again.' Catching sight of Nancy, he started across to her 'Nancy?' He saw her shocked face, he saw how she was gripping the receiver so tight, her knuckles had whitened. 'What's happened? For God's sake, tell me what's happened.'

His eldest daughter turned to him. 'It's Judy,' she whispered. 'She's been in a road accident. She's badly injured.' Suddenly she threw the receiver into its cradle. 'We have to go to the hospital.'

As she ran upstairs, Don had dropped into the armchair; staring into space. 'I knew it!' he kept mumbling. 'I had a feeling something bad would happen.' His legs were like water.

He sat for a while unable to move, blaming himself for not being strong enough, blaming his late wife for turning Judy out instead of helping her – oh, and Mac, his brother – he blamed him too.

While Nancy telephoned Brian and told him what had happened, Don got himself ready. First, he went to wash the garden muck from his hands, then he grabbed his coat and when Nancy came rushing down, he was already in the car, waiting to leave. 'Where is she?' he asked as Nancy climbed in. 'Where are we headed?'

'Bedford General Hospital,' came the reply. 'Hurry, Dad. Please, hurry!'

~

Just as he had done for the past twenty-four hours, Harry sat beside Judy, willing her to come through; asking her to think about their future together, and how wonderful it would be.

Unaware of what had happened, Judy drifted in and out of consciousness. She had injuries to her neck, her face had been pitted with shards of flying glass, and her leg was broken in two places.

Irish Kathleen was never far away; satisfying herself that Judy was all right, praying she would survive. In her heart she suspected it was not the injuries to her neck, or the broken limb that kept Judy unconscious. It was her psychological state; the trauma of years of emotional abuse and mental cruelty from the bully she had married. It was what had happened *before* the accident that had brought her to this. Even now, they were not sure of the circumstances immediately leading up to the accident.

Kathleen came in now, softly as always. 'How is she?' She glanced down on Judy's pale, injured face, and her heart shrank. 'What did her sister say when you told her?' she asked Harry. 'I'd an idea there was bad blood between them . . . certain things that happened that helped to send Judy down the wrong road, if you know what I'm saying.'

She suddenly felt ashamed, realising how this was the wrong time and place to be discussing such matters. 'So, do you think her sister will come?'

Harry looked up. 'I hope so,' he answered. Then 'I have a feeling you're right,' he mused. 'I can't help but wonder if it was because of me that Judy fell out with her family. Maybe I'm the reason they deserted her the way they did?' Deciding, like Kathleen, that this was not the time or place, he answered her question. 'Yes, Kathleen, I have a feeling her sister will come. She seemed genuinely shocked when I told her about Judy's accident.'

He thanked Kathleen. 'It's a good job you thought to look into Judy's handbag,' he sighed. 'If you hadn't, we would never have known where to find Nancy.'

'We'll have to call Aunt Rita!' Nancy said to her father as they hurried along the winding hospital corridors. 'Tell her what's happened – ask her to let Uncle Mac know. Not the children, though. There's no need for them to know. At least not yet.'

'Why tell anyone yet?' Don argued. 'They'll all find out soon enough, and we don't really know how serious it is yet. Besides, Rita will only go into one of her nervous fits. As for Mac . . . well, we don't want *him* round us just now. You know what he's like.'

The last thing he wanted was that devious bugger hanging about. The longer that one kept away from this family, the better

Don liked it. There were things going on in his brother's mind; bad things. Mac might be his own flesh and blood, but he was not to be trusted!

When they got to the ward, Kathleen was waiting outside. Nancy thought she recognised something of the Irish neighbour who had taken Harry Blake into her home after his parents died. She had been a good friend to Judy when they were young.

There was something else too; something that shook her rigid, but then it all began to fall into place. 'You're Kathleen O'Leary, aren't you?' She hurried straight to her. 'You were the woman I saw banging on Judy's door, threatening her – and now here you are at her bedside! What the devil are you up to?'

Kathleen explained. 'I've been worried about Judy for a long time,' she said. 'I've been trying to get her away from that monster of a husband. I had a feeling he was beating her. I offered her a home with me, but for some reason, she wouldn't leave him.'

Nancy believed her explanation, and thanked her. Then she said anxiously, 'Where is Judy? How is she? I have to see her.' She shivered a little.

Kathleen took hold of Nancy's hand. 'I'll take you to her,' she said, walking her to the little side-ward. 'When you see her, don't be alarmed. She's been shifting in and out of consciousness, talking incomprehensible stuff mostly.'

Harry looked up as Nancy came through the door, with Don trailing behind. 'I take it you're Judy's sister, Nancy?' Harry had known her as a young adult, but during the intervening seventeen years she had changed, and he would not have recognised her. 'I'm Harry Blake. I used to be a friend of Judy's.' In the circumstances he thought that was enough information.

Nancy knew him straight off, that tall, capable figure and those dark, quiet eyes. She nodded, then hurried past him to be with her sister.

Don stepped forward to shake Harry's hand. 'We're grateful

that you contacted us,' he said. 'Judy has not been a part of our family for too long now.' His worried gaze reached out to her, so small and helpless, and all the years of anguish overwhelmed him.

'We thought we wouldn't be able to find you,' Harry admitted. 'Then Kathleen took the liberty of looking inside Judy's bag. Luckily, she found your number and address in her notebook.'

Don smiled through his tears. 'I didn't know she had our address, let alone the phone number.' It pleased him.

'Try not to worry, Mr Roberts,' Harry told him quietly. 'The doctor is very hopeful that she'll make a full recovery.'

While Don went in search of the doctor, eager for more information, Nancy remained at the bedside whispering to her sister and comforting her. 'Where's my father?' she asked Harry.

'He was upset.' Harry had seen the look on Don's face. 'He's gone to speak with the doctor.'

'Look after her, will you? I'm going to find Dad. I'm worried about him.'

Harry did not need asking twice.

Some way along the corridor, Nancy glanced through one of the long windows and saw her father there, seated on a bench outside. His shoulders were hunched and he looked like an old, old man. He was puffing on his pipe and staring into space, as though miles away.

Nancy slipped through a nearby door and joined him in the courtyard. When she came closer she could see he had been crying. She slid her arms round his shoulders. 'She'll be all right, Dad,' she comforted him. 'She might be a little scrap of a thing, but she's strong. She's always been strong.' She thought of the night they had turned Judy out onto the streets, and the pitiful way her young sister had pleaded with them.

'Listen to me, Dad,' she whispered. 'We all do things we regret. Turning Judy out all those years ago – maybe it was wrong. Maybe you didn't have a choice – I'm not sure. All I know is, we have a chance to put things right now. Just pray she gets better, eh? That's all we need to do right now.'

Nancy had disagreed with him on the matter of contacting Aunt Rita and Uncle Mac. She brought it up again now. 'You're wrong not to want family here,' she said. 'Don't let that be another regret, eh?'

When he gave no indication that he had heard, she kissed him on the side of his face. 'I won't be long.'

Round the corner, she found a phone booth. Going inside, she dropped her pennies into the slot, and dialled the number, pressing Button B when Rita answered. 'It's Nancy,' she told her calmly. 'I need to tell you that Judy's had a bad accident, but she's recovering. Please tell Uncle Mac, but not Sammie as it will upset her and just now, it's best if she doesn't know. We're not telling David.'

A few moments later, she put the receiver back in its cradle and breathed a sigh of relief, muttering, 'Always the drama queen, my Aunt Rita!'

Then she went back to the ward at the run. Back to her sister.

Rita rang Mac at work. 'You have to come home,' she wailed. 'Nancy just rang; she's very upset. Judy's been in a terrible accident and she's in hospital in Bedford. Nancy says we mustn't tell Sammie. It's a good job she's doing that typing course in the North this week. Nancy just wanted me and you to know what's happened. Hurry, Mac!'

Half an hour later, Mac came rushing in the door. 'We'd best go now!' he said, throwing down his coat. 'Get in the car, Rita love – or you can stay at home if you'd rather?'

'No!' She hated being away from him and was horrified at the prospect. 'I'm all ready,' she said, and quickening her steps, she went down the drive and got into the car before he could change his mind.

En route, Mac asked her as many questions as came to mind. 'What exactly did Nancy say?' Eager to get to Bedord, he put his foot down hard.

'I told you – that Judy had been in a road accident, and that we should be there.' She felt uncomfortable as she saw the speed he was doing. 'If you don't slow down, we'll be the next ones in hospital!'

'Did she say how Judy was?'

'She said the doctor told them that she would recover – that she would be all right.'

'What else?' Sometimes Rita could be a bit scatty. 'Can you remember what else she said?'

'She said not to tell the children, that it would upset them.'

He glanced sideways at her. 'That's a strange thing to say!'

'That's what I wondered, but then I think she was right. Sammie would want to come and David is in the middle of his studies, and neither of them knew Judy, did they? So it makes sense to let the children get on with what they're doing. I left a note for Sammie, said we were out for the day and that she should get fish and chips from the chippie for the tea: I left her money too.'

'Mmm!' Mac was quiet for a time, then, 'Is Judy able to speak – did Nancy tell you that?'

'No.'

'Are you sure?'

'Of course I'm sure!'

'So, did she say who else was there?'

'Not really, no.'

'Was Don there?'

'What?' Rita was looking nervously at the speedometer.

'I said, was DON there?'

'I expect he was, yes.' She touched him on the shoulder. 'I wish you'd slow down. I don't like going this fast.'

'Then you shouldn't have come,' Mac snapped. 'You said yourself that Nancy wanted us to get to the hospital as soon as possible.

'Yes, but not to the Emergency Ward, which we will if you keep driving like a maniac!'

Mac was thinking about what she had told him – that Don was already there – and what about Judy? How badly injured was she?

Like it or not, Judy might wake up and start talking.

That could be dangerous!

He had to get there before it happened.

For the rest of that day, while Harry was ever-constant at Judy's bedside, Nancy shared her time between giving him breaks and tending her father, who had taken the situation badly. 'It's my fault,' he kept telling Nancy. 'I should never have allowed her to be turned out! If only I could turn back the clock. Dear God! Look what's happened to her! Look at my baby girl . . . all broken and bruised. What kind of a father am I? What kind of a man could turn his own daughter away? If I'd been a proper father, a better man, this would never have happened!'

When Nancy tried to comfort him he barely seemed to listen, locked in his own private world. Once, sitting up straight and looking her in the eye, he asked, 'What exactly happened? Who did this to her?'

At first, Nancy wasn't sure what he meant. 'They say it was an accident – that she came running out of her house, straight under the wheels of a van. She could have been killed, like the driver. But she wasn't, and when she's out of this, we can tell her how much we love her, and how sorry we are for what happened. We've got the chance now, Dad. Be grateful for that, at least.'

But Don would not be pacified. 'Why was she running from the house?' he wanted to know. 'Why did she not see the van?'

'I don't know, Dad. We can get answers when Judy is able to

tell us. Now come on inside – it's getting dark out here and you don't want to catch a chill, do you?'

A few moments later, Nancy and Don came into the ward. Don stood at a distance quietly watching his daughter, while Nancy walked to the bedside. 'How is she?' Nancy asked.

'The same.' Harry looked up at her. 'She's been through so much. I didn't understand, but I do now. She was so cruel . . . so vicious to me today. It wasn't like her at all.'

He looked at Judy and shook his head. 'I'm such an idiot,' he whispered. 'I should have known there was something else! I think I understand it now.' He held Judy's hand in his. 'It was *him* wasn't it? *He* told you to get rid of me, probably threatened you. And I didn't have the sense to realise.'

At this point, Don stepped forward. 'I'd like a word,' he whispered to Harry, then he walked away and Harry followed him out to the corridor.

Don turned to face him. 'What did you mean just now,' he asked, 'when you spoke to Judy and said, "He told you to get rid of me"?' So what exactly did you mean by that?'

Harry misinterpreted his interest. 'Oh, look, I'm sorry. I didn't mean to say it out loud,' he apologised, 'I was *thinking* aloud, that's all. I never meant to upset anyone, least of all Judy!'

'No!' Don laid his hand on Harry's arm, 'You've got me wrong. I want to know who *he* is. I want his name. I need to know everything about him. What was Judy to him? How did he treat her? Where did they live?' Then he remembered the sordid scene in the house at Jackson Street.

Harry told him everything he knew. He reminded Don of the boy who had his mind set on Judy even back then, when they were just teenagers. He explained that Judy and Phil Saunders were married and that if the rumours were anything to go by, Phil was a pig to her.

'There are stories,' he told Don. 'I know what I think, and I mean to get to the bottom of it. The thing is, you can't ever tell what's true and what's not, though one thing is certain . . .

he's a bully through and through. He'll never change. He even came to see me, warned me off talking to Judy.'

A thought occurred to him. 'The nurse mentioned that he was brought in . . . just down the corridor apparently. He'd been shot, but the bullet almost missed him and he only received a very slight flesh wound. He was fit enough to be released. He'd already gone when I heard.'

Don was anxious, 'So, he was shot, was he?' he asked nervously. 'Was it Judy, d'you think? Is that why she was running from the house? Is that why she didn't see the van – because she had tried to kill him and was in a panic?'

'The same idea crossed my mind, but right now, it's Judy who concerns me. Everything else can wait. And if Phil Saunders comes anywhere near Judy, I'll kill him with my own bare hands.'

Don nodded. 'I understand what you're saying, and that's good.'

He shook Harry by the hand; Harry was not surprised to feel that the older man's hand was trembling. 'Thank you for being there, when we weren't,' Don finished. 'You're a good man. I know you'll look after my daughter.'

Together they went back into the ward, where Nancy was seated on the chair, her two arms stretched out to Judy. When she saw the two men come in, she stood up. 'I'll see if I can get us all a drink,' she said.

'Not for me, Nancy.' Don could not take his eyes off Judy, all swathed in bandages, and looking so small and helpless. 'I need to get some more fresh air. I'll take a walk round the grounds, then I'll be back. Don't you worry about me, I'll be fine. Really.'

He took another long look at Judy, then he leaned down and kissed her on the face. 'Get well soon, my love,' he whispered. 'He can't hurt you any more.'

~

While Don went away to settle his mind, Nancy and Harry took it in turns to sit with Judy, willing her to come through.

Kathleen sat against the far wall, watching Judy's still face, and every now and then offering a prayer. After an hour or so, she got up and said her goodbyes. 'I shouldn't leave Tom too long,' she explained. 'Ruthie Bates from lower down is very capable and a lovely soul, but it's best if I'm there. The wee lad might be getting worried.'

Harry much appreciated that. 'Do what you think is right, Kathleen,' he told her. 'I want to stay here with Judy, if that's all right with you?'

Kathleen nodded. 'Ah, sure, that goes without saying, so it does. I'll give young Tom a big hug from his daddy, how about that?'

Pauline from the Bedford Arms had also got wind of the accident and she arrived to visit Judy. Seeing that the family were there, she only stayed for a while and went away devastated, blaming herself. 'Tell her I'll be waiting,' she told Harry tearfully. 'Tell her I love her.' And he promised he would. They each felt a measure of guilt with regards to Judy.

When Mac arrived for his visit, leaving Rita in the hotel, the frostiness between himself and Don was painfully apparent. Everyone took turns to sit with Judy, though as always Harry remained present, either at her side, or watching from the back.

When Mac went outside for a cigarette, Nancy followed him. She felt the need to talk, and wanted to know how Sammie was, amongst everything else. She missed her daughter. By now, they knew a little more about what had really happened. She told Mac how Phil Saunders had been found lying unconscious where he had fallen. He had been shot, but by a miracle, the bullet had skidded along his temple, leaving him alive, and concussed from the fall. Ironically, he was taken to this same hospital, treated for his head injury, and sent home.

Back on the ward, where all was quiet, Harry found himself alone with his beloved. Nancy had gone to telephone Sammie, and Mac had gone with her, to have a few words with his niece himself.

He sat down and leaned over to whisper in Judy's ear: 'Nancy's here, sweetheart. Your sister came to see you. We're all here for you, so you'll just have to get better, won't you, eh, my precious?'

He kissed her full on the mouth, caressing her hands, doing everything he could think of, to bring her back.

At the mention of Nancy, some lost, dark image seemed to penetrate Judy's subconscious. She began to stir, moaning incoherently, her hands twitching, reaching out.

'Nurse! Nurse, come quickly!' Harry called.

The Sister arrived immediately, and sent for the doctor. While Harry stepped away to give him room, the doctor gently examined Judy. 'It's all right, Mrs Saunders. Easy now.' He spoke softly, in soothing tones. 'Just lie still . . . try not to move.'

After a moment or two he went on, still in the same quiet voice: 'You were injured in an accident. You have a surgical collar around your neck and your leg is in traction. Look at me . . . can you see me, Judy?'

Leaning closer, he kept his face on a level with hers. 'Don't look up at the lights,' he warned. 'Look straight ahead. Look at me, if you can.'

Not yet fully conscious, Judy struggled, thrashing the bed with the flat of her hands, until the doctor took hold of them and held them still. 'Look at me, Judy,' he coaxed. 'Can you hear me? If you can hear me, squeeze my hands.'

A moment passed, with him persuading her to do as he asked, until suddenly he smiled. 'That's it, Judy. I felt you squeeze my hands, so now I know you can hear me. Now, can you open your eyes? Try, Judy . . . try to open your eyes. Don't look up at the lights. Look straight at me.'

Harry stood by the end of the bed, his hands gripping the bedrail so tight it hurt.

They all waited for what seemed an age, with the nurse

keeping an eye on Judy, as the doctor coaxed her through. 'Can you say your name, Judy?' he was asking. 'Say your name for me, Judy. Can you do that?'

When it seemed that the patient was incapable of speaking, he turned to the nurse. 'Stay with her, Sister,' he instructed. 'Call me the minute there is any change. Oh, and for now, it might be advisable for any visitors to leave. The patient needs to rest.'

He was heading for the door, when Judy made a small, broken sound. Spinning on his heel, the doctor hurried to her side. 'That's it, Judy. Take your time. What is it you're trying to say?'

Having re-entered the room, Mac stood by the door, his heart in his mouth. She mustn't tell! All he could think of was the terrible truth locked in Judy's tortured mind – and the awful consequences if that truth was ever revealed.

Harry though, was thrilled to hear Judy's incoherent mutterings. 'Come on, love!' he encouraged her. 'We're here, sweetheart. We're all here for you.'

When she opened her eyes, all present gave silent thanks.

The young doctor spoke to Judy in soft, careful tones. 'What is it you're trying to say?' he repeated.

Judy could hear him. She could hear what was being said, but somehow what she had in her head, would not come out of her mouth. She tried to speak but it was hard . . . so very hard.

When she looked up and saw Harry, she grew excited. The doctor beckoned Harry closer.

Harry held her hand. 'I'm here,' he assured her lovingly. 'I'm not going anywhere, sweetheart.'

She closed her eyes for a moment, then opened them again. 'Want . . . Nan . . .' She looked at Harry with such anguish, but she could say no more.

Harry knew. 'You want Nancy, is that it? Do you want me to get Nancy for you?'

Her eyes lit up, and the tiniest of smiles lifted the corners of her mouth.

While Harry went off to find Nancy, the doctor had a few words to say to Judy. 'I'll leave you with Sister Carter for now,' he told her. 'You're doing just fine. Don't overdo it, now. I'll be back to see you in a little while.' He then had a few words with the Sister who checked the monitors.

Outside, Nancy was still wandering the grounds, searching for her father. Thrilled to hear that Judy had opened her eyes and had actually asked for her, Nancy went back at the run. 'Your dad probably needs a bit of time to himself,' Harry said as he panted alongside. 'There is so much history to deal with here.' He knew enough to be aware that Judy had been sadly neglected; though this was not the time for recriminations.

By the time they got to her bedside, Judy had drifted back to sleep. It was not a contented sleep, however, but one filled with nightmares and terror.

The one thing that made her smile, made her battered heart leap with joy, was the face of a small child. Her beloved daughter.

Her daughter, not Harry's. *No, not his!*

'Judy.' Nancy's quiet voice penetrated these visions. 'Sweetheart, it's me. It's Nancy.'

With her every sense in chaos, Judy was shifting about in a strange place. She saw Nancy in her dreams; she needed Nancy now. She needed her to know something. *She needed to tell!* She had to get this secret off her chest.

In her dreams, she found her sister. She whispered things to her. Terrible, heartbreaking things. Things that had haunted her for too long. Things she could not live with any more.

And when she had imparted that shocking secret, she felt lighter of heart. All her troubles, all that long time, and now she was free, at last.

Still seated by the bedside, with her head close to Judy's, listening in horror, Nancy remained motionless, her body grown cold but her mind alive with what Judy had told her; something she had known all along on an instinctive level but which she had chosen not to acknowledge.

In a deep state of shock, she looked round, until her sorry gaze fell on the man by the door. She locked her eyes with his, and Mac knew the truth was out at last.

It was over. It was all over.

~

Don drove the car carefully along Jackson Street; he had written the address down. He checked it now, to make sure he was at the right place.

Satisfied, he parked, got out and walked up the steps to the front door. Then he knocked.

When no one came, he knocked again, this time louder.

The curtain at the ground-floor window began to twitch and a man's face appeared. 'What d'you want?' Saunders' voice was muffled by the thickness of the windowpane.

Don told him. 'Open the door. We need to talk.'

'I ain't got nothing else to say.' The curtain was abruptly closed. 'BUGGER OFF OUT OF IT!'

Don gave another forceful knock on the door.

The curtain opened again. 'I've already told you rozzers everything I remember. The bitch shot me, that's all I know. We were just talking, then she grabbed the gun and shot me! Ain't that enough?'

Ah, so he thought Don was a policeman. Don was delighted. It was working in his favour. 'If you don't open this door right now, I'll be back with another officer and a warrant,' he threatened. 'It's up to you.'

When he turned to leave, just as he had hoped, the door was flung open. 'You'd best come in then, hadn't yer?' Unshaven and bedraggled, with a bandage round his head, Saunders looked wild.

Don closed the door behind him and followed Saunders through to the sitting room. Saunders ranted. 'You ought to be ashamed, hounding a sick man like this. Anybody'd think it were me who pulled the trigger. So, come on then! What d'you want to know now?'

Don had discreetly cased the room, and now that he had the lie of the land, he knew the ways and means.

'I need you to answer a few questions,' he told Saunders. 'This time though, we want the truth.'

Saunders began throwing his arms about, threatening all and sundry. 'I've already told you! We were just talking – nothing rowdy, nothing bad, just talking. Then she had this gun . . . pointed it straight at me, she did; shot me in the head.' He rambled on incoherently. 'THE BITCH SHOT ME IN THE HEAD!'

Phil had been informed of his wife's accident and knew that she was still unconscious, with her family around her. 'There'll be time enough to deal with her later,' he had muttered to himself when the doctor had gone. And now he had returned home, to watch and wait. Every time he looked in the mirror and saw the gash on his face, he planned his vengeance step by wicked step. There had to be that one time, he thought, when she would be alone . . .

Suddenly he was going crazy, grabbing the sides of his head and saying how he was in pain, and he had to have a drink. He went into the kitchen and began pouring whisky into a cup, still raving, still calling Judy every foul name he could think of.

Then he took a great swig of the whisky and came back into the sitting room. 'She was little better than a prostitute when I picked her up out the gutter. What thanks did I get for it, eh? None, that's what! That little cow made my life a misery for years. If she dies it won't be no fault o' mine.' He laughed out loud. 'I hope she does peg out. It's what she deserves!'

As he raised the cup to take another swig, Don simply raised the poker and brought it down as hard as his strength would allow, into the back of Saunders' neck.

Without a sound Saunders slumped like a felled ox, the

blood oozing out across the carpet; his eyes wide open, frozen in shock.

Don watched as the whisky trickled from Saunders's open mouth. He saw it mingle with the blood and he smiled. 'So, you think she deserves to die, do you?' The smile slid away. 'You are wrong,' he murmured to the dying man. 'You have got it all wrong.'

He didn't bother wiping his fingerprints off the poker or making any attempt to hide the fact that he had been there. He didn't even care about the blood that was spattered across his jacket.

Instead, he walked calmly along the passageway; carefully closed the door as he went out, and walked down the steps.

Then he got into the car, started the engine and drove away. As though nothing had happened.

EPILOGUE

OVER THE COMING months, Judy was returned to the family fold. The truth was difficult, but if life was to go on, in a healing way, then that truth had to be faced. Afterwards, it must be put away, into the annals of family history.

Don Roberts was laid to rest in his local churchyard. He was found lying dead in the church in Bedford, where he had taken a lethal number of pills, stolen from the hospital for the purpose of ending it all.

He had first gone home and written two letters: one to the police, and another to Judy.

~

It was now April 1957.

With great tenderness, Judy stooped to lay the spray of spring flowers on the ground. For a moment she stood beside Harry, her gaze resting on her father's name, and in that moment, what had happened to her as a child seemed a lifetime away. She had been a child in torment and now she was a woman, and at long last, she had learned to forgive herself. For she knew now and for always, *that it was not her fault.*

After a time, she felt Harry's hand entwine with hers. 'Time to go,' he said. 'Don't forget we're getting married tomorrow.'

She smiled up at him. 'How could I ever forget that?' she

asked, her grey eyes smiling. 'Oh, Harry.' She shook her head as the tears flowed. 'How did it all happen? Why did it have to be like that?'

He held her tight. 'Life is unpredictable,' he answered, thinking of Sara, thinking of the lost past with Judy. 'We are none of us in control.'

Judy took a long look at this man who had been her saviour; this wonderful, kind man whom she had never stopped loving, and never would; and her heart was full for him, Sara and Tom.

Yet even now, there were things that had been left unsaid; things that came of the secret, and could never be revealed.

Maybe in the fullness of time it would not matter, she thought. All that really mattered was how you dealt with what life sent you, and she had not dealt with it very well.

Now though, she had Harry, and he was her strength. She too, had found her own strength: the strength to accept what had happened; the strength to give as well as take. Above all, the strength to love – this man, this wonderful life, and especially her family.

~

'For goodness' sake, will you keep still.' Nancy was exasperated.

Judy did try, though she continued to fidget while Nancy adjusted her veil. 'It's too low,' she pointed out. 'It keeps slipping over my eyes.'

'That's because you keep moving. Now please just keep still, or they'll be playing "Here Comes the Bride" and you'll still be here, complaining!'

Having secured Judy's veil, she stood back to check the results of her handiwork. 'Oh, my.' Her face was wreathed in smiles, even as the tears blossomed in her eyes. 'I never thought I would see the day.' Throwing her arms round her sister, she held her so tight, she made Judy feel faint. 'You're strangling me! Watch out for the veil!'

Nancy stepped back. 'Sorry,' she giggled. 'Take a look at yourself in the mirror – go on. There's time enough.'

Nervously, Judy stepped back and took a long look at herself. She was so moved, she could hardly speak.

'Well, what's the verdict?' Nancy wanted to know what she thought. 'Can I make a wedding dress or not?'

'Yes, you can.' Judy could hardly believe her eyes at the vision that presented itself to her. She had stood through so many fittings, with Nancy grumbling and arguing, and had never seen herself in the finished article. Now, on the very day when she would become Harry's wife, she saw what he would see, and she could not stop the tears of gratitude. 'It's perfect,' she said brokenly. 'So glamorous. Thank you, Nancy. Thank you so much.' The dress really was exquisite.

Nancy beamed with pleasure, then she was grumbling again. 'Never mind the thank yous!' she said. 'We'd best get down the stairs or they'll be leaving without us.'

A moment later they made their way down the stairs, and everyone was there, waiting to see what Judy looked like in the dress which Nancy had made in secret.

There was a spontaneous round of clapping and cries of 'Wow! You look radiant, Judy . . . oh, and the dress is amazing!'

It was amazing. And so was Judy.

The dress was fashioned in ivory satin, with a ruffled neckline and a fitted waist; the skirt spun out from the waist before falling in soft folds to her ankles. The shoes were matching ivory, as was her headdress, a perfect heart-shaped tiara, finished with sequins that glittered as she walked.

Her long fair hair was swept up and secured with two pretty combs, and her bouquet was of early spring flowers; pink and blue.

As she walked through the door to the waiting car, she paused to look back at her three bridesmaids, Pauline, Nancy and Sammie. All were dressed in a quieter version of Judy's dress, all in the colour blue, and each with a smaller version of Judy's bouquet. Judy thought she must be dreaming – but she wasn't, she assured herself. This really was her wedding day. Harry was waiting for her right now, at the church.

When they arrived at the church, Kathleen was waiting with young Tom to give her a kiss and wish her well. 'Ah, sure ye look like a little angel – so ye do!' She was already crying and they weren't even in the church yet.

Judy cuddled Tom, who clung to her, shy with her in all the finery. She whispered a promise of cake and ice cream into his ear, making him beam.

Mac stood beside her, looking proud and splendid. 'Don't be nervous,' he said, wrapping her arm round his. 'I'm nervous enough for both of us!'

When the organ music struck up and Judy made her entrance, she raised her gaze to Harry, so tall and handsome in his suit, and the smile he gave her as he turned from the altar was one from the heart. She wanted to run to him, but the music dictated her steps, until she was right there at his side. 'You look beautiful,' he whispered, and she giggled nervously. 'So do you.'

The service was wonderful, so sincere and happy, and later, when they all gathered at the local hotel for the meal and speeches, everyone had a great time, and there was much laughter and dancing.

Breathless and happy, Sammie came running to Judy. 'I'm so glad they brought you home, Aunt Judy,' she said. 'I never even knew I had you.' She gave her aunt a hug and a kiss, and ran back onto the dance floor, where she danced the night away.

Having seen Sammie talking with Judy, Nancy came across to her. 'All right, are you, Mrs Blake?' She had an idea how she must be feeling.

Judy assured her, 'I'm fine, and I'm so very grateful to you for what you did.'

'No regrets then?'

Judy wrapped her arms around her sister's neck. 'I love you,' she whispered in her ear. 'You've done a wonderful job with Sammie.' Standing back, she looked Nancy in the eye. 'Sammie is truly yours, and I promise she always will be,' she told Nancy solemnly. 'Everything is just as it should be.'

Both Nancy and Judy were emotional. The journey had been hard.

It had been a long time. A hurtful time. But it was over now.

When the evening drew to a close and most of the guests were gone, Kathleen found Harry and Judy together in the conservatory. 'Me and Tom are away to our posh beds in this posh hotel.' She gave a wink. 'There you go, me darlin's.' She handed them the key to her house. 'Make sure youse lock yourselves in. See you tomorrow.' She gave another wink. 'Or maybe not till next week. We don't mind, do we, Tom?' She ruffled his hair.

Tom was happy enough. 'It's nice here,' he yawned, and the newly married couple each gave him a kiss and a cuddle.

When it was quiet, Judy and Harry slipped away.

Back at the cottage in Fisher's Hill, Judy removed the envelope from her handbag, where she had hidden it. 'Harry?' She called him over.

'Yes, wife?' Taking off his jacket and tie, he had a certain twinkle in his eye. Then when he saw how serious she was, he was concerned. 'What's wrong, sweetheart? You haven't overdone it, have you – all that jigging about on the dance floor?'

It was not the first time he had had to remind her. 'I know you're all mended now, thank goodness, but the doctor said you won't be one hundred per cent fit for at least another few months.'

'It's not that,' she protested. 'And anyway, I'm absolutely fine, except for the occasional ache in the back of my knees and the two nasty marks on my neck.'

'So, if it's not that, what is it then?'

Judy showed him the envelope that Nancy had found on her bed last year. It was one of two; one for the police, admitting how Don had murdered Phil Saunders, and the other addressed to Judy. Because Nancy had suspected its contents, she had deliberately not delivered it to Judy, not wanting to hamper her sister's recovery. Only recently had she felt the time was right to give it to Judy.

'What should we do with this?' Judy asked now.

'Don't you want to read it?' Harry knew all about the letter.

She shook her head. 'No. Besides, we both know what's in it, don't we? And we don't want to spoil our wedding day.'

He nodded; Judy had told him everything, and for the first time he truly understood why she had been the way she was back then. 'Yes, I know he did a bad thing. All I want now though is for you to try to forget it.' He realised how ridiculous that must sound to her. 'Well, at least try your hardest to put it behind you, Judy – for all our sakes, but mostly for yours. Can you do that?' He looked at her tenderly. 'Or is it too difficult?'

She thought about that for a moment. She looked across at the coals still glowing in the fire-grate, and knew what had to be done. Slowly she went across the room and laid the envelope over the coals.

Harry drew her away into the other room, where the clock was striking the twelfth hour. When it was finished, he looked down on her with the love shining in his eyes. 'Well now, Mrs Blake,' he said. 'Do you realise this is the first day of the rest of our lives?'

'A brand new beginning,' she murmured, laughing when he swept her into his arms and carried her off upstairs to the bedroom.

Back in the sitting room, the envelope began to curl in the heat.

When the seal sprang open, the letter slid out into the grating, where it lay, scorched and fluttering as the flames licked about it. In the glowing light, her father's words could easily be seen.

Dearest Judy,

How can I ever ask you to forgive me? I never meant to hurt you. I only ever wanted to love you.

There is no way I can explain what I did, but I know your life was turned upside down because of me. Please, can you find it in your heart, after all the terrible things I did, to forgive me?

I deserve to burn in hell, I know. You though, are an innocent who was thrown to the wolves, and you deserve to be happy.

For me, it's already too late.

I hope and pray to the Lord that He may see me for what I am, a pitiful, wicked soul who is truly repentant of the sinful things I have done to my own child.

If you can, please, Judy, will you pray for me? I don't suppose you will, and I would not blame you for that, but if you do, maybe the Almighty will listen to you where He will not listen to me?

God bless you, my darling daughter.

Slowly but surely, the coals fell down one after the other, smothering the words; shrivelling the paper until it was nothing more than ashes.

It was only right that there should be no trace of what had happened to a little girl who loved and trusted. And who was bitterly betrayed.

Upstairs, after talking and planning and making love well into the early morning, Harry was still sleeping when Judy crept softly from her bed.

She went downstairs and, taking her coat from the peg, she walked out into the garden, where she stood in that same spot that Harry so liked; at the fence, from where you could see the whole night sky above.

'I didn't need to read what he said,' she whispered to an unseen Presence. 'I know what he did. I must try and forget, for Harry's sake and for the sake of the others I love, but it won't be easy.'

Recounting the events, she spoke of them now. 'I was so afraid. I didn't know how to stop it, or who to tell. I thought it was my fault. Mother would never have believed me and anyway, I was always so scared of her and her sharp tongue. She would have made my life at home even worse than it was.'

It helped to say it out loud. 'When I knew I was carrying a child, I was terrified of the future. I thought Harry would take responsibility. I lied about my age so he would make love to me; and when I told him that I thought he had made me pregnant, he left me . . . not because there was a child, but because I had deceived him, and no one should do that to someone they love.'

She thought of the conversation she and Nancy recently had. 'Nancy had an idea it was going on,' she whispered. 'She asked me and I denied it. I thought I would be blamed and put away in some terrible place, because that's what *he* told me.'

He had told her other things too. 'He said if I ever let anyone know our secret, they would drown me for being a witch.'

Then there was that time when Uncle Mac saw her running away. 'I think Uncle Mac suspected,' she recalled now. 'He would follow me everywhere, watching me, guarding me; Daddy didn't like him for that. Uncle Mac hasn't said anything, and I would never ask, but I think he knew; although he could never be sure. I think that's why he took Sammie away . . . because he wanted her to be safe.'

She thought of her daughter. 'Out of all the darkness, Sammie was the shining light. The one good thing – but then Nancy took her from me. At first I thought she was being selfish, hiding me away, persuading me not to keep my baby. But now I'm glad. I know that if Sammie ever found out the truth, she would suffer, and so it will remain a secret. I'm happy for Nancy and Brian and for David and Sammie, and I know my lovely girl will make a fine woman one day soon.'

When she grew cold and shivering, she made her peace. 'He's somewhere else now, Lord,' she whispered. 'You must know, he punished Phil, the one who hurt me, but I can't feel too sorry about that; not even my own part in it. I shot at him because he threatened to kill me . . . he saw me and Harry kiss, and he went completely wild. I explained to the police and they cautioned me, saying I must never again use a gun.'

She shuddered. 'As if I would ever want to! I wouldn't have used that one, if he hadn't tumbled over backwards in his rage and it had fallen at my feet.'

In fact, when it had seemed to go off all by itself, it frightened her so much, and that was why she ran – that and the knowledge that he truly meant to kill her.

She took a deep breath, for she had not thought she would ever say these words, but now she must. *Try to help my father, Lord, wherever he is. After all, he is what You made him. I believe that somewhere along the way, things went wrong. I've tried so hard to forgive him, but I can't. I never will. But I'm asking You, please . . . Maybe if You could forgive him, it might help me to.'*

She stayed a moment longer, watching the skies shift and move in that great heaven, and she felt a sense of peace.

Returning to the house, she went to look at the almost-dead embers in the grate. The letter was just black ashes now; except for the two words which lay charred and crumbling. *Forgive me* – that's all she could read now.

With grim determination, she picked up the poker and swished the remains about, until it was as though the letter had never existed.

She was relieved about that. She had a future now, with the man she adored.

That future was sealed when, three months later, Judy found she was having Harry's child. 'A brother or sister for Tom,' she announced.

As it turned out, the child was a sister for Tom; strong-featured and perfectly formed, Kathleen said that little Susan looked just like Harry.

A year later, Harry was promoted at work, and the couple

bought their own little house not too far away from the lovely Kathleen.

Soon after that, there was another addition to the family.

'Twin boys!' Sammie was thrilled. 'That's three boys and one girl. You'd best even it up,' Nancy laughed. 'We can't have an odd number, can we?'

Two years later, Harry and Judy obliged with another daughter, Vicky. 'That's it!' Harry declared. 'There's no more room in this house.'

As it turned out, there was room for one more – a girl, in the image of Judy.

The six children were named: Tom, Susan, James and Joseph, Victoria and little Anna.

All dearly cherished, born out of a love that refused to die. At long last, for Judy the badness was over.

Josephine Cox

A major bestselling author in her native Great Britain, **JOSEPHINE COX**'s story is as extraordinary as anything in her books. At the age of sixteen, she met and married her husband, Ken, and had two sons. When her sons began school, Cox decided to go to college, eventually gaining a place at Cambridge University, which she was unable to accept. Becoming a teacher, she set about renovating a derelict council house as the family home, coping with the problems of her own mother's unhappy home life while writing her first full-length novel—all of which earned her a Superwoman of Great Britain Award after her family secretly entered her in the contest. Currently living in Bedfordshire, England, she gave up teaching to write full time and is the author of nearly three dozen novels.